JUNG'S DEMON

A serial-killer's tale of love and murder

Abbot Trygve E. Wighdal

JUNG'S DEMON
A serial-killer's tale of love and madness

Abbot Trygve E. Wighdal

Cover Artwork by Christian Ermel
https://www.christian-ermel.com/

Editor: Chiara Corsini, Ph.D.

A. Wighdal & Sons, LLC
Publishers
276 5th Avenue
Suite 704
New York, NY 10001

Web: https://jungsdemon.com/
E-mail: contact@wighdals.com

Library of Congress Control Number: 2019905840
ISBN 978-1-7338151-0-9

1. Mystery, Thriller & Suspense – Thrillers & Suspense – Psychological Thrillers. 2. Mystery, Thriller & Suspense – Thrillers & Suspense – Crime – Serial Killers. 3. Literature & Fiction – Thrillers & Suspense – Psychological Thrillers. 4. Literature & Fiction – Genre Fiction – Psychological. 5. Health, Fitness & Dieting – Mental Health – Dissociative Disorders

A. WIGHDAL & SONS, LLC
PUBLISHERS

"People will do anything, no matter how absurd, in order to avoid facing their own soul."

Carl Gustav Jung

Table of Contents

Part IV: The Burials

Part I
SUICIDE IS PAINLESS

The Last Chapter
THE SUICIDE

"As above, so below, as within, so without, as the universe, so the soul."
Hermes Trismegistus

Oslo, December 25, 2018

Yo! Whassup ma-fuckers?

Nay, I can't really pull off some kooky slang and hold you spellbound by virtuoso writing at the very moment of my impending demise. All I could've done was to offer you an unaltered, uncompromising, raw story of the madness within and the mayhem it had caused without.

"Beauty will save the world," wrote Dostoevsky, so listen to the master and come closer, lean over, take a glance at how beautiful it is. Feel how perfect, how mighty it is. I am, of course, talking about a 9mm Luger, and a Speer Gold Dot bonded core bullet I'm loading my 9mm Luger pistol with. Once I fire it, it will bore my brain almost instantly as it swooshes at 1,210 feet per second with a whopping muzzle energy of 374 foot/pound. More importantly, once its job is done, it will have brought me solace. Comfort has always been eluding me; I've known no respite from loneliness, pain and myself. I tried many a remedy known to men: I used to drink myself to oblivion every single day, sometimes for months at a time without being sober for a single moment. Thirsty for life, I drank madness instead. I spent unseemly fortunes in whorehouses on every continent but Africa, in front of which I humbly kneel in reverence. Addicted to phony moaning, once the silence enveloped me and the putrid smell of two now separated bodies still puffing started to suffocate me, I was always left empty, lusting for more booze, more whores and even louder moanings, and yes, even more stench. "Bravely mate, much many big seas I sailed. A stranger to me, no hooker is," I emailed once to a captain friend in Moscow. Such a nice chuckle we shared. Gladys, his big-boobed blonde wife, had no clue that he was whoring in the Russian capital for weeks at the time.

A street fighter I'd never been, but many times I had provoked a vicious brawl. I remember that December night in Salvador da Bahia in Brazil where I smashed bottles and tables alike in the *Senhorita Mafalda*, a Pelourinho's small joint. As a reward for my behavior, I'd gotten severely beaten by local ruffians. I almost died that night. Only the pain of every bone that felt crushed eased the pain of living with madness and loneliness. When I laughed and yelled at the thugs, thanking them profusely for thrashing me, "*Muito obrigado,*" they left me alone, fleeing with: "*Ele é maluco*"—he's crazy, they mumbled. Of course I was crazy, you sick ass *putos*. Praise all the saints of your dirty, overrated city that I wanted you to beat me and not to stick a gun at your eager, hungry asses and pull a trigger.

Paradoxically, those were good times compared to what had been looming on the horizon. I was crazy and lonely, and I lived in pain I was unable to comprehend, but I never, unless in drunken stupor, felt like I was losing my mind. That came later.

I traveled like a restless madman, unable to stop even when the siren's song lured me into oblivion. As I ceaselessly traveled, I was hoping to sooner or later arrive to a life of my own. It never happened. I had no life, so I sunk deep into the throes of depression, into funk as deep as the darkest emptiness of space. On the paradisiacal Tahiti's island of Mo'orea, no less, I was the most depressed man that freakishly cheerful island has ever seen. I was living on the edge, pushing it really hard. It should not come as a surprise that I was a prime candidate for a stay in a mental institution anyway. There must be a cosmic joke being played on me, I think as I sit in the Gaustad sykehus psychiatric hospital in which I'm going to end it once and for all before the night is out.

Abelard and Héloïse

As fate would have it, at the very time on the verge of a pitch-black sorrow, as I lived desolate and destitute in Tijuana, I encountered love. It was the most unexpected moment. Our love was, or so I thought, conceived rather immaculately in The Glance, the first glimpse I exchanged with

Charlotte. It was a glance of deep understanding, as we've seen each other in a manner God never wanted us to see another human being—a naked soul, glorious in all its fears, magnificent in all its beauty, impalpable and everywhere at the same time. I suspect physicists played hide-and-seek with us mortals when they called the unknown substance that permeates our universe, those mysterious 85%, a dark matter. Just because you can't see it, does not mean it's dark, geniuses. I dare to dream that some sort of universal love is that elusive dark matter.

I don't give a hoot about how stupid or schmaltzy that sounds. After all, isn't love equally elusive, equally invisible as neutrinos? That does not stop either from overwhelming us. About sixty-five billion neutrinos are passing through just one square centimeter of each area on Earth and none were visible. It's the same if one thinks about love. Show me a man who says that he understands love and I'll show you a liar. Even hard-core scientific genius Richard Feynman sent a love letter to his dead wife Arlene a full year after she had died.

Charlotte was the first and last thing on my mind every day; I floated around the ugliest shithole on Earth, nevertheless happy, immersed in sweet feelings. As I loved, I felt loved. Alas, I had no clue what would happen next, as I was reveling in my newly found happiness, oblivious to the ominous signs written all over that proverbial cursed wall of my demise.

The salvation I longed for and hoped to have gotten was instead my damnation.

Life is a Dialogue

Yes, the love grappled me unexpectedly with all its might. When I met her on the Malecón de Playas de Tijuana, México, I finally saw the light, unaware that it blinded me from the start.

She immediately started to suffocate the dialogue of life. Only her own ways mattered. She had muzzled the dialogue from the beginning, imposing her will in the most cunning way as she hid behind her stated weaknesses (or illnesses) that ruled our times together. So she had silenced me and, by doing it, she took my breath, my life away. While we were both endlessly babbling like logorrheic Howler monkeys about our "relationship" and her numerous "inabilities" to be a part of it in a way she claimed that I wanted, I started to lose myself. I felt an overwhelming urge to help her get out of her rigid cage that suffocated love.

Lamia

I had no idea that she was a monster that fed upon the living. Like Lamia, the child-eating monster who morphed into a seductress only to kill and eat the flesh of their lovers, Charlotte was the soul-eating hydra. She was subtle and perfidious. Unlike other cock teasing bitches, she wasn't satisfied only by taking your flesh—she was a nymphomaniac of the soul, she feasted upon the pain she had been inflicting on others. She played the game of endless teasing while enjoying her role of a blameless victim.

In the end it was clear: she thrust a dagger into my heart. She casted a black pall over my soul. Once she had eaten up my soul and spat it out, leaving me devastated, I tried to understand why that had happened to me. It was clear to me, even when I was brokenhearted and maddeningly hurt, that it wasn't just her or her behavior that had created so much pain in me. I did not blame her even when I hated her with every fiber of my being. I needed answers, or the pain would be too much to bear. I was aware, no matter how vaguely, that she got her claws into my being because of its intrinsic weaknesses. Pain and loneliness were, throughout my life, manifestation of those weaknesses. In fact, I never saw myself as a weak person. After all, I survived many a painful loss, the war at home, homelessness in New York, prior broken heart episodes, and a life of loneliness, and yet I was open to life and love when I met her. I did not think a weakling could survive all of that and keep pulling himself together year after year, continent after continent, decade after decade. The only way out from Charlotte's induced hell was to try to understand myself. As Franz Kafka (or was it Albert Camus? Too late for me to google it now) once wrote, "stronger than comfort would be a realization: you too have a weapon." I used C.G. Jung and various alchemical writings as a tool on the journey of self-discovery. I started to write my chronicles—a totally different kind of chronicles than these—as a weapon to help me exorcise the evil spirits. Instead, like the early Christians seeking God in the desert only to find demons, I became the prey of my own inner fiends.

And then, I myself became a demoniac presence in the lives of the others I obliterated with a ferocious, savage intensity.

Suicide is Painless

Some might claim that I'm a coward for killing myself instead of facing "justice," that mythical fairytale near everyone sanctimoniously babbles about all the time, so I feel compelled to briefly comment on such a thought. What "justice" exists within confines of those barking mad societies all over the world? Societies, as much as the countries and the humanity as a whole, have been ruled by degenerate psychopaths since forever. The world has been mercilessly caught in the war-mongering clutches of sickos whose evil deeds dwarf my own crimes by multitudes of millions.

I'm not trying to exonerate myself from my heinous crimes just because the human habitat is a fucked up sadistic nightmare. I would gladly allow the families of the women I killed in a maddening rage to stone me to death should they desire to do so or to dismember my body by wrenching my limbs. My hatred would've finally met its match—the hatred of the families who had been deprived of their daughters and sisters—a match made for hell and would've finally liberated me from myself.

Every Man Dies Alone

Alas, I have to do it on my own. Hans Fallada's[1] book said it best.

Norway is closer to a civilized country than any other society on Earth. Gaustad sykehus is no ghastly Broadmoor criminal lunatic asylum but rather a pleasant, clean and filled-with-light hospital. Moreover, Dr. Sønstebø, a forensic psychiatrist in charge of my case is a tall, incomparably gorgeous, immensely intelligent cutie whose luminescent ultramarine eyes remind me of the Geirangerfjord and its deep blue waters. Ah, how much I lust for her during long, lonely nights here. However there was an obstacle, a lingering monster behind my lust. I was thinking about the global tyrant, the glorious U.S. of A. that might, as a footnote of the evil empire's voluminous opus of terror and dread, want to see me extradited so it could deploy its famous "justice" on me. Leslie was, after all, an American.

By killing myself, I will deny any pretense of "justice" the vile system would like to usurp by trying me. Fuck them!

---

1   Primo Levi called the Hans Fallada's *Every Man Dies Alone* "the greatest book ever written about the German resistance to the Nazis."

The End

It's here! It's already burning the skin of my right temple, the bullet, at its 267°C exit temperature.

This is so strange…this odd pulsating moment. Why am I not dead yet? Is this my last heartbeat? No, that would be too corny. But it feels so weird. What is the bullet waiting for? Is it giving me a last chance to reconsider? Does it want me to change my mind? Does it ask me if I want to go back? I also ask myself: do I want to change my mind at this last moment of life? But really, do I want to live, to face my life, my love, my hatred again? To go back to México, to be with Charlotte like I was once with her during that fatal summer? The day we met was the day of Atl, governed by Xiuhtecuhtli, God of Fire. Do I want to try yet again now, right now when it's finally over?

No way in hell. The devil would be much better company than she ever was.

Whoosh!!

What is that?

The space around me suddenly spreads out for miles. For millions of miles. There's nothing in my vicinity I could reach. I can't see the horizon. Finally, I'm alone in the very center of the universe that's abandoning me. Where are the *"exquisite instruments of the mystical troupe to bid me farewell,"* Constantine[2], where?

You missed the train to nowhere? Again.

Even the time, this last instant of my life, is stretching like the space before it. Endlessly, it seeks to embrace eternity. Albert Einstein was right. Screw that spooky action at a distance, it's scary now and here. Could Yma Sumac's voice escape a black hole flying on her five octaves? *Gopher Mambo* to greet Stephen Hawking as he dwells floating on the event horizon, for the duration of one single B2 note? Forever. Why do we always talk about time and so seldom about infinity?

---

2   *The God Abandons Antony* poem by the Egyptian Greek poet, Constantine P. Cavafy
     features these stanzas: *"… listen to the sounds,*
     the exquisite instruments of the mystical troupe,
     and bid her farewell, the Alexandria you are losing."

La Llorona

Why do I hear *La Llorona* by Chavela Vargas now? And why her? She has drowned her children. I had none. I always loved Frida Kahlo, that's why, I guess. *Perhaps, Perhaps, Perhaps.* I listened to a Lila Downs concert once. On that day when I saw her concert with Jackie E. in New York, Lila Downs's nipples got hard as soon as she switched singing from English to Spanish, *Quizas, Quizas, Quizas.* Dear Jackie, she's the most gorgeous, by far the most brilliant woman I ever met but, somehow, she can't find her way into the books of men that loved her, barring her own, unless she's a footnote.

I saw Frida Kahlo in real life only once. She was standing next to the *Dream of a Sunday Afternoon in the Alameda Central*, a painting by Diego Rivera on a mural in México City. She was holding a Tao Yin Yang pendant in her left hand. She was dancing to Waltz No. 2 by Dmitri Shostakovich. She was the only one Diego loved on that painting. He looked at her. She looked back at me. Others were just extras, swimming by like the catfish in the pond.

I am thirsty now. That's absurd.

I would love to have one last sip (*esetleg* two if György S. decides to pop in, but he's from a completely different world called Magyarország) of El Perdido Tequila Gold. The best comes from Arandas in Jalisco. I miss the taste of its agave-y flavor. Funny, I was never too fond of tequila. El Perdido Gold is from the place where the agave kisses the heavens, not so far from Guadalajara, where I once spend a night kissing Soledad. Soledad stands for "loneliness." She had those fiercely beautiful *ojos tapatios*—dark and alluring eyes like the night under the crescent moon, not unlikely those of Ximena Navarrete whom I never saw. When on acid, Soledad painted Frida Kahlo's hallucinogenic portraits. Poor Soledad… if only I had learned to dance tango in time. Was that a chord of Julio Sosa's *El Último Café* just now that reminded me of a wasted life as it tangles on without me? Alas, I am not that lucky to hear *el Varon del Tango* with my sweet Sophie for the last time. Where are you now, *mon chéri*, I wonder? Sosa crashed his DKW in Buenos Aires and killed himself. He was thirty-eight.

Chavela Vargas, who lived to ninety-three, sings again:

Ayer lloraba por verte, Llorona   *Yesterday I cried 'cause I wanted to see you, Llorona*
Hoy lloro porque te vi   *Now I cry because I saw you*

Really, why do I hear Chavela Vargas singing *La Llorona* again? Do I also cry for the children I might have had with Charlotte before she devoured their images and erased them from my mind, only to have them replaced by hatred?

Hatred is to Love What Devil is to God

Finally, it's here, the bullet. In less than a millisecond, rather in a 1/100,000th of a second, it will be all over. The bullet effortlessly pierces through my head. The heat is surprisingly pleasant. My brain is ruptured with a creaky sound of my shattered skull that tolled the end. What bliss. It's done.

I'm sent off.

Adiós muchachos.

The Flashback

So it's true, life flashes before your eyes at its last infinitesimal moment indeed. Flashbacks that follow are that flash.

A PUBLISHER'S NOTE

The above letter was found near Roman L.'s dead body in the Gaustad sykehus, a Norwegian psychiatric hospital in which he had died on the Christmas Eve of 2018. We'd been friends while we both lived in Paris but had lost touch for over a year or two ago. So you can imagine my shock when a mutual acquaintance sent me a link to an online version of the Oslo's daily newspaper, *Dagbladet*, prominently featuring my friend's face with one word written across the whole page: **MORDER (killer).**

I was even more startled when, several days later, I received a letter in which, in his convoluted way, Roman had confessed to his murders. He also had enclosed instructions on how to get a copy of *The Bergmannstraße Demon Chronicles*, his detailed tale of love and murders he had committed.

What follows is the terrifying reflection of the terrified monster sneering inside him. His harrowing descent into Hell.

January 10, 2019 in Paris, France

Abbot Trygve E. Wighdal, Ph.D.
Editor-In-Chief

THE LETTER FROM NORWAY

"Perhaps some day I'll crawl back home, beaten, defeated. But not as long as I can make stories out of my heartbreak, beauty out of sorrow."

Sylvia Plath

Oslo, 24 December, 2018

Trygve, my most valuable friend:

You know better than anyone—this world is bleak, grotesque, and beyond vile. How anyone could argue otherwise? Why we never listened to Denis Diderot and did not *"strangle the last king with the guts of the last priest,"* is beyond me. What a shameful monument to the cowardice of that bloody mass we call humanity. The heroes are gone and despised in the muck of political correctness of the 21st century's agendas, and all that's left is a flat-out insane mass of deranged, zombie-like lunatics voting for equally corrupt, stinking political parties all over the world.

That's why I spent most of my life without being around people. I don't go out like the young Mark Twain and search for honest decent work in order to "blend in" and "learn" either. Perhaps I never saw myself as someone who can achieve things in this world? I have been too nauseated by it and the politics that rule people like sheep to bother. I prefer to sit on the shores of magical, mystical, majestic Rapa Nui and live with my own thoughts next to the mighty *moai*. Maybe I am too lazy to think about accomplishments? You be the judge. Long since, I lost the faith in a way—of my sense of destiny, identity and with it, the purpose.

But, I can't help myself and, as usual, I've gone askew. Forgive me.

In Media Res

Trygve, I must tell you, I've gone off the handle perhaps a little bit too much, gone mad and killed. Some details about my strange path since we parted ways might surprise you. The fact that I drank the blood of the women I murdered is one of those controversial topics. But, my friend, the times in which Maasai warriors drank the blood of a lion they killed is not behind us yet. Norwegians drank the blood of bears they hunted only decades ago. Even menstrual blood is a natural cleanser.

I know I'm mad, but I drank blood as an eternal communion, longing for sweet forgiveness. Regrettably, I'm beyond forgiveness. I know that. I am burning in Hell already. Tell me, frankly, what else your God could bestow on me?

Anemones

I love anemones. They sprang out of the tears of the goddess of love and beauty, Aphrodite, while she was mourning the death of her lover, mortal Adonis. I have mourned my lost love perpetually. The vase you once saw in my miserable little flat I watered with blood of my loved ones. Yes, as you may have already guessed by your keen Jesuit mind, out of hatred for Charlotte sprung—forgive me, a pun—an endless spring of love for so many others. I loved them to death and sacrificed them to the altar of my own suffocated love. I used their warm, velvety red blood to celebrate life embodied in a single flower of the mighty Anemone. Thanatos is Eros's brother separated at birth, another bloody affair, is he not?

Yes, although their dying screams resembled orgasmic cries of some mad sky dwellers I used to fuck in Paris, I hear them as distant riffs from a long forsaken past and then I know that I did indeed really, truly, deeply love them. The chains Charlotte bolted me into with her grotesque selfishness and her callous cruelty was gone. I went on liberating them as much as I was on the path of liberating myself. On a subconscious level, I did not really kill them; I exorcised my demon(s) instead.

Yours truly,
Roman

P.S. Please, go to the Oslo airport, and with the enclosed key, open the locker 27, my friend. Therein you'll find my feeble attempt to record that intense period of life since I parted with Charlotte. It's a small, diary-like set of tales that might provoke you to utter a giggle or two as you recall our lives as "two sexy bitches" in Paris. On a more serious note, think of my *chronicles* as a legacy that may be a parting gift for my brothers and sisters from soon to be their ostracized shadow.

Damn, I am getting all mushy now. While I have taken well too much of your precious time and have some other urgent matters to attend to in the next several days, pardon your old friend and cut me some slack. I hope not for a great post-mortem literary fame should you chose to publish my humble volume. After all, I acted merely as my own chronicler, hastily scribbling down a memory or two that might be of use to students of human nature, or at least of some entertainment value, if nothing else.

I'd be happy if my memories would help even one single human being to either heal or kill.

Part II
KNOW THYSELF

Chapter 1

THE DEMON

"If you bring forth what is within you, what you bring forth will save you. If you do not bring forth what is within you, what you do not bring forth will destroy you."

Gospel of Thomas

Oslo, December 12, 2018

How to put a method, a structure in madness? Since I'd be first to cast a stone at a murderer—I am one after all—I venture on writing these truthful chronicles as a study of human suffering. Selfish perhaps, but I seek neither forgiveness nor understanding for my evil deeds. I am not excusing myself nor do I think for a second that my own suffering justifies any of my actions. But my case shows how pain could go horribly wrong if not addressed properly and how it had morphed into a horrendous monstrosity whose shallow breathing keeps me up at night.

I am that monster. This is an attempt to understand how the monster came to be.

Forensic Inquiry

"Would you like to talk about demons?" asked Dr. Anja Sønstebø flatly, as she was meticulously leafing through a pile of papers in front of her, not looking at me at all. My case, I guessed keenly. I also chuckled to myself at the word "keenly," for there I was, under the microscope of a forensic mental health assessment expert, myself a murderous guinea pig the good doctor intended to dissect with tools her dubious profession developed in order to control people and societies alike. In my case, those would serve to probe me, to dig into my soul, to extract the essence of madness. All for the enlightenment of men, I guess. What a futile endeavor this was. Like we're not all lunatics in an insane world anyway, illustrious Dr. Sønstebø included. The doctor smelled of sex and confusion that no amount of woodsy scent her generously splashed perfume managed to cover and camouflage. I knew a *courtisane* in Paris who used to apply same tools of seduction—those costly fragrances—on her silky skin.

I had to give it to her, she was courteous and composed, and while I would not go so far to call her sympathetic, she was for sure kind. She wore that legendary Norwegian distant calmness, as a barely noticeable protective cloak around her. With that perfume on her, she smelled nice and sexy.

I liked her.

I would have expected her to have started with something easier, like my mother and her early demise, or that the doctor would've tried to unsettle me by inquiring about my most gruesome murder first, but no, she went *in media res* and tried to rattle a bee hive of monsters and demons, the merry little band of ghoulish creatures that had been inhibiting my being and ravaging my soul for quite some time. The demons, you ask? Tread lightly, doctor—this is a dangerous minefield you intend to explore and maybe even hope to defuse— tread lightly.

I did not say any of this aloud.

Nevertheless, she went on probing and poking me with sharp tools of her superior intellect. She needed to package her neuropsychological assessment of me in a forensic context, asses my legal sanity, i.e. my criminal responsibility and my competency to stand trial and present her findings to the authorities as soon as possible. So she repeated, in a soothing tone only a trained therapist could muster with such ease:

"Roman, did you hear me? Would you like to talk about demons?"

"No, not really," I replied coolly and this time without hesitation, my eyes still adrift.

Unlike Charlotte, Dr. Sønstebø was a dazzlingly beautiful specimen of the same gender. I smiled at the thought. Alas, she was, as Charlotte had been, a psychiatrist, so I really could not look at her at first. I feared the Hatred might jump out of me and, by taking over, disturb the fine balance she was trying to establish during our first session together. I owed her that much, a courtesy for courtesy, a respect for politeness. She looked up at me; her luminescent ultramarine eyes flashed a tiny smile as she caught my glimpse back. My eyes riveted on her. She was indeed one of the most beautiful women I have ever seen.

"It's OK," she said.

"No, it is not," said I.

The Glance

Once you've killed, a strange sense of power overwhelms you. You feel a tremendous regret at first, but almost at the same time, a void—the vast emptiness of your own soul takes a dominating place in your life. Soon after, it feels like a load is taken off your shoulders. Then, a feeling of deprivation might come to rule you. You just crossed the line. *Thou shalt not kill* wasn't an exemption reserved only for that omnipotent entity billions worship. Think Sodom and Gomorrah in the long line of murders directly committed by Him and you'll understand how being in such great company empowers you. The humanity invented the devil, for it needed to live with an illusion of good and evil; goodness as their own being reflected in God.

Moreover, the people you encounter, even if they have no clue about your hideous past, sense in it a strange, inexplicable, subliminal way. I guess they also cringe, not knowing why. A meaning is exchanged in a glance, not unlike the one Rogozhin and Prince Myshkin exchanged in *The Idiot* [3] while Nastassia Filipovna, a femme fatale loved by both men, laid on a neatly made bed behind the closed door, stabbed to death by the former to the horror of the latter. Myshkin, once he looked at Rogozhin's eyes, needed no words to *understand* what had transpired in the dark room in which Nastassia Filipovna ceased to be, murdered by her lover.

Once you've crossed the line and committed a murder, it's like an archetypal, ancient warrior oozes out of your aura and invisibly overpowers those you meet. You look at any particular woman fully aware that you could take her at will or break her neck at any given moment, and she senses it. I

---

3   *The Idiot* is one of the great books written by Fyodor Mikhailovich Dostoevsky, a Russian writer and, I daresay, mystic. It was published in 1869 as another story of love, madness and murder. Mikhail Bakhtin, a Russian philosopher, literary critic and semanticist said of the world of Dostoevsky's books, 'A single person, remaining alone with himself, cannot make ends meet even in the deepest and most intimate spheres of his own spiritual life, he cannot manage without *another* consciousness. One person can never find complete fullness in himself alone.'

am not sure if that does not attract them mightily. I reckon you should ask Ted Bundy[4] about it.

Dr. Anja Sønstebø was a strong, highly intelligent woman. She's a top-notch mental health professional so I assumed she knew a thing or two about human minds and souls and their numerous fickle fallibilities. She's also fully protected from any outbursts; after all, I sat across her shackled like a bear on a chain. One fully armed, burly and vigorous security officer from the *Politiets sikkerhetstjeneste*, the Norwegian Police Security Service, was always nearby, a mere second or less away from stopping me from any hostile actions I might have thought of. And yet, her body posture told me she secretly cowered as she inconspicuously protected herself. The books, the yellow folders, and the pile of papers lay upon the desk in between us, creating an invisible obstacle, a physical barrier representing a defense against an attack. When she spoke to me, she leaned back, folded her arms with her hands clutching the arms. Subconsciously, I realized, she was afraid of the serial killer smiling at her from the other side of life.

I wondered how long it would take her to decipher the truth—in my case, killings were not a matter of power. On the contrary, they were a matter of utter powerlessness.

The Bergmannstraße Demon

It all started—rather, *my life* started—to rapidly crumble with a maddening speed after I met Charlotte Mørk, the woman I loved, the woman whose name spelt doom. My love for Mørk was also conceived in a chance glance we exchanged on the Malecón de Playas in Tijuana. Within the glance was a burst of emotions, a sudden reaction of two overwrought souls that unconsciously found each other once their eyes met.

There were times in which I had had foreboding premonitions regarding her and "us" but those always escaped my proper scrutiny. Love for her and pain inflicted by her actions were too irresistible, too addictive, too demanding of my attention, so that I neglected the obvious and kept rushing toward my impending downfall with each attempt to keep our moribund relationship alive. But, like undead Lamia, a spiritual vampire

---

4   Ted Bundy was born on November 24, 1946 in Burlington, Vermont and grew up to be a charming, articulate, and intelligent young man. He was also the sadistic serial killer, kidnapper, rapist, burglar, and necrophile who had confessed to thirty murders, though the actual number of his victims remains unknown.

representing our entanglement, the phantom of love did not want to leave us, and it kept luring us together. So the *demon* will be present throughout this chronicle as a memory, not unlike the memory of a corpse eaten by pigs I once saw in Slavonia[5], something I wish to but am arrantly unable to forget.

"Shall we discuss The Bergmannstraße Demon, instead?" insisted Dr. Sønstebø, kindly but firmly. "Charlotte is the only woman you... *encountered...* that you call the demon," she paused as she kept reading from her notes.

"Why's that," she asked, rising her luminous eyes up.

"The Demon," I repeated as the rush of mixed feelings engulfed me. A twinge of those claws of the maddening, soul-shattering hatred I'd talk about later stabbed me again, piercing right through my heart, splitting me in half. And, to my horror, as I trembled in physical pain the memories had invoked like a whiff of cinnamon in the Haagen-Dazs Mayan Chocolate ice cream, I sensed a distant memory, a smattering of love I once had for her. This felt even worse than hatred—much more painful.

"Are you OK?" Dr. Sønstebø asked, leaning toward me as I convulsed. She seemed genuinely concerned.

"I am," I assured her. My shaking was gone as fast as it arrived. "All is fine," I repeated.

Of course, nothing was "fine." Far from it.

The Presence

There was also something else therein, around me, somewhere, everywhere, neverwhere, perhaps even in me as well, something elusive, like a ghost, a paranormal spirit attachment I could sense but was unable to see or hear or really feel. Years ago I would've dismissed such thoughts as balderdash that drunkards babble about in deliriums, but after all that had transpired over the last year or so, I was not sure where the insanity resides; is it in my bones or in a hijacked soul, or does this represent some sort of neurological disease? A psychological disorder? A brain tumor? I have no clue. Had I happened to fall into their clutches, the church would have sent me an exorcist, that's for sure. In the United States, some noble member of the

---

5   Slavonia is a region in Croatia. Roman is referring to the scene he witnessed during the war in the former Yugoslavia when he was a war-reporter stationed in Osijek until January 2nd, 1992 when the ceasefire to the conflict was signed in Sarajevo. (note by Trygve E. Wighdal)

American Psychiatric Association would be gavaging me like a goose with chlorpromazine and would've expected me to become a healthy, well-adjusted serial killer overnight. Luckily for me, the Norwegian legal system had sent me a blue-eyed, angelic-looking doctor and, respecting my human rights, they let me cope with my own issues on my own time as long as I was calm and cooperating. They even gave me a computer to write. No internet access, alas.

But that "something" inescapably and *invisibly* stood in between me and my memories, casting an enormous shadow I was unable to see, while also being overwhelmed by it. For the moment, after Dr. Sønstebø mentioned the *Demon,* I was unable to remember how the woman who defined me and the last years of my life looked as I was trying to articulate an answer to Dr. Sønstebø's question. At that moment, I did not remember Charlotte! It felt like I was losing myself again, suddenly afraid that I'd be gone, lost in the chthonic world of a non-entity that knows nothing but the terrifying fact that it has lost itself.

Suddenly, as fast as it had arrived, in the midst of those horrifying fears, a *puff!*—the gnawing sensation was gone in an instant. A phantom— that strange presence in me that had no name, aura, smell, and shape or form—was gone, and I again remembered everything.

I was ready to address the Dr. Sønstebø's inquiry.

Chapter 2
EROS AND THANATOS

"For all sad words of tongue and pen, the saddest are these: 'It might have been'."
John Greenleaf Whittier

Tijuana, April 30, 2014 (Easter Sunday)

Cornelius Agrippa[6], the famous mystic from the 16th century, screwed me over even before Dr. Sønstebø's forensic examination of what was left of my identity. "Love is the chariot of the Soul, the most excellent of all things," Agrippa wrote. I wholeheartedly subscribed to his thoughts. Nothing matters more than love. Love is the humans' way of defeating God's jealousy and a manner of defeating death. Love was my mantra, the song my heart sang even while I was all alone. *No se puede vivir sin amar*[7] (you can't live without loving) and all that stuff I lived by doomed me. Charlotte was merely an executioner with a knack for blowjobs, someone placed in my life by devilish forces whose sole purpose was to push me over the edge.

---

6   Heinrich Cornelius Agrippa von Netteshe, 1486-1536 was Doctor of the Laws and Physick [medicine] a German secret agent, soldier, physician, orator, and law professor, making a living around Europe as an alchemist. He was counselor to Charles, the Fifth Emperor of Germany but some believed him to be not only an alchemist but a demonic magician. (note by Trygve E. Wighdal)
7   You can't live without loving. *Under the Volcano* by Malcolm Lowry, Ch. I (p. 6)

The Sun God

I once soared toward the Sun God and wrote a screenplay set under the ruins of the fabled city of Machu Picchu. The Andes are a place where magic happens: gateways to heaven and the occult world of souls. In that vast, esoteric part of the world, we shared a spiritual spark that made us one with the Sun God. Believing that "impossible is nothing," I wrote "only love is as strong as death."

Well, I might have had a change of heart since.

Charlotte had read the screenplay. She didn't care about it too much, for it spoke a strange language (of love) to her but, much worse, it left the doors into my naiveté wide open. It was a wide crack of vulnerability, an inviting opening for a dagger, that sentimental script of mine, may it rest in peace, unmolested by Hollywood's agents who were never really eager to sell it.

Zona Norte[8]

I rapidly scribble down my notes because I am in a hurry. As I harken back to the dark times of the soul Dr. Sønstebø inquired about, I also hasten to die before the night's out. Chop-chop. I recall that I was supposed to cross Wu Han's great divide in between daily misery and eternal rest much earlier, on the Easter of 2014, in Tijuana, México. TJ is not only the God-forsaken place where I first met Charlotte, but a city in which you gullibly chug a hooker of whiskey with hardened harlots whose black hearts are made of charcoal, just moments before they rob you blind. And yet, those shaved ladies of the *Zona Norte* nights were so much more honest than Charlotte ever was. Particularly when they snorted a line of coke, sucked you dry for ten bucks and pickpocketed you at the same time, God have mercy on their weary souls.

Moreover, TJ is a city whose ghastly façades keep that great Mexican sense of humor hidden and *corazónes valientes*, fearless hearts of this great nation out of sight as its unparalleled ugliness gets into your face on every corner. You need to get to know México *lindo y querido* if you want to understand and, ultimately, love México. Otherwise, mariachi bands' incessant shrieking would drive you barking mad like they'd done to León Eugene del Norte, a hacker friend of mine who ran from the TJ mariachis all

---

8   Zona Norte, a.k.a. "La Coahuila" is an infamous red lights district in Tijuana.

the way down to Terra Australis in a search for silence and is now hacking Twitter trolls from somewhere in the Gold Coast, just south of Brisbane.

Or you might end up drinking yourself to death in this strange and painfully beautiful country. With open arms, México invites you to down the hatch your booze and vanish in Tijuana's hidden tequila vortices if you're so inclined. No one would judge you there. Should you, on the other hand, prefer to further sanitize your sainthood, go with your head held high straight to the Calle Benito Juárez and attend a Sunday Mass in Catedral de Nuestra Señora de Guadalupe—it is entirely up to you. Alas, it's unlikely we'd meet there praying. My church is Iglesia de la Soledad, the Church of Solitude of the *"The Virgin for those who have nobody with."* But beware: México worships *Nuestra Señora de la Santa Muerte*, our Lady of Holy Death, maybe more than it worships God.

Unlike Frida Kahlo, who on her deathbed wrote, "I hope the exit is joyful and I hope never to return," I hoped neither for joy nor for bliss from my exit; I just wanted it to be over. Little did I know, I would have to suffer for another four and a half years, ravaging my own life and destroying the lives of others. So as luck would have it, I kept on living and killing, until the day of reckoning finally came—today, on the Christmas Eve of 2018.

C'est la vie! [9] as the French would say.

My ludicrous life has been shattered into smithereens so many times, it was hurled into garbage heaps over and over again, here, there, anywhere, everywhere, tossed overboard from the indefatigable ships that crossed oceans many times over with me on board, smashed from the TV screens by rabid *apparatchiks*[10], suffocated under the gallons of vodka I drank like there's no tomorrow when I was younger, lost like forgotten luggage on airports in Papeete, Tahiti or Mombasa, Kenya alike, sucked out of me by Lamia's hungry, cold kisses, trashed by Humberto C. who had stolen all of my earthly possessions in Brazil… so how could I hope to find my identity scattered all over the world, lost in broken glasses of *vodka com suco de naranja* I trashed with Donny A. in some dive bar in New York, vanished in a novel I wrote decades ago whose only printed copy Silvia T. lost over one

---

9   A French expression used to play down some minor disappointment, translated as "such is life." I suspect Roman is being deliberately flippant here. (note by Trygve E. Wighdal)

10 This is a reference to the attack on Roman, broadcast by the national TV in his native country, something that he wasn't willing to elaborate. But that moment marked a crucial moment in his life: he had felt abandoned by his own homeland. (note by Trygve E. Wighdal)

drunken white night she shared with cab drivers in Reykjavik, while I slept oblivious in the futuristic, obscure Galaxy Pod Hostel. How could I have hoped to find my identity once I buried it in Charlotte's house of cards? To my shame, I sacrificed it rather both lovingly and unwittingly on the altar of love and have finally lost myself.

I sat still.

Beyond Gaustad sykehus *sing the woods* like in the novel by Norwegian Trygve Gulbranssen of the same title, the cold breeze could not care less about my life's idiotic smithereens, as it was flying around, that windy image of freedom and pure innocence. I sincerely hope I manage to tell you about both of my stunts: those strange Brazil-based adventures and how I ended up living those grotesque homeless days in New York—all in due course, before the first cu–ckoo, cu–ckoos greet the Christmas Day. But, for the time being, let us move on along the dusty roads of my Mexican memories and follow the story as it unfolds.

On Easter of 2014, I was starving, having just eaten my last reserves of beans provided to me by aforementioned León, that hacking purveyor of legumes and crazy scientific stories. I miss that old mischief dearly. Moreover, I had no money for rent as my online consultancy fees had dried out. YouTube binge, as I was sitting in front of the screen watching endless funny cat videos (but in fact frozen waiting the ultimate) did not help either.

I worried myself sick, so I searched for some uplifting songs.

Don't Worry Be Happy

> *"The landlord say your rent is late*
> *He may have to litigate*
> *Don't worry, be happy"*

An a cappella song sung by Bobby McFerrin back in 1988 made millions happily dance to its tune but paid only for Mr. McFerrin's rent. Alas, the TJ landlords were not an overly litigious crowd. They'd kick you in the ass if you were lucky not to be killed and throw you out on the streets butt naked. That was going to happen to me on that holy day. Positive thinking does not help either, despite what spiritual gurus tell you. Hungry and homeless in Tijuana—that's some achievement deserving of fulfilling the promise of ending it all on the very Easter Day.

One man's resurrection is another man's descent into Hell.

Manna from Heaven (or Hell)

Out of the blue, a client who had owed me money for over four years, some $1,500.00, sent me his payment that very evening. I was saved, or at least my demise had been postponed.

Armed with a nice wad of rent money, I met with José Jaime B.—the toothless landlord who was released from prison after serving a twelve-year-long sentence for some gang related crimes in Los Angeles just before I moved from L.A. to TJ—and proudly paid him. He looked somehow disappointed but took the money anyway. I invited him for a drink and, soon after, we'd gotten drunk on Don Julio® Añejo Tequila, a smooth booze smelling of agave and wild honey. What could possibly go wrong? Truth to be told, I was already going insane, so getting smashed to pieces with a nasty son of a gun like José Jaime was, paradoxically, the only respite from mental anguish I could think of summoning. Him whining about two women he used to date at the same time—and beat the living shit out of "because he loved them so much"—was almost a refreshing change from my own suffering.

For weeks, culminating over the last seven-to-ten days, I had been going mad. The closest comparison to what was going on with me would be David Bowman's disconnecting of HAL 9000[11] and the latter's terrifying fear of creeping, crippling madness. Charlotte had been excoriating my soul for ages already, removing each and every desire for life and love I had, and I'd been losing it.

Reductio ad Absurdum

In that drunken stupor, I emailed her: "You are the only person in the world in whose expertise I'd believe enough to talk about this *creeping madness*." Once I'd sobered up, I was ashamed. Why would I write to a woman who was never there? Ten days ago she had left, again, "loving me more than ever" and my heart was falling apart; I learned the full meaning of a broken heart. It really breaks. I started to think she was also insane. Why would we have met and clung onto each other for such a long time (five, six years of endless agony) otherwise? So I fruitlessly tried to help us survive,

---

11 In the Stanley Kubrick's film *2001: A Space Odyssey*, David Bowman's character deactivates the cognitive functions of the murderous artificial intelligence computer, HAL 9000. Heuristically-programmed Algorithmic computer, or HAL, had his mental capacities rapidly diminished, ultimately reverting the powerful sentient computer to a childlike state.

live and thrive. Little did I know that "us" existed only in my imaginary world she never even dreamt of inhabiting.

"I never stopped loving you, and I have not been with anyone since we first met. And I miss your brilliance a lot," she wrote back to me from India. The hangover from hell slowed me down to a painful crawl, so it took me a lot of energy to go back to the computer and re-read our exchange. "Living in such a way is totally invalidating the life itself. Madness did not take over completely, so I keep fighting but I don't know what I am fighting against anymore."

Her comment was, "It is interesting that you write you fight but you don't know what you are fighting. That's how I always perceived your struggle," and while I read those clinical words, I remembered a dream I had the previous night.

Ulrike B.

I came home and opened the door of my room, facing its utter darkness. I stood still, disoriented and somehow trepidatious. What is this? In that instant, a spark of white light, like a pinpointed laser beam, had appeared. Follow the light they say, so I looked up as the white beam widened. It glistened like a liquid silver streak of some magical stream, calmly flowing toward the rivers of Babylon. In that glowing stream, like Aphrodite who rose from the white froth of the sea, straight out of gentle silvery ripples on the water's surface, our unborn daughter, a little child barely old enough to be able to speak and who looked like Charlotte's spitting image when she herself was a kid, Ulrike B., showed up. She was dressed in a little blue dress, matching her crystal blue-grey eyes. She was so cute and little, her shoulders tiny. I wanted to hug her but I was frozen on my end of the room.

She looked up at me and her sad blue eyes filled with tears when she quietly told me:

"If you betray me, I will die."

I panicked. Why would she think I would betray her? I woke up, or I dreamed that I woke up, but nevertheless, I grabbed a pen and paper and scribbled down what she just said. I feared I might forget her and her message given the prior's night binge. I'd fallen back into drunken stupor and kept on dreaming.

The light was gone and with it, Ulrike. That second dream felt like a continuation of the first one but now in the pitch-blackness. It felt like death. I was in that abject darkness, devoid of sights and sounds. I searched for Ulrike, called her name, but no cry or echo returned my calls. I was able to walk through the room that had become enormous but could not reach any furniture, any light fixtures, any walls. I walked blindly around that huge, disorienting space, hollering her name over and over again. My voice and my sight had been drowned in black. I started to feel like I was going to die in that dream; it felt I was going to vanish in that vacuous infinity and never wake up to see, to hug, to love my wee daughter again. But I did not want to die in that scary night in which Ulrike had disappeared, so I kept searching around and calling her name. In vain. Nothing came back and yet I knew, I felt that she was there, all by herself, so little, so lonely, so scared. I woke up screaming her name.

Once awake, I found that barely legible note I scribbled down with her cryptic words.

The Dream

I never had a dream of Ulrike before. She looked almost exactly like Charlotte did as a kid—a dead ringer. The love I felt for her was palpable, the sweet and painful unconditional love of a parent. That love stayed with me for a long time after I woke up. I still love her. She wasn't a part of my prior, "real" life due to Charlotte's "need for freedom," i.e. her refusal to have children, so she wasn't a part of a plan, or a hope and for sure not even as a remote possibility. And yet, Ulrike's first appearance in my life felt like she was always there, always in me, always a part of me, our unborn child made of filaments of what might have been. A gaping wound in my heart had been filled with love for her. It was all surreal: Ulrike and her little blue dress, the dream, the thoughts I thought, the feelings I felt. Everything was also as disorienting as Hell.

I talk about (my) "madness" but in those moments, I was as sane as Saint Dymphna[12], a devout teenage Irish Girl from the 7th century had been until her father beheaded her. While I knew my daughter was real, I also knew her "realness" wasn't of this world. So if I wasn't going mad, how to explain this strange phenomenon I was experiencing? It was a dream that did not want to go away, it was an apparition of my child that wanted to come to life, and yet, it was so scared of betrayal, which felt like death.

I had to think, to process all of that—I had to understand where she came from, which realm she lived in, who she was… these were the things I needed to understand about my daughter. Who is that little scared child so terrified of my betrayal?

Gnothi seauton[13]

Oslo, December 12, 2018

Dr. Anja Sønstebø jotted down some notes in her notebook, then looked up and glared at me carefully.
"Did you discover who she was?"
I looked at her, but my gaze was turned inward when I replied.
"Oh, yes. But not quite at once."

---

12   Saint Dymphna's mother died while Dymphna was a teenager. Her father, who loved his wife deeply, was driven to madness by her death. Delusion and mental illness overcame him, and he eventually sought to marry his own daughter because she reminded him of his departed wife. St. Dymphna, a devout Christian girl, refused to do such a wicked thing as marry her father. She resisted her father's advances and fled Ireland with her confessor, St. Gerebernus. When she was 15 y.o. her father beheaded her. (note by Trygve E. Wighdal, as extracted from Nick Rabiipour's writing on the topic)

13   Greek for "Know thyself," from the temple of Apollo at Delphi. (note by Trygve E. Wighdal)

Chapter 3
GNOTHI SEAUTON

"If you only knew what darkness I am plunged into."
Sainte-Thérèse de Lisieux

Rijeka, April 4th, 1972

It was rather an uneventful Tuesday, that April the 4th—almost dull given all the school chores I had to do since early morning, boring all the way up until 8:10 PM at which time my mother had died. She passed away alone in the Radiotherapy and Oncology department of the Clinical Hospital Center of Rijeka, in Croatia, my native country. I was watching the TV with my father when the phone rang. I observed him plodding over to the other room to pick up the phone. He looked like a man carrying a hundred tons on his shoulders. He *felt it* even before he had answered the call.

Thanatos

"Mother of God..." he groaned quietly and side-glanced at me, as he was hanging up the phone in what seemed like an endless slow motion, prolonging the moment of truth. He did not have to tell me what he has nevertheless softly said, choking back tears, for I also *knew*: "Mom died."

And that was it.

It was a loss engraved deeply on my heart. A heavy cloak of loneliness had fallen upon me and my soul as I stood forlorn of hope my mom would miraculously get well.

"Mothers are superheroes when they're battling cancer," wrote Jessica Reid Silwerski in her *Cancer Hates Kisses* book and she seems right. After a full year of a truly mighty struggle, including chemotherapy and several metastases, which my mom heroically fought against, she finally succumbed to illness. Only a few days before her premature death (she was thirty-six years old when she died) she published a final installment of her newspaper serial about battling the breast cancer. She did not say a word about her own sickness. What she was publishing was more of a booklet with instructions to women how to detect breast cancer early and how to fight it. In the early 70s of the 20th century, a breast cancer diagnosis was as close to a death sentence as any diagnosis came.

I don't remember much of the days before the funeral that took place two days after her death. Father sent me to my uncle's house in order to avoid the people coming and going to our place and be left in peace. I do remember my uncle's pandemoniacal, devilish snoring that kept me awake for hours and hours at night. As I laid awake in bed and waited for dawn to break, I was numb, remembering the cursed phone call over and over again. I also recalled that my Darwil watch had stopped at 8:10 PM that same evening, at the precise moment of my mom's death. I never hand-wound that watch again, letting it stand frozen in time, in that singular moment of deep sorrow that had changed my life.

Eros

Dostoyevsky wrote about the "moment of bliss," "enough for a lifetime" and I sought it all over the world, that moment of bliss, for the feeling of ecstasy, for the lightness of joy or for at least a moment of calmness to counter the heavy burden of sorrow that had enveloped me since I was a young boy. It mostly eluded me, but I did feel bliss once or twice in my life, I think.

I met Gabrielė F., a girl from Kaunas, Lithuania, in January of 1994, in Venice. She studied for her Master's degree in History of Arts and Conservation of Artistic Heritage at the Ca' Foscari University in the Dorsoduro district and had lived there for several years already.

It was a chance meeting. I saw her, all cute and confident, beautiful and terrifying, in one small *osteria*, Antica Osteria Ruga, close to the Rialto Bridge. She was wildly gesticulating about something that must have been of great importance to her friend, who has evaporated from my memories. I was instantly attracted to the energy emanating from her, drawn by her aura and the way she dressed and carried herself. She wore an immaculate, vintage black velvet Edwardian cloak. It was some sort of impossible steampunk Goth vintage combo, complete with black faux leather jeans and, don't ask me how and why, a worn out French cap. I complimented her on her unique style, but I'd done that because she also wore unspeakably ugly, mismatched with anything, atrocious white sandals with that stylish outfit. I faked admiration over her cloak and outrage over her footwear choice and it worked. She laughed at my compliments, even more so at my dismay over *that... that thing* (the sandals). She accepted a drink, and soon after, an invitation for a walk. She told me she lived around there, so I asked her to be my guide in Venice. She happily accepted, and we walked about the city of water and gondolas, of bridges and canals, of romance and love, me and Gabrielė who knew myriad stories about happiness of the couples that kissed on a gondola ride under *Ponte di Sospiri,* the famous Bridge of Sighs.[14]

She also had an irresistibly cute habit of naming the mermaids of Venice. "Look," she cried excitedly, as we walked up the Scala dei Giganti, the staircase leading up to the first floor of the Doge's Palace, "this is Chiara, the Ducal mermaid." And there she was, Gabrielė's Chiara, a young double-tailed mermaid. She did the same with dragons and phoenixes along the Venetian canals. "This one is Ivan Drago," she giggled, and that one is "Rocky." Neither a single gargoyle we passed by nor the smallest winged lion, nor Cerberus or Minotaur or chimaera that live in Venice was left unnamed. She was indeed a unique creature, unlike any other I have ever met.

I pinched her: "Are you for real?"

And she giggled, "stop it." She slapped my hand, laughing, and moved on across this unequalled, mystical town whose soul is made of reflections. Venice attracts so much water so she could enjoy herself, reflected from the bridges and palaces alike. A supple, reddish gondola glided by, hung with yellowish lanterns, and a gondolier's tenor started to sing *"O sole mio."* I still hear a distant echo of that Venetian gondolier we heard that day. Gabrielė shed a tear as she quietly hummed along.

We kept sauntering along and she told me all about *The Last Supper* and *San Giovanni Elemosinario* by Jacopo Tintoretto and Titian, respectively,

---

14 Ian Harvey wrote that "although the bridge is associated with romance, the story about the origins of its name has no romantic background at all. As one of the legends says, prisoners walked across the bridge on their way to the executioner or back to their cells. The view from the bridge was their last view of Venice, and their sighs of despair and depression are the ones credited with the famous name of the bridge."

the paintings we saw in Basilica di San Giorgio Maggiore (on the island of the same name) and Chiesa di San Sebastiano (in Dorsoduro). Those were works of art she admired greatly. About the paintings, she radiated enthusiasm so great that she seemed to have a glow similar to the luster Christ had about him in the corner of *The Last Supper*. She eloquently spoke about depth Tintoretto had created by using the linear perspective and that unmistakable glow that immediately delineated him from his disciples. She admired the angels floating above the feast and loved how, in contrast to the Leonardo's own Last Supper, Tintoretto's is much darker, lightened only by fire from the chandelier. It's like Christ was having the last supper in some dive bar in Dublin she said.

I was bewitched by her. She was as lively and vigorous as the chiming of the Chiesa when I kissed her. Yes, that gorgeous brunette with quick wit whose skin was as soft as a Venetian dove made me forget the time and space, as we embraced and soul-kissed for the first time. The world stood still, as the old cliché has it, but it was precisely like that. It was the first kiss in which I've totally lost myself.

After a long walk around we'd gotten hungry, so I took her for a dinner to the upscale Riviera restaurant, next to the *Il Canal de la Giudecca*, following Lena T.'s recommendation. Lena is a friend from Amsterdam who knows more about Venice than Joseph Brodsky himself. She is an exceptional character that merits her own book, but I do not have time to talk about her anymore. I can only thank her for the recommendation of that romantic space that spawned Gabrielė's and my passionate affair. Yes, dear Lena, you were right, a sunset over *La Guidecca* is a sight to behold. No woman, unless her heart is harder than the Templar's sword, could resist the pure essence of romance Riviera & La Guidecca combo produces at sunset. Gabrielė, on her merry way to give up any ideas of resisting, chose for us a *fresco* sea bass with prosciutto and crispy sage, wild mushrooms and king prawn. She had that mischievous smile and giggle that made even a simple thing like ordering a meal feel like a great, mysterious adventure.

Vini Divini

I felt a bit intimated by Gabrielė's immense physical beauty and her vivaciousness alike. Her *passione* for Venetian art and architecture oozed out of her with such charm, deep knowledge and profound understanding that I was overwhelmed just by listening to her words and how she molded them out of air and inspiration. All's fair in love and war they say, so I used a harmless little trick of mine to even the playfield with that divine creature. I asked her to choose the wine for us but asked of her to choose one of the wines I wrote about years later. Those are the choices I offered her, keen to see how she'd react:

Pietra Sacra – *excites like a young, salacious peasant girl. Deep in what she offers, suggesting what she proposes is much more than what's obvious. The wine is full, strong after 10 years in the bottle, as strong as her legs and arms. Bouquet is terrestrially opulent, coming from the depths of clay from which its grape grew, as sumptuous as curves and breasts of our little lustful rustic desire fantasy dressed in her white linen shirt.*

Tannin in the Pietra Sacra wine is like a whiff coming from the Mediterranean Sea, which gives it another layer of beauty; the tongue and the palate sing as they're smooching her. Very pleasant to imbibe. A feel of tipsiness: Dionysian. It's somehow "raw"—it feels like one drinks it directly from a moist, rustic soil as it takes it from the lips of your peasant girl.

With Pietra Sacra, one must fuck in the hay.

Mille e Una Note – *this (quite expensive) wine is like a lustful—albeit a tad aged and therefore even more exciting—rather perverted aristocrat. Now at a certain mature age, her bright blue eyes radiate life experiences. She's all smooth, velvety and, dare I say, somewhat cunning. But what a charm she possesses. She knows the game of life better than you could imagine. The wine itself has an intense, exquisite ruby color. Its bouquet mesmerizes you. You can whiff a scent of the celebrated licorice amidst a tad stronger blackberry and plum notes. One even senses a chocolate in it. Ahh, il cioccolato Siciliano, how could anyone live without you?*

Mille e Una Note makes you wish to be able to swim in it, to immerse yourself in lustful Dionysian games or at least to frantically dance under the full moon, like the renegade dervishes of yesteryear used to do.

Then you take a sip. You imbibe it gently, almost timidly kissing the lips of your aristocrat lady as it all starts slowly and deliberately. Think of Gioachino Rossini and "William Tell Overture." It does not overwhelm you at the start but then, with every bit (a sip, a kiss…) it lures you even deeper into its mystery, all the way up to the overpowering crescendo. Yes, she is reserved at first, our gorgeous aristocratic lady, but once she opens herself, she takes you to the heights of sensual pleasures you could have only dreamt of before encountering her.

Mille e Una Note is big, an exceptionally refined wine. It is as smooth and as silky as our aristocrat. So, with this big, red ruby Sicilian wine, one ought to fuck in silk.

Gabrielė giggled several times as she read my enology notes and then laughed out loud. "Really nice," she said, looking at me with those beautiful Lithuanian eyes filled with promise that made my heart race like a colt. "One must fuck no matter which one of those wines they drink."

"So, which one do you choose?" I was curious.

"Which one you think I'd choose?" She played a flirtatious game that gorgeous women had excelled in since Cleopatra had seduced Roman emperor Mark Anthony.

"The aristocrat," I guessed.

"No way," she laughed, hitting me in the shoulder. "You think I am an old pervert? You are the pervert. I'll go with the peasant girl, with Pietra Sacra and you get us some hay, just in case."

I asked myself, as my heart was melting away, what magic made her eyes flash with such erotic fire as she was mocking me? I was out of my mind, deliriously happy just to have someone as unique as Gabrielė next to me.

Keep in mind, the Riviera restaurant is in Veneto, but those vines are prides of Sicily. It was highly unlikely they'd carry any of the wines I wrote about, a true fact Luigi, our *cameriere*, the waiter, had confirmed outright. "I am sorry," he said. "We don't have Pietra Sacra."

"No need to be sorry." I smugly smiled. "I will be more than happy to pay for the corkage fee." I said as I triumphantly pulled a bottle of Pietra Sacra out of my backpack.

"You scoundrel," Gabrielė laughed and hit me in my arm again.

At that moment I knew she was mine, so I kissed her passionately in front of Luigi whose *"mamma mia, che baci sensuali"* (what sensual kisses,) cries of approval made us laugh, even when he left to get our order, still crying out loud, *"mamma mia, che baci."*

Che Bacci

It seems obvious now, in Gabrielė's arms I sought the moment of bliss to be extended forever. I was going after the freedom only love gives you as it liberates you from the hells of daily living and weeping wounds of the past.

Given all that had transpired with my life since January of 1994 and a fleeting love affair with Gabrielė, it's interesting that when she left me, I did not feel hurt. I asked her if she's going to be with me exclusively and she replied with a factual "Not likely." There's a world out there, a world she wanted to explore, a myriad of men and women she wanted to taste, fuck, leave and forget as she examined life's ups and downs. I could only hope she remembered me from time to time, at least as half as fondly as I remember her, which is more often than I'd like to admit. That was tough though, her answer. It was really hard for I was taken by her. Her decision to keep roaming free as a bird did not steer anything hostile or angry in me. Such a far cry from the future degenerate version of me that Charlotte molded in her own image.

Unlike her, Gabrielė did not lie. She did not betray me. She was honest and I was OK. For the time being.

The Road Not Taken

So, Gabrielė was gone from my life. I often thought about her and our brief encounter in Venice. Those several days were among the most memorable of my life, but she had taken the other road. Saturn entered Pisces that January. Do I need to tell you that Gabrielė was born in Pisces, in "the last of the signs who are potentially the most tolerant and least judgmental of all them all?" I am an Aries, the first sign, not as tolerant one might argue but also someone who never gives up. If only I knew how to give up Charlotte and many lives would've been saved. If only I had fought for Gabrielė, I might have had a chance for a different life, one of love and fulfillment, far from the hellish nightmares Charlotte had been creating around the clock, like her life depended on dramas and pain.

Alas, I did not take that road. On the one I had taken, some twenty years in the future, had waited with all its dangers.

Charlotte Knew

Oslo, December 12, 2018

Until I met Charlotte, I had no idea that I had been frozen in that moment of my mother's demise. I walked on a knife-edge ever since, and I had a pretty clear idea about loneliness, about the hole in my heart, about missing my mom as essential parts of my identity, but I did not think it was crucial for my spiritual development. I paid a heavy life coinage for my inability to see the truth, so I refused to accept the truth even when it sneered at my face from the mirror. At that time, I thought losing loved ones was a part of everyone's life. I was nothing special, for that matter. I knew much more painful losses than my own back in 1972, no matter how frightening and devastating it had been to have lost Mom while I was such a young boy.

On Tue, May 16, 2016 at 7:15 PM <charlotte.mørk@yahoo.no> wrote:

> It seems to me that you had fallen into the betrayed boy inside you and had been frozen in the memory and that this is what has been paralyzing your life, and in seeing it you can start to find a way to integrate it and move on.
>
> xoxo,
> Charlotte

"So see," I said to Dr. Anja Sønstebø, handing her a printout of Charlotte's e-mail. "She knew me better than I knew myself. Such deep understanding made me fall in love with her even more than I thought was possible."

"This is the first positive thing you've said about Charlotte," Dr. Sønstebø remarked.

"Really?"

"Yes. Everything else was about her being the demon—a deceptive, selfish monster. It surprises me that you have anything nice to say about her at all."

"I would have many a positive thing to say. Only that I now have the full picture of her real nature."

"And your own," Dr. Sønstebø said coldly.

"And my own, yes," I said, miffed by Dr. Sønstebø's implied suggestion. "I never tried to hurt her, despite all her deeds and all my pain, even when I was studying magic and knew how to do it."

"No, you killed her instead," she said matter-of-factly.

I sighed. "Well, you might have a valid point there, Dr. Sønstebø."

Chapter 4
SOUL FRAGMENTATIONS

"The unexamined life is not worth living."

Socrates

Oslo, December 13, 2018

The soul is not an independently existing substance but a part that gives life, its body, the potential to be. A loss of soul, the alchemical, spiritual Soul-Loss makes us wonder what it is that we are missing in our lives. It is usually love.

Today, the soulful Dr. Anja Sønstebø and I had an early morning session. She arrived immediately after I had *lakes go eggerøre*, that sumptuous Norwegian breakfast made of smoked salmon and scrambled eggs with a slice of Kneippbrød roll. It's nuts how civilized this country, populated by tall and smart descendants of Vikings, once the dread of the Northern European tribes, had come to be. This is how they feed even their worst prisoners.

Dr. Anja Sønstebø looked fresh, rested and rather jolly. No perfume today, I noticed.

"Good morning, Roman."

"Good morning to you as well, Dr. Sønstebø. You look full of kicks this morning."

"Shall we discuss Ulrike today?"

"The terrors of the forest, like all panic terrors, are inspired, Jung believed, by fear of what the unconscious may reveal," I started, a bit cryptically. "Only after Charlotte appeared in my life…"

Dr. Sønstebø cut me off, surprisingly harshly. "Forget her, please, only for today."

I looked at her nervously.

"Focus on the Ulrike dream and what it meant to you. What was your discovery after the dream you described yesterday?" she demanded.

I took a long breath as I mulled over her sudden change in demeanor. OK, as you wish, I thought, annoyed, but continued anyway.

"Easter Day of 2014 was the first day in which I finally realized the existence of *entities* in me."

"Entities?"

"Come on, Dr. Sønstebø, you know what I mean."

"Maybe. But why don't you tell me, what do you mean by entities?" She looked truly interested.

"It is self-explanatory that we all have different personalities, as we wear different *personas* on our faces. You are one person while probing me, another while having adulterous sex and cheating on your husband."

She did not bite and kept calmly looking at me like I said nothing provocative. She was good.

"A third when you are out for a dinner with family members that are not your favorites. We are all like that, aren't we? We wear one mask, displaying one personality for the job interview and quite another for a first date or grocery shopping. Luckily, those different personalities are a way we function in the society. Nothing profound or shocking in that."

"But your own entities, like Ulrike, are shocking?" Dr. Anja Sønstebø inquired. She was good, very good indeed, that blue-eyed glacial beauty Alfred Hitchcock would have loved to have tortured in one of his movies.

The First Discovery

Only after the Ulrike dream, I started to seriously think about that "betrayed boy inside me that had been frozen in the memory." As I had begun to explore the dream's meaning, the surge that opened the floodgates of feelings, discoveries and understandings seemed to have been growing by the minute. For a fleeting moment only, I was relieved, for it felt like I was on the starting point of a journey within, a long overdue trip of self-discovery I had been postponing so many times that it seemed like an impossibility to start with it now. Flashes of understanding brought light into the depths of my being, disturbed my shadow, and invoked a deep-seated need to finally understand the sources of my life-long pain and reasons for my squandered life.

Alas, very quickly I realized those were not floodgates of heaven the good Almighty Lord sent—full of blessings, to his meek worshipers. On the contrary, those were the curses residing in me, longing to be known for such a long time that now, long forgotten, they started to wreak havoc on their way out. "If you only knew what darkness I am plunged into," Sainte-Thérèse de Lisieux wrote to her sister nuns. I fell into the bottomless pit of the hellish nightmares reflecting my own soul. Unlike Sainte-Thérèse, I did not have God to turn to. Unlike Dorian Gray, I did not have an attic to hide my decaying self-image, and I went on soiling my way through life.

Truth be told, I am not doing justice to the early days of the journey I embarked upon. It had its advantages, the process of discovery of what was hidden in my own soul. But where it ultimately took me was far worse than even the most nightmarish scenarios I either lived or envisioned. I would've thought—hoped—that revelations such those of Ulrike would've brought me solace in sorrow, that the fact that every dark trip arrives at the port of hope for a new discovery meant a new step into a better, freer life. *"After all… tomorrow is another day,"* even Scarlett O'Hara in her darkest moment realized, but it was not meant to be like that for me. On the contrary.

Entities

It was so obvious, the "discovery," that I felt like an idiot for having lived life for such a long time ignoring what was patently apparent. Through the Ulrike dream, I finally realized that I carried around a young boy, that barely twelve-year-old boy in me, a boy that stayed frozen at twelve years old, since the day my mother died. I might have grown outwardly but inside I was split in between "me" who lived his life and grew with experiences and that other "me" who was frozen in memory, a "twelve-year-old boy entity," a fragment of me somehow dissociated from myself.

The concept of fragmented selves was nothing new or surprising to me. Freud originally referred to fragmentation as part of an internal catastrophe in psychotic decompensation, so it happens as a consequence of a trauma or cumulative trauma(s). Those hidden levels of subconsciousness were parts of me I wasn't aware of throughout most of my life. I did realize my "fantasy world"—the world of images, hopes and cockamamie dreams— is an unrealistic fantasy field, but because I wrote a few books and several screenplays, I thought they were the creative outlets for my inner worlds, not its dissociation from myself. Trying to understand my own fragmentation and dissociations that followed, I read Van der Kolk, who wrote, *"That the essence of trauma is that it is overwhelming, unbelievable and unbearable."*

Unaware of the lonely, depressed, abandoned, betrayed (as in Ulrike's dream) boy in me, I wasn't able to cope with, for example: depression. I did not know its roots, and ascribed it to various outside factors, like the scourge of war back home, alcohol I drank in gargantuan quantities, grave political problems, savagely slaughtered relatives, abject poverty I faced, loneliness of exile. Drawing upon the ravages of my life, Charlotte had started a pattern she had been repeating all over again throughout our relationship, a pattern that I felt as one little betrayal after another, so that the boy, to be named Abandonment Entity, had taken over and his pain started to dominate me without my own conscious awareness of what was going on.

"I thought we agreed we'll leave Charlotte out of the session today?" Dr. Sønstebø inserted herself, interrupting me in mid-sentence with her idiotic remark. And she was supposed to be smart and insightful? What the heck?

ZLY - *The Man With the White Eyes*

Almost at the same instant Dr. Sønstebø imposed her tyrannical rule, a huge dark cloud appeared again and cast its shadow over me. That ineffable "something" was there, the Presence was there. But there was more to it: Dr. Sønstebø truly enraged me by her constant interruptions. Who does that pretentious twat thinks she is? I listened to my thoughts, not quite sure I was the one thinking them. There I was, openly and honestly prostrating my heart and soul before her immaculately manicured, impeccable feet and she treated me like a swine? And for what purpose was I pouring my heart out? To amuse her? To justify obscene fees the Norwegian government had to fork out for her hogwash science? Or for the "system" she obediently served perhaps, the same evil system that sold anti-submarine warfare weapons, armored vehicles, artillery, missiles and who knew how many other tools of death for millions of dollars, for the system that judged me, the system that *would* judge me based on her interpretation of idiotic stuff like the Personality Test or the Thematic Apperception Test (TAT) or the Minnesota Multiphasic Personality Inventory (MMPI) she used to probe me with. To hell with those feeble tools. Take them and shove them up your hungry, horny ass, Dr. Sønstebø. They manufacture weapons in Norway but are unable to come up with original psychological tests of their own? I was as mad as hell.

"Roman?" she asked.

I realized that I had not uttered a word for several minutes. I could not care less. I was focused on the growing anger in me, somehow amazed by it as I observed myself and the Presence I was this time able to perceive a bit better, the presence that somewhat frightened me as it took over in almost an imperceptible but unstoppable way.

Ever since I read Leopold Tyrmand's book *The Man With the White Eyes*, published in Warsaw in the mid-fifties of the 20th century, I had the idea of the white eyes as the pinnacle of danger, within and without alike. One of the book's main characters, Philip Merynos, was a fearless crime boss in Warsaw's underworld, a powerful man unafraid of anything. That was, until The Man With the White Eyes appeared and Merynos discovered the true meaning of fear. He feared those white eyes more than death. Those were the same eyes that, as a young man, I used to imagine in my fantasies of a daring swashbuckler who went on the farthest ends of Earth, conquering unknown worlds, and they were now lingering above me, rather above the horizon, more of an portent than a real mental image but somewhere herein nevertheless. As I felt the steely white gaze I also felt, like in the times prior, how my face is narrowing, for the want of a better word. It was a strange feeling; it felt like I was myself morphing into someone else. It wasn't as dramatic as the Dr. Jekyll and Mr. Hyde transformation—not at all. They were minute, those changes; they came from inside, barely perceptible for anyone on the outside but myself. I was filled with growing rage. That furor in me was real and easily sensed by those in the room with me.

"Roman, what's wrong?" Dr. Sønstebø asked again, the smell of her sudden trepidation almost palpable. Even that ever-present security officer from the Norwegian Police Security Service moved a step closer to me.

"Take a pill, Robocop, take a pill," I hatefully addressed him, quivering with anger, but when I heard myself quoting the Primo Sidone character from Harold Ramis's 1999 flick *Analyze This,* I calmed down. The ridiculousness of the quote and how I used it made me laugh at myself.

It was like someone turned the sound off, an instant quiet. I kept chuckling to myself. "The Robocop?" I mean, really, where does such batshit crazy stuff comes from?

The Systems

"Are you OK?" Dr. Sønstebø asked for the third time. It aggravated me, her nagging.

"I heard you the first time," I snapped, regretting my outburst. "Sorry, I apologize."

"That's fine," she said. "What disturbed you so much?"

I did not really know and had decided to think about it once I was alone again. But I needed to calm down and interact with Dr. Sønstebø with more patience. After all, I did like her. Didn't I?

"You can't cut off Charlotte Mørk from any forensic examination of myself," I replied slowly and deliberately, "only because you are tired of hearing about her."

"What makes you think I am tired of hearing about her? That's not true. I only wanted you to focus on Ulrike's dream and what it meant for you, untroubled by the memories of Charlotte."

I chuckled. "You still don't get it, Dr. Sønstebø, do you? We were, and still are, of the one, same system. I was a host to her parasitical, vampire self. Ulrike would not exist without Charlotte."

"But you yourself told me that Ulrike does not really exist."

"Aren't the fantasies, the realities of psychotic patient real for her or him?"

She looked at me for a long, quiet second.

"Do you think Ulrike is a product of psychosis?" The pit bull doctor bothered me with yet another of her idiotic questions. I stood up abruptly and the burly guy jumped. A thought flashed through my mind: Did he like Dr. Sønstebø, by any chance? Is he, maybe, her lover? Frankly, I didn't give a damn. I also did not care about talking to Dr. Sønstebø anymore. I politely told her that, as required of a mental hospital patient under scrutiny immediately after an unwelcomed outburst.

"I feel tired."

"All right, Roman, we will continue tomorrow. Have a good day," she said and left. Burly shot me a mean look—what is wrong with that guy?—and accompanied me back to my cell. I was finally left alone and able to focus on these truthful *Chronicles* again.

Chapter 5
ANGELS AND DEMONS

"Love, which absolves no one beloved from loving,
seized me so strongly with his charm that,
as you see, it has not left me yet.

Love brought us to one death."

Dante Alighieri, Inferno

Sovana, Tuscany, August 11, 2018

As per American TV commercials, no one seems happier than men with erectile dysfunction, cancer patients or those poor souls suffering from severe depression. When you see them on TV, they are so hunky-dory and copacetic as they smile from the screens, glowing in between wonderful scenery shots with sunsets and waterfalls, green plains and cheerful blonde and black children together on the Ferris wheel, and loving families hugging everywhere that one wishes to have been impotent with cancer and therefore in a severe funk in order to be deliriously happy. Such happiness is only one drug prescription away.

All those miraculous drugs the pharmaceutical corporations are pushing all over the land of the free, shoveling them down unsuspecting throats in all the hospitals and homes of the brave come with a warning such as this:

"Call your doctor if your depression worsens or you have unusual changes in behavior or thoughts of suicide.

> Antidepressants can increase these in children, teens and young adults. Elderly dementia patients taking Abilify, have an increased risk of death or stroke. Call your doctor if you have high fever, stiff muscles and confusion, to address a possible life-threatening condition or if you have uncontrollable muscle movements as these could become permanent. High blood sugar has been reported with Abilify and medicines like it. In some cases, extreme high blood sugar can lead to coma or death. Other risks include decreases in white blood cells, which can be serious, dizziness upon standing, seizures, trouble swallowing and impaired judgment or motor skills."

But then a nice looking, wide-smiling lady, whose husband is likely an impotent, dying cancer patient in coma in some dreary hospice charging $500.00 or so a day given the high level of her happiness, appears at the end of the commercial, looks us straight in the eye and says: "Adding Abilify has made a difference for me." Suddenly the "risk of coma or death" or "thoughts of suicide" the drug makers mention in passing are not important anymore. The happiness they peddle is.

People only hear what they want to hear. If someone would've told me that loving Charlotte Mørk came with a high risk of being hurt like I'd never been hurt before because she was a selfish, indifferent monster, I would've loved her nevertheless. Even if a small print as long as Abilify's came with her, stating that I have a real chance of becoming a serial killer who'll end his life in the psychiatric hospital as a result of loving her, I would still be head over heels in love with her.

Such is the madness of human minds in love. Such is the feebleness of human hearts in love.

Un Amore Maledetto (A Cursed Love)

When I was dawdling around Italy after my love-thirst with Sophie (her story comes up later—I spent a wonderful and terrifyingly revealing time with her earlier, before I went to Sovana) I knew I was going to give myself up. At the time I was still trying to understand how all these spine-chilling events I provoked came to be.

I drove around Tuscany like a headless chicken. Maremma—adorned with delightful stretches of the Tyrrhenian Sea coast, which hides treasures

like ancient Spanish towers and white dunes and filled with dreamlike hills—
is a natural miracle, but I did not know what to do with it. I felt so ugly inside
that it was unseemly for me to be amidst all that beauty; it strangely made
me feel guilty. I ran away from the heat, the summer crowds, and myself to
the tiny village of Sovana, a *frazione* (commune) of Sorano, and entered a
small museum in *Palazzo Pretorio*, the Pretorio Palace on its main square.
There, I found, quite unknowingly, what I was subconsciously looking
for. It was there where I encountered a perfect example of Etruscan magic
practices, *un amore maledetto* of the two lead statuettes depicting two figures
from Sovana, Zertur Cecnas and Velia Satnea, a man and a woman, both
nude and with their hands behind their back, exuding mystery and intrigue.

That seemed like a sign to me. A tiny sculpture in a minute hamlet off
the beaten path in the middle of Tuscany must have been placed there with
a purpose; it was there in order to tell me a story. Perhaps a story of my own?
Having the hands of Zertur and Velia tied behind their backs suggested a
curse was placed upon them. Throughout the relationship with Charlotte,
I felt like my hands were tied—my love was eternally strangled by her. My
time with her felt like being under the spell of black magic, unable to leave
even when being with her pointed to utter fruitfulness and danger.

In recent history, there had been only one Frenchman who spoke
the ancient language of Carthage and only another human who spoke the
forgotten Etruscan tongue, Charles Godfrey Leland, a connoisseur of *la
stregheria*, the old Etruscan witchcraft, also since long deceased. No help
there. I was left to my own faculties to deal with in the search for truth. And
then I received quite dubious help from the last apparition in the world I
would ever dreamed of "helping me."

Magyar the Priest

Just in between the Pretorio Palace and *Chiesa di Santa Maria* on
the Piazza del Pretorio, there's a small brown bench on which I hid from
the scorching sun. I blinked and a strange man appeared in front of me. I
recognized him instantaneously! It was Magyar the Priest—a man in his
fifties who impishly looked around like he wanted to be sure there was no
one but us on the square. When he was sure we were alone, he approached
me with a crooked smile. He has a huge head and is as nearly as wide as he
is tall. He is oily and he is remarkably ugly. His one eye is black, the other

blue and blind. He is also not real, being rather a character from my own screenplay—a figment of my own imagination. I shuddered.

"*Quid est veritas?*" (what is truth,) he asked grimly.

"Truth?" I asked, stupefied. I couldn't count how many times I fantasized about my screenplay(s) being made into movies (Benicio del Toro should've played Magyar the Priest) and now I had a character from it in front of me, speaking directly to me. He looked exactly as I imagined him, only more terrifying. The glow of summer haze was suffocating, and I was sweating profusely. Magyar the Priest, despite his heavy cassock, did not seem to care about the hellish heat; he rather looked like a phantasm borne out the sultry air. He came closer and leaned over me. The day suddenly darkened as he whispered:

"Do you really wanna know? Do you really wanna know the truth, you wussy, forlorn boy?" I sat unable to answer as he continued, "Do you have guts to handle the truth?" he panted laboriously. "I longed for Charlotte, you vain idiot. I lusted madly for her. I loved her from the moment she came to Cusco, before you came prancing around. And I had a real chance with her because she was alone and lonely, fucking only an occasional tourist."

I blinked in pain, silent, an icy needle of fear nested itself in my heart. Magyar the Priest took a step back and looked me up and down, measuring me with disdain, his eyes filled with pure hatred.

"And then you came. With your cute curly hair and your mellow voice, and your mouth full of teeth, you... you... rich, manicured Yale monkey."

I was not rich.

I did not have curly hair.

I'd never been to Yale.

Charlotte had never been to Cusco.

But every word he uttered, with such immense, soul-shattering hatred, rang true. He continued, his voice making me cringe. I tried to avert my eyes.

"The truth is, it is cold, it is lonely, and it lasts forever—the old friend Death." Magyar the Priest smiled horribly. "And it awaits you."

Then he yelled at me with a voice so terrible that I froze: "And Charlotte? She's already dead. Do you hear me? She's stiff, decomposing cold meat. Vanished, gone. She's no more, checked out for good, a lifeless, frozen, half-eaten cadaver. And YOU are to blame! She's dead because of YOU!"

And then, as sudden as he had appeared, he was gone.

The Triumph of Death

Sovana, Italy, where I sat on Piazza del Pretorio, is 10,493 kilometers away from the magnificent Machu Picchu, where I wrote the screenplay with Magyar the Priest in it. He's a product of my imagination. His words that scared the living shit out of me were my own words from the screenplay Charlotte once ignored.

Moreover, on that Saturday, August 11, 2018, with its partial New Moon Solar Eclipse and retrograde Saturn, she was alive and well, reading her daily horoscope in Norway. "She's dead because of YOU," words by Magyar the Priest felt like malediction, like an old Etruscan black magic curse. After all, he was an excommunicated Catholic priest, a character so repugnant that the devil himself would expel him from Hell, so no treacherous means were beyond him.

I remembered a perfect reproduction of Pieter Brueghel the Elder's *The Triumph of Death* that was hanging on Magyar's house's wall and I recalled that it was alive. In the screenplay I wrote in Cusco, he told me menacingly, "Look here, armies of skeletons kill the living in many creative ways—slitting throats, hanging, drowning, smothering—but there's no God here, no haven, no hope." And I felt like there was no hope indeed.

And then, like the Magyar the Priest hallucination—what else it could've been? —wasn't enough, *The Triumph of Death* came alive in front of me, like some fraught melodrama. Death, in the form of multiple skeletons, leads an army of executioners to kill the king, a cardinal, chess players, a loving couple, and a knight—everyone. It was a medieval orgy of death before my eyes but then the paintings became blurred. Roman soldiers and Etruscan magicians popped up from every corner, invading the orgy of death. They were pointing their decaying fingers at me, whispering curses in a language I did not understand. I wanted to run and, suddenly, somehow, like in a dream, I drifted away and soared above Sovana, trying to escape toward the heavens. Beneath me, a sea of blood, blood gushing from the dead. Slaughtered, bludgeoned, massacred, disemboweled women started to rise rapidly as it threatened to engulf and drown me.

One huge Roman soldier, so broad that his shoulders obscured the setting sun, a spitting image of the Bulgakov's centurion Mark Muribellum who faithfully served "the cruel Procurator of Judaea, fifth in that office, the knight Pontius Pilate[15]", appeared and pierced me with his spear. I screamed in pain as I died, hanging from the blade that killed me.

Achath Ruach Elohirn Chum

Who woke me up by throwing a splash of cold water on my face was none other than Aleister Crowley, one more character from my other writing. "One is the spirit (not air) of the Gods of the Living?" he said and continued, telling me: "Upon the blade, accordingly, is inscribed the word of the law. This word sends forth a blaze of light, dispersing the dark clouds of the mind."

After swooning seconds ago, I was still groggy and dazed, unable to process what was going on in that long episode of horror. When Crowley raised another bucket of water to splash me again, I realized it wasn't him, rather, it was Giacomo, the kindest ice-cream parlor owner that ever existed, who had set up a shop across the street. He laughted heartily as he commented on the hellish heat that must have been the cause of my brief loss of consciousness, brought some normalcy into my day.

And it also brought hunger for I suddenly felt famished.

Crowley's Daughter

Trying to shake off the experience I just went through, I was eating *Pappardelle al Ragù di Cinghiale* (a ragout with pasta noodles and wild boar) in "La Taverna Etrusca" when it dawned on me: Aleister Crowley did not have a daughter, but I wrote a whole book around the premise that he indeed had one. I myself did not have a child either and yet my fantasy world had produced a daughter in my mind and heart who was as alive as anyone else. But, with Ulrike B., "my fantasy world" went one step further, so it seemed that, since I had met Charlotte, I had started to create all those "entities" in me at a more rapid pace.

Today's episode of invoking Magyar the Priest, Brueghel the Elder's painting and Aleister Crowley, all from my own writing straight into my hallucinations showed me that my fantasy started to compartmentalize and dissociate in me. When "Crowley" told me the spear the centurion Mark Muribellum's doppelgänger killed me with means "dispersing the dark

---

15   Here is Roman quoting the last words of *Master and Margareta* by Michael Bulgakov, one of the books he cherished throughout his life. (note by Trygve E. Wighdal)

clouds of the mind," he might have given me hope that I would perhaps gain some understanding of what had happened to me before I turned myself in.

The guilt and remorse over all those murders I yet have to tell you about were eating me alive and I needed to end all of that, all those nightmares. I needed to know WHY all of that happened and then I could admit to my crimes and, ultimately, die.

Oslo, December 13, 2018 (night)

Remembering that Sovana episode that felt like had happened in some other life, I realized that I badly needed to go back to my past, to dig a bit deeper.

Deep chasms of unknowing, a yawning fissure of ignorance about myself was a huge gap to fill and a monumental task I avoided to embark on for the most of my life. Visions and hallucinations like the Sovana's should've told me that I had been throwing them into my work only to be chased by them, deformed in my subconsciousness. Instead of facing my inner world and learning from it I was just chasing my tail, hidden behind a role of a romantic boozing globetrotter, aimlessly soiling my way through life. Perhaps I should write an essay for Dr. Sønstebø so she could better understand my and Charlotte Mørk's damned symbiosis? And then maybe she'll also provide me with insight I so desperately need?

I liked the idea, so I started to write and wrote throughout the night.

Chapter 6

CRIME AND PUNISHMENT

"People who develop PTSD are often naïve; and then they encounter something that's not within their framework of thinking, and it's usually something bad. And because there isn't anything in their philosophy, their way of looking at the world that has prepared them for that, they end up fragmented and devastated."
Dr. Jordan Peterson

Oslo, December 14, 2018

For the first time since I met her, Dr. Anja Sønstebø wore worn out, dark blue jeans beneath her white coat. Manière De Voir black sneakers were a nice touch of elegance. It made her look younger and even more desirable.

"What is this?" she inquired when I handed her a neatly printed out bunch of papers I'd worked on the previous night. Yes, despite my net access being cut off, I had a new Dell computer and a decent HP printer in my cell. Such is the Norwegian Correctional Service standard. The prison utopia in which "an offender should have all the same rights as other people living in Norway, and life inside should resemble life outside as much as possible," as they say. Speaking of which, my cell contained three rooms: one for sleeping, one for studying, one for exercising—plus daily access to the exercise yard. I'd guess many an American on the shorter end of the American Dream would gladly exchange their wretched, mortgaged living for a place such as a prison in the secure ward of my psychiatric hospital here in Norway. And I'll say zilch, nothing about the food. But I am not here to brag.

"My essay for you," I replied, smiling.

"What about?"

"An essay on Charlotte Mørk and me, so you'd have an easier time understanding my constant references to her."

Dr. Sønstebø took the essay and started to carefully leaf through the pages. "This is a lot," she said, looking quizzically at me, almost surprised by the essay's thickness. "You know what?" she uttered pensively, "I am going to read this today and we'll continue our discussion tomorrow, once I have processed what's inside. Would that be OK with you?"

"Okey dokey, doc!"

My attempt to repartee fell flat.

Crime and Punishment

(Mørk Essay)

Before I met her, I was poverty-stricken. Humberto C., a thief who, in Rio de Janeiro, had forged my signatures on a Power of Attorney, stole everything I had. The situation that ensued revealed something worse: a distorted image of myself. I might have been a tad too brash at times, sometimes even unpleasant and obnoxious, especially when I drank, but I was someone whose good deeds outweighed the bad ones. Or at least I thought so.

Well, I was wrong. Some people I deemed friends not only refused to help me after I ended up destitute and virtually begging for help but relished upon hearing about my misery and humiliation. It was a sobering revelation about my own fantasy-image. I was lost in the sea of indifference. That was the final indignity—to be ignored in moments of gravest need—for the unspoken, crushing message was I did not deserve a helping hand.

Somehow, that dark despair made me wanna be a better man.

The alchemical answer to the situation was obvious. My circumstances without were a mere reflection of the circumstances within, and not vice versa. Only by changing my inner self, I would be able to change my world and turn my life around.

The Comet

Around that time, Charlotte had appeared like a comet, brightening my world and obscuring everything else. While she was rather like the burst of Tycho Brahe Supernova after centuries of long, dark, cold winters, she did indeed enter my life during the worst possible times ever. I did not scream *"De nova stella! De nova stella!!"* after I saw her, as Jepp the Dwarf, Tycho Brahe's assistant, had yelled upon seeing a burst of the "B Cassiopeia" in 1572 for the first time, but I was, while ashamed of my living conditions, equally exuberant as that old, odd jolter head[16] had been. I lived in squalor, and I was losing all hope. I did not know where the next meal was coming from. That fear does not only eat the soul but paralyzes and freezes you further. All in all, I was near bottom, having suicidal thoughts daily, so the last thing I'd expected to happen under those dark circumstances was a romantic encounter. I felt like an utterly worthless, unattractive loser whose chances of bare survival were diminishing on a daily basis. Love, companionship, sex, warmth, friendship—those were for other people, for decent, happy people that barbeque on Sundays and attend their children's school plays—well outside my miserable circle of sorrow and self-pity.

However, when we met, it was an instant, supernatural, subconscious attraction that wiped out reality like a tsunami. We spent two or so hours talking about everything that came to our minds: Paris I loved and she hated; Carl Gustav Jung I gobbled up but she found him a poor writer; Mozart I admired but she avoided, for he was too loud. Differences in opinions on various topics felt more like complimentary parts of the whole than obstacles to deeper understanding. Soon after, she left for the States, and we hadn't met since. For two months after she left, I couldn't stop thinking about her, and, despite my down-and-out circumstances, I somehow found courage to look her up online. After a bit of hesitation, I sent her an e-mail. She replied quickly, within hours—the longest few hours of my life—and we started a long, epistolary love affair that lasted for months. We were insatiable for each other. Despite the distance, I was smoldering with passion. We'd fallen in love more and more with every passing minute, by every exchanged e-mail. This is what she wrote when I asked her why she loved me:

---

16 Roman is here quoting from his screenplay *Tycho Brahe Secret*. It surprises me he had not written more, or used more from the script, given how much he loved it and how many high expectations he had for the said screenplay. He saw it as his one-way ticket out of Tijuana's inner hell. (note by Trygve E. Wighdal)

On Thu, December 6, 2012 at 11:45 PM <charlotte.mørk@yahoo.no> wrote:

> Oh I felt attracted to you at the Zhi Cafe because you were interesting and interested, intelligent, mysterious, intense, loud, serious, funny, direct, curious, argumentative; and because I find you physically very attractive and because you have beautiful eyes, and because you really looked at me and really saw me.
>
> And then with every single mail I fell more in love with you, and couldn't believe what was happening and it just kept getting deeper and funnier and wilder and more intense and better every day and with every mail, and I started to miss your mails more and more - and this still doesn't explain why I have fallen for you. :)))
>
> Because of your honesty and maturity and your beautiful writing style and your humor and how you challenge me and how intelligent and witty you are and how you make fun of me and tease me and how you write about yourself and your intense and extremely unusual and adventurous life; and your sensitivity and vulnerability and compassion and beauty and openness. And the variety and depth and how you switch between modes and moods, and your interest in so many things, and your fast mind and your gift with words. And I love how you draw me out, and make me write and express myself, which I usually don't do at all (like I would have never written this!). I am usually totally focused on just listening, and am glad if no one asks me anything. But I notice how much I enjoy this challenge to open up and how exciting it is.
>
> I talked to my best friend today (we are extremely close and like sisters, we are so much alike and so connected. She already knew you even though I hadn't described you yet, she can sense what I experience in a psychic way). I described to her that you are like a real man and grown-up compared to most men who are kids; you have such a mature way of dealing with things (and having a temper does not make this

any different), but it doesn't mean you don't have the lightness and playfulness and enthusiasm that is so beautiful in children. And you also see yourself and don't take yourself too seriously. And I also told her that I never felt so much seen before by a man. I have known men who recognized a certain side of me, but who didn't see everything else - I have never felt seen so completely before. And you really listen, and ask, and care, and are interested, and understand. You have no idea how rare that is in a man! I can live without it, but it makes it so one-sided and more like a client-therapist deal than a relationship between two equals. And it is such a joy to experience mutuality like this. And I also told her that I can be myself with you and be honest and that you can handle it and feel responsible for your own reactions, and we are both interested in keeping it real (and with me there is such a big risk that I adjust because I can sense what the other person wants me to be and I try to be that for them, and I don't want to disappoint their expectations or trigger a strong reaction, but then of course I can't keep that up forever. And it is so hard for me to dare to be me, especially if I have to worry that the other person is fragile and can't handle it). (Difficult to not fall into writing about myself instead of why I have fallen for YOU. I guess that is because there is things I want to talk about because I want to give the complete picture, and they bubble up at the same time).

I am so grateful to have met you, no matter how this continues..."

xoxo,
Charlotte

Had I not been deprived of my liberty, I could add that I love long strolls on the beach and cuddling with a good book and put her words on my Match dot com profile as a letter of recommendation, don't you think, Dr. Sønstebø?

That was a time of pure bliss, a moment I had been waiting for all my life: a love letter from an incredible woman I also loved. Her words were suffused with so much… *positivity* about myself that I felt everything was possible again. I was flying high and did not even notice so many obvious obstacles she hinted about in her letter.

Icarus did not come to my mind, but Kundalini did.

Kundalini

I have been like Pollyanna, blindingly optimistic. My dream, the same night after I received a love letter from her, was a brief one and it only reinforced my beliefs that "impossible is nothing." I dreamed of two snakes as they entered my body, through my spine, and vanished there.

In *Man and His Symbols*, Jung writes, "perhaps the commonest dream symbol of transcendence is the snake. This was originally a nonpoisonous tree snake; as we see it, coiled around the staff of the healing god, it seems to embody a kind of mediation between earth and heaven."

"The coiled snake may be indicative of the Kundalini Shakti energy. Kundalini is the Sanskrit word for 'coiled up' and is symbolic of the cosmic feminine energy that fuels spiritual awakening. In Kundalini Yoga, the snake is curled at the base of the spine and it moves up through all the chakras as one awakens spiritually. Play with the idea of the coiled snake being an indicator of moving into higher consciousness."

Charlotte spent a lot of time in India, the home of Kundalini, so I took that dream seriously, as the most hopeful sign that I was going to start my inner transformation alongside someone that had been on the same path of self-realization already and much further ahead of me. My love for Charlotte was my first real, deep, grown-up love, something that would not succumb to any ridiculous whims our different temperaments might produce. It was real to me, the love, those dreams, and the future.

Sadly, as I was going to learn soon, nothing was real at all.

Disentanglement

All the beauty of love had happened before Charlotte and I met for the second time and before we kissed or slept together for the first time. She came back to Tijuana to see me, despite my (feeble) protests regarding the living conditions I was in. I had been scrubbing the Rathole I lived in for a full three days and nights prior to her arrival. It was that dirty. But even the clean Rathole still looked like, well, a rathole—a windowless, dark, dumpy hole never meant to house a human being. Anyone who dared to rent such a ghastly, mold-infested shithole should be summarily executed on the spot.

She assured me none of that meant anything to her and that all that matters was for us to get together and see what was going to happen once we met. Hours before her arrival, I was as crazy and excited as a seventeen-year-old boy before the first date. Better yet, I was as worked up as the Bird of Paradise before mating, given how meticulously I'd prepared my own nest, scrubbing the dirt like devil, from everywhere, trying to make the Rathole spic and span. I was shaking out of passion and also fear of what was going to happen.

The Hug

And then the agonizing wait was over, and she was there. She was as trepidatious as I was, but her glowing eyes were happy to see me. We hugged and stayed in the hug for a long time. It allowed our nervous systems to calm down, for we were both more than nervous, each for our own reasons.

After we made love for the first time, her "WOW!" told us both everything we needed to know. The chemistry was there, the attraction was insane, the intimacy simultaneously dirty, deep and divine. She was too skinny; I was too fat, and yet we were a perfect for each other. It was real. I had never ever loved a woman or made love to a woman like I had loved and made love to Charlotte Mørk that first afternoon together, in my soul-eating place that had briefly become our love nest.

But even that fantastic sex wasn't as nearly as good as the embrace after it. We were one. We fell asleep holding hands. When we went for a walk, we walked hand in hand. Neither of us had ever walked hand in hand with another person. Two lonely weirdoes had finally found each other. Our souls clung onto each other with every breath, with every glance exchanged, with every word or wordless bit of communication. It was something exceptional, the feeling of connection we had on every level. I looked at her mesmerizing eyes and I saw oceans of love and time in which I could have spent an eternity. And even those greyish-green eyes of hers aroused my wild sexual desires. It was exceptional, the splendor of love we'd encountered.

Everything had pointed to a fantastic start.

And Thus the Struggle Had Begun

The very same evening she had insisted that two people couldn't really be together and how each one had to live his or her own life, independent of the other's. "I believe I can love someone my whole life, but I don't believe in lasting romantic relationships, or the need for one," she said curiously. And then she added, "I believe we meet because we have something to share, give to each other, learn from each other, and sometimes that can happen in one single meeting and the transaction is complete. Sometimes it takes more time, but at some point, it is completed, and we move on."

I was perplexed and a bit upset. Her Asperger-like terminology—love described as a *transaction*—did not bode well, but I still found it cute and fascinating. While she had not put an expiration date on our *transaction*(s), she did put a lid on it at once.

And, after only twenty-three days in Tijuana with me, she had left.

Oslo, December 15, 2018

The next day, after Dr. Sønstebø arrived to our session she asked outright, without her usual polite greeting, "Shall we now discuss your essay?"

"Sure."

"You titled your essay *Crime and Punishment*. What do you think was Charlotte's single biggest 'crime' during the times you were together?"

With the full benefit of hindsight, I never thought about Charlotte's 'crimes' in these terms; her whole presence in my life felt like a full-fledged criminal activity endlessly robbing me of my soul. But I understood the importance of what Dr. Sønstebø was asking. I mulled over her question and realized all those obvious "crimes" of "betrayal" were only the surface of Charlotte's dark nature that sucked me in. As I sunk back into my memories, the sounds around me quieted and I myself quiesced as I kept reflecting. A flash or two of memories, both wonderful, like encounters on railway stations in Germany, and ugly, like disconnection in Karlovy Vary where we went to reconnect—but that wasn't it, that wasn't the very deep core of her "crime(s)."

"Take your time, Roman," Dr. Sønstebø encouraged me to ponder her question carefully, but I already knew rather a surprising answer, which I told her.

"Curiosity. She has taken away the curiosity from me."

Chapter 7
THE SYSTEM

"The spirit doesn't die, of course, it turns into a monster."

Christopher Koch

Oslo, December 15, 2018

A year later, on Fri, December 6, 2013 at 6:54 PM <charlotte.mørk@ yahoo.no> wrote:

> It does hurt when the kisses are missing and in a strange way it does feel like we were meant for each other despite the impossibility. I really wonder what existence wants us both to do with this situation...?
>
> xoxo,
> Charlotte

That was a classic Charlotte. It was the existence that "wanted us to do something," like it had nothing to do with her. (or me) However, later in the same day she wrote the following:

On Fri, December 6, 2013 at 10:27 PM <charlotte.mørk@yahoo.no> wrote:

> I just told Wenche what I am grateful for in what a gift you are to me - and it was so much, I couldn't summarize it in one thing - you made me aware of so much that I was cutting off form my life and running from and denying - starting with my

body and sexuality and being a woman and having talents and using them in the world, my past and childhood stuff and fears and limitations - and your way of loving me with your strong unafraid total overflowing love opened my heart so much wider - and you letting yourself being touched by our alchemy and going through such an intense and deep transformation, and your incredible creativity and beauty of language and brilliance and intelligence and funniness...

xoxo,
Charlotte

The System Denied

Two people bonded together in an intimate relationship are a SYSTEM, no matter if it is a wonderful loving marriage or a dysfunctional partnership of inequality at any given moment, but a system nevertheless. This whole world is made of relationships. One can't truly entangle herself into a relationship and pretend that it does not mean anything, trying to be in that same relationship independently of the system it creates.

She kept insisting on "impossibility" of our relationship with a fanatical ardor of the Kali Ma's most zealous devotee. And yet, she had kept inundating me with praises and exclamations of love that I had always seen as a door ajar to all the possibilities she was denying us. We expended so much energy debating instead of creating. She kept telling me that our connection is like a Shakespearean tragedy, so I suggested to write a Shakespearean comedy about the cosmic joke our relationship represented instead. She kept hammering the differences as something bad, so I invented a Turkish therapist persona, as a third party to our marathon debates, who helped us build upon the differences and see them as opportunities. When we noted how we are prone to being triggered by the other's words or actions, I suggested a comical "Trigger Alert" the triggered one would use to stop the trigger. All in vain—she preferred her own narrative, impervious to editing.

The Sliver

I took a small, narrow sliver of the woman I loved and mistook it for the whole. It was a mistake, but the love only grew in me. The "alchemy" she wrote about was best seen in my increased visions I used to achieve deeper understandings of us and my life-long pain. Through her presence in my life, I started to see the past that hunted me, clearer than ever before. I even started to remember my mother—a memory that had been buried deep down in me for decades. Discoveries manifested themselves more often in dreams, but sometimes even during the daytime as I daydreamed. Those elaborate fantasies I conjured up during my walks or when I was simply sitting under some mighty redwood tree were rare instances in which I'd seen my "fantasy world" as something good and productive. I had recovered financially since the rock bottom I hit on the April 30, 2014, so the money was not the problem anymore. I started to work more and more toward the goal of regaining full financial independence. I even managed to start investing, which would soon bring real monies into my life and with it so much needed freedom. But she, without having to get married, had behaved like a runaway bride anyway, only to come back to me after long periods of separation, claiming her love again.

On Sun, January 11, 2015 at 0:09 AM <charlotte.mørk@yahoo.no> wrote:

> Imagining my life without you it feels empty and dull and sad – with all the beauty and magic and joy and aliveness that you bring into it. There is nobody I would like to talk to as much as I want to talk to you. And my heart just wants to hold and be held by your heart and feel home with you..."
>
> xoxo,
> Charlotte

It felt like we were two broken parts of some ancient, cursed sword. To me, these parts strove, or should have striven to unite. To her, it seemed to me, these parts served only to hurt each other. Even when nothing made sense anymore, for we spent 84% of our time separated (she mocked my statistics), our unconscious attraction never waned. The longing for her, and her stated longing for me, grew stronger and stronger, so we kept reconnecting and the merry-go-round of her "impossibilities" and my "efforts" started all over again.

Jung's Grandson

Charlotte had a deep understanding of the intricacies of the human mind, which attracted me to her. What I felt when I read her e-mails or spoke to her over the Skype was the very definition of sapiosexuality. I once mentioned how I'd "go to Barcelona, right now" after being sick. This was her answer:

On Wed, March 23, 2015 at 10:10 AM Charlotte Mørk <charlotte.mørk@yahoo.no> wrote:

> Oh oh oh - nooooo! I was just joking because that's what I thought you wanted to hear to have an excuse to fly to Barcelona! What I really meant is that you would be wise to employ your alchemical skills and Jung's grandson genius to go to the root of the issue and find out what the fever is really about and how to resolve whatever frozen in time energy from the past is causing it so you are truly free and can go to Barcelona because you enjoy going and not to run from an unresolved past pattern that will find another opportunity to come back if not released and integrated properly...
>
> xoxo,
> Charlotte

In one off-hand remark, she perfectly diagnosed my situation. I ran and ran, from "an unresolved past pattern" as she had put it, or from myself as I saw it. I was like a hunted beast running away, unaware that there's no place to hide, and even more so, that I was the prey and the predator at the same time—both living alongside in one lost soul, my own. An acquaintance I knew back home once wrote about me: "Roman L. lost himself in the slums of Brazil as he went further away from home. Seeking Kurtz, he became Kurtz. This is a problem with the *Heart of Darkness*, where evil is a primordial anxiety, followed by the parrots squawking and snakes hissing. The lost soul, stranded in whore houses in Brazil, is awaiting a new breakthrough, and by then it he might have enough cheap alcohol to last from sunset to dawn." That was as close to my life as I lead it as it could be.

But once the "whore houses" and their revolving doors closed behind my ass, and "cheap alcohol" stopped flowing down my throat, Charlotte took their place in my life as an addiction stronger than any I ever knew. She had also established a clear pattern—a few days, up to max few weeks allocated for us to spend together were always followed by several months we were separated.

Aikido

I'd been constantly under attacks of avoidance (a small wonder she had an aikido black belt with thin gold stripe) and suffered needlessly. She knew I was severely PTSD-ed. She knew I had abandonment issues. She knew I had at least one sign of a dissociative disorder: I had almost completely forgotten my mother. I had no recollections of our times together, just a fragment or two or shattered episodes, which is highly unusual for a boy who was already twelve years old when she died. She was of your profession, Dr. Sønstebø, and she knew, or at least she must have known, how damaging her repetitious patterns of running away, coming back, rhapsodizing about myself but rejecting me (sexual rejections started soon after as well) were, and yet she insisted on the same old same old.

"User"

I came close to realizing how deeply hurtful that relationship might have been for me and how bad it might end. I did not think—not even in my worst nightmares—that I'd end up a killer, but something bad was lingering above. Given how much time we were separated, that ridiculous 84% of the time, it was clear that she had lived her life mingling with a lot of other people, away from me. We were in touch daily, and we loved each other, so I bought in her claims about her need to spend time alone, to heal, think, to perhaps write. So it came as a shock when a friend of hers from those spiritual circles she frequented in India and Thailand wrote a strange, strongly worded e-mail he even strangely Cc-ed to everyone he knew. I also got a copy. Here's what he wrote from some beach resort in Thailand:

On Wed, March 16, 2014 at 23:27 PM <antoine.t74@hotmail.com> wrote:

> I feel that you didn't hesitate to "use" me on a number of occasions when you asked me to keep you aware of social gatherings, your appreciation for my introducing you to a number of my friends, inviting you to dinners, bringing you to two special parties, and music gatherings with my other friends.
>
> I didn't actively seek to have that one meeting with you because I initially believed your statements that you needed to heal, did not wish to socialize with anyone, and preferred to spend time alone.
>
> It now seems obvious to me that you were not open and honest in your sharing with me that you were unable to meet with me because you were needing to rest in your room, and were avoiding being social with anyone, and needed to spend as much time as possible alone.
>
> The reality is, you were meeting with other friends throughout most of the time your were on Samui, which is wonderful, but, you were intentionally not interested in our briefly meeting.
>
> And, this is certainly understandable if you really had no interest in even briefly connecting as friends...which I naïvely assumed we were, based upon what I thought was our enjoyable and active friendship that you stated very clearly in Tiru that you deeply appreciated, and my offering editing suggestions for your and Helen's book proposal that you had requested, and actively introducing you to my friends, bringing you to a few social gatherings, and other Tiru events.
>
> Yes, I assumed, and again ~ naïvely ~ that we had a genuine friendship that appeared more evident in Tiru. Quite honestly, my intuitive feelings are ~ that you are a "User."
>
> Yes. A very strong observation and judgment. Only You, and possibly a few past friends and lovers know if your life pattern

under certain conditions which meets your needs, is to be a "User."

Antoine

That should've been a huge red flag, worthy of deeper examination, but she assured me that he wanted much more than just a friendship, something she was unwilling to give given her love for me. Like all idiots throughout the history of human interactions, I heard what I wanted to hear and forgot about that episode. I chose to forget. That was my first fatal mistake.

Jealousy

Almost at the same time, she went on a dinner with a former lover, Karl. I am not a jealous type, otherwise I would not have been capable of staying in a long-distance relationship with a woman who spent time mostly mingling with other men. But when she went to meet Karl, I went crazy, like an animal in a cage, sensing an earthquake, running in circles, terrified. Decades ago, a woman I loved went to meet—again away from me for I was busy and could not travel for a summer holiday she went on enjoying alone—another guy I knew. The moment an acquaintance told me they were going to meet, I went crazy, for I knew, I sensed, that they were going to hook up. They did and ended up married after she left me that summer. So I had a similar feeling every time Charlotte was meeting Karl. I was a wounded animal in fear.

Charlotte could not care less. She coldly explained to me that Karl was just a friend, that a dinner was not a big deal etc. I could not tell her not to meet the guy—it's not my right, but what was scary was that she totally ignored my pain and my guilt over my overreaction. I tried to ease up the conflict—the only one we had—and told her, great, take a selfie while having a dinner, make fun of my jealousy, anything just to assuage my fears. She did not. She only told me that having sex with Karl ages ago was a mistake and that she was not at all attracted to him, and for her that was it.

Despite the dark clouds over my head and my heart clogged by fear and jealousy, I spent time torturing myself over my jealousy and inability to either break up with her if her indifference was so hurtful or to get over it and trust her fully. That was my second fatal mistake. I chose to forget that incident and to keep living in the grotesque long-term relationship, prepping myself for a disaster to come. I chose loyalty and tenderness over jealousy, love and trust over mistrust, and by doing that I sentenced myself to death.

Oslo, December 15, 2018

"What did you mean when you said that she had taken your *curiosity* away?" Dr. Sønstebø asked.

"She was ambivalent. But what reigned in her thinking and behavior was absolute. The "absolute" being no, we can't be together, and the ambivalence was in her coming back to me over and over again. She said that she would love for me to be with a woman who'd be able to return my love and sexual desires in a manner she, Charlotte, was unable to give. And then she made love to me. Then, while she was making love to me, she stopped, unable to continue. It was insane. Take that episode with Karl. She claimed she loved me so deeply and then goes on hurting me, no matter how irrational my fears might have been."

"How did you cope with all of that?"

"I didn't, damn it. I suffered all the time. *'I can't'* was her magical mantra," I said, starting to feel that familiar, unpleasant twinge of nervousness.

"I understand that her *magical mantra* might have been enervating you. But maybe she really could not have been with you in a way you wanted? Or anyone else for that matter? Did you think about it?" Dr. Sønstebø had said. "I still fail to see her *dishonesty*."

Dishonesty

"An example of Charlotte's dishonesty is what you're aiming at hearing?"

"It would help."

"She shared with me her vision of us in previous lives being separated in the concentration camp. That trauma of separation made us, our souls, long to be re-united. To me, if we were separated once, we were given a second chance now. And we would need to fight for it with our dear lives. When Charlotte spoke about her own inabilities and fears when relationships were in question and how she thought "disentanglement" was the only way of co-existing, I took her seriously. I tried hard to cope with all of that. I believed her, hook line and sinker, and was doing my best to find a solution for us."

I started to feel annoyed, I feeling like I am explaining myself while talking about her.

"She once scolded me by saying, 'I don't know why you can't look at me independently of yourself for a moment, and accept that I maybe have a disability.' *Disability* being her inability to do anything together despite her stated love and her supposed efforts."

"I can see how those memories are upsetting you," Dr. Sønstebø said in a soothing tone I imagine her peers used to address feebleminded refugee children who spoke neither Norwegian nor English.

I let her get away with that shite this time.

"I'd been living under the cloud of what she called her "disability" for over four years. I suffered because of it, I fought it, I tried to understand it and, I learned to live with it, to embrace it and, ultimately to love it. I ended up believing some sort of compromise in our relationship was possible—that was how much I valued and loved her. Compromise being a way for us to live and love each other, to grow together, to learn instead of those constant struggles. I accepted an idea of living in separate houses. Mind you, we had already been sleeping in separate rooms during those rare times of being physically together, but the most beautiful part of our day were mornings. She used to come to my bed in mornings, all sleepy and cute, sometimes all babbly in her slumber but always damn sexy. I helped her wake up by loving her in the morning. It was wonderful, those morning hugs, embraces, kisses—that passionate, smoldering sex in the morning. So, by forfeiting that sort of beauty, we'd be both deprived of a wonderful way to start a day. Losing that was a painful compromise to me but if she really needed it, to hell, I was going to give it to her. Obviously, it did not help at all. Unlike some people that always wanted more and were never satisfied, she always wanted more of less and the more I gave up, sort to speak, she wanted me to give up even more," I ended angrily.

I had difficulty breathing for I said all of that in seemingly one breath. Suffocation I lived with while with Charlotte reflected in my gasps; I struggled to breathe.

"Understanding"

"I realize how it must have been painful for you, difficult to understand and to accept. But I still do not see dishonesty in her behavior. Perhaps she was just confused?"

"Confused by fucking what?" I blurted loudly. "She wasn't confused, she was fucking dishonest, since day one." I banged my fist on the table.

"I see you're getting really angry, Roman."

There she went again, in that phony soothing voice. Charlotte was also full of it, she had that bullshit way of repeating what you just said to "let you know you are being heard" and she always "understood," she had always fucking "understood" everything without understanding anything.

"I understand how upset you must be—" she continued.

"You understand?" I yelled.

Then, *screaming is not an efficient way of communicating,* a voice in my head said, so I obediently calmed down. I took a deep breath and looked at Dr. Sønstebø as she was sitting across me, all sexy and clean, smart and educated in the same dark knowledge as Charlotte had been, that legalized *macumba* practice of torturing, drugging, abusing and degrading other human beings, psychiatry, "full of understanding" and free as a bird to live, fuck and buy those fucking fancy sneakers.

I was calm outwardly, but I felt rage that from deep down in my guts, from the very root of my being, from the first Muldahara chakra as that deceiving bitch Charlotte would have called it if she had sat in Anja's place, starting to slowly move up. Deep in the base of my spine, where the Kundalini snakes from my happy dream entered my body once, that white rage was now roaring in the distance. Like lava deep down under the volcano, on its unstoppable way toward the surface, it was coming. Above, same as the volcano's ring before the eruption, my face showed only calm. I think I even smiled a tiny crooked smile at this Grand Inquisitor across from me. However it was composed, that Smile of Rage on my face was as cold as death. But it wasn't alone, the Rage. I also felt my old chum Hatred finding its way up to the core of my being, through my plexus, overwhelming my heart as it went up through my third eye into my brain, and then way up, all the way up to the subconsciousness that fed on my enraged self.

"You *understand*, but you *do not* see her *dishonesty*," I said, slowly emphasizing each syllable. "I told you she knew about my mental health issues. She, as much as you, good doctor, had been a mental health professional. She knew that '*if the elements of trauma are replayed again and again, the accompanying stress hormones engrave those memories even more*

JUNG'S DEMON | 75

deeply in the mind. [17] Did you note, doctor—*even more deeply*? She knew very well about the existence of what we named Abandonment Entity but she kept repeating the same pattern. I love you, I love you so much, you are the most incredible lover, you are this or that in a way of uncritical praises of me. Only a mother could utter words of such extravagant enthusiasm to her child and for sure not a grown-up lover. And then she died. And died again. By leaving me again and again and again."

"Do you need to take a break? A glass of water perhaps? I see you are really agitated," asked Dr. Sønstebø with worry in her voice. "I see you are in pain."

---

17 Here is Roman quoting, verbatim, from Bessel van der Kolk's book *The Body Keeps The Score: Brain, Mind, and Body in the Healing of Trauma* he seemed to have studied only after arriving to the Gaustad sykehus. (note by Trygve E. Wighdal)

Chapter 8
THE MAN WITH
THE WHITE EYES

"Did you lose your mind all at once, or was it a slow, gradual process?"

Jack Lucas[18]

Oslo, December 15, 2018

Here we go again.

This is how it all always starts.

This is how Charlotte had been bullshitting me, exactly like that: "I see you are in pain." I am in pain, you demon from Hell, I scream inside because of you.

"When I see and feel what you wrote, I can see how total you have been in doing everything you can to make my life more wonderful," Charlotte once wrote to me. She had always been writing some such shite, that fraud, like this Anja fraud here masquerading as a psychiatrist, going on about "what she is losing when she clings on her rigid ideas about disentanglement" but had never ever done anything for that "us" she "was losing," insane monstrosity of a woman that took all my life's energy from me under a disguise of "love" and her phantasmagorical "disability." If there

---

18   Jack Lucas is a fictional character, played by Jeff Bridges, from *The Fisher King* (1992), a Terry Gilliam flick. Also with Robin Williams as Parry, whose insanity was, ultimately, healed by love.

were an ounce of truth in her words she would not have stayed with me for a single moment, damn soulless vampire.

I had not said a word since the lovely Anja's "understanding of my pain" bit, but Hatred and Rage had now started to surge toward the surface, to the very front of my frontal lobe. I trembled inside and I had problems containing them, but I wanted to further examine what I had been thinking about for quite a while: Charlotte's deep-seated deceptiveness and duplicity.

"Conscious, intentional exaggeration of someone's pain is not only dishonest, it is pure evil. She had been deliberately, purposely and methodically reinforcing my deepest traumas all over again. She was coming and going; aiming squarely at my Abandonment Entity, the easiest one to hurt, and she kept coming and abandoning me all over again. As a psychiatrist herself, she knew how to do it in the most painful way. Repeatedly, in the same manner so it could hurt to the maximum. She was hurting me on purpose!"

"I see how you might feel that way—"

That soothing voice started to pierce my ears. I interrupted her.

"And do you know what happened next?" I asked as calmly as I could, unable to listen to her prattling anymore.

The inner emotional storm kept brewing in me; the dark clouds were gathering. I was overwhelmed by images, sounds, e-mails, Skype calls and numerous fruitless discussions I had with Charlotte over the years that now felt like an endless pandemonium of the same old same old *magic mantras* as Dr. Sønstebø called them—or was that me?—that Charlotte always deployed. I heard them in an ever louder cacophony of deceit that ate my heart as rust slowly ate away at the iron.

"Tell me please," the creature across me asked in a manner of those that care.

ICE train #1050

"Since I realized the abandonment issue, I started to recognize its patterns. Once we traveled together in the ICE 1050, a high-speed train from Berlin to Köln Hauptbahnhof. I was going to Amsterdam and she was going to Wuppertal where she was going to catch another train, and then proceed to a flight to India. At Wuppertal, as she was disembarking the train, my heart just broke and stopped beating for a while. It was incredibly painful, even though we were going to meet again in less than a month. It just made no sense, such an overreaction. Sure, she stayed in India for almost a year and kept lying over subsequent months, but I did not know it would happen at the time. I had no reasons whatsoever for a painful reaction like that."

"What happened next?"

Does this "doctor" ever stop interrupting?

"What happens *next, doctor,* is that I went through such a grotesquely exaggerated burst of inexplicable pain on that ICE train, but afterward, I managed to understand the abandonment and its mechanisms. So in the future, it did not bother me that much. Once we reconnected, Charlotte continued the pattern of loving/escaping, but her actions did not produce any pain in me anymore. Just a whiff or two had shaken me from time to time. I learnt to expect them and learned how to cope with them, those 'abandonment triggers.' I even became calm when she was leaving me, as long as we both knew she would be back. In fact, those moments when her train was leaving, or she vanished in the boarding tunnel in an airport started to feel like beautiful moments. I wasn't 'losing her' anymore, she wasn't 'abandoning me' anymore—it was a wonderful, temporary separation that would be followed by even stronger love once we met again. It felt like a huge load of my shoulders."

"How did she react to your breakthrough? Was she supportive?"

I looked at her with an open, intense animosity, already filled with hatred to the brim for Anja, 'Doctor Sønstebø,' as she liked to call herself. You should've seen her try to understand. She was so calm and composed while I was opening my heart and soul and all she had to offer was that phony understanding, in a manner exactly like Charlotte's. They even looked alike at this moment. Strange, I hadn't noticed such similarities before. That was perhaps because Anja was so much more beautiful than Charlotte. I would've really liked to fuck her, our Anja. Speaking of which, I continued:

"Oh, yes, as supportive as Dr. Mengele to his patients—are you deaf or what? Since her recurring escapes did not produce the desired effect in me anymore, Charlotte started to intensify her sexual rejections. It was a perpetual *coitus interruptus,* encounters with her, courtesy of Charlotte."

"That must have been painful for you."

Steppenwolf

I sneered at her as a wolf would. I could hear myself growl inside, and I started to speak again, very slowly, deliberately emphasizing every word in order to keep calm despite the storm that was rapidly approaching.

"Yes, Dr. Sønstebø, it had been *painful*. She understood better than me that the Abandonment Entity also existed on a primordial level, one deeper and murkier—that of sexuality—and lured me into more confrontations with the unknown. I was unable to understand what was going with her or to detect what was going on within me. She kept repeating a winning pattern. She was coming and going, aiming squarely at my deep, hidden abandoned parts all over again. She knew how to do it in the most painful way, leaving me in the most intimate moments, my body and my soul naked, my manhood denied. Repeatedly, in the same manner as before so it could hurt even more than before. And again, over and over again, she was hurting me on purpose, over and over again, over and over again..." I started to lose it. I growled the last words in almost unrecognizable voice.

As I was repeating "over and over again" I started to bang on the desk in between us, in the rhythm of my words. "Over," BANG! "and over" BANG!!, "again," BANG!!, "She was doing it over," BANG!!, and "over and BANG!! over again," BANG!! I was now maniacally pounding the desk, "until the traumas were engraved even more deeply"—BANG! BANG!!, BANG!!!—"*even more deeply*, you motherfucking piece of shit!" I was roaring to curse the heavens.

"Roman," cried Dr. Sønstebø, "try to calm yourself down, please."

Fuck you!

BANG! BANG! BANG! A crack in the desk. I was losing it. I stood up as I kept pounding the desk. Then I saw Mozart, my only ally over the long decades of loneliness, nodding from the corner of the room. *Go for it*, he said, and I started to sing from his magnificent *Requiem*. *Dies irae, dies illa...*

I kept singing and I kept hitting the desk with so much power, reflecting the might of my hatred like I was trying to pulverize the universe and myself in it. I sang Mozart.

Agnus dei... my lost love...
Dies irae, dies illa
Solvet saeclum in favilla[19]

---

19 *Day of wrath, day of anger will dissolve the world in ashes.*
(translation by Trygve E. Wighdal)

I sang in Latin, a language I do not speak, as I was banging on the desk I did not recognize the horrible bass-baritone coming out of my throat. It was divine, that hellish insanity I encountered digging through the unknown Mozart's grave, and I succumbed to his unspeakable might. It gave me insane power myself. I was outside of the power and myself multiplied. BANG! Now with both hands I continued to clobber that fucking desk. *Dies irae, dies illa* motherfuckers. *Imago dei*, my ass, it was Anja's *imago* of the utterly petrified little tart. She was trembling like Charlotte had trembled during her last moments. The Burly was standing nearby, frozen, unsure of what to do, waiting for Anja to issue an order, that sniveling little weasel piece of shit without a single thought of his own in his puny, testosterone-laden brain.

BANG! I pondered the desk with ferocious savagery. It was beautiful. It was liberating. *Dies irae* hears the wrath of the doomed. BANG! My hands started to bleed. BANG! The bitch's computer fell off the desk. Or should it be called a table? Fuck it, it would break no matter its name. The computer fell off that thingy with a BANG!!

Confutatis (Accused)

Confutatis maledictis
Flammis acribus addictis
Voca me cum benedictis[20]

I sang maniacally. "Do you hear me?"—BANG! —"you damned, do you hear the cursed?"—BANG!! —"*Confutatis maledictis!*" The crack on the damn desk widened. "Do you hear me, you infernal demon? When the accused, when the accursed are confounded, they are doomed to the flames of Hell where you burn. Apage Satanas! Tornjaj se Sotono, Begone, you Satan," I bawled vehemently as the flames of Hell were engulfing me. It was wonderful. It was madness in motion. I hurled the printer through the window, shattering the glass. I saw Anja shudder in the corner of my eye. Good. Keep shaking. It will do you some good when you meditate tonight before sucking on some dick, you horny slut from hell.

"*Flammis acribus addictis* the flames will eat you up, you false prophet of mental health. Be afraid, be very afraid, they are coming after you, the

---

20 *When the accursed have been condemned. And doomed to the searing flames, Summon me with the saved.*
    (translation by Trygve E. Wighdal)

infernal demons, brace yourself." I laughed in her face. *"Ego te absolvo a peccatis tuis in nomine Patris, et Filii, et Spiritus Sancti,"* I sneered at her fear. "I absolve you, but Hell wouldn't."

"Spare some cutter me brother. Spare some Xanax me sister," I laughed at her as she was shivering like the little frightened twat that she was. And then I saw her. Right in front of my eyes, I saw cursed Charlotte Mørk as she looked when I came to see her for the last time. BANG! and suddenly I was there, in her damned abode, where I "wasn't unwanted" as she had so lovingly put it, clutching a morning star in my hands so hard that my knuckles were all white. No, not the fucking Venus you idiot, how one could clutch a star, it was the morning star, a club-like weapon, the mace like thing with a bulbous head, a heavy tool, did you get it now, sweetheart? And I smashed her with it, across the face. How do you like this *'transaction?'* I hit her with all my hatred. I bludgeoned her with all the devilish strength my dead love possessed. And again. A dull thud was the only sound. Boring. So I hit her again. And then yet again as her blood splattered all over the morning star, soiling my hands and face. It was salty and disgusting—like her rotten soul, the blood. I spit it out. *Apage Satanas!*

"*Confutatis maledictis,*" I roared again. BANG!! The desk split apart. Charlotte's skull cracked wide open. Bingo! That's the sound I wanted to hear. *Ding-dong, when your lover is gone, gone, gone Sing ding-ding-dong. Ding dang dong.* BANG!! *Confutatis maledictis* and a BANG, the chair was gone. Charlotte's brain scattered all over the walls, ceilings, and her Indian fucking rags. You couldn't meditate in Oslo, you phony spiritual 'seeker.' "*Confutatis maledictis,*" I howled in supernatural voices not from this world. I loved them, the voices. They had me at *Dies irae.* They complete me. BANG! Another chair was gone. Charlotte's skull was unrecognizable. *Confutatis maledictis* monster. *Dies irae, dies illa.* BANG, I raised Anja's computer and smashed it at the wall. I started to contort, to convulse, suffused with the white light of hatred and death as those white eyes of dread were lingering over me again, gazing at me approvingly.

I had nothing to bang at anymore so now, standing and screaming in horrible rage, I kept hitting Charlotte's dead body with my bloody morning star as I was waving my empty hands in the air, like I was conducting my own Requiem. "*Confutatis maledictis!*" I howled and growled and screamed, "*Confutatis maledictis* motherfuckers," and I kept shattering her cursed body into smithereens resembling the bloody smithereens, what the fuck is wrong with me and these fucking smithereens, pieces of my life she ravaged and I was losing for good.

Then the Burly finally realized Charlotte—or was it Anja?—whoever, will never tell him what to do so he unfroze and moved like the trained animal he is and hit me. Fucker knew how to throw a punch, so he hit me so hard that I coalesced in pain. Two panicky nurses that ran into our sessions room injected me with some horse tranquilizer or some such atrocity. Its effect was instant. I fell down to my knees and rolled over on my back like a giant deflated cockroach crawling back to his inferno. Charlotte's bloody, broken, bludgeoned, unrecognizable body was gone, along with the morning star that vanished into the thin air from which it had appeared. Only my bloody hands and ravaged psychiatric evaluation room stood there as silent witnesses to what had just happened. Even the Mozart was gone. *Et tu, Wolfie?*

The silence enveloped me.

Bohemian Rhapsody

Finally, a respite of the *understandings* conceived in Hell where psychiatrists dwell, screwing with the minds of their victims, all of them oh so superior to the mere mortals they had entered and blessed my world. As I was losing consciousness, I saw those four morons standing above me and looking at me like I was some freakish curiosity. Burly, Anja and the two nurses positioned themselves like the "Queen" guys from the "Bohemian Rhapsody" video from that legendary 1975 album named *A Night at the Opera* and stared down. Idiots.

But high above them, like the Mozart's oboe from *Serenade For Winds, K.361: 3rd Movement,* the White Eyes still quietly lingered. Those burning white eyes looked down on and me and they were telling me that while maybe my life was so unbearable and my pain so intense, that I might choose an abrupt end to it. And if I do choose to do so, the White Eyes were telling me almost lovingly, I will *understand.* I burst into laughter at that cosmic joke and I screamed in pain; the bastard seems to have broken a rib or two when he hit me, and I finally passed out.

Chapter 9
GREEN GREEN GRASS OF HOME

"I believe that I am in hell, therefore I am there."

Arthur Rimbaud

Oslo, December 16, 2018

I woke up quite groggy after yesterday's little episode with Dr. Sønstebø, but did not recall much of it, only that I was enraged by her behavior and broke a glass or something. However, my hands were severely bruised, and they ached. My body felt injured. I had problems inhaling, for it was painful, and my head was spinning as I suffered from vertigo. It must have been interesting, the session—perhaps a bit more intense than I previously thought. Two disinterested nurses, bland young women I've never seen before, came to my cell and took me for X-rays and a medical examination, which was a nice change of routine. An older gentleman, a nice general practice doctor whose name eluded me but whose long silvery gray hair was quite unforgettable, nodded politely, greeting me, and went on wordlessly examining my back and lungs. He wasn't a chatty chap. Luckily, my ribs were not broken but definitively hurt as he concluded after touching and probing me, using percussion techniques and, finally, by placing his stethoscope on my back and chest. The drug they administered yesterday must have been diazepam—a horse size vial of Valium given how strongly it affected me, basically knocking me out. But the real clue was in administration of flumazenil they injected me with. As the nurse was injecting the dose, the silvery doctor explained that it was a benzodiazepine receptor antagonist—some thingy used to reverse the effects of the horse injection from yesterday. That was all anyone told me the whole morning.

They escorted me back to the cell and left me alone for a day. I went back to writing my chronicles.

Rijeka, November 15, 2018

Winged Victory, *The Nike of Samothrace,* is one of the most memorable works of Hellenistic art in the world. She had been in the Louvre Museum, the world's largest art museum in Paris, for over a hundred years, spellbinding and seducing everyone lucky enough to have seen her up close. A small wonder that Victoria's Secret supermodels wear wings molded on the image of Nike. I was ten years old when my mother took me to Paris and to the Louvre.

The Nike was big and powerful, beautiful. I did not even notice that her head and arms were missing but I remember quite vividly that her wet *chitōn,* sensually pressed against her body, more revealing than concealing her breasts and legs. She represented my first sexual arousal and my first erotic fantasies afterward. Her headless allure had followed me since.

On the top of the Victory Lighthouse of Trieste, there's another Nike sculpture. Trieste, an Italian port city and the capital of the Friuli-Venezia Giulia province, used to be the place where we—my mother, father and I—went shopping in the 60s and an early 70s, for the food was much better and cheaper in Italy than at home. This still might be the case, I reckon. We passed her by many times, remembering Paris and the original. The sculptor of Trieste's Nike was a certain Giovanni Mayer, who had also sculpted an angel on the top of the magnificent Steffula-Pavletich tomb in Rijeka, my native city.

My mother took me there often. She loved angels. She used to tell me that I was her angel.

The Three Wise Monkeys

All those images flashed through my head as I walked toward my Mom's and Dad's tomb located in the beautiful, tree-lined Trsat Cemetery in Rijeka. I wobbled. Forty-six and a half years ago, as my mom lay dying in her hospital bed, she wrote me a letter. In the letter filled with love and sadness—she died mere hours after finishing it and the letter was stolen from me some nineteen years ago—she gave me a couple pieces of advice. One sentence she wrote stayed deeply etched in my mind forever: "Never accept compromises."

She herself was a very brave, uncompromising woman. Not only that, she wrote a sort of hospital bulletin from her hospital bed, about breast cancer and how to early detect it in order to help other women with prevention, but she was politically brave as well. I recall how she had received an anonymous package with "The three wise monkeys" figurines in it once. "Shut the fuck up or else…" was written in an enclosed note, but she had never shut up. When I followed her steps as a journalist myself, I was also never able to shut up despite quite real threats to my life. I remember how once a crazy guy who had just returned from the front combat zone approached me on Korzo, the main pedestrian city of Rijeka, as I was walking with Asja, a girl I just met. He was enraged by some political column I wrote against the holy president of the country. He pulled a gun and fired it above my head and growled: "The next time, I will aim in between your fucking eyes, motherfucker. This is your last warning," and left. Well, that was interesting. I looked at Asja. The poor girl had peed in her pants, mortified. I took her to the taxi stand and sent her home, never to see her again.

After Asja

Several days later, a nice, polite man dressed immaculately yet casually knocked at my door. I never saw him before; I had no clue what he wanted. He asked me if I'd kindly let him in, for he had something important to discuss with me. I let him in, and we sat at the big mahogany kitchen desk I was so proud of. He declined a drink I offered and told me that he was Asja's father. Fuck me. Then he took a brand new Heckler & Koch USP ("universal self-loading pistol") from his pocket and laid it on the pride of my kitchen. Fuck me twice.

"If you ever come near Asja again, I will not waste a bullet warning you. Are we clear?"

We were clear.

After he left, I wrote an unrelated column that made me fear for my life more than ever but had no other choice but to write it and to deliver it to my Editor-in-Chief personally, so to avoid it being intercepted by the ever watchful sentinels of the government.

"Roman, if I publish it, we're both screwed," he said.

Two days later, he published the article and we were both screwed for real. I ended up with political asylum in the United States, and Veljko Vičević, the editor I loved almost like my own father, died of a massive heart attack a year later, as only a forty-four year old man. He was as strong as a bull, but he had carried the whole newspaper on his shoulders and his heart had just burst.

The uncompromising stance with which I lived my life wasn't too kind to me. It had created a lot of misunderstandings, even hate from too many people, including some well-intentioned people, and I paid a pretty penny for my life's energy supply because of it. I don't regret sticking to my principles. Granted, I soiled myself by drinking at that time, which might have created a myopic vision of myself, but tell me, my most learned reader, who does not carry a small weakness in them? If anyone of you, my valuable readers, is a sinless, weakness-less hero of tomorrow, feel free to cast the first stone at me as a punishment for the sins of my own.

The only time I did not listen to my mother's words and compromised, compromised endlessly and unwittingly, was after I met Charlotte. By giving in to her bullshit—I thought it was love at the time, not that I see that as any excuse—I had also, a bit by bit, given up my identity and got sucked into perpetual fondling of her own flat-out-of-her mind deceptive persona. Such surrender accelerated the split in me that ended up so horrendously.

The Grave

My mom asked of me only two things. First was her request that I, from time to time, bring her *Kutijica koja svira* (little music box), to the grave and let it play for her. The tune was "Waves of Danube", which she loved. That little music box made in Vienna over seventy-five years ago from Bolivian rosewood and quilted maple was my father's present to her, something he bought the very same day she phoned him (he was in Vienna on business at the time) to tell him she was pregnant with me. No matter how insane my life turned out to be, I never parted with the little music box, not even when I was homeless and desolate, nor when I drank, nor when I traveled around the world losing golden watches and luggage alike. That little wooden box made me feel, even during the hard times of worst self-loathing or hunger on the streets, that a man who kept it and guarded it over the decades couldn't be all that bad. I let it play for my mother on her every birthday, on every anniversary of her death, no matter where I'd been in the world at any given time. Over the years it had played for many others that have passed.

Her second request was for me to tell her when I visited her what was new in my life: if I loved someone, if I was loved. She wanted to know. And every time I visited her grave, I told her stories and news about my life. After I left my hometown, I was absent for decades but had managed to visit her resting place where she was now accompanied by my father, who died twenty-eight years after her, only twice. The first time was in 2013, on the heights of my love for Charlotte, and again on November 15, 2018, only a month or so ago. I knew that was my last visit to my parents grave and that I would never go there to clean and polish the tomb slab, to put some flowers in the vase, to light a candle again. To let the Little Music Box play its tune. To tell her stories.

I also knew I couldn't tell her that I was a murderer.

I stopped some twenty meters away and looked at that simple, beautiful grave under the green cypress trees. Somber bells were tolling in the distance. I guess a funeral was going on the other end of the cemetery. I strained to see Mom's faded photo on the headstone from afar with such a heavy heart that I almost turned back and ran away. The sense of guilt and shame was that powerful. But I was done running, so I finally went to my parents' last resting place and suddenly drooped. I felt listless. I fell on my knees, my head on the tombstone. I almost embraced it. I was crying.

I was also lying. The last words I had spoken to my parents were lies.

I cleaned the tomb and then I winded the Little Music Box's revolving cylinder (it contained a set of pins placed on a disc to pluck the tuned teeth of a steel comb) and let it play its tune. The very first time it played on that same spot was a few days after her funeral, forty-six and a half years ago. I was there with my father who had been holding my shoulder but, given his white knuckles and how much it hurt as he clutched me, it seemed like he needed me as much as I needed him. He never recovered from her early demise and never remarried. Several years after I left for America, he fell ill and died. I am sure that he had died of loneliness. I greatly contributed to it, and I always felt guilty about that. As I stood there, I told them that I was not lonely, that Charlotte still loved me and that I was happy as I choked in front of the grave, lying.

Forgiveness

> *He asked me if I could forgive others*
> *I said I could do that*
> *Do you believe that God forgave you?*
> *Yes, I said, I believe that*
> *Then he said, can you forgive yourself?*
> *And I said, "No."*
> (**Dan H.**, Marine Corps rifleman)

I kneeled next to the grave, burning with the desire to ask God for forgiveness and ask of my parents to forgive me but I knew I was beyond forgiveness or redemption. "If you deserve forgiveness, then you don't need it," another U.S. marine, Jerry S., once told me. I could not utter a single word more. I did not deserve them, my mother and my father. I knew that with every fiber of my being, my heart, in my soul, as unforgivable as I was. So I left, not turning back, silently bidding them farewell, my parents I'd lost for the second time.

The Grady Twins

As I was walking away, I had the strangest feeling. I felt like my mother's and my father's eyes were riveted at the nape of my neck. I wasn't turning back, but I was getting a very clear mental image of them. It was like my third eye was not located at the sixth chakra, slightly above my eyebrows, but in the very center of my nape, and it gazed back at them as much as they were gazing at me. They were standing at the grave holding hands like the twins in Stanley Kubrick's movie, *The Shining*, and quietly looking at me as I was walking away.

They were not as freakish looking or creepy as the Grady's daughters[21] and did not lie bloody and dead like the twins in the movie, but there was something eerie in the image frozen in the air behind me. I didn't recall seeing them holding hands when they were alive and in love, but they were holding them now. They looked like they were around their respective ages when they died. My mom was a thirty-six-year-old woman, still healthy and beautiful—only her hair was old-fashioned and styled in the manner of

---

21   Grady's daughters refer to the two girls in blue Danny Torrance sees while riding in the Overlook Hotel's West Wing in Kubrick's masterpiece movie from 1980, *The Shining*.

Jacqueline Kennedy's. My father looked like he had the last time I'd seen him, back when he visited me in New York in November of 2000—an elegant, charming sixty-nine-year-old man with a distinguished moustache on his face.

While I trembled inside me, I also smiled. Together they'd be able to cope with the *discovery* about me, for I knew they *knew*. Because of that, I was unable to turn and look them in the eyes. I was too ashamed, too cowardly to face them as I observed them through that strange third eye. But I also knew for sure that they were together again and that all was going to be fine for them from then on. As I walked, I recalled a vision in which they were together for the first time since 1972, and what was going on now was a confirmation of the vision I had a while ago.

San Francisco Train

As an engineer my father was mightily impressed by the Golden Gate Bridge in San Francisco. When I was a little boy, I listened in awe to his stories about that majestic monument to men's ingenuity and how it has been built and maintained. He died in January of 2001. Later that year, for my birthday, I walked across the bridge in memory of him. That very April he was supposed to come and visit me and the Golden Gate city for the first time. We had planned to cross the bridge on foot together. All his admiration was based on books and engineering data, so he planned to finally see it firsthand. It was not meant to happen.

That is perhaps why I had the most enchanting vision in San Francisco. I crossed the bridge on foot, like I had in reality, and walked toward the train station. It was huge, like The Gare du Nord (North Station in Paris, France)—bustling and crazy and, yet, still somehow in San Francisco. I was there with him, waiting for his train to come. I don't recall where was he traveling. Once the train arrived, much to our surprise, my mom was in it. She smiled at me, but her eyes riveted on my father. They loved each other. They touched hands through the train's window, and he rushed in. I saw them hug and kiss and laugh and, as the train started to leave the station, they both came to the window and looked at me. They were smiling. I was smiling. It was quiet. It was nice. I felt like I had been holding my father back with me, selfishly, after his demise, for I needed his presence to help me live through all the difficulties I encountered and this was the moment in which I set him free to finally re-unite with his wife. I walked along the train as it accelerated, and we kept looking at each other. Then, my mother embraced him, buried her head against his shoulder and they were gone.

I was happy to see them together. In that rare moment of peace, I felt hope that my life could finally turn around and that I might find the wholeness I missed. The Abandonment Entity did not appear at all. If it was in me, awake at that time, it had made his peace with the fact they were gone.

On the road again

Those memories were overflowing in me as I left the cemetery. Present and past, calmness from the San Franciso's Gare du Nord train station, and somehow strangely quiet dread and shame from the graveyard comingled in me, but I wasn't torn apart like many times before. At least I had one closure in my life—well, closed. Likely the very last, that with Charlotte, still lies in front of me.

Once outside the cemetery, I started the car and left for Norway. There was a long, long drive waiting in front of me. What I was going to do was even worse from anything I'd done thus far. A long, painful, convoluted trip of a madman, my own *Journey to the End of the Night*[22], would end up at the very same place where it had started, in Norway, in Charlotte's cozy home up in the woods.

But before I did that, a lot had to happen.

---

22 *Journey to the End of the Night* is a novel by Louis-Ferdinand Céline Roman loved. He used to carry that book with him on the *Route Nationale 6* in France, when he was 14 y.o., walking from Paris to Marseille. (note by Trygve E. Wighdal)

Part III
THE FLYING
DUTCHMAN

Chapter 10

DR. ELLINOR
TYRY GELIASSEN

"What do we live for, if it is not to make life less difficult to each other?"
George Eliot

Oslo, December 17, 2018

The Burly sentinel who was always in the room with me and Dr. Anja Sønstebø, lovingly watching over her, seemed to have been replaced by the two disagreeable looking, thickset-yet-scraggy police officers. Both of them were almost a half-head taller than me, and I stand at a not-too-shabby 6'2" (188 cm). They were too Aryan for my taste—two identical, blue-eyed, blond replicants. A pair of perfect fighting/killing machines devoid of humanity, created in some not-too-creative Hollywood lab churning out cliché after cliché, I thought. They escorted me to an interview room—other than the one I got used to and trashed the last time I had a session with Dr. Sønstebø. There was a mounted big-screen HDTV on the wall and not much else. It felt bad being there in that barren room painted in the sickish green tones Henri de Toulouse-Lautrec loathed so much, alone with those two replicants breathing down my neck. That was, until a short and plump but energetic woman in her late-sixties/early-seventies appeared like a tornado whirling the air about her. She had the most energetic presence I have ever seen. She had a purple lock in her salt-and-pepper grey hair and wore purple vintage eyeglasses made of fake tortoise shell. She carried a thick folder with her. In addition, she had a pipe in her hand. A bloody Sherlock Holmes pipe.

That strange human ball of energy, as I was about to learn later, was no one other than the very legend of the dissociative identity disorder (DID) trauma research, its pioneer, celebrated and revered all over the world, Dr. Ellinor Tyri Geliassen. Who could say they got traumatized in this clean and educated, rich and peaceful Kingdom of Norway? I guess it must have been the polar nights? Those endless nights drive me insane, if you would forgive me a pun.

Nevertheless, having a DID pioneering mastermind present was a slightly unnerving fact. The DSM–5, the standard classification of mental disorders in the United States, provides several criteria for its diagnosis, of which the first one reads: "two or more distinct identities or personality states are present, each with its own relatively enduring pattern of perceiving, relating to, and thinking about the environment and self." What do they think? I am like Sybil with her sixteen personalities? They have the freaking multiple personality disorder issues, bloody fraudsters. Did you know that the geniuses that wrote the DMS (Diagnostic and Statistical Manual of Mental Disorders—its fifth Edition is therefore called DSM-5) once listed homosexuality as a mental disorder in the DSM-II, the Manual's fabled second edition? Today they claim that believing homosexuality is a mental disorder is in itself a mental disorder. What a bunch of clowns. I believe writing for the DSM is a mental disorder. Are their deranged, worshipped-as-the-Bible guidelines going to be the framework with which Dr. Ellinor Tyri Geliassen will judge me? I hope not.

DSM-5

Norway is a civilized country in comparison to that barbaric cesspool of drugged lunatics, the United States, where psychiatry, as prescribed by the mental illness bible of evil, the aforementioned DSM-5, sees grief as a "Major Depressive Disorder" (buy Pfizer Pharmaceuticals shares). They drug children if their concentration is not that of Immanuel Kant's and label them as tiny sufferers of the "Disruptive Mood Dysregulation Disorder." One can't invent such shit. Run and buy some Shire Pharmaceuticals shares, the makers of Adderall, a pharmaceutical bridge to suicide. Or rather, buy the shares of its owner's Takeda Pharmaceutical Company Ltd. The more children these monsters drug, the more profit your shares would get you.

Excessive eating is now a psychiatric illness as well; in the DSM-5 it is called "Binge Eating Disorder" (buy more shares). Even your normal worries of paying for your kid's tuition would now be a "Generalized Anxiety Disorder" (Xanax sales would skyrocket. Ergo, buy more Pfizer, PFE, shares. It even pays you a nice little dividend as of today). Hell, I was working myself up. What they are going to do? Lock me up? I chuckled.

"I'll explain," Dr. Ellinor Tyri Geliassen said, whirling like a dervish dwarf. OK, she did not really whirl around but the whole room seemed to have been suffused by energy emanating from her. What a sight to behold.

"What's to explain?" I asked with a peculiar whiff of arrogance. Strange, for I liked this new doctor immediately.

"I am here to replace Dr. Sønstebø."

"Well, I gathered that much," I uttered through my teeth. I was not sure why she had annoyed me a bit given that I liked her. Was it fear? Or was I still upset over all those hellish abbreviations, DSM–5, DDI. Why not BBC, LSD, CIA? She had seen it or sensed it, my agitation, and that made her even more cheerful.

"A clever chap you are, aren't you, right?" she said. "That's great. We'll get along just fine." She plopped down in a chair by the table. And she went to light the pipe, almost embarrassed as she asked me for permission.

"Do you mind?"

"No," I granted her request. I saw the replicants exchange something remotely resembling a smile. Whatever that grimace was, they exchanged it with each other with some sort of creepy, robotically conspiratorial understanding between them. They must be the life of every party, the replicants. The whole hospital is strictly a non-smoking area and yet, Dr. Ellinor Tyri Geliassen seemed to have some special privileges. She took a first puff and sighed with so much pleasure that I thought "I'll have what she's having" line would be even more appropriate in this context than it was in the scene in which Meg Ryan famously faked orgasm in a restaurant.

Then she extinguished the pipe. One puff was all? Was she messing with me?

"Doctor's orders," she said with a disarming Hobbit smile. "Shall we start?"

"Shoot away."

"My name is Dr. Ellinor Tyri Geliassen. It is the hospital's standard procedure after a patient attacks his or her therapist for the doctor to be replaced, at least temporarily. You will not be working with Dr. Sønstebø until I decide it is safe for her to return to examining you."

"I did not attack her." I did not like my defensive stance. This dwarfish Dr. Geliassen somehow intimidated me, it seemed.

"Well, we shall discuss the event," Dr. Ellinor Tyri Geliassen said. "But first, I must ask you for your permission."

"What for?"

"A permission to interrupt you when you speak, to re-direct your attention, simple things like that, should I feel it was needed," she smiled, "it might help you not to get agitated again."

"Sure, no problem," I said begrudgingly.

"You do not sound convincing, dear." The darn Hobbit smiled again. "So let us just dive into it, shall we? Do you mind seeing a little movie? You love movies, don't you?"

"I do. Which movie you would like us to see? *Kalifornia*[23]?"

"No, you rascal," she smiled with an over emphasized mirth in her voice. "Your drama performance," she said.

"Unless you object to it, Roman, I'd like you to tell me what you see when you are watching the incident as an neutral observer would. We'll start slowly. I will show you just a tiny bit of the tape and then I will stop the player. Is that OK with you?"

"Sure."

"*In media res.*" She giggled. "You do speak Latin, I gather," she said rhetorically and pressed play on the remote.

The Laurence Olivier Award

And there I was, flat out of my mind, screaming from the TV set—*Dies irae, dies illa*—from the top of my lungs, like my life depended on it. I was hitting the poor Dr. Sønstebø's desk like a maniac. Dr. Geliassen stopped the tape.

"What did you see?" Dr. Geliassen asked.

"Well, a raging maniac," I admitted.

"But, was that you?"

"Who else? It wasn't Rocky."

---

23   *Kalifornia* is a savage 1993 thriller directed by Dominic Sena, staring Brad Pitt, Juliette Lewis, David Duchovny, and Michelle Forbes, in which Pitt plays a serial killer. I thought it was funny, my remark.

Dr. Ellinor Tyri Geliassen clapped her hands—only once, but with such enthusiasm that I felt like I'd just won the Olympic gold medal in speed skating for Norway. WTF was wrong with that woman?

"That's it," she exclaimed. "The agitation is coming." She pointed her little finger at me, then she made a little circle in the air with it, like she was drawing a circle around my face. *What sort of psychological voodoo is that shite?* I wondered, suddenly amused by her little performance. Whatever it was, I concluded that it worked, for I started to enjoy the little ploy, curious to see where she was going with it.

"Tell me—" She leaned toward me, as if she was going to tell me something in confidence. "Who annoys you more, me or Dr. Sønstebø?"

"I am not sure what you mean," I told her sincerely. She addressed the replicants, "Leave us alone for a moment, please."

"Men doktor…" one replicant started in a surprisingly pleasant, neutral sounding baritone but she insisted. "A minute. Please. It's OK. I'll scream if I need you," she said in Norwegian and winked at me.

"You have a soft spot for Dr. Sønstebø, do you? Rather a hard spot," she said giggling to herself, quite amused by a thought she pondered.

"What does that even mean?" I asked, annoyed.

"You'll see," she said and pressed the play button on the player. "I have edited the footage myself to protect your privacy." Was that the wink again? Did she think she was Porfiry Petrovitch to my Raskolnikov[24]? I looked at myself screaming on the screen. I looked like a rabid dog. It was embarrassing. Then a zoom in focused on my trousers where I had, no doubt whatsoever, a boner.

"You see, Roman, I think you are full of shit."

"Excuse me?" Since when doctors speak like that?

"I think you created your little drama with Dr. Sønstebø because she arouses you sexually. You could not/cannot have her and that frustrates the living hell in you. Therefore, because you could not kill her either, you wanted to scare her with that theatrical screaming, Mozart quotes, a maddening display of aggression. But you had control over it all the time, didn't you?" She asked and banged her pipe on the table. Twice.

---

24 There is a psychologically important scene in Dostoyevsky's *Crime and Punishment* in which *Porphyry Petrovitch*, the 'leading investigator' in the double murder Rodion Romanovich Raskolnikov had committed, during the investigation interview, winks at the murderer as if he was telling him: "I know you killed them. (but I can wait for you to confess)" (note by Trygve E. Wighdal)

"Didn't you?"

I had to pause and think. She confused me.

"No, Dr. Geliassen, you are wrong. It wasn't a performance; I really did lose it."

"What did Dr. Sønstebø do to provoke you so much?"

Killing Fields

"She pretends that she's my therapist while her only job is to assess if I am clinically insane or not. Her phony understanding of this or that reminded me of Charlotte's phoniness and how she had understood..." I made an air quote, "... 'everything' without really getting anything. I guess that triggered me. Thus the rage episode," I explained.

"Thus indeed," Dr. Geliassen said nonsensically.

"Should I have said hence, instead?" I asked belligerently, but she ignored me. Instead, the little dwarfish doctor startled me again with her following question. This was not how an interview with a murderer should go. Or was it?

"Would you have killed Dr. Sønstebø if the security officer and the nurses weren't there to contain you?" Dr. Geliassen asked with what seemed to be genuine curiosity in her expression. She leaned in a bit, eagerly waiting for my answer.

I had to think again.

"Frankly, as I reflect back, I think there was a fifty-fifty chance that I wouldn't."

"Not that you would?" Dr. Geliassen asked looking surprised as she kept smiling innocently, like the friendliest of the Hobbits in the Middle-earth. "You did not say the chances were fifty-fifty that you *would* kill her. Why's that?"

"It is fifty-fifty chance, no matter how you look at it. It does not matter in which order you put it."

"OK, let us stop. Have a glass of water. I do not want you to get agitated."

"I am not agitated," I said, raising my voice.

"My point exactly." She smiled. I felt embarrassed. She was getting under my skin quite rapidly.

I took a sip of water and looked at her. She gazed back at me, nodding, as if she was pondering her next move. It was barely noticeable, her nodding, but she did think and nod, while she had all along kept gazing at me. Her stare was piercing but not unpleasant or unsettling at all. I was curious to find out what is coming next.

"So she has triggered you, Dr. Sønstebø, by her *phoniness* as you put it?"

"Yes she did. I think it was obvious from the footage."

"But you remember the episode, right?"

"I think I do. Yes, I do now. Why?"

Dr. Ellinor Tyri Geliassen reached for the pile of papers in front of her. She took one paper, with the *Politidirektoratet* letterhead and a logo on it, obviously a police report. She was not concealing the document, so I saw the date on it—*6. December 2018*—the day in which I confessed my murders to the Majorstuen Police Station officers in Oslo. It was written in Norwegian, but I knew what was inside.

"It says here that you did not remember your murders or anything about them until September, when all the memories rushed back to you, all at once? Is that still correct?" Dr. Geliassen asked.

"Yes."

"So it seems you have two levels of losing it, one in which you forget your murder and another in which you do not?"

"Well, Dr. Geliassen, you are wrong. Must I remind you that I did not kill Dr. Sønstebø. Hence my memory was intact, for no further trauma triggered the amnesia."

"Indeed," the funny dwarf gave me that one. "So shall we discuss the women you had killed?"

I did not reply.

"How did it start?" Dr. Geliassen insisted.

Chapter 11
LESLIE DIES

"'When I see a pretty girl walking down the street, I think two things. One part of me wants to take her out, talk to her, be real nice and sweet and treat her right ... and the other part of me wonders... what her head would look like on a stick."
Edmund Kemper

Velebit Mountain, Croatia, July 19, 2018

She was funny and smart, Leslie, an angelic-looking all-American girl about 28 y.o. when I met her. Her strawberry blonde hair reminded me of the Niagara Falls during autumn, when foliage is yellow and orange like her hair, and brown and bright like her eyes. When I told her that, she laughed and told me that she was born in Niagara Falls, a city on the Niagara River in New York State.

"You must be kidding me?"

"I shit you not. I was born on the first day of spring in Niagara Falls. Then all went downhill, and I am now condemned to live in Tulsa, Oklahoma, an ex oil capital of the world, now just another dreary dump in the United States of America," she replied as sunny as a head cheerleader would be upon accepting the dazzling quarterback of her dream's marriage proposal. I instantly liked her. She was so lovely and lively and, it seemed, open to all possibilities.

The disconnection from women that I started to experience in Rio de Janeiro, Auckland and Kenya—developments I will tell you about later—truly scared me. I did not want to have that triple-cursed Charlotte's legacy in my life to be that of aloneness. I did not want to live a solitary life. I did not want to die alone like my father did. I felt like Roy Orbison in that I still "have some love to give" but I also felt like my time was running out. Then, like a ray of sunshine that cute, sexy and interesting Leslie and her freckled face showed up and brightened my day. Yes, she instantly gave me hope. My fantasies overtook me again. When that happens, I have no defense mechanism left; I go all in, no matter how ill-timed or inappropriate it could be. Meeting Leslie was a wonderful encounter—manna from heaven, I felt.

She was camping in the Kamp Velebit on the Velebit Mountain in Croatia for the mindful adventure retreat by Solar Spirit (conscious movements system was her shtick). The majestic Northern Velebit National Park is every nature-trekker's dream. I drove around. I was not much of a hiker, but I loved to roam alone around beautiful places. This is what I was doing when she appeared from the trek. It was an entrance worthy of a Hollywood movie; the Sun was behind her, so she was glowing in an aura of sunrays.

"Hi," she said, smiling. Her gaze was lucid, honest and open. Her voice crystal clear. I liked her.

"Right back atcha, pilgrim," I replied with a smile and she smiled back at me and introduced herself. She had a firm handshake despite her small hands. I had a bottle of cold water I had just opened, and we shared it along with those famous Croatian Kraš *bajaderas*—a sort of praline candy from nougat enriched with almond, hazelnuts from the species of *Corylus avellana*—I had bought in Split the day before.

"Yummy," she said, melting away as the *bajadera* melted in her sweet mouth. Nothing gets you closer to the girl's heart like a nice box of chocolate. Only perhaps humor. And a tireless, hard cock.

We spoke about our respective travels. She loved South America and Brazil in particular, places where I'd spent quite a lot of time. She laughed her head off when I told her about my acquaintance from Italy, Giacomino Bacigaloppo, an Italian bookseller from Padova, a purveyor of medieval literature books and about his love life in Salvador da Bahia. If there were ever a walking cliché of a bookworm devoid of any chance to score even miniscule success with a beautiful woman, such as getting her Instagram username, that was Giacomino. A small, somewhat squiggly man with a pencil thin moustache that really looked like it had been drawn on his face using a pencil. "Giacomino looked a bit like Antonio Griffo Focas Flavio

Angelo Ducas Comneno Porfirogenito Gagliardi De Curtis di Bisanzio," I told her and she snorted, laughing.

"This cannot be a real name," she exclaimed with suspicion.

Well, it is a real name. Moreover, that was the full name of the famous Italian actor Totò, who would, had you drawn a moustache on his gaunt face, look like Giacomino's spitting image. Only that Giacomino was not really haggard in his appearance—he was rather wider than he was tall, his belly bulging against his white, 100% linen guayabera shirt in Ernest Hamingway style that he wore with excessive pride. And Giacomino decided to invest and had subsequently lost all $100,000.00 in no other business but a gym. Let me know about a less suitable investment and I'll pass that on to Giacomino. Luigi, our mutual friend who played an important role in Giacomino's life even prior to Brazil, assured him after he had lost everything that it was not really a loss. On the contrary—he had in fact won so much, our dear confused Giacomino. He, who had arrived in Brazil for business negotiations as a virgin, now had three girlfriends at the same time. He had learned a lot, had even acquired a raunchy skill or two. He could now go back home to Italy with his head held high and find himself a nice little chubby Giacomina and start a family with her, something he had always wanted. Especially now, since he's broke and his many girlfriends have left for more solvent investors Luigi had procured on a 24/7 basis.

Leslie could not stop laughing. Then she did something strange. She hugged me, pressing her firm, well shaped body into mine and kissed me on the cheek. "I gotta pee," she said and ran away to do her deed in the nearby bushes.

I've Heard That Song Before

I invited her to come with me to a small guesthouse in *Kuća Krasna* (a beautiful house) in a little village named *Krasno Polje* (a beautiful field) where I had a room, luckily not also named *krasna*, reserved, to take a shower and get some rest. She accepted my invitation as if it was the most natural thing in the world to do.

I felt great.

After she had taken a shower, she came back to the room barefooted and clad in a big, fluffy white towel and sat on my bed where I was immersed in reading of *The Language of Demons and Angels, Cornelius Agrippa's Occult Philosophy* by Christopher I. Lehrich. An interesting book, I might add. But the look on her face and scent from her body were more interesting than the book. I took her hand, feeling strangely liberated. All those weird and scary encounters I had with women since Rio de Janeiro faded. I was focused, energized, excited and, it should not be denied, aroused. She noticed my erection and smiled.

"Roman, I don't want to be too forward, but if we sleep together, you must know one thing."

"Tell me," I rose in my bed.

"I travel in two days."

Damn. It hit me. I could feel how the Abandonment Entity in me got upset. My cheeks started to burn a little. I controlled it, though.

"Where to, if you don't mind me asking?"

"No, why? To India," she said.

No way, I thought. I mustered enough strength to ask, "India? Why?"

"I go to India as often as possible. I've been doing it for years. I like the extremes and intensity of India, but only in an impersonal setting—India easily gets too much in a more personal constellation."

"Why don't you just kill me outright," I asked. It surprised her.

"What? Why? What are you saying?"

"What you are telling me about your reasons to go there sounded, almost verbatim, what my ex was telling me. This brings so many bad memories back. It was a really bad breakup."

She stood up, moved to her bed and sat again. "I am so sorry," she said. "Do you want me to leave?"

"No. Why? Please stay. It's only a bit shocking to hear almost the exact same words from a person so different from my ex."

"How different am I?"

They never fail in that game.

"Well, for one, you are much kinder. You are also much more beautiful."

"And still you don't want me?"

They never fail to tease.

"I do. But not now. We'll go for a hike tomorrow. Until then, I'll forget about her completely."

"It's your choice, mister," she smiled and came back to me. She jokingly placed a nice wet smooch on my lips. Her own were soft and red, like kneaded cherries, inviting and sensual. What was wrong with me?

Tiruvannamalai

Before she went to her bed opposite mine, Leslie took a small framed photo out of her backpack and placed it on the bedside cabinet. I could not believe my eyes. It was Ramana Maharshi, some sort of a guru there. Charlotte was going to Tiruvannamalai almost every single time she ran away from me. Even more so, she, the person that was cynically mocking religious people, used to place that guy's photos all over every damn place we shared.

Maharshi photo was in her wallet. Another one on the wall. The third one of the same holy guy next to her bed. Even in the bathroom. Then his book. She had plastered his photos all over the place like some rabid Stalinist would have his mustached hero. It was weird. Moreover, while he claimed, "Happiness is your nature," Charlotte did not embrace his key message. That was her *modus operandi*, she took only what suited her needs and gave almost nothing in return. Luckily, Leslie had only one small black and white photo of the same guy, but that was still incredible, the coincidence. I was struck by it. The first woman I really liked since I parted with Charlotte had shared the same teachings and went to holy pilgrimage to the same places as she did. I wondered if she had sex with the same guy? Charlotte had told me about her ex-boyfriend, whose specialty, for the want of a more appropriate word for the sophisticated spiritual fuck circles around the foot of Arunachala, was to shag Western "seekers," just like her or Leslie. Hey, I assume when a full-fledged sage is not available, a guru's guru would do it.

Leslie fell asleep quite fast, but I stayed up all night. My hatred toward Charlotte took over again. I felt like a miserable wimp; here, in the same room with me was a young and willing, sexy and exciting young woman ready to sleep with me and I was going in a next loop of my hatred and impotence. For yes, I was impotent toward Charlotte's bullshit—sucked in into her world and played by her rules I did not even understand. So many fruitless talks with her were going through my mind, sucking up all my energy. When the dawn broke, I was worked up, nervous and tired.

I promised myself I would not let Leslie see any of that and made her a nice cup of coffee and a breakfast like they'd done in old Western movies: sausage and eggs.

"Aww, so cute, thank you. But I am a vegan," she smiled, gratefully accepting the coffee.

"Of course you are, damn cow—you all are," I said. Did I say it out loud? Nope, thanks God, Leslie was enjoying her coffee and did not seem to have heard anything of what I just said. I must have just thought it.

A Morning Hike

Leslie had a quick breakfast of her own, some sort of incongruous looking, borsch-like shitty smelling stuff, and we went out for a brisk morning walk just after she had finished. It was chilly but sunny, a perfect day for a hike.

"You look tired," Leslie said. "Did you sleep at all last night?"

"A bit," I replied begrudgingly. She shrugged my foul mood off and we kept walking in silence. It wasn't as pleasant as it should have been. Instead of enjoying Leslie's company, I hated Charlotte more and more with every passing step. I must have been emanating the negativity that enveloped me because Leslie gave me an uneasy side-glance and stopped.

"Roman, I don't like this," she said. "You are obviously still upset over the similarities in between me and your ex, but this is not my fault. Your silence and demeanor seem like punishment."

"What do you mean?" I asked her but I knew she was right. That annoyed me even more.

"You changed since I brought up India. This silent treatment… you … you are not a pleasant company anymore. Sorry. I feel like you are punishing me for whatever she has done to you."

We were standing next to the ravine and looked at each other. Her eyes were now glistering with pain and intelligence at the same time. She was right in her assumptions. Alas, I was consumed by hatred for Charlotte to the point where I was unable to admit I was wrong or to think clearly. I had nothing to say, so I suddenly blurted, "Fuck you." What an idiot.

"What?" Leslie seemed hurt.

"You were ready to sleep with me only after an hour or so but were ready to leave in a day or two." I heard myself babbling childish nonsense and I hated myself for it. But I hated Charlotte—or was it Leslie?—even more.

"Yes, I did. And I was honest about it."

"Well, fuck your honesty. You care only about your own ass being filled by a stranger's fat cock and not about his feelings."

"Roman," she said trembling. Was that sadness? "Roman, I see you have been hurt horribly. And I am truly, deeply sorry about it," her words were like tiny little needles hitting me all over my skin. I knew she was right, and I knew I was horribly wrong. I could see that I deeply hurt her, but the Hatred did not let me step back, apologize, fall on my knees, retract, retreat, accept. It only pushed me harder, the Hatred.

"You are not sorry enough," I said to Charlotte.

"What? I did nothing to you to be treated like that," Leslie said, hurt and sad. "But I am not responsible for what you're feeling at the moment."

That was it.

Those words were Charlotte's words.

Do they all quote from the same "for Dummies" book on human interactions? She was never fucking responsible for anything. For a moment that stretched for eternity I looked at Charlotte, not seeing Leslie, who asked, now a bit afraid, "Roman, what's going on…" and felt how my face is narrowing, suffused by the white light. I had problems breathing. I started to hyperventilate as my heart was pounding like mad. And then I could not breathe at all, I was drowning in the oceans of time Charlotte had stolen from me. I had to rip off my jacket and my shirt from my chest as my heart wanted to jump out.

Charlotte came to me, fear in her eyes. "Roman, what's going on? Please, breathe, breathe—it will pass," and then she touched me, trying to console me.

"Don't you dare touch me." I shook down her hands and then I saw Charlotte in India laughing with some "guru" as she was *coming*, all holy and enlightened like all the Tiruvannamalai female "seekers" and it felt like she was laughing at me. It tore me apart. I could not bear it anymore. I pushed her over the edge of the ravine.

Leslie had a surprised look in her eyes as she was stumbling back, and, ultimately fell down the ravine. I realized it wasn't Charlotte I pushed, and I tried to catch Leslie. It was too late. She fell down the ravine, straight into a vipers' pit.

Then the screams started.

The Screams

I drove down the 405 scenic road and almost crashed the car several times. I could not see the road, weeping along with God over Leslie's dying breaths. I could hear her piercing screams from the snake's pit as the *poskoci*, the nose-horned vipers' diabolical fangs were injecting their lethal neurotoxins all over her body. As her blood was congealing, soon to kill her with massive blood clots, I drove like a maniac downhill, running away from the painful cries, but her screams multiplied in a pandemonium that only grew louder and louder every passing second.

"What have I done," I screamed as I was trashing the steering wheel with my fist. "What have I done, what have I done!" almost as if I were trying to make the noise of my own yelling quiet Leslie's dying screams in my head. I wanted to expel them, those horrifying screeching sounds of my damnation, as I ran and ran, further away from the crime scene that never really left me. "Help me run away from my day," I once begged a friend of mine, when the pain of relapse, some ten years ago, was too hard to bear. Well, one cannot escape from oneself; I was going to learn soon. From then on, until the day I die, Leslie from Tulsa, Oklahoma was going to keep living in me, a ghost of damnation, an innocent, beautiful human being who did nothing wrong had been murdered by me and was now becoming a part of me, mingling with my other parts in a blend of horror. I was cursed. At that moment, I condemned myself to Hell.

The Hitchhiker's Guide to the Galaxy

As I cursed myself driving downhill like a madman, I saw two hitchhikers, cheerfully standing on the edge of a large ravine, next to the sharp curve. The bastards were all smiling, all happy under the sun, smugly enjoying the view of the Adriatic Sea beneath the foot of the Velebit Mountain. Life was good for those bloody motherfuckers, unaware of the pain and suffering of a girl that could have been their lover, their healer, their wife, a mother of their children, an angel watching over their dreams. No, the bastard motherfuckers were enjoying the sun and the wind instead, all oblivious and all so cool and with the nature. They even had a cute little sign—"STINICA"—written on a cardboard and a translation—I could not believe my eyes, the stupid hippies had a damn translation of the Croatian name of the village they were heading to, a line that read: "Little Rock, far from Arkansas.[25]" Did they really think they were funny, these bloody bastards, while Leslie was dying of viper's poison only a few kilometers uphill?

I broke hard. The car swerved, the tires squealing. I stopped next to them.

---

25   Croatian name *Stinica* derives from a dialect, *mala stina*, and means a little rock. (note by Trygve E. Wighdal)

"WOW, man, you know how to drive," they cheerfully exclaimed. Nothing could upset those chirpy freaks. I exited the car, as angry as hell at them. I was all puffed up, my eyes and face red, tears trickling down my cheeks.

"Man, what's wrong?" they asked in unison. What was this, a mountain opera? Not talking, I rushed up to them and took a swing at the taller one. The moron wore blond dreadlocks, the idiotic, atavistic hippie wuss. His nose broke, his skin cracked open. He bled like a slaughtered pig and conked. I hit him again as he was falling down. The other one was smaller—but as they say oysters are better when small—his mouth agape. He looked dumbfounded.

"What the hell…" he uttered when I smashed him across his left ear and then right hooked him at the jaw. What a feeble pussy this other hippie was, even weaker than the first one. He just plopped down on the road like a spineless scarecrow.

"You wanna go to 'the Little Rock, far from Arkansas,' motherfuckers?" I yelled at them as they were rolling on the ground groaning in pain.

Leslie was dying in the pit and you morons want to have fun. An adventure. So here's your adventure. I started to kick them. I could hear how their ribs broke, how their noses cracked. I saw their broken teeth as they flung around. They were crying like the two little bitches they were. I hated when they whine like that. "This will teach you compassion, motherfuckers," I growled and kept hitting them until I got too tired to move my arms or legs anymore.

I spat on them, jumped in the car and split.

Oslo, December 17, 2018

Dr. Ellinor Tyri Geliassen listened to my recounting of Leslie's murder without interrupting me once. Then she finally spoke.

"That was a horrible murder."

I could not utter a word for a while, looking inward and trembling. It was horrible, indeed. As I spoke, I felt the dread, I heard the screams. It was a crushing recollection, but I needed to continue, to disclose the darkness, to face the monster in me.

Dr. Geliassen looked at her papers.

"Leslie was your first murder. You killed your second victim, Viridiana, short afterwards. Why didn't you stop if you felt so much remorse and guilt as you claim?"

"Brigitte was my second, not Viridiana. She was third." I corrected her.

"I beg your pardon?" Dr. Geliassen started to frantically leaf through the thick police report. Then she raised her eyes and looked at me.

"There's not a word about Brigitte in your confessions to the police. There was Leslie you killed first. Then Viridiana. Are you telling me that you killed another woman, someone you did not mention before? Are you confessing to another murder?"

"I forgot to mention it at the time."

"You forgot? Right…" she kept staring at me.

"We must stop this session now," said Dr. Geliassen. "I ought to call the police—this is in their jurisdiction. Are you ready to amend your confession to them?"

"Absolutely," I said.

Majorstuen Police Station

It was fast. I described in detail what had happened in the Joshua Tree Park where I went with Brigitte. They asked me to confirm other elements in my confessions. It was a surprisingly uneventful chat with the police. They were professional and somehow detached and indifferent, so I did not feel any need to go inside my guilt and grief during that hour or so with them. I was rather annoyed by their lack of interest, but it was soon over, and they delivered me back to the hospital.

Chapter 12

THE HATRED

"Hatred eats the soul of the hater, not the hated."

Alice Herz Sommer[26]

Oslo, December 18, 2018

The next morning, Dr. Ellinor Tyri Geliassen perused a copy of my (amended) statement to the police quite carefully, glancing at me from time to time. She read it thoroughly and finally looked up at me with a cold, penetrating gaze.

"These are bloody serious proceedings. You are under a charge of multiple murders you have confessed. We have given you every opportunity to tell your story. Lying to us is not only dishonest but makes conducting the process for all the professionals impossible." She was angry at me.

"I am truly sorry."

Dr. Gelianssen kept staring at me, expressionless. Silent. I felt I needed to explain myself, like a little pupil. It miffed me, but I felt guilty in front of her.

"I was interrogated only once, when I was bloody, tired, after I'd had a drink or two, hungry and was out of my mind. I did not remember everything that day. They rushed me here quite rapidly. Dr. Sønstebø's assessment started very soon after and we got entangled into her approach."

"Did you kill anyone else?" She asked sternly.

"No, I did not."

---

26   Alice Herz-Sommer, lover of Chopin's Etudes, was a Prague-born Jewish pianist and
      music teacher who survived Theresienstadt concentration camp and lived to 110 years.

"OK," Dr. Gelianssen sighed, "let us go back to your murders. You killed Leslie and then you killed Brigitte, very soon after you'd killed your first victim. If you'd tell me one singular reason for killing these women, what it would be?"

"It is not that easy, Dr. Geliassen."

"Killing them was not easy?" I felt a whiff of her mockery might be back.

"No. I sincerely cannot pinpoint to one singular reason. I did not start killing outright. It was a long process of falling down."

"So tell me, how did it start, then?"

"With hatred," I replied. "With maddening, crushing hatred."

Berlin, April 10, 2016

I have been an assertive guy almost all my life. Sure, I must have had a predisposition or two for an inner disaster in me. After all, I drank like there was no tomorrow, gulping down gargantuan quantities of booze in a suicidal manner, but I somehow managed to go through life as a highly functional alcoholic for quite some time until I quit. As I looked back, it was so obvious that I had coped with life by avoiding it. It seemed so funny, given that I'd been to all the continents and had a wild life filled with adventures, but truth be told, I had never done more than scratch the surface of life. Certain talents I might have had developed, like playing chess on a higher level, or alchemical inner insights, always frightened me. I wasn't really aware of those fears, but I had not embarked on the path in front of me as the only way to live a full life, a path of inner discovery.

I neglected the dreams that might have been significant. When my former girlfriend back home, a psychologist, told me that I was "afraid of madness" after an encounter with a madman that shook me, I did not stop and ponder such a statement, not for a moment. I neglected every single sign the universe threw at me. I enjoyed loud, outwardly insanities of my theatrical bullshit and ascribed all of that to my youth and need for an audience one can easily find in dive bars, even after I reached thirty and beyond. Not a big deal—everyone was an insane drunkard anyway, I thought. In my writings I had left clues about the state of my mind many times, in sentences like this one, *"Bone-dry, I am sipping on doubts about truthfulness of Queen Margot's very existence and I am going to wrestle in*

beforehand lost battles with the phantoms I myself have created and who are
not letting me down no matter the price they demanded for their existence."
That very sentence even had a title.

Mezzotempo of Despair on the Way to Madness

So, all was there, seeds of madness to come, black on white. I wrote it
without understanding a single word coming out of my own pen. In a short
novel I published in 1993, I ended the story in a similar fashion. The demon,
always the damned "demons" in my life, approached the protagonist, a writer,
from behind. The writer turns, recognizes the visitor and utters in terror:
"This is impossible. I created you," I said.
"Really?" I replied.
So, that was another "demon" that I had created, the one that finished
me off in that novel. So while Charlotte was a real person, her bludgeoned
body was living proof of her violent death. I must have invoked The
Bergmannstraße Demon from those truthful Chronicles.
Schrödinger's cat would meow even if she never existed.

Naiveté

Only once all the miseries I'd encountered started to dissolve my
resilience, I began to melt down. My confidence was gone first—my ability to
assess myself, the people around me and the world as a whole as well. Point
in case: I once invited an acquaintance of mine, Garry W., an ex-convict who
had spent forty-seven years of his life in a penitentiary for a double murder
he had committed in Los Angeles as a service to the *cartel*, to a lunch. As
we ate, I told him that I think I lacked street smarts and survival skills to
move forward.
"Bullshit!" Garry said in his gruff voice. "You did survive. Don't sell
yourself short."
So, while it may appear that I was more resilient than I thought, I
did not acknowledge that, not even after Garry scolded me. Since an early
age, I had some sense of the fact that I was not entirely aligned with the
realities of life. I lived in a fantasy world, depending on magical thinking.
I had "magic coins," traveled the world in my fantasies. I had been writing
short stories since I was eight years old and started to play very good chess
even earlier, at seven. None of these teach you how to deal with the real life.

When I started to drink, the naiveté did not go away. On the contrary, it had only gained a patina of bohemian romanticism. I dibbled in poetry. I read Gérard de Nerval, Charles Baudelaire, Arthur Rimbaud and France's "Prince of Poets," Paul Verlaine. I drank absinthe. I ran away from home when I was only a fourteen-year-old boy after I flunked out of the school (because my writing was of a political nature even at that age). In Marseille, I was naïve and stupid enough to board an Arab ship going to America as a stowaway. The crew caught me, handed me to the police and, after I refused to join the *Légion étrangère,* they sent me back home.

My extreme naiveté resulted in me being robbed of my possessions by wrongly chosen business partners twice. Once back home, another time in Brazil. Moreover, once in New York, while I was homeless, that same credulity put me in a serious trouble with the FBI. I was a victim of fraud, a long story to be told elsewhere, for I did not have even the most basic self-protection mechanisms set in place. But again, I naïvely ascribed those events as results of various circumstances, not as something I invited into my life myself. I neglected to ponder and research the causes of such events and lived with their consequences, oblivious of the fault in my stars and my behavior.

Hating with a vengeance

Only when the Hatred for Charlotte came into my life with such a soul-shattering vengeance, I realized there is much more of "me" than I realized. I moan about Charlotte all the time like a little bitch. But I do not want to give her too much credit, too much power. She was like heroin, a conductor, a wormhole that transported me from one state of mind to another. Without me and my journey, she's nobody. Ultimately, it was me allowing her malign presence to distort me into a mirror image of a raging, murderous maniac. I was chasing the dragon but had no other drug, or woman, to wean me off of her. I am ashamed.

Oslo, December 18, 2018

This time Dr. Ellinor Tyri Geliassen interrupted me.
"Of what? Could you specify?"
"Addicts know their addiction is going to kill them. But what they say about the euphoria and blissful apathy heroin produces as it temporarily rids you of the pain is only a half of the story. They know that bliss is bad. Very

bad. My phony bliss was 'love'," I made an air quote gesture, "and I was doing everything for her 'love'." Air quotes again. I was getting agitated.

Dr. Geliassen interrupted me again. "Water time." She slid a glass of water across the table as they used to do in old Western movies. I caught it and took a sip. "Good," she said. "Please continue."

"It was so obvious she was full of shit. But I chose not to see it."

"Specifics, Roman, specifics. How one goes from 'full of shit' to 'maddening, crushing hatred' as you put it?"

I took a deep breath. There were so many.

"Once she suggested that I get a puppy from Sergio O., a friend of mine who bred dogs, and added that I could always give it back to him, once I was able to leave. That's cruel. Even better, I asked her for an investment only once and only after she had ample chance to observe my work ethic, my almost fanatical devotion to the project I believed in, and you know what was her response?"

"Please tell me."

"She told me that I am a genius. That the project was brilliant and needed in the world and that would make all the difference. She said that she believed in me, that she did have the money but then refused to invest despite all the safety nets I'd put in the proposal. I've been told to fuck off an die with more kindness and sincerity than in her refusal."

I saw Dr. Geliassen open her mouth as to ask something.

"Just don't ask me how that made me feel!"

She smiled.

"Before that, two or three years prior, while I was still destitute, she went on blathering how she had been blessed with money she did not earn and how she sees no reason why she would not share that money with me. Mind you, I never asked her for anything. I managed to survive homelessness and abject poverty all on my own. I started to make money again and work on the projects again, all by myself. [27]"

I was calm, so Dr. Geliassen's gaze encouraged me to continue.

"Speaking of specifics, Dr. Geliassen, probably the most disgusting display of her selfish persona was when I got sick. I had problems with my

---

27 Roman is not telling the full truth here. While some of his oldest friends did indeed turn their backs on him, some people like Luigi from Salvador, Marina, a childhood friend from Osijek and The Captain from Moscow helped him, by lending him some money to survive, to eat and to be able to procure consultants' gigs. Those weren't gigantic sums, but I think that he would not have made it without their help. He told me that himself once in Paris. (note by Trygve E. Wighdal)

back for a long time, namely with my vertebrae. Scoliosis and a herniated disk that used to create sometimes unbearable pain. We once stayed in a cheap Airbnb with a horrible bed that completely messed me up. I could not walk; this is how horrible the pain has become during the course of only a few days of sleeping in that atrocity. Her reaction? She was thinking only about herself. Mind you, she 'loved me more and more every day,"—an air quote—"but did not even think about helping. As a Norwegian, she could've married me for the health insurance. As a person with some means, she could've helped me get medical care in some cheaper country with good medical services. Anything. No, she was thinking only about running away to India again. She freaked out when I was in pain. What kind of love was such shit?"

"How did you resolve the back problem?"

"By walking. I remember it was a very cold day in Berlin and we went for a walk. For the first one hundred meters, two hundred meters, even five hundred meters, I was in excruciating pain. I was barely able to put one foot in front of the other. I knew that if I gave up, that would be the end of me, so I continued. The body started to help me, and I was getting better and better with every step and walked and walked and walked for kilometers until I've gotten much better."

"That's horrible how she had treated you," Dr. Geliassen said. "Why didn't you just break up with her?"

"I was too ashamed of my problems, first the money related and then those regarding health. I saw that as a huge problem I was bringing to the system of 'us' and felt solely responsible for it, at the time unable to even notice her utter selfishness in coping with them. Listen, I went all alone from homelessness and from a guy who had to accept her charity *just to eat*, from a guy who had made her seventeen times her investment and who earned enough money to travel around the world in the business class, visiting very expensive places like Easter Island, Tahiti, Sydney, Singapore, you name it. That by itself was no mean feat and worthy of celebration. A huge load off our system's chest had been lifted. Instead of enjoying this financial freedom that we now both had, she started to manipulate with sexuality. Given that I gained a lot of weight and lived with a very strong physical pain in my back that almost fully incapacitated me, something I alone have also resolved later, I was again on the beginning of the vicious cycle of feeling guilty. She was of no help—on the contrary. The question you should ask yourself, Dr. Geliassen, is why she did not break up with me?"

"Will get back to it later. Now tell me more about hatred."

You are a Genius. Now Fuck off and Die

Berlin, April 10, 2016

I knew dysthymia for ages. I knew these deep throes of depression as I was plummeting into hell ever so often. Sometimes I was catatonic, and in that stupor, I binge ate. Junk food and sugar were my ill-chosen remedies. I greatly admire Andrew Solomon and his *"The Noonday Demon"* book on depression[28]. But I disagree with him. To me, depression is not "the flaw in love" as he claims; it's rather an absence of it. If you're unloved that's painful but still fine, you can cope with aloneness and even loneliness, but when you're unable to love the world, to love the fellow human beings (or that "one" you love fully) and ultimately if you are unable to love yourself, than you start to sink into the deepest throes of depression, whose other name is Hell. I also always somehow had seen both love and depression as something that happened to you, like something coming to you from the outside.

Little did I know.

King Solomon

If depression is an absence of love; the opposite of love is not hate. It is power. Hate is a sad, often tragic manifestation of powerlessness. If you're not loved, you are indeed powerless—try and "force" someone to love you. Well, unless you are really vile and gamble on the Stockholm syndrome as your tool of seduction in order to make someone love you, you're up for a rude awakening.

Those days I was working virtually twenty hours a day on the documentary project with the orphans in Kenya and the David Sheldrick Wildlife Trust, an orphanage for elephants. Think of a slow peeling of the bandages from the deep wounds both human & elephant orphans feel for being abandoned, until we find the point of newly found hope, love and life in an encounter of a child and a baby elephant. I really hoped Charlotte would fund this documentary, so I asked her to invest rather a modest sum. She said no. Then, as she was prancing around on some holy festival under her holy Indian mountain, she sent me a PayPal "gift" of $300.00, with a note, *"This is unrelated to what you wrote about the project and just in response that you need to eat c."*

---

28 "To be creatures who love, we must be creatures who can despair at what we lose, and depression is the mechanism of that despair. When it comes, it degrades one's self and ultimately eclipses the capacity to give or receive affection," writes Solomon.

I accepted that money. I ate with it. I was crushed. I was ashamed of myself. I hated myself. And why? That was the manifestation of her power over me, that's why I feel that power is the opposite of love. While she refused my request, she had decided to send me "food money," at the time of her choosing. She decided how much—how much should I eat, for how much money. All of which from afar while dismissing my project, the only thing I ever asked of her. My track record was good enough that I warranted some minute risk, especially given how I had structured the investment (in very small steps).

What a damn idiot. Instead of living in my fantasy world where magical thinking roams free, I should've gotten a job in McDonald's or anything and acted like a man. Like this, I was reduced to a beggar. Moreover, to a rejected beggar. But in my infinite wisdom, I truly believed if someone works almost twenty hours a day on a project aimed at not only helping children but creating a wonderful journey for those beautiful little orphans, a project that might have even earned us some money, that it's justified. I did not need or ask anything for myself—no salary, nothing. I had barely eaten those days.

Seeds of Hatred

"What do you regard as most humane? To spare someone shame," wrote Friedrich Nietzsche. So there I was, a double deranged idiot, a man living on fumes, believing he had love in his life, and a man working on a project that had zero chances of taking off. Try to have zero dollars, Euros or yens in your pocket and see where it would take you. I was depressed, I despised myself. Self-loathing grew in me, hour after an hour.

When Charlotte had taken away love from me by ripping my heart out of my chest and feeding it to the rabid dogs, I was in a real, heart-breaking physical pain. I felt it all the time. I could not sleep or focus on anything else. And yet, still, because it was inflicted from the outside, it felt like something foreign, even the pain in my own heart. But nothing had prepared me for the outbursts of hate I experienced soon after she disappeared under the "sacred" mountain in India and rejected me, the "genius," she "loved" and "believed" in yet again. Moreover, nothing had prepared me for the discovery that I had that horrible hateful persona in me. It was indeed unmistakably me, the mirror image of myself, the Hatred persona that came to life out of me and, for a while, had completely taken over my mind and heart.

A way of describing how it operated, the overwhelming hatred, would be a *next loop* metaphor. The loops in an old Commodore 64 computer basic program are repeated executions of one or more lines in a program. The GOTO tells you to go back to the same old same old. In the case of my Hatred, I just kept repeating the most hateful insults, the most dreaded curses, all aimed at Charlotte. While those were aimed at her, I kept telling them to myself all the time, like magic mantras of insanity, dozens or more a minute, like a full-blown obsession. No other thoughts but those of hatred were allowed. A better comparison might be *All work and no play makes Jack a dull boy* sentence(s) from Stanley Kubrick's movie *The Shining*:

"All work and no play makes Jack a dull boy. All work and no play makes Jack a dull boy. All work and no play makes Jack a dull boy. All work and no play makes Jack a dull boy. All work and no play makes Jack adult boy. All work and no play makes Jack a dull boy. All work and no play makes Jack a dull boy. All work and no play makes Jack a dull boy. All work and no play makes Jack adult boy. All work and no play makes Jack a dull boy. All work and no play makes Jack a dull boy. All work and no play makes Jack a dull boy. All work and no play makes Jack a dull boy. All work and no play makes Jack adult boy. All work and no play makes Jack a dull boy. All work and no play makes Jack a dull boy. All work and no play makes Jack a dull boy. All work and no play makes Jack a dull boy..."

And like that for over five hundred pages, so now imagine telling it to yourself, out loud, over and over again twenty hours a day, seven days a week, each and every minute of each and every waking hour. You'd be drowning in a maddening pandemonium of your own making in no time. So had I.

This was what Hatred looked and felt like. Luckily, I knew since beginning of the Hatred's life in me that this is a manifestation of some sort of mental illness, for want of a better definition. It gave me hope, that notion. Paradoxically, I did not think it was *my* mental illness specifically but I thought that hatred, any hatred, was a mental illness, some sort of devilish possession. I had to expel it from me. If I wanted to live, I had to amputate a malign tumor on my soul, the Hatred.

Oslo, December 18, 2018

Dr. Ellinor Tyri Geliassen stopped me by the slight movement of her smallish hand.

"Yes?"

"This is important, what you're telling me. But first help me organize the order, if you wish, of the existence of your *personas*, or *entities*. I am with you only the second day today, and after we had another murder I wasn't aware of to discuss, I need to catch up with everything. You said that you developed an Abandonment Entity and now you talk about the Hatred persona, as different parts of you, correct?"

"Yes, it is."

"You don't drink now?"

"Not anymore. Why? I did relapse and drank quite a lot over the last six months, after a decade of sobriety."

"So there is an Alcoholic Persona as well?"

"Funny that you should ask that, Dr. Geliassen. I have never drunk alone at home. I never even drank from hotels' minibars. I always needed to get out for a drink. Firstly, I thought that was because, as an aspiring writer in my youth, I needed—as Nietzsche would say—an audience, even if it would be oxen. Then, given my propensity for loud burlesque and theatrical exaggerations, I saw myself as someone desperately needing attention. I was wrong. What I needed was, I know now, help."

"Everyone does."

Dr. Ellinor Tyri Geliassen surprised me.

"Please continue."

"Anyone who's being loud and inconsiderate at best and obnoxious and rude at worst while drunk like I had been does not really induce people to dig under the slurring words' surfaces and recognize the offender's cry for help. Drunken babble is rarely an inspiring sight one wishes to emulate or join, much less to engage in a meaningful interaction. That is why normal people turn their backs on you, form an opinion about you and put you on the 'a fuckup drunkard' pile, while those you drink with could not care less about you or your life. They have their own and the lives of those close to them to screw up. The vicious cycle of dehumanizing the pain and coloring it with whiskey, vodka, and rum closes and further isolates the drunk. What's left is even more pain."

"Should I quote you in my next paper on alcoholism?"

Is Dr. Geliassen messing with me?

"Did you enjoy drinking?"

"You bet your ass I did, doctor. Duality of every drunk's feelings. You hate it and you love it. I guess it's the same with drugs. At the end it consumes you completely."

"As much as love," said Dr. Geliassen flatly.

Boulevard of Broken Dreams

"As much as love," I concurred with the wise doctor.

"Do you think you have an Alcoholic Entity in you?" Dr. Geliassen asked.

"Most certainly," I replied. "It's interesting to me that I think the barfly in me became Bozo the Clown only once I stopped drinking."

"How so?"

"I have that clownish persona in me. That part thrived, briefly, with Charlotte when I entertained her with my theatrics. But I think it's one and the same with the alcoholic part. All in all we have Abandonment part, Hatred part, Depressed part, the sad clown alcoholic part…"

"So which one of your parts had murdered all those girls?"

She stunned me again, Dr. Ellinor Tyri Geliassen, with this unexpected question. I thought long and hard.

"Neither, I am afraid. I truly don't know. All those amnesias do not help at all."

"And Charlotte, who killed Charlotte?"

"Oh, that was me. Most definitively me," I replied without hesitation.

"All right, Roman. Thank you for the session," Dr. Ellinor Tyri Geliassen said and called a quittin' time.

I was escorted back to my cell where I got on with writing again.

Chapter 13
THE WANDERER

"Oh God, let it be over with,
this miserable wandering
under a vault as deaf as stone.

Because I crave a powerful word,
because I crave an answering voice,
someone to love, or holy death."

Tin Ujević, *Daily Lament*[29]

Oslo, December 19, 2018

The feeling of being mentally ill, as I thought I was, as I was possessed by Hate and its soul-splitting reverberations, made me study the very word "hatred." It's a noun, therefore it represents a state of mind, an emotion that in one might have been hidden for ages while in another it rages and ravages incessantly. I suspect that Charlotte was infected by hatred, but she was unable to face it within herself until she had to face it without, in myself, in the face of a man who loved her and whom she supposedly loved, only to

---

29   The Croatian poet Augustin (Tin) Ujević (1891 -1955) is one of the finest Southern Slav lyric poets and one of the great poets of Europe in the first half of the 20th century. 'Svakidašnja jadikovka' ('Daily Lament') is Tin's lyrical masterpiece. Unrhymed, but with an inescapable, incessant, pounding rhythm, it insists, with slow inevitability, on successive waves of feeling that tumble over one another in rapid succession, oscillating between unease, anxiety, angst, anger, anguish and despair. (Richard Berengarten) Tin's translated from Croatian by Daša Marić and Richard Berengarten. Roman L. had a copy of Tin's 'Daily Lament' next to him when he died. (note by Trygve E. Wighdal)

be murdered by him. Such is the irony of life. I use the word "hate"/"hatred" with a purpose, for it delineates danger. It transgresses the emotion and embeds itself in the body until it becomes a visceral part of one's being. I truly believe poets and psychologists, sociologists and philosophers alike should study hatred and its metaphysical implications even more in depth, especially nowadays when hatred is so prevalent in both social media and political discourse.

The word "hatred" surprised me. Pokorny Etymon, rather a Proto-Indo-European (PIE) etymon reveals its interesting roots. Some Indo-European reflexes of the word *hate* are Old Celtic *cath* which means *battle*, as well as Old Frisian *hatia* for *hate*, or Old English *hati (ge) an* for the same word. Digging deeper reveals Old Norse *hatað* as *hate*, but then Hellenic ἀκηδής and κῆδος are not "hate" anymore but rather *grief* and *sorrow*. In an extinct Tocharian language (such a shame it vanished, the Brahmi script is wonderful) the root of *hate* is *kat* or *destruction*. So the path from sorrow and hate to destruction has been imprinted in the very word that depicted that horrible emotion of HATRED.

I fought against it mightily. While I had indeed, well, *hated* Charlotte with all my heart, I think I was rather *disgusted* by her behavior, *despised* her selfishness and ultimately *abhorred* what she has done to me and other people who were unlucky enough to have crossed her path, and I wanted to get rid of that sickening emotion that was tearing me apart. I went on a quest—destined to fail, for I wasn't near ready—of meeting other women first. It was a wonderful clusterfuck.

Brussels, August 4, 2017

Wholeness breeds and represents charisma, so charismatic people are admired, respected and, ultimately, loved. When people know who they are and where are they going with their lives, they are irresistible. A force to be reckoned with. I've been shattered and unloved for the most of my life. My destiny was to walk alone no matter how much I longed for company. I have been an unwilling aberration throughout my lifetime. The Gazelle, a beautiful African woman I met in Kenya and who Léopold Senghor must have dreamed of when he wrote "Black Woman" poem (*"Naked woman, black woman / Clothed with your color / which is life with your / form which is beauty"*) told me that I "am not a human" if I do not have anyone. While I did not have anyone and lived in an utter isolation from the rest of humanity for decades, I had her briefly before I moved away from Africa, a continent which frightens and fascinates me, to Beirut were I truly experienced fear. In Lebanon I also missed meeting the Victorian Ghost, but that's a completely different story. L., if you read this, know that I never drank from that bottle of the "Chateau Musar Lebanon Rouge 2010" I wanted us to share.

Being on the road felt like fulfillment, or at least a useful contentedness to fill the void, while in reality it had been like a runaway train without brakes on a downward slope. Traveling was my bliss, my burden and my transgression. The Fool, the first card of Tarot was ideal match for my Zodiac sign, the first in line, Aries, "the pioneer and trailblazer of the horoscope wheel" who kicks of spring and disasters. The Fool is also an unnumbered card, representing freedom and the start of any journey. I searched for freedom only to be enslaved by the search. *"None are more hopelessly enslaved than those who falsely believe they are free,"* said Johann von Goethe, whose quote I once used in an argument with Charlotte about her "need for freedom," a freedom that to me looked more like a rigid cage from which she did not want to escape. I did not realize I was the same, enslaved by my delusions of free will as I roamed the world, never letting roots grow to help me connect with the Mother Earth, the other people and, ultimately, myself.

Wanderer

I traveled as I ran away from the pain, only to end up running away from love and life. Strangely, while I lament about not being loved, I had, in fact, had a surprisingly high number of love affairs, especially if one would bear in mind that I spent half of my life drinking heavily and most of my years depressed or overweight. I guess I had been an ungrateful bastard for most of the time. Some of these wonderful, or perhaps equally disturbed women even professed how much they loved me, and a few of them repeated those claims after the brain-eating amoeba era of Facebook entered our lives and fake-connected us all, some twenty years since the last time we'd seen or slept with each other. Barbara M. was one of these women, someone who played a minor but a very important role in these narratives.

After Charlotte had expelled me from my life and the Hatred had crushed me, I started to wander like *The Flying Dutchman* or Goethe's eternal wanderer. One might say that I was rather like a headless fly going nowhere. Should you take a look at my first month or two traveling after I left Norway, the white puppies of my mind, and Charlotte behind you'd see a map of a madman's journey:

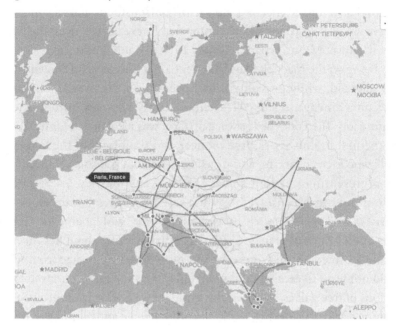

I was also a lunatic who was unable to read the messages given to me from almost every woman I met. I went to Berlin where I was rejected by Stephanie, a meek looking girl whose wonderfully intelligent eyes were somehow hidden by the glasses that also camouflaged her as tough as nails character. While I was sitting with Stephanie, I told her how I was able to "see" what's behind people's façades, namely her immense intelligence, and, to further prove my point, I'd stopped one extremely, beyond painfully beautiful young woman. Jasmine was her name. She was from Sarajevo, well too perfect for anyone not to be strangely upset sitting next to her. I was on a roll, performing a loud psychic burlesque for my eager audience; I guessed where she was born. I knew she wanted to be a writer but was afraid of publishing her work, for it was too intimate and she did not believe it was any good. I knew she was an orphan—OK, that wasn't an insight worthy of Thomas Aquinas; I lived through times of The Siege of Sarajevo[30] so I knew how many people had been killed there. I also guessed her immense

---

30   The Siege of Sarajevo started in 1992 and lasted for 1,425 days and was by far the longest siege in modern history. It was even a year longer even than the Siege of Leningrad during World War II. Official figures list 11,541 people killed in Sarajevo during the siege but the correct figure will never be known.

sensitivity and even, after she approved such a bold attempt, ventured into describing her love and sex lives, and I was correct in every aspect of her deep, dark nature. Occasionally, she shot at me a bewildered glance. Sometimes she blushed and sometimes she just stared at me motionlessly. I get it now: Stephanie was attracted to Jasmin. A small wonder given Jasmin's ravishing beauty. Alas, my mighty intuition accompanied with violent excitement did not produce the desired effect. My paroxysms of insight had worn out both Stephanie and Jasmin by its violent nature, so the former told me that something was really wrong with me. They also declined my kind offer to smoke a joint or two in my hotel room. I mean, who in Berlin declines such an invitation nowadays?

That was the first and final blow; the rest was just a routine.

Routine Rejections

I realize it's rather deranged when someone goes jumping from woman to woman if one is not committed to serious possibilities or even to a one-night stand, a fling. For I did not really want them. I do not even know what I would've done if some of these girls expressed a wish to sleep with me; I was spaced out in perpetuity. No clue why I did not opt for solitary drinking either. I guess I was too lonely and hurt. I went from woman to woman, talking, babbling, clowning around and therefore counting rejections like some half-baked nitwit accountant on a path toward oblivion, almost enjoying how the number of rejections grew. I counted my brushoffs like blessings.

Heba followed Stephanie few days later, claiming that I had something strangely unpleasant and scary in me despite the correct words I used in interacting with her. She was very kind to me, but there was a granite firewall she'd erected in between us, negating any idea of accepting me into her life for even a moment after I had left the restaurant in which I had approached her. So I went to Prague, hoping my Slavic madness would blend with a somehow subdued Czech craziness of the Golden City better than with the Germanic precision of those ultra-smart Berliners, half of whom are high on weed and another half on post-doctoral studies.

Alas, in the city of a thousand spires, I experienced a piercing rejection, a betrayal from a fellow Slav. Alla from Moscow turned me down with flirtatious laughter: "it was fun meeting you but now I have to go." Those fashionable *Moskvichkas* have style even when they deny your advances, and Alla was one of the most stylish women I ever saw. So, naturally, I flew to the fashion center that is Milano, took a train to Florence and Pisa where I was unmolested by rejections but still bothered by *The Florentine Pieta* by Michelangelo and by The Leaning Tower of Pisa, the only Italian city I disliked. Then I went to Porto Azzurro on the island Elba, where Napoleon was exiled, and where the rejection saga started all over again. Sophia, the hotel's director, told me that I was not normal as she rejected me on daily basis like she would a cockroach. I did not blame her; she looked like a supermodel and drove a 1969 Ferrari Dino 246 GT she'd inherited from her father, an automotive engineer who had worked in the Ferrari factory in Maranello for three decades. In the same "Hotel Plaza" overlooking the Tyrrhenian Sea, I had a glimpse of a chance with one young, somehow sluttish American girl. Maya was her name, I think, but at the end she elected to go to bed with her boyfriend instead. A youthful folly, I thought, not paying attention to the simple fact that I was older than both of them put together. The boyfriend did hint that we might have a threesome, but I am a deeply conservative chap—the threesome for me always meant one man—myself—and two women not the other way around. Even though I did try it once with a former friend of mine and his female colleague over one drunken night in New Orleans. His body was stronger and more attractive than mine so I guess many would say I was traumatized and therefore wary of young and vigorous competition over Maya's erotic flair, which could have been the case, but I guess we'll never know.

After Porto Azzurro, I rushed back to Athens without any reason whatsoever and then to Istanbul, a unique city that spanned two continents and which was where I wanted to cross from Europe to Asia on a ferry. After that sacred pilgrimage had been done and crossed off of the bucket list, I flew back to Italy, to *La città eterna*, the eternal city of Rome. There I was spurned once again by one older noble woman in the historic "Harry's Bar" on the famous Via Veneto, just around the corner of the beautiful Park Villa Borghese. This woman did not succumb to my advances, not even after the ten cocktails I paid for in a vain hope that she'd lower her guard. Alas no, she defended herself like an old Gothic castle would defend itself from the Barbarians. She had a body of a young hippie in Woodstock and the contemptuous, albeit still beautiful face of a destitute aristocrat who refused to accept reality. Federica wasn't like Sylvia from *La Dolce Vita*, Fellini's 1960 flick, and *"love, love, love"* wasn't in her heart anymore—just distain, mostly for me. That did not preclude her from ungratefully imbibing my drinks. I saw a glint of sorrow in the singer's eyes when she glanced at us from time to time, but I was getting too sloshed to consider an attempt to conquer yet another likely impenetrable castle. Federica aside, I must tell you, everyone should at least once in their lives see the sunset from the Villa Borghese and enjoy its scarlet glow.

Ancona was my next destination. I went there to catch another ferry, the one that sails across the Adriatic Sea to Split, Croatia. On the ferry, Magda, an unattractive school teacher from Rtina, an important village in northern Dalmatia that even has its own Wikipedia page, discarded my futile attempts to offer her a warm body and skillful hands fully at her service, so I went back to the ship's bar and drank the night away with a couple of bleary-eyed tourists from Ann Arbor, Michigan. From Split, after I had been drinking "Dingač," an exquisite Croatian red wine famous for its donkey label and the fact it had been exposed to the "three suns," as its grapes matured, and ate seafood in abundance, I left for Zagreb and then Budapest, capitals of Croatia and Hungary respectively. Then I found myself in Vienna, Austria and thereafter, after indulging on some *Sachertorte mit rum*, I went to Kiev and Odessa, Ukraine where I was awe-stricken by the lure and allure of those peerlessly beautiful Ukrainian women.

They also have a great sense of humor in Odessa. I daresay nothing in this world is more powerful and horrifying than the gorgeous women of Odessa when they look at you with a glint of a smile that tells you they effortlessly see you and through you. Yes, Irina, I am talking about you. I stopped talking to women somewhere around Split. It wasn't a conscious decision or my own vengeful rejection of women after all those experiences, it just happened naturally. I was unable to connect all those rejections and create a comprehensive self-image of someone off the rails with whom something was seriously going amok. When I look back it seems to me that those days, I walked the life somehow blurred, almost like my aura or my spiritual body had been disturbed and out of place. I definitively wasn't myself. Truth be told, why would any woman go to bed with a man who was still obsessing over someone else and drank to drown the sorrow? There's hardly anything more pathetic than a sorry sight of such a man.

Finally, in Odessa, to my surprise, I met the first woman that attracted me madly, Victoria. With the benefit of hindsight, I realized even sadder truth: she somehow resembled Charlotte, especially when a shadow covered half of her face, revealing only her luminous eyes and a perfect body beneath her sexy white silk blouse. She drove me nuts with desire but after she had rejected me repeatedly with the most magnificent indifference I ever encountered, I went to Paris, France, the very City of Love. Decades ago in Paris, I gave up approaching women with any romantic ideas. The chic Parisienne women were in a league whose rules I am utterly unable to master. To me they live in a parallel universe. However, I felt safe, safe from women that were walking around the 5th Arrondissement as I was drinking wine on Rue Mongee and reading Kierkegaard. *I can also be blasé, you creatures from another planet.* Then I took a train to Brussels. Why Brussels, I had no clue. I must have thought I was going to Bruges.

My head was already spinning. That zigzagging of Europe without any purpose did not seem to have produced any apparent benefits. And my soul was left behind, maniacally scrambling to catch up with me and my breathless marathon of futility.

The Beginning of the End

In Brussels, out of blue, I received a most unexpected e-mail from one of the women from my past, that very same Barbara, the woman I always wanted. She was Frieda Kahlo to my Diego Riviera, which is to say that we were quite different and not really complimentary in sizes and volumes of our bodies, but she had that incredible sexual appeal I always found irresistible. There was also something in her character that at the same time repelled and insanely attracted me. I could not put my finger on it, but out of all women from my past, she was the one I never forgot and often daydreamed about. In the past, we had a chance or two to consume our respective passions—respective for she claimed that she wanted and loved me until the present day—but I mostly screwed it up by drinking I craved more than her it seems. Or was I just afraid? Her appearance in my virtual world felt like manna from heaven. I could not think of any other woman I desired as much as I desired Barbara and, given the state I was in, she was the only woman I felt I could be real with and love and have sex with truly out of lust for her and not because Charlotte was gone. When I was in Zagreb only days before, it did not even occur to me to contact her myself. She was a married, respectable and well-known clinician, so I did not want to bother her and upset her neatly organized life in which she "controls her family and her husband" as she confidently claimed. So her e-mail came as a very pleasant surprise and at the right moment, when I needed her most without even knowing it.

That very day, we had virtual sex, and a bit later, we agreed that we'd meet the very next day. I'd reserved a room in the Hotel "Esplanade," and bought a ticket for Zagreb when she suddenly bailed, giving me some lame excuse. Even more, she has totally vanished from my life since. Strange—until this day completely inexplicable—outcome. Or maybe she simply took revenge for my failures to shag her in the past? Women rarely tolerate such neglect once they have given you a chance.

Perhaps it was the vacuum Charlotte had left that made me so insanely wanting Barbara, and maybe she had sensed it somehow and decided not to risk meeting me? I will never know. But as I was sitting in "La Porte Noire" bar in Brussels, drinking one beer after another, it finally dawned on me: I was messed up beyond words. Barbara's rejection had felt so real; the possibility of our tryst strangely hurt me. I was virtually shaking from desire when I was purchasing my ticket to get to meet her, so losing that night or two with her felt like a profound loss of any hope. I will never find another woman to replace the illusions that bred false hope and false life, neither as a lover or sex partner, unless I make some profound changes in myself. A recovery from a breakup as painful as that breakup I went through does not happen overnight, and no amount of Barbaras in the world, no matter how desirable they are or how dirty their sexual fantasies might be, would heal me overnight. After all, no one wanted me those days; women do not seem to be natural healers of those in mental disarray.

Anyway, I had already relapsed, so I wasn't too keen on any "profound spiritual changes" that required the hero's journey and its twelve stages. At those times, I had a rather trivial penchant for spirits of a more immediately obtainable order. I also loved to fly, so instead of going to Zagreb, I downed the hatch one more cold beer and flew to Rio de Janeiro instead. It had been a pleasant flight in the KLM's Boing 787-9 Dreamliner's business class. (I went to Amsterdam by train and there I got on a KLM 705 flight)

Rio is a city whose every dark erotic secret I knew by heart. "Sex is the lingam franca of the world," Philipp G. used to say over the Eva Vollmer's "Bruder Dornfelder" wine, and I dare you to tell me who speaks the *linguagem do lingam* (and that *do coração*, of the heart) better than *cariocas*. If anything could help me, that's Rio de Janeiro, the City of God.

Blame it on Rio

Rio de Janeiro, August 18, 2017

A stentorian voice of an enormous cab driver, João, made my day after we landed. He boomed with pride when I, in my broken Portuguese of what's left of Jorge Amado's language in me, told him that he looks like Zumbi dos Palmares, the slave king and one of bravest warriors in Brazilian history that fought against slavery. Even though Zumbi's head ended up on a pike after the Portuguese defeated him, my new friend João was unfazed. I almost flew out of the car when, out of pure joy, he hit me in my shoulder after I told him that his name should not have been João but rather Grandão ("Big guy") like the famous capoeira master's name, Mestre Grandão.

"Eu não jogo," João said sadly. ("I don't play capoeira") *Então.* Well then, I told him, you must know, João, that once I almost made a documentary about capoeira, *O Jogo Que Pode Matar* (*The Game that Can Kill*). That was enough to make a real friend out of João. These Brazilians are something else.

Alas, bafflement would best describe the look in João's eyes after I told him I would be staying at the opulent, luxurious "Copacabana Palace" hotel. I guess his sympathy for me fell a notch or two. At that time, I had the money, but I was dressed worse than while I was homeless. I did not do it on purpose for some snobbish disdain for the rich frequenting *The Palace*; I simply, truly did not care. Brazilians are, in their hearts, despite all the freedom samba gives them, a truly hierarchical bunch. They dress up for a long flight or for a visit to the iconic places like the stucco on the beach, that legendary meeting place of Rio's high society and a hotel that had hosted Orson Welles and Madonna, Nelson Mandela and Princess Diana, Justin Bieber and The Rolling Stones alike, so to look like a bum while going to *The Palace* was a sign of disrespect. I apologized to João for my appearance, explaining that my wardrobe was part of a lost luggage saga, and that I'd dress properly as soon as I could buy myself a new outfit. This restored both order in the universe and the smile on João's face.

Despite a twelve hour long flight across the Atlantic Ocean, I had no jet lag, thanks to the Boeing Dreamliner's cabin pressure simulates an elevation of just 6,000 feet (1,828 meters) which is a much higher air pressure than in other aircrafts. Flying business in an airplane almost completely made of composite carbon fiber like the Dreamliner is certainly a stress-free experience. What I am saying is that I arrived in Rio rested and ready for some old in-out in-out.

Termas Centaurus

'When in Rome, do as the Romans do' when applied to single, brokenhearted men in Rio de Janeiro means only one thing: going to the *termas*. No, while the word means "spa"/"spas", one does not go there for a hot bath. It would be a grave *faux pas* in Brazil to call termas by their real purpose—that of a bordello, but this is what they are.

I went to visit likely the most famous and best *spa* in Rio's Ipanema, "Termas Centaurus," in a search for my *Garota de Ipanema*, "The Girl from Ipanema" from the Antônio Carlos Jobim unbearable popular song. I did not find one, I have found twelve. Yes, over the course of one deeply insane night, I have been with twelve of the most skilled sex consultants Rio had to offer that night, thanks to the precisely measured combo of "Viagra" and *vodka com suco de laranja* (a simple screwdriver drink made with vodka and orange juice). I am not bragging here—nope. I do not possess any special prowess to carry me through the night, just madness and loneliness. What's important for this narrative is what happened next.

So I spent over ten hours in the termas, drinking and having sex with all these women. At the wee hour of the morning, I was too tired even to walk or think anymore, so I was ready to leave. For the casual observer, that must have been a blast of performance, for I'd danced with the cleaning ladies in my underwear, drank vodka from the girls' brassiere, sang karaoke with equally drunk hoodlums from Warsaw, went into rooms with one girl after another while I was laughing like a maniac, and danced and drank again... too many too embarrassing theatrical, nonsensical exorbitances to count or to be proud of.

I left "Centaurus" and went into a night that was lonelier than ever.

Self-flagellation at "Cervantes"

Squeezed in between some other bland looking businesses on the Avenida Prado Júnior in Copacabana, there's a wonderful night-snacks joint whose unappealing yellow façade you'd most likely fail to notice—a bar and restaurant named "Cervantes." It's a dive bar famous for its *estupidamente gelada* (literally: stupidly cold) draft beer and much more for its pineapple sandwiches, bohemians and occasional lady of the night gathering for *bate-papo* (shooting the breeze) at dawn.

I was exhausted. The alcohol I'd been drinking all night wore off; I was hungry, lonely and confused. All the sensations of smell and touch with these beautiful women I spent a night with were gone. All of that felt like it had happened a lifetime ago, from times past and never to come back. I ordered one *estupidamente gelada* and a pineapple sandwich and looked around. Everyone was having fun. A lot of couples enjoyed each other. A life I would never have again, I felt.

At that moment, one dangerous looking guy, walking like a rapacious tiger as he was displaying his muscular physique, entered "Cervantes" with his feline looking companion. Ana Vânia was her name. She came to Rio from Belo Horizonte, some 500 kilometers north from here, to be a model. Someone should've told her that São Paulo was the place to be, not Rio, but I was sure the tiger guy would be the last one to tell her that. She was supple and subtle, her beauty wasn't flashy, but she oozed stygian depths from her mysterious beauty. Like Helen of Troy, she brought life and death to this world. Her cinnamon color emphasized her commanding, inebriating presence and those green eyes so rare on mulatto skin made her stand out in millions of people. Ana Vânia was an absolutely unique looking human being.

I was looking at her with growing longing. I did not desire her at all—she was an image of perfection beyond my reach or dreams, a personification of the life and love I longed for. I desired living; I was yearning for a meaning in life that I had lost over the years I spent clenched in the deadly grip of my relationship with Charlotte. The utter meaninglessness of that degrading night in "Centaurus" was catching up with me. I shook off my fatigue a bit, and I was in a mental haze. Rejections in Old Lady Europe somehow seemed better, or at least more real, than that cheaply bought "love." But now, there she was, a lovely, lively, absolutely stunning woman who seemed to have arrived from a Jorge Amadu novel to spread wonder in a world filled with pain. I did not understand how men did not die in her arms. She noticed my gaze, so the boyfriend followed her glance and looked at me. Immense animosity was his immediate visceral reaction; I sensed it as a shark would sense a drop of blood from kilometers away. Only the blood would be mine.

I approached them with a smile and asked for a permission to offer them a drink. Ana Vânia asked me for a name and provided her own and looked at the guy, apparently seeking a permission to accept a drink. He curtly said that he could buy his own beer. There was a palpable danger in his demeanor. All the red lights in me started blinking *this is not going to end up well*. I had zero chances against that lean, mean, fighting machine. Good.

So I looked at his kitschy gold watch and told him, pointing dismissively at it, "of course you could buy your own beer, given that you're with such a precious woman." Then I made almost a fatal mistake and touched her bare shoulder with the back side of my fingers, saying something along the lines that she's like a fragrance come to walk among us mere mortals, unworthy of her. He did not hit me but pushed me so forcefully that I flung over the bar and smashed a barstool.

"Fuck off," he barked at me.

Ana Vânia looked at me with deep sadness in her eyes. It was like she knew I was losing not only her, but also every other woman in the world on my early way out. I made another mistake. I sneered at him, matching his contempt, and turned to leave with a dismissive hand movement. "Motherfucking baboon," I said through my teeth.

I knew it was coming. I wanted it to come, although I did not see where it came from, but he kicked me with such a monster force that I instantly fell to the ground. Capoeira practitioners call such a leg kick a *"queixada."* Its power comes from someone executing the kick twisting their upper body as he hits you with the upper edge of his foot. It is a basic capoeira kick but a monster one. As I was falling down, he kicked one more time with his knee, breaking one of my teeth.

He grabbed Ana Vânia's hand, jerking her as a true baboon would, ready to flee. From the floor, bleeding, I glanced up at her legs, which looked like Michelangelo Buonarroti had sculpted them, when he was possessed with the mad lust for life such mesmerizing creatures give to us. My gaze led me all the way up to the "passport to heaven" as Al Pacino's character said in that overrated movie, hidden only by sexy lace thong panties. They were pink. The baboon caught my indecent glimpse and kicked me in the ribs so forcefully that he broke one, bloody bastard. But as I convulsed on the floor, I felt a wave of happiness overflowing me. In those few kicks, he had given me more respite from anguish that all the "Centaurus" women put together.

Hoo-haa!

Chapter 14

THE CRUEL CITY

"I needed a cruel city."

René Daumal

Oslo, December 20, 2019

"The pain provided you with relief? How so?" Dr. Geliassen asked.

"It was different, the physical pain, much better than the mental anguish and a much needed change from it."

"You could not have gone for a run instead? Lift some weights?" She asked without a hint of irony in her voice.

"Well, in fact, I did walk twelve kilometers that day. I made a loop from the hotel to Leme and then over the Botafogo and passed the Rodrigo de Freitas Lagoon, and then all the way up, via Ipanema to the Avenida Niemeyer. There I had an orange juice, the very same drink at the very same place I drank it some fifteen years ago, after I'd lost everything."

Dr. Geliassen nodded, encouraging me to continue.

"On that day, when I was going to fly to San Francisco by using my frequent flyer miles, and, with the last hundred dollars in my pocket that represented everything that I had left, I thought I would never be back. I almost lost my life because of what transpired in Brazil at that time, and I wasn't sure I wanted to face that harsh reality—where it started—again."

"Your homelessness?"

"Yes."

"It seems it has left a strong imprint on you. Would you mind telling me about your homeless days?"

"Not at all," I replied.

"It was the night of the Blizzard of '06 in New York City..."

New York City, February 11, 2006

It was the night of the Blizzard of '06 in New York City, Saturday, February 11-12, 2006, a bit after midnight, when the kindhearted people in charge of care for those among the least fortunate denizens of that glistering megalopolis threw me out of the former Bellevue Psychiatric Hospital, turned into The 30th Street Men's Shelter. This place was the essence of New York's cruelty and its arcane symbol. Despite the record 26.9 inches of snow that fell on Central Park during that freezing-ass cold, frigid night, the homeless shelter's dwelling stood in all its ghastly glory, unmolested by the romantic snowfall and its winter beauty. It was that everlasting, horrid, red brick building, separated from the New York's bustling life by tall-spiked wrought-iron fences. I walked toward Mid-Manhattan, barren of any ideas whatsoever where I'd land that night, leaving the shelter behind. A prototypical New Yorker, Woody Allen, once adopted the old Yiddish proverb, "We plan, God laughs" and made it his own by saying, "If you want to make God laugh, tell him about your plans." I certainly did not plan for any of those dubiously exciting developments, but the gods were nevertheless laughing at me. What else they would do? There I was, limping into the icy cold night, carrying a heavy pinkish duffel bag with me, a sore caricature of a human.

The Identity

The bag was filled with several pieces of smelly clothing, one baloney sandwich I'd cherished since lunch and vigorously guarded like a blushing debutante guards her innocence until nightfall, and, more importantly, about thirty kilograms of books in it. No matter how difficult was to walk with all that weight, I could not get rid of them. Those books were perhaps the only guardians of my identity left, the identity that laid squeezed and forgotten somewhere among the numerous lines filled with pain and beauty, love and hatred, war and peace alike. I seemed to have existed only in between those majestic pages of the world's literature, which I'd gobbled up all my life. I loved like Mark Antony loved Cleopatra, drank like British consul Geoffrey

Firmin drank in *Under the Volcano*, traveled across the American wasteland like Dean Moriarty, soared over the oceans of time like Jonathan Livingston, suffered in Saint Petersburg like prince Myshkin, fought like Doc Holiday fought Ike Clanton at the O.K. Corral, or searched for the life's meaning like Ulrich in Vienna and wanted to invent words like Buck Mulligan did with *snotgreen*. Ah, *"The snotgreen sea. The scrotumtightening sea"* [31] how I wished you'd wash away my pain of loneliness yet again, like you did once when we were young in Monfalcone, Italy, me and Luisa G., a girl of my dreams. Sometimes I clowned around like *dobréhi voják* Švejk, but more often than I'd like to admit, I felt like Gregor Samsa's insect, clad with and suffocating by Don Quixote's armor. [32]

Back in New York's winter of 2006, I was like a ghost in the ghastly city whose cruelty I was about to face in all its callous might. Frankly, as any born and bred Manhattanite would confirm, it's not that bad, that New York City. No need to worry if you plan to visit it. One out of every ten or so persons living in Manhattan is a millionaire, some of them I guess are also kind people who love their art and their pets, so this diverse, bustling, smoldering-at-4-AM city is also full of joy and sex, fueled by money and cocaine, both of which it has in copious abundance. Just ask anyone who frequented the "Studio 54" in the old days or those who will tell you what—if asked around Washington Heights in a properly respectful tone—the question *have you seen Fats* means nowadays. The Devil himself confirmed that sentiment when he, in a devilishly convincing portrayal by Al Pacino had said, high above Manhattan in one of the Mammon's high rises: *"Money, ha-ha-ha, yeah, that's the easy part."* Of course, if you have it.

That pulsating heart of capitalism where everything was on sale was not too kind to me that night. I had nothing for sale and no money to buy anything, so I was a non-entity in the soulless mercantile capital of the world, just another of the Big Apple's numerous personas. In my jacket, though, I had another book, a pocket-sized *A Night of Serious Drinking* by René Daumal. He had found his "cruel city" in this same New York about

---

31 Characters from William Shakespeare tragedy *Antony and Cleopatra*, Malcolm Lowry's *Under the Volcano*, Jack Kerouac's *On the Road*, Richard Bach's *Jonathan Livingston Seagull*, Fyodor Dostoyevsky's *Idiot*, Doc by Mary Doria Russell, *Man Without Qualities* by Robert Musil and *Ulysses* by James Joyce. (note by Trygve E. Wighdal)

32 Another set of characters from *The Good Soldier Švejk* by Jaroslav Hašek, *The Metamorphosis* by Franz Kafka and *The Ingenious Nobleman Sir Quixote of La Mancha* by Miguel de Cervantes Saavedra. (note by Trygve E. Wighdal)

whose cruel streets I'd started to learn. I laughed, like a maniac would, as I was singing, like a lunatic would, on these freezing temperatures:

> *If I can make it there*
> *I'll make it anywhere*
> *It's up to you*
> *New York, New York.*

Laughing in the face of difficulties had been the defense mechanism I had to employ too often in order not to be daunted by a life I had managed to reduce to a caricature of living. Daumal, perhaps due to the lack of humor those mortally serious para-surrealists lived with, did not make it. He left New York with his tail between his legs and went back to Paris to drink with his buddies and died young—at my mom's age of thirty-six—from tuberculosis.

Decades ago, while I was still a teenager, I recalled that I'd also walked alone through the night that time, from Daumal's Paris to Marseille over the Route Nationale 6 (I wanted to get to this same damn New York City, as a stowaway on some rusty Arabian merchant ship, but that is a totally different story that I have no time to share with you now) and at that time I also carried quite a few books with me. The one I had in my pocket was a novel of another Frenchman, Louis-Ferdinand Céline, whose *Journey to the End of the Night*, a hilariously cynical take about human beings and our deranged, obscene societies, I read in reverence those days.

Memories

Only two years earlier, I'd seen New York's more glamorous side. When, on March 13th of 2004, Luciano Pavarotti gave his last performance at the New York's Metropolitan Opera, I was there, clad in a brand new suit, watching and listening to Pavarotti alongside Jackie E. I also recalled what Dante Alighieri wrote almost a millennium ago, stating: "there is no greater sorrow than to recall happiness in times of misery."

Such is an unplanned life, still provoking mirth and joy in the Goddess Fortuna.

I was cold. I was homeless. And—can you think of a greater irony?—I was just expelled from the homeless shelter created to help people like me. The snow was falling, and New York looked like it came from a magical fairytale, so at first, I did not feel miserable at all. Overwhelmed and perhaps delusional, I refused to accept the reality of what lay ahead. I was also strangely, insanely exulted.

I left the confines of that maddening homeless shelter, avoided a transfer to another forsaken shelter somewhere north in upstate New York, a place where I would not only be without any access to job offers and the libraries with their internet services, but also a horrid shelter where only the worst addicts and the most violent offenders were sent to rot. Despite the serious, rather grave circumstances I found myself in as I walked the now completely snow covered streets of New York, I started to hum another song made famous by Frank Sinatra: "My Way."

No matter where I'd end up, from now on things are going to be my way.

My Way

Exuberantly, rather maniacally singing "My Way", I already crossed a bit of Manhattan and had reached Park Avenue. The burden of the books I carried with me started to weigh me down. The cold did not help either. My duffel bag's belt started to cut into my skin. I think I was already bleeding a bit. I was also sweating under all that weight plus my own not-insignificant extra pounds, so it all started to feel quite unpleasant.

The maniacal phase of my unfounded exuberance ended as quickly as it had begun, and the reality started to creep in. I was getting more and more tired with each new step. It started to be difficult to walk. I stopped at windows of the "Churchill Tavern" on East 28th Street and Park Avenue and glanced through the windows, and I realized I was famished. The last chuckle of the day was given to me by *The Little Match Girl* a short story by Hans Christian Andersen I recalled as I salivated at the sight of the food and beer, listening to the girls' sultry laughter in that opulent tavern, all of which was utterly out of my reach. I was literally penniless; I could not even afford a one dollar nugget at a nearby McDonald's.

I was hungry.

I was as lonely as it gets.

I was hot, and I was very cold.

I was homeless. I had nowhere to go.

It is a fucking hellish nightmare, living as a homeless person in New York City.

The "A" Train (Eighth Avenue Express)

Each weekday, approximately 800,000 subway trips include the A or C lines, which is about 14% of all New York City subway trips. Most of these people seem to have arrived directly from Charlie Chaplin's *Modern Times* dystopian sequel—dehumanized, lifeless, stupefied people, their souls pulverized. But at least most of them had a home at the end of their subway ride. All I could do, however, was to ride the longest trip in NYC and stay warm: from the 207th Street Inwood/Broadway station to the Rockaway Park Station - Beach 116 Street. It takes approximately 1 hour, 42 minutes in a car, far from the outside's chill and then back.

So I sat and rode the "A" train. It was Saturday night, very cold outside so there weren't many passengers inside. An occasional homeless person, like myself, hiding from the blizzard and that was it. Then the question of the day finally arose as I was riding the trains for whole nights and until the early hours of the next day—what am I going to do now?

The Whole Picture

New York City, February 12, 2006

La Notti Di Cabiria (Nights of Cabiria), a 1957 drama directed by the great Federico Fellini, has one of the most powerful final scenes in the movie history. In a nutshell, Cabiria was a prostitute who had finally found love but ended up betrayed just when she was starting to be happy. Her new fiancé was going to kill her for money. She realizes his real intentions and completely falls apart in pain, sobbing and begging him to kill her. Her life lost meaning and only death would be a way out. The anguish Giulietta Masina, the actress playing Cabiria, was able to convey and portray in that scene makes me want to hug her every time I watch the movie. The fiancé runs away with her life savings and she is left sobbing, broke, broken, utterly alone and rolling on the ground in a heart-shattering scene. She picks up a flower that thieving Romeo of a fiancé brought her and wobbles through the woods, aimless, in despair only a broken heart knows.

At that moment, a group of young boys and girls join her on the road, singing and dancing, like coming from another Universe. But those two worlds of youthful hope and Cabiria's hopelessness did not collude, they merged instead. She walked with them and finally started to smile through her tears. At the very last scene of that movie, Cabiria/Messina looks at the camera, straight into ours eyes, nods as her smile widened. *Yes, life is cruel and indifferent, but I will live,* that smile tells us, *I will survive.* The film ends ambiguously as we do not know what happens next. Fellini himself said, "I myself have worried about her fate ever since."

My Cabiria was in the book by Professor Richard Walter (Professor Emeritus at the UCLA) I read in the "A" line on that cold night. Had Walter stuck with that inextinguishable American optimism and merely told his readers that you fail only to rise up again (and succeed) I would've likely jumped under the train. But he went a step further and wrote that you fail and rise only to "gloriously fail yet again" and that was the moment in which I decided, for the second time, that I would live, no matter the cold or hunger.

A Dinner for a Homeless Man

I can't remember how I ended up in some alley street in Queens. I think I was looking for a job in a storage house or something but got lost. I was famished and dehydrated after I had been walking around for hours. It was surreal—those empty alleys with garbage everywhere. Was that really in the richest country the civilization had ever seen? That squalor, decrepit façades with homeless like myself, hungry ghosts prowling around?

Then I saw it. A dead mouse lying in the street, its guts out.

I stood there for minutes, like a catatonic patient, with only one thought in my mind: should I eat it? It made me nauseated, the very thought, I almost puked, but my stomach was empty. It's a rich source of proteins, I thought but the concept was so grotesquely absurd that laughter made me gave up gobbling up the dead mouse.

Even after I continued walking, I stopped once or twice and looked back, still thinking about eating it. At that time, I had no clue about soup kitchens for homeless people; homelessness happened so suddenly to me that I was abjectly unprepared for my new life. As I kept walking, I passed a garage and asked the guys for some water and they gave me a full liter and a half in a fresh, cold bottle. I drank it and violently threw up.

I had finally reached the bottom as I hid behind a wall, puking blood and shaking. *I will fucking live, I will fucking survive that shit. I am not leaving like this,* I swore. Not for the first time. I had a flashback.

Berimbau Perdido

In late August of 2006, absorbed in my insignificance, forlorn and suddenly destitute, I was sitting beneath Morro Dois Irmãos (Two Brothers Hill) in the notorious shantytown *favela* Vidigal in Rio de Janeiro. Just as I was about to embark on the long walk down the steep and dangerous hill, I heard a *berimbau* playing inside a small yellowish house. An invisible man's gravelly voice sang Vinicius de Morais's lyrics:

Quem de dentro de si Não sai	*He who doesn't come out from inside himself*
Vai morrer sem amar Ninguém!	*will die without loving anyone*

I always loved classical music and opera, not really a big fan of samba, but as I listened to that captivating afro-samba tune, I had an epiphany. Though my soul had been crushed on my way up Avenida Niemeyer just an hour ago, I no longer despaired. That gravelly voice had made me fall in love with the grandiose opera of life all over again: "I will participate in the game," I declared, "no matter the pain."

Better still, fuck the pain.

I also had a flashback to Milos Forman's movie, *Amadeus*.

"Too many notes, Herr Mozart."

I thought of myself as Salieri thought of Mozart's oboe from "Serenade For Winds, K.361: 3rd Movement," and chuckled. Without that single note, the serenade might have been reduced to a dulcet vaudeville tune, removed from God. Without my own life, it would be like James Joyce had never written "Three quarks for Muster Mark!" in *Finnegan's Wake*, I thought, and I laughed and danced away, as clumsily as a tipsy bear, toward the Ipanema beach. One day, I hoped, I might meet the mysterious berimbau player and have a glass of Sicilian red wine with him.

Oslo, December 20, 2018

"You never met him?" Dr. Ellinor Tyri Geliassen had asked rhetorically, and paused, fixing all her attention on my eyes, piercing through my brain with her intelligent gaze that saw it all.

Chapter 15

FALLING DOWN

"Home? I have no home. Hunted, despised, living like an animal."

Béla Lugosi

Oslo, December 20, 2018

"Thank you for telling me about your homelessness days," Dr. Geliassen said after almost a minute spent scribbling notes down in silence. All I could hear was the keybord's clicking. "It must not have been easy for you."

Well, what to say to that, I thought.

"Let us move on, shall we. What happened next?" she asked.

"More than any other woman, I loved Ingrid Bergman," I said.

"What do you mean?"

"Do you know her?"

"Everybody in Scandinavia does. I also love her. What do you mean by loving Ingrid Bergman?"

"Do you remember her line in Casablanca, *'One woman has hurt you, and you take your revenge on the rest of the world',* she told to Humphrey Bogart?"

"Yes. But what does any of that has to do with our conversation?"

Serial Killers

In Hollywood movies, serial killers tend to be presented like geniuses, akin to Hannibal Lecter whose crimes are portrayed as a superior dance of wit. *Zodiac*, a 2007 movie about the Zodiac Killer focuses on his ability to avoid the police. Gruesome murders are just a backdrop. In my case, there wasn't anything witty or especially clever. Had I not surrendered myself, I might have gotten away with them—not because I was a cunning criminal covering his tracks, but because of the circumstances. I traveled the world; I had no prior contacts with any of the girls I murdered. It all happened in remote places without witnesses. Even Charlotte had managed to keep our relationship out of daylight. No one even knew I existed in her life. But I had not just woken up one day and, because she had hurt me, started killing. It was a long trip. I did not take my revenge on the rest of the world outright. It was a falling down process. Slow, hard, inevitable.

Svullrya, Norway, May 5, 2017

While we were temporarily living in Die Bergmannstraße in Berlin, one of the coolest streets in that exceptional, sultry and smart metropolis, Charlotte had gotten a job through The Norwegian Association for Children's Palliative Care, in some reclusive, uber elite private hospice about thirty kilometers north of her house—a holiday cabin in that area of Norway. The hospice was hidden in the woods, located on the outskirts of the protected natural area, called Vestre Lukashaugen og Bornoberget. It operated in a magnificent manor house that once belonged to the distinguished Mohr family and which they bestowed on The Association. Painted in white, it featured an herb garden and a little colorful playground that mostly stood empty as the kids were dying. I could not imagine a more painful job, but she was up for it after years of not working (she lived out of her inheritance. The Mørk family had made a fortune in lumber business).

She did not want me to go with her, she "needed her space" to organize herself. It would be too much stress to handle a new job and myself at the same time, she claimed. "I don't have the capacity for all of you at the same time." I was already used to so many of her idiosyncrasies and wasn't bothered by it at all. If she did not want a big, strong man to carry her furniture, that was fine with me. God bless strong, independent women—more power to them. We agreed that I would join her in a month or so and I was free to stay in Berlin or to move around a bit. Always a globetrotter ready to fly on a minute's notice, I've chosen the latter and left for Oslo, flying to Berlin first to visit a friend and then to Athens, Greece. The months of the continual travels were already in my cards, but I did not know that at the time. The Fool, the number zero card of Thoth Tarot represents vacuum and a start of a journey. The most exciting journey of my life—that with Charlotte—was in front of me. The affirmation with The Fool goes *"I tread the path of life with joy in my heart and a smile on my lips."* The travels without and within were in my cards, I felt, and everything seemed great.

At these times, my travels were still enjoyable. I knew where I was going, for I knew where I would end up: back with her. So as my first step, I went to climb The Pantheon in Athens and then I went on the Greek island jumping tour. Syros and Naxos, Mikonos and Paros, Sifnos and my favorite, small and magical Folengadros, where Natasha and Maria, a tavern owner and her waitress were crying when I was leaving. During my Greek adventures I was in touch with Charlotte daily, entertaining her with "for her eyes only" vlogs and essays about the trip.

Svullrya, Norway, June 15, 2017

When I came back to visit Charlotte after she had settled in her new job, she went berserk. Underneath her nervous reactions, I sensed some strange hatred that I was unable to pinpoint, but it felt not only like she unconsciously did not want me there, but more like she abhorred me for being there. That was communicated to me via collective unconsciousness, over some strange cosmic strings. I had no clue, but it felt horrible to come to her for love but encounter not only a lack of love but sheer animosity. She did everything to hide it; she might not have been even fully aware what was going on with her, but it was surreal, the whole nightmarish episode. I had to leave because her whole being was vibrating with rejection. The walls were hostile, the air heavy.

I was numb, the shock was too great, but I did not feel its impact as of yet. Almost the same had happened on October of 2016 when I visited Charlotte in Norway for the first time. She was so freaked out over the idea of me living with her there that I had to leave for the first time. Needless to say, over the 216 days we were separated after I had left, she had sent me numerous love letters, repeating all over again how much she loved and missed me. Why else would I come back?

But I did ask myself what sort of masochistic insanity took me there again to go through the same old same old. I packed myself in haze. She was helping me, she was a master of packing, but all of that was happening like in a silent movie. We did not talk; we did not look at each other. Once I was done, I looked at her and I shrugged. There was nothing left to say; that madness needed to end, and it ended that day. Or so I thought when I left.

Like years earlier when I was homeless in New York and carried all my life stuffed in one duffel bag, I dragged myself and my two heavy suitcases all the way down to the Svullrya Shell gas station from which I called a Svein Kalheim taxi. It took me over three hours to finally get to the train station in Kongsvinger, where I then took a train to Lillestrøm, and then, due to some damn engine failure, I had to take another to Oslo Central Station.

As I sat in the L14 train, heading in the direction of Asker, I could not even laugh at the grotesque life I'd lived over the years, entangled with that woman whose philosophy and magic mantra of relationships was against everything love and life represent. People affect each other—you can't pretend it is otherwise; they affect each other daily and deeply, unless you are Charlotte Mørk. I observed myself from afar, and what I saw was a deeply lonely man, a human being without a single soul in this world, whose only "home" was in Charlotte's embrace and who was just kicked out from that home he'd wanted so badly. I had no idea where to go, what to do. I had done everything that was humanly possible to accommodate her peculiarities. I wasn't in Tijuana anymore. I wasn't hungry anymore. I had the money, not some vast fortune yet, but quite a lot given the prior circumstances. I wasn't sick, drunk or crazy. When you feel loved, you don't have to be crazy and in my cursed naiveté and blindness I felt, I thought she loved me.

Moreover, I accepted her fully and did not even care about children we might have had but would not; I could not care less about anything that would put pressure on her precious soul. I'd been away for month and a half so she could organize herself and her new job, and even when I arrived to Svullrya, I devised a useful little trick to further ease her anxieties. Given the 2016 episode, I did not say I was going to move in with her, not even that I was going to live nearby—no, I played the game of a tourist. I was going to visit her, continue to the magical land of Lapland, enjoy the midnight sun and then, once I was back in Oslo, we'll see.

And yet, it did not work. I was tired, my soul pulverized. I was lost in space, alone and lonely. As a loving person, I needed love but was denied it. As a homeless, stateless person, I needed home I thought I had found in her arms, but I was denied it as well. As an abandoned person, I needed to be accepted but was rejected all over again. She really did a number on me, in an absolute brilliant coup. She crushed me. She thrust a dagger into my heart. She cast a black pall over my soul. As I was leaving, little did I know I was going to pay her one more visit, the last one at that, in early December of 2018.

As they say, third time was a charm.

Oslo, December 20, 2018

"That was the last time you were together as a couple?" Dr. Ellinor Tyri Geliassen asked.

"I thought we were the couple. She obviously did not."

"What happened next? You started to kill after you left Norway in June?"

"Wrong! I started to travel and then the disentanglement started, as the first phase. I started to fall down straight to perdition and did not stop until I reached the Ninth Circle of Hell."

"Disentanglement?" I surprised Dr. Geliassen. It made me feel smug.

"That was her mantra. In a relationship as the only way of relating to each other."

"That's an interesting concept," Dr. Geliassen said.

Chapter 16

DISENTANGLEMENT

"Our capacity to destroy one another is matched by our capacity to heal one another."

Bessel van der Kolk, M.D.

Oslo, December 20, 2018

Dr. Ellinor Tyri Geliassen leaned toward me, "homelessness played a big part in your life and traumatized you," she said, "but how did you go from being homeless to having all that money for the cars and luxurious travels all over the world?"

"I got lucky."

"In what way?"

"After I started to earn money by my online consulting business, internet marketing, stuff like that, I invested every single penny I did not need for rent and food into dividend paying shares. Then I went on margin and started to play with options and made a hefty profit. At that time in mid-2017, I took the profits and re-invested them heavily into crypto currencies and got extremely lucky with ICOs—"

Dr. Geliassen raised her eyebrows.

"—that is Initial Coin Offerings, and made profit of several thousand percentage points. The money just multiplied. I spent about $25K on business class travel around the world but that was just a fraction of the profit I made. Basically, I went from $5K to $500K in several months."

"Maybe I should ask you for an investment tip?" Not a hint of irony.

"Never trust anyone's investment tips." I smiled at her.

"Good advice. So, back to Brazil," Dr. Geliassen said. "You were beaten because you wanted to get hurt."

"Correct."

"What happened next?"

Salvador da Bahia, September 30, 2017

It took more than a month, rather some six weeks, before my rib cage healed itself after I was trashed in "Cervantes." I moved out of the "Copacabana Palace" for it would have been a waste of good money to stay in such an overpriced hotel over a month, money better spent on the skillful ladies in love-making consulting services, so I moved to Salvador to heal. Its full name was a mouthful that reads: *São Salvador da Bahía de Todos os Santos* ("Holy Savior of All Saints' Bay"), a city where Jorge Amado lived and a city where I hoped to find my salvation—yet again, after I had lived there some ten years ago. I had a sinking feeling that I was losing any connection to the world. If the twelve women I slept with in Rio de Janeiro did not help me find a moment of respite, what else would? I couldn't go around offering my ribs to be broken by hoodlums in a vain hope that some modern Eva would jump out in front of me and make me happy.

While I stayed on the other part of the city, called *Jardim de Alah*, because of the wonderful beach there where under the palm trees one could swim, enjoy coconut water, *caipirinha* (sugarcane liquor, sugar, and lime) and women all at the same time, I went to the old city, Pelourinho. I wanted to visit Jorge Amado Museum, eat in the Museum of Gastronomy of Bahia where kids from the culinary school prepared and served typical food. The cuisine there was not too good, for they were still learning, but I always enjoyed their efforts and the enthusiasm with which they carried themselves and their wonderful smiles around.

A Hooker from Lagos

Just across the Museum of Gastronomy, on the Rua Alfredo de Brito, sits an ugly, quite small and malodorous joint named "Nosso Bar" (Our Bar), where I went for a drink. It was a kind of place tourists avoid in fear for their lives, wallets and sneakers alike. It stunk. It was ugly, a brawl or two was always happening in between dignified patrons, so it oozed unpleasantness, our bar. It was also noisy and its food seemed like hellish, poisonous borscht waiting to end your Earthy travels and travails on a low note. Even *dendê oil*, that wonderful, thick palm oil that normally smells like violet at the "Nosso Bar" had a special flair. It stank like the unwashed clothing of a mentally sick homeless person, John M., whom I'd befriended in New York City, and God bless his meek, desperately lost soul.

Toothless patrons do not inspire confidence either. My kind of place I go to when I am not enjoying snobbery on the other side of poverty line. I took a couple of selfies with the *distintos cavalheiros,* distinguished gentlemen of the "Our Bar" and I blended in perfectly, drinking and dancing on the street.

Tom Waits' *"Christmas Card from a Hooker in Minneapolis"* was blasting from some ancient speakers that distorted his voice when I heard, in a very loud, thick nasal baritone voice yelling in a perfect Croatian, "No one will ever love you like a hooker from Lagos, Roman!" What? I turned and to my great surprise, what I saw was a white bushy beard and beneath it no one else but my good friend, Andrija P., a maritime captain from Rijeka. I hadn't seen him for over twenty years. I also had no idea that he was sailing those seas around Brazil.

To say that he was sloshed to the ears would be an understatement of monumental proportions. He was drowning in alcohol. Otto von Bismarck once said that "God has a special providence for fools, drunkards, and the United States of America," and while I was not so sure about the accuracy of his quip when the United States was in question, since that day in which I'd seen Andrija plastered like some bull fighters in Linares, Andalucía on the fatal day of 29 August 1947 in which Manolete had died, I was positive that all the ancient gods, the good Lord of the *Igreja de Nosso Senhor do Bonfim* in Salvador and all the orixás of Africa and Brazil put together are indeed protecting fools and drunkards. They had for sure protected him and went an extra mile to keep him safe. There was no other explanation for what I'd seen in the dark corner of the dive bar in which I encountered my friend again after so many years.

Andrija had disembarked from the merchant ship that very morning, in Santos, and had flown to Salvador for a brief visit. He had thousands of dollars in cash on him, and hundred dollars bills were falling out of his pockets and yet, miraculously, no one had killed or even robbed him. Do not get me wrong, Brazilians are fantastic people, but even among them you have a murderous thug or two here and there. One has a feeling that Pelourinho had attracted a few of those unsavory characters who are better to be avoided at any cost. You can get killed on Pelourinho for hundred times less money than what was laying on the floor next to Andrija's feet, but he stood there unmolested, like a mighty, rugged mast that once powered "Preussen." Regretfully, he was way too drunk for any meaningful interaction, so as my good deed for the day, I took him to the hotel amidst his loud, incomprehensible protests. I hadn't seen him again because his seaman's visa did not allow him to stay in Brazil, so his company's agent took him to the airport early morning the next day. He left without saying good-bye. I doubt he remembered he had seen me at all. It was a brief, strange encounter with my past that just popped up out of thin air and with a *puff!* it just vanished as fast as it has appeared.

Gabriela, Clove and Cinnamon

Jorge Amado, whose book *Gabriela, Clove and Cinnamon* I gobbled up as a young man dreaming of my Gabriela, was a grand old man of Brazilian modernistic literature whose work had been translated to forty-six-plus languages. He was honored as Obá de Xangô, one of the Candomblé's mightiest orixás and was a living legend of Salvador and Brazil. Candomblé is primarily an African religion, basically a realm of powerful African deities—over four hundred of them—that correspond to natural forces. Once again back in Salvador, I observed, frightened and saddened by the fact, how the clepsydra of my ideas and dreams was running empty. In that same Salvador I once wrote a screenplay titled *Berimbau Perdido* (*Lost Berimbau*, a berimbau being a one string musical bow used in capoeira) about sex slavery. Ah, how inspiringly I wrote about menacing capoeira movements—*Forquilhas*, *Meia Lua de Compasso*, *Cinture Robusta* and my favorite *Vôo do Morcego*, the bat's flight—with so much passion. A triple *Giro da Sereia* smashed my main villain's head with a forceful stroke. I loved Bahia, *minha quierida terra*, my dear land, those days that they called me *Baiano Lindo*, a beautiful Baiano. If ever there were a misnomer, that was it. It never failed to produce a guffaw in those baianos and baianas always ready for sex, brawl and laughter.

I also saw myself almost as Exú, the crosser of boundaries, with one leg in the realm of gods and another in our human world. I wrote, obsessed with all of them, but more beautifully about Iemanjá, the goddess of the sea and the mother and protector of the fishermen. I wrote about Preto Velho (wise old man) having my late friend, Marc Anthony-Thomas as a model for Preto Velho. That Brooklyn-based choreographer and theatre director,

despite his impediment—that of an American, had the essential goodness
of Africa in him. And Salvador was the very essence of Africa in South
America. I cried when I wrote about King Zumbi's murder:

```
EXT. - QUILOMBO, RIVER NEAR THE OCEAN

Slaughter in Quilombo de Palamares is taking
place. Slaves are outnumbered by heavily armed
enemies and are being killed one after another.
Portuguese warrior first wounds King Zumbi. His
blood spills on the ground and in the river and
floating in the Ocean, calls for Iemanjá's help.

            FANTASY: IEMANJÁ - DAY

Iemanjá stands up, her hair is now red like the
blood, her face is changed with rage, her eyes
look like an evil cat's eyes, greener than ever
before, her nipples are hard, her nails grow,
her breath is short, fast and heavy, is getting
crazy in pain and hatred towards the Portuguese
army that killed King Zumbi.

She heightens, grows, enlarges to gigantic
proportions and starts destroying Portuguese
army and Quilombo with the heavy rain, eerie
thunderstorms, gushy winds in wide, horrifying
destruction.

Dead bodies are vanishing into skies and the
Ocean.

After the destruction of Quilombo, which was
wiped out from the face of Earth together with
the easing of weather, Iemanjá's fury withdraws,
she calms down like the elements also. She is a
beautiful deity again. She suffers like a human
and in tears vanishes in the Ocean, leaving King
Zumbi's dead body behind her.
```

I stood on the shore and looked at the ocean. It was even rougher than usual, the Atlantic—wild, mighty, dark and terrifying. Far, far away, through the salt and gushes of water, I saw what looked like the same small boat I described in the script, the boat that took Zumbi's family to their deaths. It was distant, only the silhouettes of the people on board were visible, so I wasn't sure I was really seeing the boat, or was it a vision from my own words written here decade or more ago? Gusty wind gave that image—real or concocted in my mind—an eerie feeling while I silently witnessed the vision of the past.

Losing Myself for the World

Something profoundly sad had fallen upon my soul. I realized I had a stronger connection to the characters from my own screenplay than to the real people around me. Given my rib cage pain, I interacted with the ladies of the night only on an oral level. No, we did not engage in witty oratory, but rather in reduced sexual activity, connecting their hands and mouths and my intimate parts, but I felt no intimacy at all. As they were pleasuring me with avid enthusiasm, I was disconnected, disentangled, disassociated. While my body physically worked, my mind and soul were absent. I felt like I was floating further away from reality.

Blowjobs and hand jobs exchanged for money became, firstly, annoying and then frightening. I started to withdraw into my past, but only visiting its safe landscapes. I did not think of or hate Charlotte Mørk too much those days—she was an irrelevant, vacuous phantasm of my mind those days. Only if that notion had stayed with me. I re-read what I'd written years ago and, while I enjoyed the worlds I had created, I could not recognize that idealistic man I had been but lost along the way. That recovery time in Salvador was the last time I had a real chance to stop sinking into madness, to recover, to regain control of my life. But I did not. As I rummaged through my past, I found an old "Manifesto" of mine that went back to the fatal day in which Facebook introduced its "Like" button, one of the most devastating social engineering tools ever invented. During those times, I thought a lot about "unheard voices" of the people all over the world and their suffering, their will to live and love despite the unbearable pain of living. I read the "Manifesto" in its entirety and am copying it here. Feel free to skip it, but I am making a point by quoting my own words with a purpose.

Unheard Voices Manifesto

Have you ever looked up into the starry sky at night and tried to count all those flickering stars high above your head? Sure you did, at least as a child; after all, humans are blessed curious minds capable of tackling such enormous questions like, "what is the purpose of life?"

The sun zips through the cosmos in an astounding pace of 483,000 miles per hour, every minute of every hour of every year and it takes a full 225 million years for the sun to make a trip around our Milky Way Galaxy, while rushing through the universe altogether with about a hundred billion other stars.

And a human, that infinitesimal blink of a divine eye, that fragile creature made of water, carbon, bones and dreams, has the incredible ability to ponder the vastness of the universe and the spiritual power to find a place in it all, not at all insignificant but as rightly here as the stars

Where Have You Gone…

People were dying in corporate wars that one religious fanatic waged against other religious fanatics, only to have his insanity replaced by the insanity of a new corporate tool, a one-time "savior" that occasionally had waged six wars, all paid for by our blood and money while billions starve all over the world; at least one genocide is ongoing somewhere in the world at any given time; 200 million children work as slaves all over the globe any given day; nearly three billion people in the world live on less than two dollars a day; and more than 30,000 children die each day due to hunger or avoidable disease.

Do you need a better understanding of this number? During an average Seinfeld re-run episode in length of 30 minutes 600 children around the world will die due to the poverty and hunger!

A typical American child watches twenty-four hours of TV weekly and during that time 28,800 of her or his peers around the world will perish. A million girls work as sex slaves only in Asia. Over a million kids in the U.S. run away from violence and rape every day. And thanks to the numbing media tidbits we're served around the clock, we are more concerned about some idiotic reality star new scandal than about any of those persecuted children.

There is more humanity in one single Mozart tune than in all Congressional decisions combined. Should we really let those cold, money-grubbing, power-hungry, soulless shells decide matters of life and death?

One of the most famous speeches in American political history is titled "I Have a Dream" and guess what? Its author, Dr. King, was assassinated just like other dreamers, such as John and Bobby Kennedy. The message is: "Don't you dare to dream!" The corporate cubicle needs you focused, the ammunition manufacturer needs you sharp. Let us kill the spirit; let us kill the soul, let us enslave the mind by propaganda and let us have George W. Bush or Donald J. Trump in Kennedy's place and let us have Al Sharpton speaking for Dr. King.

Do they dream, politicians of today? What are the dreams of the camarilla we still call the Congress of the United States? Dreams are not good for business. A war is gift from heavens made for profits, so draw your own conclusion. They come to the national TV and look straight into your eyes and tell you that, unless you die for their blood money in a war they wage for Halliburton's or Exxon's profits, you an anti-American traitor. How dare they?

So when you go shopping into the Mall of America, just five minutes from the infamous toilet turn monument of our nation's pissing pride and you fear that some mutilated kid from Iraq, a country we ravaged with bombs, bullets and torture, would throw a stone over the ocean and harm you. That's the perverted idea of democracy and promotion of tyranny of fear where you have to dread your government instead of having your government answer for its actions to you.

You sit at your couch, tired after a long day in a factory (are there any left?) or a cubicle, afraid that you might lose your job or your house; you sit and munch on your pizza slice and enjoy your Coke or Bud. The TV does not relax you; it numbs you, and occupies you, rallying with hatred wrapped in comical morsels of a quasi-commentary. Let us be honest: it is repulsive, today's media, but it's fun on a most primitive level, arousing hate and disgust. But we have our mortgages to pay, to kids to protect from this pervert's Internet "invention," we have our corporate king's bottom line to support with our blood, sweat and tears so who has the time to worry about the global warming? It is baloney anyway. (just ask Bill O'Reilly)

A Man and the Burning Inferno

But, there is so much beauty in the world, so much strength in a human being. We are unique creatures capable of caring, of loving, of creating art, music and literature. Shakespeare's *Hamlet*, Dostoyevsky's *Crime and Punishment*, Proust's search for the lost time, Mozart's *Requiem*, *agnus dei* and need of a human to create despite the pain and suffering. A man is a unique creature, capable of remarkable tenderness and love; it is a being capable to laugh and to dream. A man rushes into a burning inferno and sacrifices his own life trying to save a fellow human being.

We ought not be helpless slaves anymore unless we accept to be, brainwashed meat that feeds the war or corporate machines; we can speak, we can think, we can yell, we can communicate; they can spy to our talk but they cannot silence us; we can act and above all, we can choose to change. If we do not act to stop the madness of a mindless corporate king and his soulless political serfs ready to sell you out in a heartbeat, the burning rubles of Baghdad would be seen in Los Angeles and the starving children of Africa would be your own.

FOR EVIL TO FLOURISH TAKES ONLY GOOD MEN TO DO NOTHING.

Aren't Auschwitz survivor and famous author Viktor Frankl's words:

> *Since Auschwitz, we know what man is capable of.*
> *And since Hiroshima, we know what is at stake.*

An ominous warning of what could happen if we are not vigorous defenders of our own humanity? Humankind should reach the stars instead of killing Mother Earth; it should think freely and create passionately and love fully instead of being enslaved by the corporate monster, filled with hatred, killing fellow human beings for corporate profit. We want humans to take the responsibility into our own hands and thwart this disastrous course the soulless scoundrels we call politicians lead by corporatism that is swallowing us all. We long to see the day when humankind will be liberated from the enslaving chains of bloodthirsty propaganda and finally make this world a better place for all living creatures.

We cannot be free as human beings as long a single child suffers anywhere in this world we share, as long a single mother starves and has to choose which one of her children she's going to feed today.

We cannot be free as humans as long as the wars ravage distant lands and mutilate and kill fellow human beings.

We cannot be free as long child as slave laborers produce cheap sneakers for our own kids and we do not want to see our children growing up in the world plagued with such a mortal inequality as it is today.

We cannot be free human beings as long as there is a single enslaved, illiterate, hungry fellow human being!

I wrote that *manifesto* ten years ago. However, I do not remember a single word of it, even now, after I copied it word by word. I know for certain that I did write it, but it felt like it belonged to another world, to another life, to another me. It was scary not to be able to recognize my own words, my own thinking, my own life. So the question was, who was this man holding a grudge against some character by whom he was moonstruck once, a woman who was, in the large scale of life, an irrelevant, selfish quasi-lover? Really, who was she? Just another of those vile people, no matter her exquisite talent in hiding her true nature? I would have kept wasting my life because of her as I whined in an incessant babble about her, about how "she had expelled me from my life," but that would've hidden the real question.

Was that life really so cheap, so meaningless, so weak that I'd sacrificed it to the altar of false love to a woman that was never there for me? I got it, she never was the problem and I was, as I always had been. But I had no clue what to do, how to help myself, what to do with that revelation.

At that moment, I wasn't even sure that Charlotte Mørk was a real person and not yet another apparition, a figment of my imagination. However, given that I felt she had stolen that life from me, the depression and hatred were real. And they were back with a vengeance, ravaging me. I had to leave Salvador and all of its saints and all of its women behind. The loneliness started to manifest itself in the most peculiar way.

Chapter 17

DEPRESSION

*"The s(**m**)adness will last forever."*

Vincent van Gogh[33]

Oslo, December 20, 2018

"How so," Dr. Ellinor Tyri Geliassen asked?

"The depression kicked in first. I started to cry over nothing. It was maddening. I felt like a self-loathing, whiny wuss all the time. While I was still in Salvador, I went out to provoke a brawl and beat the living shit out of one otherwise totally normal guy in a bar, just to feel that I was not that miserable crybaby. I will get back to it in a moment, for that was a very important moment I missed at the time. Afterward, I went home and watched a movie. It was *There's Something About Mary* and I was blubbering like a baby during the closing credits."

"Isn't that movie a light romantic comedy?" asked Dr. Geliassen?

"Indeed."

I realized that I cried at every scene that had people's interactions in it, any loving interaction, any human interaction. Friendship in between movie characters was enough for me to cry. *Thelma & Louise* and their bond that took them to death together made me wail for minutes. That fabled

---

33   Vincent van Gogh, a Dutch artist and one of the most famous and influential painters of all time, apocryphally uttered those words, *"the sadness will last forever,"* as his last, after he had shot himself. (or was shot, the historical accounts vary) Roman had altered the sentence with the wordplay *sadness/madness*. (note by Tryghve E. Wighdal)

Casablanca ending, Ingrid Bergman's *"Good-bye, Rick, God bless you"* and then the legendary *"Louis, I think this is a beginning of a beautiful friendship"* made me cry my eyes out. It was maddening; I had no control over my emotions and reactions. It was so over the top how I felt and was unable to have any say in my own feelings that I started to hurt myself. The last scene, a three minute long montage of kisses from old movies in the *Cinema Paradiso* made me sob the whole time, so afterward, I trashed my hotel room in a rage of self-hatred. I hit the mirror for I could not look at my bloated face, red nose and all those tears trickling down, smashing it to pieces, hurting my fist, which bled like crazy. How in the name of God anyone could keep reacting like that? I was aware depression could do that to a man, to cry without reason. That was well too much for me to bear.

But then, I incomprehensibly started to search for the scenes to cry. Almost like I was seeking a drug. I was absolutely unable to understand myself, like I was possessed by a blubbering baby. Was I searching for a Hitchcockian "good cry"? Not likely. A "Candy Colored Clown" surreal performance from the *Blue Velvet* made me cry as much as Jack Heke & Beth Heke song "Here Is My Heart" from *Once Were Warriors*. I cried over the display of love as much as over the brutal pulverizing of the Uncle Bully by Jake the Muss. When Jennifer Connelly's character had showed *"what is real"* by touching him and then said *"I need to believe that something extraordinary is possible"* to Russell Crowe's character in *A Beautiful Mind,* I looked at her eyes, filled with so much love for her husband, that I cried for hours. "Impossible is nothing" my mother wrote to me on her deathbed and I spend a lifetime believing in it. I built my life on that conviction, only to see it utterly shattered, but what was happening was beyond me. I was hiding in my hotel room for I was ashamed of myself. I had no problems shedding a tear over an emotional scene, *"real men also cry"* said that other Lebowski in the cult-movie *The Big Lebowski* but to blubber for hours and days at time was beyond comprehension.

I wanted to purge my pain, so I told myself I would tolerate one day of crying over scene after a scene, and no one would ever know anyway. I had a photographic memory for movies, so I was just going from one to another, for hours and hours at time. Warren Beatty asks Halle Berry, *"are you coming or not"* in *Bulworth* and I wail for half an hour. Every interaction in between Pablo Neruda and Mario Ruoppolo in the 1996 movie, *Il Postino* made me cry. I knew for ages that Massimo Troisi, an actor who played Mario Rouppolo's character had died only hours after the main filming had finished, likely a result of his decision to postpone surgery but, when I went to read his obituary again, I cried for half a day. Don't let me even start about *Mary and Max* and they are damn animated characters. When Crowe's character, Josh Nash, spoke about "love" at the end of *A Beautiful Mind* in his Nobel acceptance speech I thought my heart was going to explode, that is how enormous the pain felt.

Korsakoff Syndrome

I felt like a patient suffering from Alcoholic Korsakoff Syndrome who keeps waiting for the dinner just after he had eaten. I had waited for the train of love to come back and Charlotte in it—on the train station she had left never to come back.

Chapter 18
LONELINESS

"Make someone happy,
Make just one someone happy,
And you will be happy, too."

Betty Comden & Adolph Green

Oslo, December 21, 2018

Dr. Ellinor Tyri Geliassen ended our session, which had lasted for hours—until late evening yesterday. We continued in the early morning of Friday the 21st. She kept being subdued, not even once flashing her Sherlock Holmes pipe or gently mocking me.

I had a video of Dr. Geliassen's joint lecture with Dr. Bessel van der Kolk she gave several years ago in Boston, MA titled "Convergence of Trauma," in which they talked about energetic reactions to traumatic events. It was on my computer's hard disk, but I never watched it. After the incident in Salvador in which I'd beat that guy, my friends told me that I had better leave as soon as possible. He was some big shot, or his father was a bigwig—something like that, I don't really remember—with strong connections both to the corrupt police and several vicious gangs in Salvador, so I could have ended up paying a hefty price for my savagery had I stayed. Not a risk I was willing to take. I was ready to leave anyway, for I could not face myself anymore. I was going to continue my "miserable wandering under deaf heavens" (un)aware that I have kept running from the same city Constantine P. Cavafy so aptly described in his poem "The City:"

New lands you will not find, you will not find other seas.
The city will follow you. You will roam the same
streets. And you will age in the same neighborhoods;
in these same houses you will grow gray.
Always you will arrive in this city. To another land -- do not hope --
there is no ship for you, there is no road.
As you have ruined your life here
in this little corner, you have destroyed it in the whole world.

While I was painfully aware of what great that Greek poet from Alexandria, Egypt wrote and what seemed like a prophecy of my own life, I was unable to stop ruining my own in every little corner I visited. I kept perpetuating the curse for "every effort of mine is condemned by fate" so I left for Santiago de Chile. I will have wasted my life once it ends, here, there, anywhere.

From there, I flew to Rapa Nui, the majestic Easter Island I always wanted to see. I finally watched Dr. Geliassen and Dr. van der Kolk's lecture during the five and a half hours long flight in the LATAM's wonderful 787-9 Dreamliner.

Trauma Attached to Memory

The most relatable bit from their talk was "a need for an energetic reaction" to the traumatic event. Remains of the trauma stay attached to the memory, they claimed, and, unless these are "discharged" by an action, "be it tears or an act of revenge," the effects of the trauma would not go away. It helped me realize two key factors from the Salvador incident I wasn't aware of earlier. The guy I beat up so severely had a striking resemblance to Asja's father, the guy who had visited me in my Rijeka home with the Heckler & Koch pistol and threatened me almost two decades ago. At that time I had absolutely nothing against him; after all, he was a father protecting the daughter I unwittingly put in danger and had every right to act as he had acted. I was lucky that he had not blown my head off given how devastated Asja had been after the event. But now, decades later, I realized I had been nesting a deep resentment in me, not only for him, but for the whole history of mine in the land where I grew up and was left ostracized. I felt like my homeland, my own tribe, had abandoned me because of my political writings at the time. So my old friend Abandonment was acting up again, it seemed, without me being even cognizant of it. I had been like a Vogon back home, I thought, chuckling at myself, recalling the wonderful scene in the *The Hitchhiker's Guide to the Galaxy* in which Vogon, after reciting some unbearable poetry asks Arthur Dent, *"so what you're saying is, I write poetry because underneath this mean, callous, heartless exterior I just want to be loved?"* but instead of being loved, I ended up being hated by so many. So, I was a fertile soil for hatred for ages and blissfully unaware of it, even when I posted a video a friend of mine, Vedrana, made in Rijeka, titled *"From Vukovar, Without Hatred."* Lack of hatred, an ability to fight it off and to forgive and even love (your enemy) instead of hating them, was always a highly ranked quality in my eyes.

But I also remembered how the American guy's girlfriend, I am talking about the guy I senselessly pulverized in Salvador—a nice looking, all-American blonde girl—had attacked me in a vain attempt to protect him. She was brave. Normally, I would have respected her courage, but at that moment I looked at her with such a blazing hatred in my eyes that she recoiled in dread and went to cower in a corner, crying. I am sure I looked like someone ready to kill her. And I was for sure capable of killing her. That was a crucial moment, the first moment in which I felt burning hatred for someone other than Charlotte or myself.

The seeds of what was yet to come were firmly planted in me and started to grow.

Hanga Roa, Rapa Nui, October 2, 2017

Although I arrived to the majestic, mythical and mysterious Easter Island in a lazy manner and in full comfort of business class, I felt like Thor Heyerdahl, a legendary Norwegian explorer who, in 1947 had built a raft of pure balsawood, and followed the footsteps of Kon-Tiki[34] Viracocha, an Indian chief who sailed from Peru to Polynesia on a 5,000 mile (8,046 kilometers) long sea journey. Thor Heyerdahl's Kon-Tiki Expedition inspired awe in me when I was a young boy and listened to my father's stories about Thor and his motley crew of brave sailors. In fact, only one of his six crew members had any maritime experience, no other had a faintest clue about sea or sailing and yet, they had succeeded in proving Thor's point: South American indigenous peoples discovered and inhabited Polynesia for

---

34 Kon-Tiki was a name of the Sun God in the ancient Inca language. He was banished from Peru and vanished toward Polynesia.

hundreds of years, as well as those from the West, on such a primitive raft. Later in his life Thor Heyerdahl went to Easter Island to discover the secrets of *moai*, those huge, imposing, wonderful monolithic stone statues scattered all over the island. From the above Rapa Nui looks like a triangle, covering only sixty-three square miles (163 square kilometers) and yet, despite its minute size, it is a place like no other on this "blue dot" of ours, Earth.

Remote and so isolated that the natives joke how the closest land to their island is the moon, Easter Island mesmerizes everyone. I love the ocean, so Easter Island seemed like a perfect place for me to find peace. There I was, sitting on the top of Easter Island, on the "Mirador", with the Rano Kau volcano on my left and the Pacific Ocean on my right and yet I kept feeling depressed as hell. As recovering alcoholics say on their path to recovery, they used to be tired of being tired and I was in despair over the depression.

I wanted to kill myself out of sheer anger. I was visiting one of the most magical places on earth, touching The Big *Moai* Thor Heyerdahl touched decades ago but was nevertheless unable to enjoy the unique privilege of being there. What was the point of wailing like a little bitch for hours and days in Salvador if there was no discharge of whatever cursed trauma shattered me? Why did I pulverize that poor defenseless guy like the worst bully would if there was no discharge, no respite, and no relief? How could I even hope to get well if I couldn't get rid of the demons, *The Bergmannstraße Demon* that clung onto me, sucking the living life out of me. I'd go on YouTube and cry over a comment of some anonymous guy losing his wife years ago, then go and beat the shit out of someone only to go back to watch a movie and cry yet again. I hated myself over such a wussy display of unmanliness, which I was utterly unable to comprehend. Nothing was helping; on the contrary, I was getting worse, seemingly on a daily basis. The only explanation I had was that I was regressing back to childhood, to the position of absolute helplessness yet hoping for an outside salvation that would've been given to a child. But children do not weigh above 140 kilograms and do not go around beating other people or getting themselves beaten by mean street fighters. I did not entertain that thought, to my peril, because of the new inner developments that had occupied me; it was something new and unexpected.

I spent all day on Anakena Beach—the only real Polynesian beach on that whole volcanic island—ate lobster, drank lemonade and enjoyed the sun. The self-loathing and depression subsided a bit, for I swam in the ocean, took numerous photos of the Anakena *moai* (all of them look inward, watching over their descendants) and shot some breeze with an American eternal tourist, Donna from Berkeley, CA. As an anthropologist, she was a very interesting conversationalist, so we had a great time prattling about our respective travels throughout Spain and Italy.

Detaching

After I returned to the hotel, I watched a Clint Eastwood movie, titled *Hereafter*, staring Matt Damon and Cécile de France. Ah, those French women. Reneé always comes to mind but she belonged both to another man and another story so I will let her be at peace in their Paris abode. I somehow drifted away, like I was not watching the actors on the screen, rather like I was there with them, above them, observing their interaction from a bird's perspective. I liked them both—hell, I loved them. But I loved them like one loves strange creatures—a bunny in the park, an antelope on the safari, a whale in Baja California, from afar, not like one of them. These talented actors represented the humanity that I was detached from. I watched a big Hollywood star like Matt Damon and felt tenderness for him, almost sorrow, like one would feel watching a magnificent tiger in a zoo. I could not recognize the feeling but it was quite a grotesque outlook on the slice of reality Clint Eastwood, the director of the movie, depicted for our enjoyment.

After my delicate "tenderness" for Matt Damon went away, I found a copy of the Bible in the drawer of the room's nightstand and started to read the good book.

Deuteronomy 28-28

If you do not obey the LORD your God by carefully following all His commandments and statutes, *"The LORD will afflict you with madness, blindness, and confusion of mind,"* says the good book Bible in the appropriately titled *"The Blessings of Obedience"* chapter. I looked up the King James' Version of Deuteronomy 28-28 for I knew it was more poetic. It indeed was, as it beautifully said: *"The LORD shall smite thee with madness, and blindness, and astonishment of heart."* Smiting someone with *astonishment of heart*, that's a pure poetry of cruelty. I could not help myself and started to laugh. It's a small wonder the verb "smite" means "to inflict a heavy blow," the Lord's favorable approach to humans, as well as "to enamor."

So after you got smitten by the beauty and charms of your loved one, the good Lord enters into the picture and he smites you as well.

Hope you not, my learned reader, there's no way you'd get out of the love predicament without paying an exorbitant extortion charge for the dubious privilege of being alive. For everything else, there's a MasterCard. HE, our loving father, also promises you, firmly, "a bubonic plague". Also, he *"will strike you with wasting disease, with fever and inflammation, with severe heat and drought, and with blight and mildew; these will pursue you until you perish. The sky over your head will be bronze, and the earth beneath you iron,"* that is if you do not obey him fully. I mean, really? What is wrong with that Lord guy? I asked myself, finally finding some comic relief in all that nonsense. Then I suddenly felt dread. The Bible states that God will strike sinners with madness as a curse and while I think there's more humane feelings in one episode of "Asterix" than in all those Testaments put together, I felt as if I was really cursed by madness.

The terror of losing one's mind in that "sinking into the terrifying hell of my own soul, a cold, utter darkness of the scariest, most painful insanity that peels off your skin while your brain screams, crushed by madness," as I once wrote to my friend Trygve, was the most palpable fear I had ever experienced. I did not fear losing my life as much as I dreaded losing my mind. But on one of those days on Easter Island, for the first time in my life, I thought that insanity—crossing the line from being aware of your mind feeling like it had been splitting in half to it actually being split—might not be that bad at all? Going mad would have meant not being me anymore and therefore it would have meant being free, not only from myself but from the anguish of loneliness and absolute isolation from the life I never really lived?

What a strange thought.

Oslo, December 21, 2018

Dr. Ellinor Tyri Geliassen inserted herself.

"It is not that strange, Roman," she said. "In fact in my colleague Dr. Bessel van der Kolk's book[35], one of his patients, Charlotte—"*You must be fucking kidding me,* I thought. Dr. Geliassen caught me flinching upon hearing my *demon's very* name.

---

35   *The Body Keeps the Score: Brain, Mind, and Body in the Healing of Trauma.* (note by Trygve E. Wighdal)

"—it was her name, sorry," and continued to explain. "So, she told Dr. van der Kolk that *'Without the split, she would not have been able to come back to life.'*"

"How so?"

"She was an Auschwitz survivor and she told Bessel, Dr. Kolk, 'the self who was in Auschwitz wasn't her. It was too unbelievable,' so *the split* had helped her function and live a normal life."

I understood what Dr. Geliassen was saying. But, damn! An Auschwitz survivor, in comparison to my trivial issues? Sure, my mother had died. Yes, I had been attacked and hated by the state media back home and forced to flee. I have been, and am, an alcoholic. Granted, some very dear members of my family had been slaughtered in the war. When I was only eight years old, a relative tried to strangle me, and he would have almost assuredly killed me had his father not arrived at the moment I was turning blue and kicked him in his arse. It is beyond doubt that homelessness left a deep scar on me as well. I guess that I have established how Charlotte bled my soul to death. I had no home, homeland or a puppy. "Hunted, despised, living like an animal," as Lugosi had said, but none of those—"OK, I give you that one, Dr. Geliassen," I said after she raised her eyebrows and said "Come, on!"—not entirely trivial issues amount to the horrors of years living in a concentration camp, or years of being sexually molested, or having to bury your own children.

Being a mere reporter, I did not kill in the war. I had not been wounded either. And yet, I was spiraling down faster than I could have imagined, getting worse than some blind and guilt-laden war veterans that I knew in San Diego.

I never took my own traumas seriously. After all, it was not because of some macho bullshit that I had been a chess player as a young boy instead of an athlete, but I simply did not think or feel any of what had happened to me was exceptional in any shape or form. It was life: a bloody confusing mess of suffering we all endure, living sometimes as happy as a clam at high tide and sometimes as miserable as sin, but still just life. Each of us paints his or her own totally unique hue of pain for ourselves. Take my granny Katica (Kate), for example. She was virtually a slave-child as a six-year-old little girl whose only salvation was in her faith in God. Myself, even as a kid, I had a freedom to deny the very existence of God to my dear granny—God have mercy on her wonderful soul—a highly religious woman. No one punished me for that blasphemy; on the contrary, my father and mother were proud of me and my independence, while teaching me to respect the boundaries of the other people's freedoms and, yes, their religious beliefs. When I was nine, I was so mesmerized by the science that put Neil Armstrong and Apollo Lunar Module Eagle of the Apollo 11 Mission on the moon on that glorious Sunday, July 20, 1969. I was glued to the TV screen like the millions all over the world and was imbibing every word Dr. Josip Kotnik, an astronautic expert par excellence (for that brief period of time, Dr. Kotnik was our Carl Sagan), shared with his viewers before and during the moon landing. As a kid I must have been insufferable, for I knew so many technical details about the Apollo missions. Those were the times of global hope and private joy. What I am saying is that I had a healthy foundation from my childhood. Nothing pointed out that I'd morph into a murdering monster? Or had it?

The only abuse I suffered growing up was my father's permission to read Albert Camus, Fyodor Dostoyevsky and Franz Kafka as a fourteen-year-old boy.

Hanga Roa, Rapa Nui, October 2, 2017

I sat across the fifteen *moai* statues of Ahu Tongariki (*ahu* are stone platforms on the Rapa Nui) or hours and just breathed, gazing at them. Their white coral eyes looked back at me as they had been doing for centuries, overlooking their island.

They did provide a powerful sense of tranquility, those *moai*, as majestic and stoical as they were, so I wanted to sit there forever for in front of them and the "Traveling Moai." I felt peaceful like never before and as I said to myself, "I will keep traveling and will travel until I arrive at the life of my own,[36]" I knew I had decided the rest of my life would be that of a wanderer in a search of life ("of my own").

Mo'orea, French Polynesia, October 4, 2017

Love is all that matters, no matter what that idiot woman thinks, it is the only truly mysterious force. Sure, but do not tell this to anyone. I still can't control my damn weeping nonsense as I listen to "The Traveling Wilburys," their *"Handle With Care"* hit, obviously Roy Orbison's line, *"I'm so*

---

36   Roman put those words in the quotation marks because those come from Dr. Stephen Fleming, brilliantly played by Jeremy Irons, in the 1992 movie by Louis Malle, *Damage.* Irons's character had a fatal tryst with his own son's wife, Anna, equally brilliantly played by Juliete Binoche, an actress Roman loved almost as much as he had loved Ingrid Bergman. (note by Trygve E. Wighdal)

tired of being lonely / I still have some love to give," but yes, I do, I do have love in me. I will travel, I will live and, ultimately, I will be free, and I will love. So I went to French Polynesia, to the mythical place of love and beauty, and I landed in Mo'orea, another volcanic island in the land of smile and delight.

I started to laugh at the first sight of the turquoise waters and the emerald green cliffs hovering above the ocean like a floating mirage. In French Polynesia, one has a feeling of being in a perfect computer simulation. The beauty of Mo'orea simply made no sense at all; it was insane—no pun intended. Nothing can be *that* stunningly beautiful, no way in hell. Or paradise if you wish. To get there one needs to cross the "Sea of the Moon," from Tahiti's capital Papeete and enter heaven on earth. While soil on Easter Island is so poor that it could have barely sustained its population over the years, Tahiti's is so fertile that they have some four hundred types of fruits on Mo'orea alone. Being so damn hospitable and lively and filled with boundless *joie de vivre,* they kept giving me fruits until they started to snort out of my nose. Give me seafood and wine, Polynesians, and I'll dance with you like an elephantine Pollyanna, just please, for the love of Tangaroa, the god of the oceans, stop overfeeding me with those fruits, no matter how rare and special they are.

Love Grows (Where My Rosemary Goes)

My enthusiasm for living and loving did not last too long. I stayed in a wonderful Hôtel "Fenua Mata'i'oa," Madame Eileen's own Garden of Eden. That was a mesmerizing property whose lush tropical garden sat on the edge of a wonderful, turquoise lagoon. Eileen, whom I promptly renamed to Madame Brigitte for her uncanny resemblance to Brigitte Bardot, herself also a Parisienne who had lived on Mo'orea for twenty plus years, had created pure perfection out of her edifice. Later that day, for dinner, Madame Brigitte sat me next to the Pacific Ocean and adorned the dinner table with the most exquisite bouquet I ever saw. She told me they were gardenia, heliconia and orchids. Well, if she says so—I only knew that they were beautiful and that made me unspeakably sad. Sumptuous, gorgeously decorated and exquisitely prepared food that followed did it for me. I was drinking the *Chablis Grand Cru* with the lobster and listening to Francoise Hardy and her *"Tous les garcons et les filles"* hit from another era (*"... I walk the streets alone, the lost soul /... I am alone, because nobody loves me..."*) when Madame Briggite came to check on me.

"*Très romantique*, isn't it?" She asked me with a coquettish smile those French women most likely master in their mothers' wombs; it came so naturally and beautifully to them. "Very romantic?"

"Too *très* romantic, Madame Brigitte, don't you see I am sitting alone here?" I asked her. She was unperturbed. It was *très romantique* nevertheless. It became *très* unbearably romantic once the coral reef sharks—harmless, I was told—arrived and swam virtually a few inches from my table that stood on the deck next to the lagoon. Then something astonishing happened. Stingrays arrived and looked at me from the ocean. I cried for Madame Brigitte, "Am I hallucinating again?"

"*Non, monsieur,*" she said, "they look at you because they want you to feed them."

Damn fish look at a human and expect us to feed them? Bread, she explained, they are fond of the bread. They have mouths further below their heads so I had to reach into the sea, under their bellies to feed them.

Who, in the name of the merciful God Lord ready to gleefully smite you, would feel miserable after an experience like that one in this very heaven on earth? Well, I did. I felt a bit tipsy after imbibing some nice red wine, whose label I do not remember, and talking with Brigitte's transvestite waitresses. They were quite confusing. Their perky bottoms were swaying around, as sexy as Polynesians and equally inviting, but they were as tall as Jar Jar Binks (6"4' or 193cm) and had the gigantic hands of street fighters. It was difficult to decide should one shag or fear them. But that French accent… anyway, I finished my dinner with crêpes with chocolate mousse filling and went back to my suite. It had a large private terrace on the lagoon, an appropriate accommodation for a single man. I sat on the deckchair next to the sea and the garden and went to watch on YouTube a one-hit wonder, *"Love Grows (Where My Rosemary Goes)"* and read the comments below the video:

> "My sister was Rose Marie, some people called her Rosemary. She loved this song. She passed away on this past Saturday. I am listening to it in her memory."

That story broke my heart and I burst into tears. Again?

To the Life of My Own

At that point, all of that rubbish was too much. Was this life I wanted for myself? Screw the pain; no pain merits that endless blubbering. Screw depression. That was not normal, that was not me. I screamed into the pillow until I almost passed out, for I was ashamed of myself. I kneeled and started banging my head onto the floor until I bled from my forehead profusely. Then I stopped like nothing had happened and laughed at myself. The concept of Fenua Mata'i'oa restaurant is such that each couple's dinner table is secluded from all the others. *Très romantique* intimacy assured. But if you try, you could still hear them talk. I listened to all those "awwws" and "awesomes," mostly from the romantique-ly inclined women as they were gorging on the ambrosial food the giant transvestites were tirelessly bringing to their tables and had a very similar feeling like that one in Rio de Janeiro. I felt sad that those people were enjoying Tahiti so much, a place I would be happy to visit. I kid you not, that was the thought that popped up in my mind as I was sitting on that very Tahitian island, that I would like to see it, but as forlorn as I was, I might not?

So I sat on my luxurious deck under the wonderful Tahitian sky, still bleeding, confused, angry, afraid, and, above it all, flabbergasted over thinking that was invading my mind like hordes of rabid, out of their minds Mongolians. It did not bother me at all that I was bleeding, and I sat and looked at small boats gliding on the horizon, and for the first time since all this confusion started, I finally asked myself the crucial question, who in the name of God has been crying all this time?

Chapter 19

VICTORIAN GHOSTS IN BEIRUT

"We had learned that there were pangs too sharp, grief too deep, ecstasies too high for our finite selves to register."

T.E. Lawrence

Oslo, December 21, 2018

Dr. Ellinor Tyri Geliassen leaned closer. "Did you get the answer?"

"Yes, but about two, three months later on another end of the planet, in Beirut, Lebanon. But it was rather a partial one," I replied enigmatically.

"You spent several months on Tahiti?"

"No. After Madame Brigitte's housekeeper further confused me, I went to New Zealand, then to Sydney and then continued my tour around the world."

"I would think that the transvestites would have confused you more," Dr. Geliassen mischievous smile was back.

"No, they were more of a curiosity—so big, so fast, so perky—but that girl was something else."

"What happened?"

"Nothing really. She was working next to me as I was writing on a computer, so I could smell her, hear her breathing, enjoy stealing a glance at her long limbs while she was stretching as she was reaching the most remote dust mites hidden in the room's corners. Her small tattoo of a sacred union of Rangi and Papa[37] was also sexy. Her accent inviting."

Dr. Geliassen beamed. Something in her smile told me that she also must have been seduced by the French accent once. Perhaps by a woman? I liked the idea.

"She was really attractive. She had the most mesmerizing bright brown eyes with a greenish hue and she looked at me expectantly, so I had a feeling that she would be open for some sort of an arrangement of a more private nature."

Mo'orea, French Polynesia, October 5, 2017

My disentanglement from women started when I felt not only that I would never be with a woman again, much less be *loved* by a woman, but felt also like I had never been with a woman in my life before—a confusing notion given my propensity to forget even those I loved, like my mother, or events I loathed, like the war. So when that tattooed Polynesian beauty with such a sexy accent gave me look that would instantly heal impotence and death at the same time, I should've been ready to lose my virginity again. Alas, I hadn't. She stood next to the huge glass door, stretched herself toward the top, revealing her sexy belly, her head-spinning pear-shaped breasts and those perfectly toned legs, and asked me if I needed it cleaned. Her eyes were glistering at me, but I was distant and, perhaps, even afraid. I had the most peculiar sensation at that moment. I had an erection just by looking at her, but at the same time I, again, looked at her like she was in a different dimension, not within my reach. I felt like I was in a bubble.

Should she reach toward me or me toward her, it felt like the protective bubble, for this is what it was, would burst and would have destroyed me. I trembled, barely noticeably, but my whole body language was that of a squeamish rejection. Even if I imagined the potential of eventual negotiations with her, I was awkward, and I felt awkwardly embarrassed. She left without giving me a second look. I also packed and left French Polynesia soon after she had vanished into the world that I was never going to get to know, the mythical world of Polynesian erotic mysteries that had seduced even a philandering maniac like that wild sex demigod, Marlon Brando[38].

---

37   According to the Maori people of New Zealand, Rangi was the Sky Father and his wife was the Mother Earth, Papa.

38   Legendary Don Corleone from *The Godfather*, a 1972 movie, owned a private island in French Polynesia, called Tetiaroa. (note by Trygve Wighdal)

The Curse of the Flying Dutchman

What followed was a rapid succession of countries, cities, rejections and escapades, almost like I started to mimic Charlotte's avoidances. In Auckland, New Zealand, I had a dinner with an eye surgeon from London I picked up at the restaurant's doorsteps after I lured her with the promise of some tasty Brazilian barbecue and New Zealand wines in the "Wildfire" on the waterfront. As we drank "Craggy Range Syrah le Sol," I tested some "Charlotte teachings" on her by telling her what Charlotte had always preached, "I am not responsible for your reactions to what I say." In return, she told me to fuck off and abruptly left—quite livid, I might add. I guess that is how normal people react to nonsense? Or perhaps her reaction told me that Charlotte wasn't that off the mark, and the eye doctor was the crazy one? I reckon I will never know.

Later that same evening, in "The Grand Millennium" Auckland's swimming pool, I was alone with the Emirates' flight attendant from Korea who told me straightforwardly that she was lonely and that she had only twelve hours left in Auckland before she took off back to Dubai. I pretended that I did not understand what she was saying, so she left in a fury. Women rarely forgive a man who could have them but pass at the opportunity.

A few days later in Sydney, I met two French girls, Nathalie and Noëlle, and joked about an idea of an old fashioned threesome along the lines of a Marquise de Sade depravity. To my surprise, they were ready to engage and explore. Immediately after I was given a promise, I was terrified. I was double their size, but I had a feeling like they were too strong for me—such was a nonsensical source of fear. I guess all that blubbering made me feel weak. We were drinking, so I should not have had any inhibitions whatsoever, no matter how depressed, flat out of my mind or heart-broken I had been since forever. Viagra and vodka combo worked for the infamous Rio's Twelve, so for sure it would've worked in Auckland for only two girls, had I decided to take them to my hotel. I chose to drink alone instead, for I wasn't up for the ultimate sexual fantasy Nathalie and Noëlle represented—a bloody moron. Who would not want them? He himself needed to be rammed in, tarred and feathered and then publicly executed by hanging. The execution should be performed by spinsters as head executioners. A body of such an unnatural idiot should then be cremated, his ashes thrown in the River Lethe and utterly forgotten.

So I ran again, this time from those girls as I slunk away like a coward to another bar around the Harbor road. Then, I kept running and went from Sydney, leaving Australia behind after only five days, to Singapore and Hanoi and Ha Long Bay in Vietnam. In Vietnam, I felt sickish, so I decided to stop that maniacal run around the world and go back to Europe. I like to break my flights into shorter legs, so I had flown back to Singapore and gotten onto an easily manageable seven hours and fifteen minutes Singapore Airlines flight to Dubai, one of the most bizarre places I'd ever visited. It was a hell on earth hidden behind its heat, opulence, and shiny veneer. I stayed in "Taj Dubai" hotel, notorious for brunches that every Sunday witnessed the drunkest throng of young women I ever saw in one place. "Taj Dubai" offered food and booze on steep discount during their brunch, so the women arrive there at 10 – 11 AM and drink until the wee hours next day. They were stumbling and vomiting, screaming and crying all over the place, like in some post-apocalyptical movie Guillermo del Toro had made in hell on a high wardrobe budget. There, at the bar, one super sexy Lithuanian lady of the night who was prowling for clients with means nevertheless refused my advances even after several glasses of some Sauvignon Blanc that I was given in exchange for my soul—such was the price of booze in Dubai (not a part of the brunch). Damn, even a hooker steered clear of me, and I was comparatively sober, in that drunken mayhem the mostly British young women had created.

Hakuna Matata

There, on a whim, I decided to buy a camera in that hellish "Dubai Mall" (at least the fountain show is quite spectacular) and went to the land of Hakuna Matata (no worries), a stunning beauty of vast nature and wonderful people with the most beautiful smiles in the world: Kenya. Nothing warms the heart more than the early morning sight of Kenyan kids that, all so serious, go to the school carrying schoolbags bigger than them. Once they spot you as you wave or smile at them, they wave back and flash that disarming smile of sheer happiness. I fell in love with every smile in Kenya. Only Maasai warriors do not smile that easily, but then they have their reputation as lion hunters to preserve. I felt I needed the last really unspoiled nature to help me stop those maddening travels, to try to recover and to start healing, for where I was going internally seemed like someplace very dark, threatening and final. Alas, I never stopped and pondered that insane jumping from place to place, as I also relapsed and seemingly enjoyed what my renewed life of drinking did to my already severely disturbed psyche.

The Land of the Lion King

Tsavo East National Park, October 15, 2017

ROAR!! At first, we didn't see him. We knew he was somewhere nearby as we looked around from an underground tunnel connecting the "Voi Wildlife Lodge" and a waterhole where animals come to drink, but he wasn't to be seen yet. Another ROAR! but still not a sight. The space is phenomenal, those African landscapes, so we were excited knowing he was around. At the third ROAR! so terrifying that even our goose bumps wanted to jump off our skin and run for dear life, we fully got it. One could have seen thousands of movies and listened to thousands of MP3 of a roar, but nothing prepares you for the sheer power of that sound in real life. He could've been a few meters away or a mile, for he gets all the energy from the mighty Africa and its land, and roars with such power that it shakes every bone and nerve in your body. That is how it confuses its prey; that deep primordial sound coming from everywhere at the same time unmistakingly told us, this is the King of Africa. Yes, elephants are mighty, wonderful and smart, and ancient rhinos, my personal favorites, possess such a brutal force that inspire fear, but nothing matches the power and majesty of Simba, the Lion King. Once he appeared, only ten meters away from us, we stood there in reverence, motionless, admiring the king with trepidation despite the thick glass that separated us from His Majesty.

"We" were The Gazelle and me. The Gazelle was A.B.O. (her initials) a wonderful, supermodel-like woman I met in a restaurant on Diani Beach near Mombasa and had, taken by both her beauty and calm wit, invited her to go on the safari with me. She happily went, became my lover and also a litmus test for my curse. After a long day on the safari filled with miraculous encounters with the Big Fives, we laid down on the bed to get some rest and, perhaps do the bad thing but, for about a half an hour which felt like an eternity, I could not get an erection. That had never happened to me before when I was teetotaling like I had been all my time in Africa, where I finally sobered up. Even worse, I got a splitting headache next to the generous, young and ready body of a woman who wanted me. It was tearing me apart, the headache, my first ever with a naked woman next to me. It was embarrassing and scary and very painful and quite disorienting at the same time. I had no clue what was happening, why my whole being was rejecting such a wonderful woman. She had the patience of a saintly nun and had lovingly seduced me into submission nevertheless.

We had sex and made love almost that whole night, until 4 AM, according to her bookkeeping account that also counted three orgasms by herself alone. But, despite all that erotic beauty she gave me so generously, I wasn't there. Imagine being in a bed with a gorgeous woman, touching her silky, sexy black skin and having sex all night and yet feel dissociated from her? A totally new experience for me, I read about in books about PTSD-ed war veterans as a symptom they sometimes display, to their horror I'd reckon. It was like I was forcing myself to make love to her in the middle of majestic Africa, after a day in the nature. We'd seen lions and leopards, elephants and buffalos, giraffes and zebras and so many other game and lizards and birds enough to fill someone's heart and nutsacks alike. After the day on safari, I had a long swim in icy cold water in the swimming pool that was open only for me.

It was a perfect day with a perfect woman and should have resulted with perfect lovemaking, steamy sex, wild fuck. And yet, I could not be with her in a manner she deserved me to be. I was losing it completely. It was that much scarier because I was immersed in majestic beauty that I enjoyed. I was sober, I wanted a new life and I felt like I could muster the patience—her example would have provided me some—to achieve it. Perhaps even with The Gazelle, for her subdued sexuality knew how to erupt at the right moments; her fine mind and patience seemed exactly what I needed. All in vain.

Our safari guide and driver, a super funny, smallish nervous guy with a charming laugh, told me the story of her life and a tragedy she had experienced. To cut a long story short, because of a calamity, she had to interrupt her studies and ended up without the diploma of an environmental scientist, which was her major and her dream. After hearing that I had decided to offer to pay for her studies, a few days later she left for another country to the university, to re-enroll. It was nice to be able to help someone.

She left and I was alone again on Diani Beach, next to Mombasa, where in "The Villa Luxury Suites Hotel" I had spent my days and nights, left to ponder my now total dissociation from women and the life they represent. This included a hysterical display of madness with The Sexy Dozen in Rio de Janeiro, another drunken avoidance of women in Auckland and Sydney but quite a different thing had transpired here. In Africa, I had been almost depression and hatred-free for a few days. I was there with a woman I liked and who liked me back. I slept with her, more than once, and yet I was totally absent, disentangled and more alone than ever. Death of the soul would be the only way to describe how I felt. If hatred was a painful, soul-splitting experience, if depression was like living in darkness without end, this felt even worse. My heart and my soul seemed to have inhabited this empty shell of my former self, but I was already a living dead.

In Africa, of all places, in the Africa I dreamed of while I lived in Rijeka or New York, Salvador or Montréal alike, in Africa whose beauty and savagery surpassed everything I had expected from her. The soulful Africa of the smiles and open hearts had witnessed the demise of my own heart and soul, so I was ashamed and afraid, and I had to run again. I had absolutely no idea what to do with myself, so I went to Beirut, Lebanon. Why not?

Beirut, December 15, 2017

"Sanremo has the ramshackle charm of a dying spa. Once the place to be for gay-ish British gentlemen during wintertime, now became a beautiful, but rotting *centro storico* and a yacht port for Russian snobs," I read in Philipp's e-mail I received once I landed to Beirut, after a brief stint in Addis Ababa, Ethiopia, where, to my great surprise, nothing had happened.

"Sanremo? I am in Beirut, man," I replied, to which he immediately suggested that I should meet his super-ultra-smart, perhaps a little bit weird friend, the Victorian Ghost from the vast forgotten lands in ancient Scandinavia. I was never one who would refuse meeting a Viking or a ghost, so I eagerly accepted the idea. Regretfully, The Ghost never materialized, which created an indescribable sorrow in me, but somehow, her absence also produced a strangely nice feeling of relief. Ghosts can't really hurt you, despite popular beliefs and Baba Yaga. Hurting you is within the purview of the people you love, deeply care for or, God forbid, depend on.

I had strolled around that mythical and heroic city, whose people left me in awe with both their resilience and special sort of firm kindness. Disrespect them at your own peril. After I had walked for hours and hours, I went into the T-Marbouta restaurant—arguably one of the best small joints in the whole of Beirut—for a quick bite. At least that was the idea. There, I had experienced one of the strangest events in my already outlandish life. The cast of characters I spent the night with was typical for Beirut—an eccentric bevy of multinational, colorful characters. First one was a Canadian, Stephen Sumner, a fabled "logger, a fisherman, a photo model, a fisherman again and a hobo-drifter" who had lost his leg in a freakish accident in Toscana.

He was hit, run over and left for dead in a farmer's field but miraculously survived. He was living with devastating bouts of phantom limb pain that was "enough to make him just want to sign off," when he discovered so-called mirror-therapy that had helped him. Since then, he cruised the world on his bicycle and helped fellow amputees, be it in Afghanistan, Sri Lanka, Lebanon or Cambodia or wherever his two wheels took him. Stephen was an extraordinary character whom I happily provided with a very modest assistance. I am so sorry, Stephen, that I wasted so much money on stupidity before we met, but *c'est la vie*.

The next one was Juliette from Paris, France. She was one of the heirs of the vast Renault fortune and was getting her Ph.D. in Cell and Molecular Biology at the American University of Beirut. She was immensely intelligent, one of the type of people who never wasted a single word; each syllable she uttered had a deep meaning. I'd liked her but had no chance with her not only because I wasn't a match for her intellect but also because she had her eyes fixed on N., a Jewish Zen-lawyer obsessed with the Chin People of Myanmar, whom he had been visiting for the last decade. He was in Lebanon on his third passport—a Bulgarian one. He was helping Palestinian people from Gaza escape Israeli occupation, but no one who went to Israel was welcomed in Lebanon. His first passport was Israeli—not a document anyone would like to have on them when traveling to the Middle East but especially to Lebanon. Until this day, I still do not know how many passports N. had or how many nationalities he had acquired.

We also had two Austrian diplomats briefly joining us, one wonderful lady whose blue eyes had seen hell, and an over two-meter-tall Adonis-type of a superhuman species. After they'd left, a sharp Kenyan human rights lawyer, Awino was her name, joined us. She was pleased that I recognized that she was from Kenya—out of all African countries I could've chosen as her origin. It's easy, I said, you're the most beautiful and also the smartest people in Africa. I did not mention The Gazelle to her—who knows why. Perhaps her beauty was the reason.

Piss Poor Protoplasm Poorly Put Together

While humans may mostly be P.P.P.P.P.T., that was a wonderful pool of human genes at the same time in one place I encountered. I felt privileged to sit with these exceptional people only Beirut could bring together, despite that nagging, rather horrible feeling of not belonging, of being dissociated with the world and, increasingly, from myself. I had also somehow disconnected with the time. It was sipping from its clepsydra in a rhythm that felt as a nightmare lasting for one heartbeat of a gigantic heart and an eternity in hell at the same time. I was totally disoriented, time-space wise, and one peculiar manifestation of disconnection was that I lost a sense of what was left, where's West or East. Strange. But I was fascinated by the company, and had no problems sitting with them for hours. When João, a Portuguese barkeep from São Paolo owning a bar in Beirut—don't ask—also joined us with his companion, a smallish Japanese woman, Michiko, who laughed like Tinker Bell, we were ready to go full throttle into the night and ordered enough drinks to take us all into oblivion.

Stephen told us stories about healing the people with phantom limb pain in Cambodia he circled on his "BENNO" cargo bike, and then he and N. realized they shared the same passion for Myanmarese people and the culture of ancient Burma, the Land of Gold. The stories they exchanged at that table would have sufficed for a book of its own, but I am not going to write that one, unless the devil provides me with a pen and paper in Hell. A proverbial snowball comes to mind.

I noted one ruggedly handsome Palestinian Arabic guy who sat alone at the bar drinking "Chateau Mussar", the same wine I had bought while hoping to meet with The Ghost, and he was looking at our table quite openly. In fact, he had looked at me despite Juliette and Awino at our table. I have bad memories with Arabs and their glances, for they wanted to have sex with me in Marseilles when I was a fourteen-year-old running away from home, but that man did not look like someone having overly romantic feelings toward me. It was more of a search for a connection that had no name. Juliette followed my glance and, what else would *la Parisienne* in Beirut do, invited him to join us. Haydar, that was his name, meaning "the lion," gladly joined us. *Nomen est omen* indeed, for he did walk like a lion.

Parallel Universe

At first, he was silent as I yelled across the room, attempting to communicate with two Russian girls, putting Fyodor Dostoyevsky and Dmitri Hvorostovsky, Vladimir Visotsky and Mefistofelos Bar in Moscow in one sentence. It did not work. The waiter came and warned me that they were off limits due to some unsavory connections to the Beirut underworld, which they cherished as much as the gold they were lavished with, so I went quiet and all our attention was again re-focused to the stories, this time from Kenya, where homosexuals were brutally persecuted while Awino, who told us that fact, was helping them *pro bono*.

Then it was Haydar's turn. He used to be a math professor at the "Einstein Institute of Mathematics" in Jerusalem and then went on to work for Goldman Sachs in Beirut. Those bastards always got the best ones to work on the most senseless computer trading algorithms. What a waste of talent. The life was good for him and his young wife. But suddenly, that beautiful, healthy wife of his died in her sleep, without any apparent reason. To say that he was devastated would be like saying the sun is lukewarm. Since that day, he just drank his two, three bottles of wine in the quiet of his sorrow, without the faintest clue in the world how to continue living without her. As he spoke, he kept looking mostly at me. Soon we realized that his wife died at thirty-six years old, the same age my mother had died. Then he exchanged something with N. in Hebrew—no clue what it was—and continued in English. Another discovery stunned us. His wife had died on the same day and date my mother had died. He was five years older than her, exactly as was my father to my mother. Haydar looked at me, but now like I was the ghost. And his birthday was also on the same day as my father's birthday. That felt like too much. He did not believe me, so I had to produce photos of my parent's grave in order to show him the dates engraved as proof of my claims.

No one spoke for a moment. "Pure coincidence is a rare quality," Ian Flaming's brother Peter once wrote, but I did not know what to take out of those staggering coincidences. Hayder asked me how my father and I had coped with my mother's early death, so I went somewhere deep and shared with him the most painful moments of our lives—mine and my father's. All of us around that table were pretty inebriated already, but that connection bridged the continents and decades, and it felt like my experience had helped him a bit. Interestingly, no one at our table offered any thoughts and prayers or their idiotic equivalents, not even condolences, to Haydar. It would've been shallow to comment on such a senseless, painful loss that he had suffered at the peak of their happiness together. That was another parallel with my mom's and dad's happiness during 1972, a year in which both of them had gotten promotions and bought a wonderful, spacey and sunny new apartment, until the day she came home from a hospital with a diagnosis that spelled death.

Haydar then had shown me a photo of his wife's grave. It was flanked, embraced by sunrays from both sides, only the tombstone was in the shadow, exactly like my parents grave the last time I visited them. Philipp's Ghost might not have been there with us, but all of that was a ghastly reminder of my own mental state. I dug into it for I had a reason—Haydar and his pain and his loneliness that mirrored my own—so I started to tell him about memory of trauma, how it got embedded in the body and how he was in for a long ride. I did not mean to be mean; on the contrary, I shared with him what my father had told me after my mom died. "You are going to miss her more as the time passes," but will have to find a way to live with it.

"How?" he cried.

"I don't know."

But then I remembered something else. "*One day the pain will go away but not the memories,*' Arthur C. Clarke wrote in *Childhood's End*. I said.

"But, I do not want pain to go away," Haydar uttered through tears.

Childhood's End

At that moment, his words, *"I do not want pain to go away,"* took me away. I drifted from the table, to some other dimension, as I sunk inside myself still not really sure what was happening. Everyone at that table was suddenly miles away from me; I did not hear their voices. Their movements were slow, all around me was in slow motion until it froze, and I was alone in my own time-space. The voice said, *it is time for your own childhood to end.* Who said that? Was it Juliette? Stephen? No, they were too far away to be heard, and motionless at that. It must have come from inside. I felt dizzy—well too drunk for the amount of wine I had so far, but those were my first drinks after Kenya's teetotaling months, and I felt it. It hit me hard. Then I saw an opening in me as my eyes were turned inward, and the deep depths of my soul were revealed. It was the space I had never gone to before—the ultimate frontier, the darkness I dreaded to visit all my life. Haydar's wife danced with my own mother, and it was a marvelous gala they attended. I played chess against Fisher as a twelve-year-old boy. My father thought me how to swim. I remembered the day when I swim-floated for the first time free of any help—what an intoxicating moment of freedom. Then I was riding a bike for the first time. He taught me to swim and to ride a bike. The electricity burned through my right hand when I was a very little boy. My father, who worked on the roof at the time, jumped back in the house and saved my life by disconnecting me from some open wire I'd grabbed like a stupid child would. I saw a fetus rotating in darkness, glowing, filled with stars. Was that me? It was a nonsensical mess of images and sounds but I knew there was something else inside that wanted to tell me something.

Was that Ulrike in me? Yes, she ran over the green fields of Krnjevo back home—what a word, it sounds like a broken tooth in Croatian—but if that was Ulrike, she was not aware of me. No, it was not her, it was my granny as a six-year-old. She prayed to God. Gosh, she was so small. I could hear her prayers. Jesus, she begged of him for a slice of bread; she was hungry. My six-year-old granny was hungry. I sobbed. I had never seen my granny dressed in anything but black and now I saw her in a little blue dress as a child. Death had defined her life since an early age. There, she's like a little angel. She did look like a bit like Ulrike. Yes! They both wore the same blue dress. I smiled through the tears, enveloped in silence, because my father came to her and gave her a loaf of bread. He also gave her a puppy. It looked like my own puppy I had once back in America. She was happy. She was walking the puppy. It was my own Puppy (yes, that ended up being his name) I was happily crying. She was not alone or hungry anymore.

Everyone at our table looked at me, for I was absent, silent with tears trickling down my cheeks. N. later told me I looked like I was in a trance, but Awino remarked that I looked like a saint, hovering over myself. Haydar's eyes were fixed on me like he was going inside as well, following my lead. But I was unaware of any of that.

My mother showed up. She hid Click-Clacks[39], a toy that had been banned in 1985 due to the hellish noise it produced and asked me what do I think about it. I said it was stupid. I'd lied, for I wanted it but did not want to ask for it. She smiled sadly and, behind her back, click-clacked the toy as she looked at me with sorrow, for it was a present for me she thought I'd love. I spoiled her surprise.

"I don't want you to be sad, Mom."

"You will be sorry when I die," she said.

Why would she say that? Then, she was gone. Now, there was Christmas. My father sang "A Christmas Carol". He had a clear, beautiful

---

39 Click-Clacks or Clackers "consisted of two large acrylic balls, which hung on either end of a heavy string. The two balls would swing apart and together, making the loud clacking noise that gave the toy its name. If swung too hard, the acrylic balls would shatter, sending flying shrapnel everywhere." (note by Trygve E. Wighdal, used from the Banned Toy Museum's website)

singing voice. The communist police came and took him. He was in jail for celebrating Christmas?

I was on a ship. Bombs started to fall on Dubrovnik. No, I did not want to go back there, where Ane and Periša, little kids I met during that cold, war torn winter, had perished in 1991. "Take me with you," Periša said. I couldn't. I went on reporting. Periša died. Guilt, eternal crushing guilt while I was sitting on Stradun. "Why am I here, in Dubrovnik" asked the London "Times" journalist. Why? It represented me, all of us, my identity, our identity. Identity, the keyword of my times with Charlotte, the lost identity drowned in our respective madnesses. I could not stay in that period anymore; it was too painful. I searched for my granny or my mom, but my mom had been dead for almost two decades already. Where was she? Where was the memory? The opening started to close. No, no! No, don't close, I did not learn a thing, please do not close yet. A ray of light stopped the darkness from enveloping me.

My mom smiled at me again, from the inside. She was so serene, so beautiful, as only a mother can be. Then she started to age. I remember her only as a young woman but now she was aging. She was fifty years old. Her hair getting grey and then white. She walked away as an old lady, much older than my granny when she had died. Charlotte appeared and she started to age. She was a hundred years old, she was two hundred years old, she was aging in front of me, in me. It was a vision in color in which her white hair was in a stark contrast to the green forest around us and the deep blue waters of Siskiyou Lake on the Mount Shasta in California. She was going to die, the woman I hated but at that moment, deep in me, as she was dying, I felt tenderness for her. I told her, "It is not your fault." But how was that possible? "It is OK, you are not guilty of anything," and then she died as I held her hand I used to love holding so much. She was fucking guilty of everything, where did that damn forgiveness come from?

At that moment, I had to call Charlotte. She was the only person in this wide world able to help me understand, to penetrate through that darkness that had, for the first experienced light and contained her own being as a two hundred years old, white haired, surreally beautiful old woman. I went to the bathroom to call her. Sure, I was drunk and spaced out, but she would understand.

Then in the bathroom, as I was dialing, I stopped, for it hit me like a ton of bricks. No, I could not reveal another vulnerability of mine to her. She was evil. Every time I gave away some of my vulnerabilities, she used them against me. Not this time. So I did not call her. That was likely the first time my self-preservation instinct kicked in. Living a life with my heart on my sleeve had not brought me too much good, but this time I was not going to trick myself. I went back to our table and kept drinking.

A tiny voice, more of a thought, seemed to have told me, "don't go," but the noise of the world I came back to drowned it out, so I took another swig of red wine and forgot everything, desiring Awino who gave me a long, deep gaze and then left without a word.

Chapter 20
MORE GHOSTS FROM THE PAST

"I shut my eyes and all the world drops dead;
I lift my lids and all is born again.

(I think I made you up inside my head.)"

Sylvia Plath, *Mad Girl's Love Song*

Oslo, December 21, 2018

"I wonder about something," Dr. Ellinor Tyri Geliassen started.
"Yes?"
"How come you never asked for help? Didn't you worry?"
"About what?"

Dr. Geliassen took some papers out of my file and checked them against her computer files. "When the police brought you to the hospital, you gave your initial interview. I am looking at the Admission Intake and Assessment," she pointed to the document, "where it says that your grandmother suffered from the Parkinson's disease dementia. Also, it says your father had become suddenly demented, only weeks before his death."

I flinched.

"I am sorry," she said. "I know this is painful to remember."

"You gotta do what you gotta do, doctor." My feelings were the opposite.

"You also stated that well before your killing spree and the amnesia that followed, you had experienced a long period of lost memory—due to heavy drinking, I suppose."

"If it says there…" I felt defensive and afraid.

"It does."

She looked at me for a long minute.

"You never worried about your family's and your own history?"

"Did I worry I'd get Parkinson's?"

"Something like that. You seem to have been very well aware of yourself—your lack of memories about your mother, your alcohol abuse, your loneliness, even your disconnection from the awareness. And yet, you did nothing to help yourself?"

I sat for a while, motionless, unable to answer her question.

A Chess Player with a Flaw

This is a position[40] from the famous game in between Robert James Fisher, when he was a thirteen-year-old prodigy and Donald Byrne, another strong American chess player. The match was played in New York on October 17, 1956.

It was called "the game of the century" ever since. Fisher's move 17… Be6! with which he sacrifices his Queen, the strongest piece on the board, is

---

40   The chessboard found next to Roman's dead body was set to this exact position. (note by Trygve E. Wighdal)

a stroke of genius. He wins the game twenty-four moves later— it's a feat of superhuman ability to see and calculate moves that far forward. It's unheard of. For decades, "The Game of the Century" had been lauded, analyzed, reproduced, talked about and admired by millions.

I was a good chess player. I'd beaten my father, a strong amateur player, the fourth day after he had taught me to play. A week later, after I had beaten all his colleagues. He took me to the chess club where a FIDE Master of Chess, Mr. Emilio Fućak, set up a game against one of the strongest players in my age range. We played for almost two hours, but at the end, I beat him. It was a moment of incredible pride for both my father and me. My first serious game and I'd won.

Soon after, I started to compete on tournaments. I wasn't bad at all. It had a sad outcome, my brief love affair with chess, better described elsewhere, but that's not the point. I had a strange propensity to make blunders. I often lost a game by some tactical oversight, not seeing a very obvious threat, mostly against players much weaker than myself in easily winning positions. When I look back, it feels almost like I invoked those losses, somehow boycotting myself, as much as I invoked so many disasters in my life, Charlotte being by far one of the biggest.

But no, I never stopped and mulled over any of this. Drinking, which I had discovered at seventeen, had immediately become a panacea that rendered my world a chaotic bohemian nightmare, which I loved inhabiting. Even after I stopped drinking, chaos was my natural element. To my peril, I guess, I had loved drinking first and then romanticized the madness, oblivious to its maddening dangers.

"That wasn't really smart," Dr. Ellinor Tyri Geliassen said. For the first time, I noted a genuine feeling behind her professional façade, and it was that of sadness.

"I realize that. I would give anything to go back to the past and tell myself to stop being an idiot. Too late now, I guess."

"Not only for you," Dr. Geliassen concluded.

The Desert Winds

At that moment, two police officers arrived and beckoned Dr. Geliassen to get out of the room. Three days before, I had given them the scope of what had happened with Brigitte in the Joshua Tree Park and answered some questions about other murders for which they needed a clarification or two.

I might have mentioned, in passing, the hippie hitchhikers I had badly beaten on the Velebit Mountain. I was bragging, I guess, for the police's bizarrely indifferent interrogation annoyed me. However, those two cheerful freaks were the very reason why the police had arrived and interrupted my nice session with Dr. Geliassen. They spoke to the doctor, whispering in the hallway. All of them were giving me side-glances the whole time. What was I, a circus freak again? What was going on? I stood up, intending to go to inquire, but one of the replicants pushed me down, back to the seat. That monster had an iron arm; I felt overpowered in that brief second. The Burly was a little kid in comparison to them and yet, he had knocked me out cold the other day.

When three of them finally entered the room, Dr. Geliassen was looking pretty gloomy, gazing at me with a piercing look. She should trademark that gaze. But, what was going on? I was to find out instantaneously. One of the policemen said, in a somehow ceremonial tone, "Roman L., we are hereby charging you for the first-degree murder of Henrik Olaf Svensson and for the first-degree murder of Per Lund Kvakkestad, both citizen of Sweden, residing in Fagersta at the moment of their death, you committed on July 19, 2018."

Well, I did not expect that.

I killed those freakish hippie guys?

Damn, this bloody nightmare just keeps on giving.

"Here goes your insanity plea, you excrement," one policeman hurled this strange insult at me.

"Stop it," the other cut him off curtly.

Because of that somehow shocking discovery, I was too dizzy to ponder whether it was some Norwegian idiosyncrasy, that *"excrement"* of his, or whatever, but I still had to be a smart-ass.

"No need to stop being a lady," I told him, deriving no pleasure out of my lame attempt to stay cool.

The police officers left. I was already apprehended, so nothing more for them to do but to re-arrest me for formal reasons. I looked up at Dr. Ellinor Tyri Geliassen whose *understanding* for my crushing sense of guilt I suddenly needed. I was a pussy after all, craving that *understanding* that would, in prior times, have always enraged me, no matter its form.

It was clear that I was not going to get any.

Dr. Geliassen's eyes were cold and calculated as she assessed my demeanor. She did not like me at all, it was obvious. I somehow felt like a cockroach, even a fraud in the most curious way. And like K. in *The Process,* I felt the shame would outlive me. I had no inner excuses for those murders. Nothing had "triggered me." I remembered vividly that I did not own Leslie's murder at that time and that, after pushing Leslie in that snake's pit, I had cowardly transferred my sense of guilt onto them. But that would have been a sorry excuse should I ever wanted to use one.

"Fuck me," I thought I'd thought that. In fact, I said it out loud.

"Yes, Roman. Fuck you," Dr. Ellinor Tyri Geliassen said gravely and left. What a gutsy lady.

The Mind Slinking Away

Somehow, I realized upon her abrupt departure, that I had hoped Dr. Geliassen would be an ally in the last leg of my self-discovery process, a helping hand rather a brain to help me find that "something" in me that was still missing the answers. Especially since that sexy fraud, Dr. Sønstebø, had been taken off my case. But I knew my neuropsychological assessment was on the fast track to its natural conclusion now. Even if she would keep on assessing my legal sanity, i.e. my criminal responsibility, she would have no inclination to dig deeper into my proverbial soul. I'd dug myself into an even deeper hole. With the murdered hippies, my crimes had lost any meaning. There aren't enough Charlottes in this world to put it on them. I was just a mindless, sadistic killer—a vile, heartless monster.

One of the replicants kept looking at me with hatred. I could not have cared less about his hatred. In fact, not only did I deserve that loathsome, murderous gaze, but I wanted the shame to outlive me. Give me your gun, you replicant, and I will blow my brains out this very moment. I did not say a word when the darkness, that "black pall over my soul," fell upon me again. I wanted to vanish in that darkness, once and for all, but instead they just took me to my cell and threw me into it like a ragtag doll.

I kept thinking about Dr. Ellinor Tyri Geliassen, her penetrating gaze and her "fuck you, Roman" and how I'd lost her. I was also fully aware how delusional I was, thinking about "losing" a mental health legend whose relationship with me was on a purely professional level. Before Dr. Geliassen had replaced Dr. Sønstebø, I'd read her books on "fragmented selves" and on "integration of parts" and hoped she'd work with me. I hated Dr. Sønstebø for pretending to be a therapist while her job was purely to assess me, but now, I wanted my mental health assessor to act as a therapist?

Duh!

Unlikely for me, I could not even laugh at the bizarre absurdity of my own magical and rather deranged thinking. I was just sad, stricken by the "loss" of that dwarfish genius, Doctor Geliassen. Sadness, the beauty of which Boris Vian[41] beautifully spoke once when he wrote about Édith Piaf[42], took over.

But there was also something deeper in that sorrow. Something tangible in me but elusive in the dark depths of my being. I desperately searched for it, for it gave me a hint of hope. I grasped at straws, rather figments of meaning hidden in the feelings that were getting stronger. And I started to get it: not only that I was fine with the "loss," but it felt like I almost wanted that "loss."

After all, who did Dr. Ellinor Tyri Geliassen think she was?

She and her high-strung books. The pink lock of hair… give me a break. Who did she think she was, a teenager? The bloody Sherlock Holmes pipe. Those were, I was certain, just quasi-eccentric displays of who knows what disturbances she carried in herself. And I got it. I did not need her. We did not need her! I felt like I had made peace with my Abandonment Entity.

Not only her, we did not need anyone. The darkness and abandonment were at peace in me.

We were one.

We were fine.

I was fine.

I would continue on my own. This was the only way that it should be from then on. Fuck them all.

---

41 Boris Vian was, as Alexandra Schwartz wrote in *The New Yorker*, "a French writer who loved America and its culture but never visited." (Duke Ellington was the godfather to his daughter though.) He was also a polymath: writer, poet, musician, singer, translator, critic, actor, inventor and engineer. He died abruptly, at thirty-nine years old, during the premiere of the screen adaptation of his novel *I will Spit on Your Graves* on June 23, 1959. (note by Trygve E. Wighdal)

42 Édith Piaf, "the Sparrow" was a legendary French singer who defied her life tragedies in her final global hit *"Non, je ne regrette rien"* (No, I do not regret anything). While I could not find any confirmation that Boris Vian had said that her life was too sad not to be beautiful, something Roman quoted many times over absinthe, I find it interesting that he had made this remark at this stage of his final loss. It's like he wanted to live and die without regretting anything while, in fact, he had died regretting everything, including to have lived such a wasted life. But my guess is as good as yours. (note by Trygve E. Wighdal)

Abaissement

"Abaissement du niveau mental can be the result of physical and mental fatigue, bodily illness, violent emotions, and shock, of which the last has a particularly deleterious effect on one's self-assurance. The abaissement always has a restrictive influence on a personality as a whole. It reduces one's self-confidence and the spirit of enterprise, and, as a result of increasing egocentricity, narrows the mental horizon. In the end it may lead to the development of an essentially negative personality, which means that a falsification of the original personality has supervened."

Carl Gustav Jung

Part IV
THE BURIALS

Chapter 21
BRIGITTE DIES

"Only those who forget why they came to this world will lose their way. They will disappear in the wilderness and be forgotten."

Gogyeng Sowuhti, Spider Grandmother[43]

Las Vegas, July 24, 2018

Just kill me outright. All the Venetian bells Joseph Brodsky knew so well were clamoring in my head like disjointed steel factory mills, screeching and hammering on what was left of my brain cells with merciless precision. Each heartbeat felt like a strike of a heavy hammer, producing infernal noises. I had been feeling crappy after drinking many times before, but this was something else. I must have miscalculated the amount of booze or the combo I imbibed, for something for sure went seriously wrong. Bright red spots, emanating thorns in lieu of light were popping in front of my closed eyes, like merry, little devils poking me with their tridents. I could not move my eyelids, for it felt it would crush my head should I even try. I groaned. I

---

43 "Among the Hopi people, the Spider is thought as a powerful spirit and can be referred to as Spider Woman, Old Woman, Spider Lady, Grandmother or Grandma. Her Hopi name is Gogyeng Sowuhti, and she appears either as an old lady or small spider. She is regarded as living medicine, often gives medical advice, aids people in danger, and is kind and can cope with any situation. The spider is also considered a trickster because she is frequently in creation myths," partially adopted from Leeming, David, Jake Page. *The Mythology of Native North America*. Roman had used the same quote in his aforementioned script that Charlotte had disregarded.

was parched. But at the very idea of putting anything in my mouth, I almost puked, and I laid down on my stomach.

Was that the sound of water running in the bathroom? No, rather, it was a jackhammer. Fuck no, it was someone brushing his or her teeth. Water. Teeth. Condom. Blowjob. I palpated my thighs and groin.

I was naked.

I remembered.

Brigitte

She had lost a boyfriend and all her money, Brigitte from Copenhagen. Her somehow feminine partner, Valdemar, just that day had decided that he was gay as they were playing roulette with a couple of uber humanly handsome black guys from Harlem, NYC. I was at the same table, enjoying copious amounts of cocktails from "The Dorsey". I had *Penicillin* and *Grand Bambino,* one after another and, when I started to win my "27" corner bets, *Joie de Vivre.*

A small wonder I felt so shitty next morning. But I had fun, observing those Harlem semi-gods, high rollers clad in custom made Versace outfits and the air of unfaltering joy and masculine superiority they emanated. I couldn't recall their names, but I remembered how our good Valdemar was taken by the taller one and, like a puppy craving a treat, followed him to his suite in the nearby Bellagio. He never came back.

Brigitte was devastated. She was humiliated. Left alone in damn Las Vegas, at the roulette table, for a guy. She let a pearly white Danish tear trickle down her intelligent, beautiful face. I did not think anyone but me really cared about the little human drama she was going through. I told her that it seemed to me she needed a bit of some old *Joie de Vivre.* At first, she looked at me like she was going to strangle me on the spot, but as soon as she realized I was talking about cocktails and not mocking her, she relaxed and accepted the drink, graceful as a princess on her throne. After a few more drinks, the *joy of living* overwhelmed her and she started to gamble really recklessly, like she was a high roller herself.

Well, she wasn't. It did not take long for her to max out her credit cards and lose everything.

Baiana Linda Cock's Tails

Brigitte laughed with some sort of resigned, bitter mirth, "I lost everything" she exclaimed. I lavished her with a dozen $500.00 chips, for I won big on my "27" corners.

"Not everything." I smiled cunningly. "Let's celebrate your freedom," I said, and I invited her to "The Dorsey."

We were already tipsy when I asked Michael, the bartender, to make us a couple of cocktails I myself had invented for Baiana Linda, my Brazilian dream bar that never materialized a decade or so ago. Now was my chance. We started with *Suco de Orgasmo*, orgasmic juice: 2/3 champagne, 1/3 *suco de laranja* (orange juice) & a bonus shot of chilled vodka.

"Orgasmic juice," Brigitte mocked me. "That is so lame."

As soon as she tasted it, she changed her mind. "Quite orgasmic," she said, praising Michael. Damn, the real creator never gets a credit. I'd gotten over myself and instructed Michael to make us *Cheiro da Jacqueline* (scent of the Jacqueline woman), made of mamey aka zapote, ice and a bit of cachaça. He wholeheartedly approved of my choices and got down to business.

"Who is that Jacqueline woman?" Brigitte asked, emphasizing "Jacqueline" and slurring "woman."

"Someone whose heart was also broken," I replied and turned to Michael. Make us *Coraçao Partido* (the Broken Heart), please, but create it yourself. I tipped him handsomely.

"Who are you?" Brigitte asked.

"Just another Indian run amok, left only with madness to enjoy."

"You are not an Indian." She mockingly slapped me on the wrist.

"I might have been. Time-space of the Continents, I'm afraid, made me of a spiritually dying race. A cruel cosmic joke. But today we celebrate. What is left is a glass of Syrah. *Vino tinto*! Every new drink is like a perpetual baptism." I was working myself up. "However, it is not so difficult to stay pure in a day of endless fucks like there is no tomorrow. *Carpe Diem* is, above all, the said Chilean Reserve Syrah."

"You are crazy," Brigitte said, laughing.

"You bet. But not as nutty as The Little Mermaid statue in Copenhagen after being blown up so many times."

I turned to the bartender. "Michael, Michael, a bottle of Syrah please, two dozen oysters and twelve *Joie de Vivre* cocktails. Have the guys deliver it to my suite."

It did not look like Brigitte needed a special invitation; I assumed she'd come. Never assume, but in this case, it worked. I threw another generous tip at Michael and he smiled, winking approvingly as he nodded toward Brigitte. What happened next stayed in Vegas, for I do not remember a thing after the wink.

Levanta Defunto, the Corpse Reviver

So, the next morning, as I was dying of hangover, I asked room service to make us a *Corpse Reviver* cocktail: 1 oz. Calvados; 1oz. vermouth sweet, 1 oz. brandy, Prairie Oysters, 1 egg yolk, a dash of olive oil, a dash of Tabasco sauce, salt and pepper and 2 dashes of lemon juice. And soon after, the *Corpse Reviver*, another of my specialties from Brazil, arrived and did indeed revive me. One must give it to those Las Vegas people in "The Venetian Palazzo," the service is above first rate.

Brigitte did not seem hungover at all. Those Nordic types never cease to amaze me.

"What do we do now?" she asked. She proposed a blowjob and a quickie, an offer I could not refuse, and I slowly started to recover from the last night's binge.

Joshua Tree Park, July 25, 2018

While still in the Las Vegas hotel, perplexed—I remembered I was in Beirut and had vague memories of flying to Split, over Munich, but I had no recollection of leaving Croatia, nor getting to the flight and getting here—I rummaged through my stuff. I had found a direct flight ticket from Rome to Los Angeles on Alitalia's flight 620, in their Boeing 777-200's 1-2-1-layout business class. I must have driven to Rome after crossing the Adriatic Sea or something? I had no clue. I had similar blackouts in my past, forgetting that I drove for hundreds of kilometers or losing an occasional day or two when I was drinking heavily. Maybe I'd started drinking again in Croatia, I wondered.

This blackout was a bit extreme, even though not fully unusual. After all, I almost completely forgot my mother and the war back home. I'd never spoken about it, I'd never even really thought about it, but I think forgetting one's mother is not a highly usual occurrence. I wasn't twelve days old when she died, rather twelve years old. I still remember, move by move, some of the chess games I played when I was ten, I remember how I waited for Doris in her dark hallway, well past my bed time, asking her to kiss me when I was five (she was eighteen), but not my mom? As far as the war, I had people dying next to me that I'd forgotten. I saw hogs eating human flesh and had forgotten even that. I could, however, invoke horrific memories with some mental effort and be back in Osijek on Christmas of 1991 during the heavy bombing of that Croatian city, or on the ferryboat "Slavija" on which I sailed for Dubrovnik on October 28, 1991 on *"Convoy Libertas"*, but I can't "invoke" memories of my mother. It must have been some deep psychological defense mechanism in play, something I neglected at my peril, it seemed.

Then, as I was going through my stuff, I saw, to my surprise, a valet parking ticket. I had a car? A rental perhaps? I searched for the papers only to see that I bought an eighteen-year-old Mercedes S-500 at the used car dealership in L.A., next to the LAX. Damn. That was a lot of work for an amnesiac. Now I had one old Mercedes S-class in Europe and another, even older, in the U.S.? It just made no sense, any of that. I looked further and realized that I had a full five days erased from my memory. I remembered buying bajaderas candies in Split, on the nineteenth. They were my favorite childhood treat, that's likely why. I checked my online credit card accounts and saw that I had sailed on the ferryboat "Zadar" from the port of Zadar to the port of Ancona, Italy. I also spent two nights in the "Nun Assisi Relais & Spa Museum" hotel in Assisi, Umbria, the very birthplace of St. Francis of Assisi. I knew that place, but from a prior visit to that exquisite ex-nunnery built over an ancient Roman amphitheater, but I could not remember a thing from this recent stay. For the rest of my five days, I had no records or recollections.

A few books I'd read on the topic pointed me toward believing that I might have experienced "dissociative fugue" during the memory losses like this one. It would align with the Dissociative Identity Disorder diagnosis, but its most common cause is extreme physical, sexual, and/or emotional abuse, none of which I experienced as a kid. A psychogenic origin of it is possible. "Physiologically, the insult appears to disrupt the affective learning circuit formed between amygdala, hippocampus, striatum, and prefrontal cortex. TGA could be viewed as an illness of temporary hippocampal insufficiency, where its inhibitory effects to the amygdala are disrupted, which could precipitate a disruption in memory formation," wrote David R. Spiegel, also hinting at the possibility of PTSD being one of the culprits. He also confirmed my suspicions. "Psychogenic amnesia can be linked to several psychiatric disorders including posttraumatic stress disorder and dissociative disorders, where the loss of memory could be considered a defensive psychological mechanism." I was not looking for the insanity plea;

my jig was up, so the names or diagnosis of what was happening to me was not that important. "A rose by any other name would smell as sweet."

You can always blame it on amygdala.

Losing such a big chunk of my life in amnesia was worrying, but the combo of *Levanta Defunto* and Brigitte's not unsubstantial oral sex-related skills made me forget all that bugaboo for now. What I did not forget was that this particular part of America, endless deserts of Arizona, Nevada and New Mexico, was someplace we—Charlotte and I, that is—used to call "Mørk's America."

"No Fucks Given"

While I was mostly a city rat, Charlotte loved the desert. She used to live in some remote places in Arizona, California and New Mexico and she knew her deserts. Back in 2013, we drove from Tijuana/San Diego to Phoenix to catch a flight to New York and Europe, where some botched project awaited us in Portugal. We passed the Salton Sea and stopped over at the doozy Slab City and its crazy Salvation Mountain, West Satan and East Jesus. The Art Garden there is one of the last monuments to the human's thirst for freedom. "No fucks given," they say in East Jesus. Shame that we just breezed through, because she did not like the vibe. Or was it the weather?

Anyway, our destination was the Joshua Tree National Park, where I was going to perform what I called the "Wedge Removal" ritual.

Dorje (Vajra in Sanskrit)

Joshua Tree Park, Christmas Eve, 2013

Charlotte, to her credit, had one inspiring, utterly selfless moment. I had one dying dream after another, which I told her about while she was living in the States, so she rushed to Tijuana to "get me out" and to, basically, rescue me from the place in which I was rotting depressed and, seemingly, on the verge of dying. (The Portugal project might have helped her make her choice, for we went there less than a month later. I was supposed to be paid for my work.) In Tijuana, during those times of despair, I had clung onto a dorje (or Vajra), a small bronze object with five spokes that were cast in a lotus shape, for its supposed magical powers. In tantric Buddhism, the vajra are used in ceremonies because it represents the nature of reality and its endless creativity. I used it to ward off evil spirits that must have been attacking me given the weakness of my own spirit and to provide me with a proverbial light at the end of the tunnel during calamitous times.

I felt my dorje had been poisoned after so many years of suffering and that it now represented a wedge in between me and a life I longed for—a life free of pain, a life filled with love. Thus, I thought, "my" dorje needed an eternal cleansing. Nothing better, I reckoned, than to bury it in the sandy soil of the Joshua Tree Park and let it heal, liberating me from the evil spirits. Charlotte was all in for cockamamie spiritual stuff and was very supportive of my cuckoo approach to healing.

Alas, as I was getting rid of the dorje, I forgot to banish the demons, and instead of unblocking my life, I led them straight into it, free to ravage me at will.

Joshua Tree Park, July 25, 2018

Several years later, I was back in the Joshua Tree Park, this time with Brigitte, another Nordic girl. I searched for the dorje I buried on that Christmas Eve and wanted it back. Wanted it, now presumably clean and ready, to help me. But this time, the "wedge" I was thinking about was the wedge in between Charlotte and me, and I wanted to put the wedge back. I also wanted to get back to pre-Charlotte times. I desperately wanted to forget. Only deliberate efforts toward forgetfulness and in creation of beauty, in a Nietzschean sense, could guarantee my future and my freedom, I believed. Nonsense, I know now. I did not know then that the only way to forget is to remember, fully and truthfully, and then to understand and, ultimately to integrate. Unconsciously, it seems to me now, I'd tried to do with Charlotte what the little boy had done with my mom—repress and forget—instead of integrate, resulting in a really bad outcome.

Perhaps it was the Devil I sought? "Reducing the long story of the Devil to its roots, there was an archangel called Lucifer (light bringer) who said 'I'm born to be free—I don't serve!'" wrote the publisher of the Raven's Tarot website. I needed my freedom back from that demoniacal woman, even if I had to sell my soul to the Devil.

Alas, with all the crazy weather, winds, flash flooding, snakes slithering around over the years, no way in hell the dorje would be in the same spot where I'd buried it. Somehow, it felt real there and then—this notion that it must be there, patiently waiting for my return. Sometimes, returning is as important as leaving had been. It was almost like I was going to go mad—I do understand the paradox of that sentiment—unless I protect myself from all these memories of the *demon* and her evil deeds.

I remembered I had buried the dorje next to the Hidden Valley Nature Trail off of Park Boulevard. From the photos I took the last time I was there, I recognized the curve on the road where we'd pulled over. I remembered where the rock and the nearby cactus stood. I was confident I would find my dorje's healing place in no time. I searched in the scorching heat of 42°C – 43°C (about 107°F – 110°F) but was unable to find it. Like a maniac, I dug here and there, all in vain. I grabbed a stick that had fallen off the tree some years ago and poked and probed the Earth with it, far and wide, high and low. All in vain. I went back to the road and re-created my walk around the cacti and rocks several times. I found nothing but one dead kangaroo rat some bucolic people had photographed with morbid excitement. A selfie with the rat, the spitting image of this deranged world, damn degenerates.

Brigitte came looking after me. She was hiding from the miserable hellish heat in the car, but it must have been too much for her, and she called me out.

"Let's go. The heat will kill you."

"Kindly go back to the shadow. I hate garrulous women's blathering while I dig for gold," I attempted a joke, but the hangover remnants and the hellish heat made me sound rather coarse and stupid. She scoffed.

"Suit yourself," she said through her teeth and went back to the car. As I kept digging, I started to feel dizzy.

Crowley's Daughter

It's damn hot. I stumbled once or twice and almost fell. The hangover was back. I was parched but too lazy to get some water or too haughty after my idiotic joke to ask Brigitte to bring me some. Red dots started to pop up in front of me. I had vertigo. The cacti around me started to spin. I sat on the rock to catch a breath when I heard a rustle behind me. I turned. A young girl, about sixteen year old with the most unusual, radiating emerald eyes and strong eyebrows walked toward me, holding an ancient Egyptian pen in her hand.

"You seem so lonely," she said softly.

I blinked in disbelief but she was gone in an instant. I looked around and there she was again, coming toward me from a different direction.

That girl was Osiris Maàt, from my own unpublished novel, *Crowley's Daughter*, and she had reappeared as a mirage, arriving straight from the desert's sun. She looked at me and said, "Like a small boat striving to reach far away shores and borrows the ocean for that purpose, we borrow the time for our journeys, just for a while. We are not even a part of it, like the boat isn't a part of the ocean, much less capable of changing, or even challenging it!"

I was dumbfounded, not that much over the words I had written in the novel, or that it was she reciting them to me like a hallucination in the damn desert would, but over the the sorry fact that I did not understand what she was telling me in my own words. What was it she wanted to tell me?

"What are you saying?" I asked hoarsely.

"Use your time wisely," she replied and *puff!* vanished just like that, back into the thin air from which she had appeared.

As she left, the sun above the Joshua Park Tree darkened. Thank God for the shadow and the respite from the heat. I hoped I'd feel better in a jiffy. Alas, the respite from the sun did not last long. I was now in the center of a dark, hurricane-like whirlwind. The wind stopped suddenly as it has begun, and the black fog started to dissipate very fast.

Wadi Kubbaniya, Africa

I was there, in 17,000 B.C., under the sizzling sun of mighty Africa. The first people, twenty black warriors, dark like the first night must have been, half-naked and motionless, stood in a circle around me and held stone arrows pointed at me as their blazing eyes fixed upon me. Then the circle broke, and an enormous shadow appeared. A dreadful Devil Choronzon, the Dweller of the Abyss, showed up. I drew a circle in the sand, cowering. I heard Osiris Maàt telling me, "He is not real. He just wants you to make him real."

Choronzon rose like a mountain in front of me, laughing. "Ah, Puny one? I will tear your phallus with my teeth, and I will bray your testicles in a mortar, and make poison thereof, to slay Crowley's Daughter with the remnants of your venomous cock."

He moved toward me, a desert dust riding beneath his feet. I heard Osiris Maàt whispering frantically in my ear, "Remember, no matter what he says or does, do not leave the circle." I could not see her. From the plume of desert dust emerged Lilith, the evil spirit. Her skin was coated in black, painted with orange stripes. She was naked. Lilith spoke in Osiris Maàt's girlish voice, too young for its sultry shape. "You want me, don't you, Roman? Confess, you want to fuck me really bad."

But she did not provoke a desire in me, only revulsion.

"You cannot trick me, Chronozon. Send her back," I yelled.

Lilith, still in Osiris Maàt's voice, "Fuck me, Roman, fuck me. I want your mighty cock. Come and fuck me, Roman, fuck me. You know you want me," she said sweetly. Her face was sneering though.

I started to yell banishing words. "I am ordering you, go back to your cell! *Vade retro*, Lilith!"

Lilith screamed, deformed into a screeching apparition and vanished.

I heard another voice calling me "Roman. My baby... come to me... come..."

Was that my mother's voice? My God, I'd forgotten how my mom sounded. I looked around. I could not see her. Was that really my mom? I hadn't seen her for almost half a century. I never even dreamed of her. "Yes, my baby, yes... that's me. I missed you so much."

"You died so many years ago..." I stuttered.

"I live in you, baby."

The thought occurs to me, she never called me a "baby." I looked around and finally saw her. She was much younger than I recalled her, almost like a teenage girl I could barely recognize.

Who was she?

Suddenly, that young woman that might have been my mother moaned. She fell on the sand and moved erratically, like she was having an epileptic seizure. It was painful to watch.

"Stand still," Osiris Maàt ordered.

Then what might have been my mom turned and got on her knees. She moved her body to-and-fro, partially obscured by the gusts of wind. This was not my mother, she couldn't be.

Osiris Maàt whispered again, "No, she is not. They are not real, don't forget. They all want you to make them real. Fear not and they would leave."

Wind cleared the air. She was in the Gargoyle's Square. Was this Cairo? Two huge Gryphon Gargoyles with a lion's body and eagle's wings guard a Pentagram. Lilich, the incubus, cast in black with orange stripes on his naked body, swaggered in from the Gargoyle's Square and started making love to my mother, or her doppelgänger, taking her from behind. I couldn't look at it. That was not my mother. I moved forward, I wanted to stop this obscenity from happening. Osiris Maàt's voice was harsh and sharp.

"Stay inside!"

Lilich came with a loud, orgasmic cry and turned to me with a smirk.

"Liked the show?" he asked.

My muscles were ready to pounce.

"Stay inside!" Osiris Maàt had repeated firmly.

Pregnancy

My mom's doppelgänger was pregnant. Her belly grew rapidly in front of my flabbergasted eyes. She gave birth to a baby and died, rapidly decomposing and vanishing in the sand. Baby Roman grew in front of my eyes. "They are not real!" He kept growing up and moved toward me. I stepped back in horror. That was me. Baby Roman kept growing rapidly; he was a pre-teen, then an adolescent, then an adult. "They are not real. Do not leave the circle," I hear Osiris Maàt. The other Roman grew old in front of me and moved slowly toward me. The flesh fell off his body as he kept coming my way, now as a terrifying skeleton. I looked at my own death's dead eyes and wanted to run as fast as possible.

Osiris Maàt yelled at me, "Do not move. He is not real, Roman, he is not real."

Skeleton, in my own voice, beckoned me. "Join me. Death is a bliss, not the curse." It shattered and Chronozon reappeared from his ashes, icy vapor steaming out of his mouth. "From me comes leprosy and pox and plague and cancer and cholera and madness and the falling sickness. You would wish you had died when your mother had died." Those were the words Aleister Crowley wrote in his "*The Equinox Vol. 1. No. 5.*" I used the quote, slightly altered, for my novel. It terrified me that I was hearing them now as a curse.

At that point, I lost consciousness. Those that were not real left my realm with screams. "The light has gone out of my life." Was that a Teddy Roosevelt quote? And what did Teddy Roosevelt have to do with any of this?

Coming back

"Roman, Roman…" Brigitte was kneeling over me, her face a frozen mask of worry. She was not that beautiful at all, I thought. She had splashed some water over my face. It tasted like acid rains or that dead kangaroo rat's piss. I spit it out.

"What happened?"

"You passed out. I told you to get away from the heat."

"Where is Osiris Maàt?"

"Who?"

"Osiris Maàt, that's who. Where is she?"

"I don't know what you are talking about. There's no one here. You must have imagined things. It's the heat. You walked around like a sleepwalker and talked to yourself. Let's go to the car."

Blame it on Amygdala

I was reeling from the encounter with the mighty Devil Choronzon, the Dweller of the Abyss, tired like a miner who had crawled from the pits of Hell. I had no clue what had happened. My memories were vague but visceral. The body remembers. And the body keeps the score. Fear was so deeply rooted in the very core of my amygdala that I thought it would never leave me. I started the car and turned the radio on. Jim Morrison sang from decades ago:

> *"This is the end*
> *Beautiful friend*
> *This is the end*
> *My only friend*
> *The end."*

The Lizard King (one of Morrison's nicknames) reminded me of the lizard king I saw in Kenya. Why him now? Morrison once said, "Life hurts a lot more than death." I repeated that aloud.

"What?" Brigitte asked.

Is she deaf? And who is this creature anyway?

"It's not like I'd be knocking at your door with a nice bottle of Chianti any time soon."

"Roman, what are you saying? You are making no sense."

Sense? Is she demanding "sense" of me, the woman in the mask?

"Sense?" I asked her. "Didn't you fucking see what had happened? My mother was raped in front of my eyes."

"What are you talking about?"

"Chronozon wanted to kill me."

She looked at me, horrified.

"And I died in front of me," I yelled at her with a horrible voice I did not recognize. "And you demand some fucking sense? Are you out of your mind?"

"You're scaring me. Stop that please."

"From me comes leprosy and pox and plague and cancer and cholera and madness and the falling sickness. You would wish you have died when my mother had died."

Is this Choronzon talking or am I talking in his tongue?

Brigitte cowered and sobbed. This how Charlotte sobbed when she was acting hurt. Someone give that damn woman an Oscar already. I could not look at that BS anymore. I broke like a maniac and pulled over.

"Get the fuck out."

"What?"

"What *what*? Do you ever listen? Get the fuck out."

"Roman, please calm down. It's fifty degrees outside—"

"Out!"

"No, you can't do that to me."

I looked at her. Her forked tongue was flicking, and she was spitting her toxic saliva all over the car. Damn poisonous lizard woman.

"Get out!"

The lizard was crying hysterically. "No, no, don't do that, no…"

I was afraid she'd bite me. The Gila monster lizard is truly lethal. A very dangerous animal. I must protect myself. I lived all of my life unprotected, naïvely wearing my heart on my sleeve. Not anymore. I hit her in the neck with the blade of my palm and crushed her larynx. She was choking. I dragged her out of the car and mercifully broke her neck so she would not suffer. But she will bite no more. I threw her dead body behind one big gray rock.

The dorje wasn't even there.

Music Heals All Wounds

I put a CD with Shostakovich's "Waltz No. 2," Mozart's "Turkish March," Boccherini's "Minuet from String Quintet in E," Albinoni's "Adagio in G minor" and Chopin's etudes, all of them recorded together, in my car's CD player, blasted the speakers to the maximum and zipped away, leaving the triple damned Joshua Tree Park and its hellish heat behind forever. I left and entered blissful oblivion.

Chapter 22
VIRIDIANA DIES

"The greatest sources of our suffering are the lies we tell ourselves."
Dr. Elvin V. Semrad

Tijuana, July 27, 2018

As I left the Joshua Tree Park behind me, I felt invigorated, like a bull-calf after mating with a whole herd of merry cows in an open field of some grassy green bovine heaven. I felt resurrected and exulted, as though I had never been nailed on the cross of my own crucifying madness. I felt as free as an eagle soaring over the majestic Andes and their snowy peaks. "Mørk's America", where I was now roaming alone, and its enormous open spaces made me feel liberated from all the bullshit this damned humanity puts on us. I had no clue if it was a drink or divine inspiration that made me come to this glorious United States of America but, nevertheless I felt compelled to toast life. "Hear! Hear! *Slàinte* my little elephants[44]. *À votre santé,*" I yelled, laughing. "*Nazdrovia. Salut e cento anni alla tutta famiglia.* Cheers. *Prost* to great Senna[45], *saúde* and *saudade*" I saluted the universe with a bottle of

---

44 Slàinte when said out loud sounds like a "little elephant" in Croatian.
45 As an ardent Formula 1 aficionado, Roman sneaked in some wordplay. A German word for cheers, "prost" is also a four time F1 world champion Alain Prost's last name. Ayron Senna, himself a three time world champion, was Prost's greatest rival until his untimely death in 1994 at the peak of his power. Saúde and saudade, Roman placed immediately after Prost and Senna are Portuguese words for cheers and a sort of longing nostalgia. ("saudade" is a notoriously untranslatable Portuguese word, note by Trygve E. Wighdal)

ice-cold brewsky. It was that wonderfully loony Belgium strong pale ale beer, with its blue label and a pink elephant on it, "Delirium Tremens." I wondered where the expression "seeing pink elephant" came from. I was there in the America and I was enjoying every second of it.

I decided to drive to the Petrified Forest in Arizona and take a look at the bones of Yietso, a mythological monster the Navajo ancestors defeated and annihilated so they could roam free around the mesmerizing landscapes of the Painted Desert. Then I could perhaps go and climb the sacred, crimson red rocks of Sedona, also in Arizona, if the vortices seeking freaks are not thronging around too obnoxiously. The opportunities are endless. What a land.

I always wanted to go around the cowboy country saying, "howdy pilgrim" and/or "howdy ma'am" and even more so, given that I never drink it, "that's one damn fine cup of coffee, ma'am" as I dabble in being a cowboy. I would find some ancient diner on the mythical Route 66, near Kingman, AZ and enjoy bacon strip pancakes, bread-n-butter waffles and a wonderfully gooey chocolate cinnamon bun. Or two. Perhaps several. Screw those Whole Foods cultists and their damn arugula salad. Who would eat food that requires of you to put a beak on mug in order to eat?

Sex on a Selfie Stick

Yes! I should do precisely that, go and drink beer and shots of whiskey with rugged gold miners from Bisbee, a city in the Mule Mountains. Fuck sobriety. Dervishes would have never known wisdom if they were whirling sober. I could go to Walmart and buy a gigantic whiskey bottle, pick up some hitchhikers and have sex with them perhaps? The Merc has ample space for all sorts of lewd and lascivious activities; the only limit is that of imagination. Or I could listen to Rush Limbaugh bitching about "snowflake liberals" in NYC and L.A., and while *on the road,* laugh with Jack Kerouac over the societal conformities that put so many good men straight into a straitjacket. Mortgage means dead pledge anyway. We're all here on borrowed time from the universe, so why waste it? After all, we pay quite a usurious rate for the meager few decades we are allowed to be alive, for we will be dead for eternity. As I drove, I toasted to the beatniks. You magnificent bastards, you were right. "The Doors" would have never existed without you. And without them, I would never fall in love with Pamela Susan Courson, Jim Morrison's deadly muse, her snow-white face and her devilish urges. God bless her insatiable flesh and curious soul. I wondered if kids of today (or tomorrow for all that it matters) love like Courson and Morrison had loved? Or are they too busy Instagramming all day long and taking selfies with a selfie stick? Imagine a life lived with instant memories, hanging on the other end of the damn stick, only to be replaced with another one in the moment that follows. "Like me, like me, please," sings the chorus of long lost humanity hooked on Facebook and its idiotic, vapid likes.

I would be a Facebook-less, genuine rednecks' luddite redneck, I thought. That would be something. I was having the time of my life just pondering the options. Clear-cut fun, interwoven with figments of madness. My own had found its mighty match in the irresistible insanity of this vast, crazy, unmatchable land. Forgive this lonely soul such a babbling display of exuberance over the land like no other, but America's immense space is an intoxicating marvel.

I put *"Don't Stop Me Now"* by "Queen" in the CD player and had the speakers blasting at maximum. So much energy in Freddie Mercury's voice.

> *"Tonight I'm gonna have myself a real good time*
> *I feel alive*
> *And the world, I'll turn it inside out, yeah*
> *I'm floating around in ecstasy."*

I started to sing with him, as loud as I could. That incredible voice soaring over the American desert had made me fall in love with the grandiose opera of life all over again: "I will participate in the game," I yelled to the desert, "no matter the pain," I screamed like once in Brazil.

Better still, fuck the pain. I said that once, I said it twice and I am saying it again. *Repetitio mater studiorum est.* Repetition is the mother of all learning, the old Latin proverb says. I was exuberant.

Sex Machine Ready to Reload

I popped a top of another cold brewsky and took an eager swig out of it. It tasted like metal and smelled of yeast, that creamy delirium. Those Belgians know how to make real beer. I was just passing through Blythe, California (I always loved the name "Blythe") when it dawned on me. I was in "Mørk's America" and what's south? The magnificent and painful country of México. On its northern part, in Baja California, lies one of the ugliest places on earth, Tijuana, with its silver arch and clock at the end of the Avenida Revolución, the place where humor and wisdom live alongside misery and pain as an unholy alliance no gringo can ever fully comprehend. Further toward the ocean is *Malecón de Playas*, the very place where I met the cursed demon from these chronicles. Is this the real reason why I ended up here, an oblivious amnesiac chasing his tail? Wasn't the right time for me to look at my own face in the town where I'd known despair like no other?

And enjoy that newly found *joy de vivre* to the fullest?

Zona Norte with its narrow, alley-like Calle Coahuila should've been the right place for me at that point in time, no? As invigorated as I felt, I needed a touch of a skillful lady of the night, and there was nothing comparable to it in the desert, no matter how magical it was. Why wouldn't I indulge in some old fashioned in-and-out to lubricate my senses, so to speak, to get me back among the living, breathing, fucking human beings, given its proximity to California, on this side of Hell? Zona Norte was its own universe. Amidst drugs and depravity that rule *La Coahuila* with its blind cruelty, there were shoe shiners whose ancient eyes had seen depths of humans' degenerate nature and all you had to do, as they're focused on your shoes, was to ask them about the life on the streets. Ahh, the stories you might hear if you were lucky, excruciatingly real narratives in which *love* rhymes with *agave*, which gave us mezcal, Malcolm Lowry and decapitated bodies thrown away in some gorge, ravine or an alley street at dawn. There were *tacos* and *churros* and *tamales* luring you with their scent all over the streets, almost as cheap and tasty as blowjobs. Mariachis were cock-a-doodle-dooing and screaming their famous *grito del mariachi* until your ears fell off and you go deaf and dumb while street barkers are trying to out-yell them, beckoning and promising you a paradise in an embrace of some chubby, lonely señorita they portray as Miss Universe waiting for her prince. The prince was, of course, you. And if she was missing a tooth, that could've been a match made in TJ heaven.

There's a side alley, a small forsaken place off the Avenida Constitución where I once bought drugs for an American junkie girl. She had the most beautiful legs I had ever seen. She waddled nervously in front of me but somehow felt my hungry gaze and turned back and looked at me. That sixth sense never leaves them; the radar they were born with dies last, only after they expired. She attempted a smile but all she managed to produce was a maddening grimace. I was startled. She had those black, decaying teeth methamphetamine crystal is known to produce in people, a small cockroach like windows into inner infernos of an addict. Her breasts had evaporated;

her eyes were insane, her face filled with pockmarks, scared like she had had smallpox. Somehow, even beneath that deadly mask, one could perceive the remarkable beauty she must have possessed years ago. All that was left now were those incredible, shapely, perfect legs. Such a surreal sight. She begged me to buy her meth. It was only forty dollars, she claimed. I was tipsy and I was curious, so we went into that dark side alley where I gave the money to a wryly-mustachioed guy and then we waited for him to bring her the goods. Those were real pros. He gave me a cold "Dos Equis XX Amber Lager," free of charge. While we waited, I observed the clientele frequenting his small drug-peddling joint. Businessman and businesswomen, the people nicely dressed and in rags, young and old, beautiful and decrepit, seemingly everyone from all walks of life were passing there for their hit and were readily served by his minions. Damn, and I'd thought I had it bad.

The guy came back with a "rig"—that is a needle and syringe—and gave it to her, again free of charge. Many big corporations could do well with the level of customer service excellence those street guys provided. He moved us into the room for her to do her deed, a small dirty space where a forty kW lamp shone some light onto his face. I marveled at his snot mop, a thick, unruly moustache I could now see in all its magnificence, and, to his great satisfaction, I gave him a thumb up for it. The American junkie girl with those fantastic legs and smallpox face slammed the drug into her vein and, almost instantaneously, she got off, sighing with relief.

The Moustache beckoned me and, through some voodoo magic only street peddlers possessed after acquiring such skills over the years, got another twenty dollars out of me and pushed me and the American girl into a nearby black hole he called his room. It was smaller than my Merc. It smelled of urine and stale sperm. It was supposed to be the American girl's and my love nest for an hour. Affixed with rose thumbtacks on the wall, he had a small photo of *Nossa Senhora da Santa Muerte* and Brittney Spears's very small, black and white photo clipped from *El Sol de Tijuana (The Tijuana Sun)*, a local newspaper.

I wanted those legs, but everything else on the American girl's body was like her smallpox face—untouchable. So I left. She did not even notice me while I was there, and for sure she did not notice when I left. That was the lure and lore of Tijuana, the private hell of mine that I suddenly wanted to see again. Sometimes returning was as needed as leaving had been. I broke as a madman, made a 180-degree turn and headed back to México *lindo y querido*.

Zona Norte, TJ

I may have been a madman, but I was not a fool. I left the car at the Border Station Parking in San Ysidro and crossed the border to México on foot. There I grabbed a cab. *"La Coahuila, por favor."* That was all I had to tell the driver. Everyone in TJ knew where it was, what it meant and what it entailed. It was already 11 PM when I arrived, famished. My first step was Alejandro's. That guy was a great cook from Buenos Aires who had a very small place on the very Calle Coahuila, across "Hong Kong", the biggest and the most lecherous "gentlemen's club" in all of the Zona Norte.

I enjoyed my T-bone steak, medium rare of course, as I drank "Corona" I bought in a nearby "Oxxo" store and imbibed on mescal he poured illegally. The liquor license fees were exorbitant, but a man must make his living, that way or another. I observed the ladies and their clients as they were going in and out the love hotel adjunct to the club, those horny bastards. Once satiated and plied with booze, I crossed the street and entered "Hong Kong," like a wolf in a search for a mate. "Let's FUCK! I'll fuck anything that moves," I wanted to yell as I channeled Frank Booth from the movie *Blue Velvet*[46]. But then I somehow suspected his gas huffing lunatic character must have been impotent, so I kept quiet. One never knew what karmic joke waited just around the corner.

"Of all the gin joints…"

Girls mud wrestling on a stage never did much to me. Lesbian show in a bubble bath, hell, yeah, that's another story. Alas, I'd been drinking too much and somehow that night I did not like any of the girls enough to take them for a session of passion, lust and sadness. I just wasn't attracted to any them for whatever reason. Trauma does that to a man, I joked with myself, so I decided to call it a night in *La Coahuilla* and visit an old friend who had a restaurant on the Playas. When the taxi arrived there, I kissed the doors. It was closed; the Jaime's damn joint. Well, it was 2 AM already.

I used to live there, in that very same Miramar next to the Jaime's restaurant and its "Estudios Amueblados," (furnished studio apartments) during my times in The Rathole as I called my *estudio amueblado*—a shithole so horrid that not even the worst squalors of Mombassa would it accept as

---

46   Frank Booth is a fictional character from David Lynch's 1986 psychological noir film, *Blue Velvet*, played by Denis Hopper. (note by Trygve E. Wighdal)

their neighbor and peer. The *Malecón* just a few steps below was empty. I felt a surge of nostalgia; it felt like I had been innocent in Tijuana during those times of suffering. Strange. I would've never thought I'd feel like that, in the place I abhorred and feared when I was living hungry there.

It was a warm, pleasant night, at around a very nice 20°C. The Full Moon made it magical, so the Pacific Ocean was alluring, calm and inviting. All the dreadful mysteries beneath its dark silvery surface were also asleep, so I decided to go for a walk. I was hunted by my own writing, it seemed, wherever I went. I finished my novel titled *Jules and Jim* on the shores of the Pacific, in Valparaiso, Chile with these words: "... *so he is here, on the Pacific Ocean, guarding peace that only that great water could give him*," I recalled and laughed at myself. There I was, the cursed globetrotter, going from Brescia to Brescia[47], from Tijuana to Tijuana in a search for a peace that had been eluding me since forever.

Did I finally find it here—of all the towns in all the world—in Tijuana?

Viridiana

"*Señor, señor, discúlpeme, ¿tiene partidos?,*" (do you have matches?) a pleasant female voice asked from the dark. I turned and saw her. Her name was Viridiana and she came to Tijuana from Mexicali, looking to make a quick buck out of tourists. Why she was there on the beach at almost 3 AM was beyond me, but Tijuana in 2018 wasn't as dangerous as Tijuana from 2012, when finding decapitated bodies was a daily occurrence. She was skinny and a bit on the ugly side, but her perfect boobs, booze and the moonlight made her look very sexy. She skillfully caught my glance, grabbed her boobs, showing them off and asked coquettishly, "*¿Te gustan?,*" do you like them? Well, I guess the stupid smirk on my face gave her the answer she wanted.

She grabbed my hand and pressed it to her breast. She asked for $50.00 "for everything" and started to suck me in no time. Efficiency ruled TJ's shadow economy those days. Foreplay was for pussies. I pushed her

---

47   Erich Maria Remarque, in his 1936 novel *Three Comrades* uses the expression, "from Brescia to Brescia." Roman, who would have done everything for love, often quoted Remarque. A love story in between two main characters Robert Lohkamp and Patrice Hollmann took a tragic turn after she had suffered a near-fatal lung hemorrhage. When her health worsens, the two remaining comrades (the third had been killed, supposedly by a Nazi) drove the thousand kilometers to the tuberculosis sanatorium in the Alps to see her.

onto the sand, took off her panties and started to do her. I was as hard as ever. Alas, the bitch started to moan the very second I entered her, like she was having the best sex ever during the last night of humankind whose very continuation depends on two of us copulating and having a nice bunch of sand kids out of which a new, better humanity would emerge. Why did she need to pretend in those first few seconds? I started to fuck her even harder, almost maniacally, revengefully, a kind of intercourse everyone who had tried revenge sex knows is not that bad at all. She started to scream and demanded, "Come, come, you are so good, come, come please…" the bitch now spoke English? That really started to annoy me. It was like, thirty seconds in, what did she think I was, a seventeen-year-old on a first date, ready to cum in his pants? I covered her mouth just not to hear that bullshit, but she removed my hand and said, "Come Papi, come, please, I am coming… Papi…"

Papi? Puppy? She thinks I am her fucking puppy?

Puppy and Bunny

There's a devil lurking in each and every one of us. The shadow that occupies our souls should be neglected only to our own peril. I will get back to that shortly. Likely, the most embarrassing aspect of my relationship with Charlotte was the "Puppy" and "Bunny" dynamics. I was desperately trying to make it work so, given her escapades and constant escapes and her tiresome struggles against love she proclaimed as something special, I called her a bunny. I wanted to make it light and funny, these endless complications she had been creating with a passion of "Great Complication" watchmakers at Patek Philippe Geneva factory. We both needed a respite from endless, recurring dramas.

"What does that make you?" she asked laughing.

"A puppy, obviously," I replied.

So we became Puppy and Bunny. Alas, unlike her who had nothing of a bunny in her core, I was somehow childish and really puppy-like in my clownish behavior. She jumped on the puppy wagon and started to push "us" and me into these infantile roles as though her life depended on it. At the beginning, it was almost a relief to be a "Puppy" to her "Bunny." While infantile, our interactions since those misnomers had been introduced into our communication had not been as painful as usual. A friend of hers, a therapist, was appalled when Charlotte told about us speaking like a "bunny" and a "puppy" to each other. It nullified the idea that grown-ups could work on their differences or break up, and introduced a whole new layer of lunacy into our weird, harmful symbiosis. I did not realize how dangerous sinking into such a role could be for my psyche. Charlotte was in India or Thailand or Norway for most of the time, so for months at a time, we were interacting only online. It seemed safe. But as the "puppy entity" grew in me and I became more and more infantile in my behavior, feeling and thinking toward her, all in order to ease the pain of our grotesque relationship I left the doors open for the devil to enter my world and myself. I became a victim of its demonic powers, unaware of what was happening to me.

At the end, Charlotte's Puppy was overpowered by the shadow left unhinged to ravage my world and, ultimately, it had written a death sentence, not only to Viridiana, but ultimately to herself. The "Puppy" hit a snag in his development, and it tore him apart. What was left was the shadow ruling unchallenged.

California Sea Current

Viridiana continued to pretend and fake it. Her phony moaning enraged me, but not as nearly as her stupid "Pupi," and her disgusting "Come Pupi, come, you are the best, come, Pupi, come" calls. Pupi—Puppy, Pupi—Puppy, fucking bullshit after fucking bullshit, why couldn't she let me be and enjoy a single intercourse without grand complications and endless dramas once in my fucking life? I moved my body senselessly and mechanically as I looked and listened to that creature beneath me as she was moaning and smirking and snarling with those triple-cursed annoying "puppy" screams. And then she wanted me to stop—as Charlotte would've—to slink away, to abandon me in the moment that should have led me to ecstasy and not emptiness. "Stop Pupi, stop, let me go..." she demanded, damn bitch, so I pressed her mouth and squeezed her neck, just to stop her annoying blathering.

And the bitch bit me!

Chihuahua Beach

It did not even hurt. She had small teeth like a Chihuahua and had bitten me like that rat-dog would have—without any real strength. However, that enraged me even further. I wanted to keep fucking until the world ended, was I not the best you ever had, you fucking Charlotte? Didn't you have the "most amazing sex" with me, you duplicitous, miserable hypocrite?

I started to strangle Charlotte—or was it that Viridiana character?—with her skinny legs and great silicon boobies. It did not matter. I squeezed her neck. She died as fast as a Chihuahua would, without any real resistance; it was all done in a blink of an eye. Strange how easily she was gone. "I forgive you," I told her as I kissed her mouth for the first time and came into her dead body.

I dressed up and dragged her to the water. Ebb, the falling tide will take her away from the shore, toward the California current that travels at 0.03 to 0.07 m/s. The current would take over and carry her corpse to the open seas where she would find peace only the great Pacific Ocean could give her short-lived soul. Pray for Viridiana, Nossa Señora da Santa Morte, pray to God to also forgive her.

Nothing else for me to do in Tijuana. So, I left the Playas, crossed the San Ysidro border on foot again and left TJ behind, this time for good, and at around 5 AM, I was in my car driving to San Diego. I checked into in The U.S. Grant Hotel in the Gaslamp Quarter, by far the most expensive, overrated hotel there, but I needed to wash away the stench of the squalor I just visited. I also needed to get seriously drunk. The Grant had been the first one that popped up in my booking dot.com app. The minibar was filled with beer and whiskey. As long as there was beer and whiskey, all was fine.

For now.

Chapter 23
SOPHIE'S CHOICE

"Love, love, love, that is the soul of genius."

Wolfgang Amadeus Mozart

Boschi di Montecalvi, Tuscany, September 9, 2018

As I drank my last in San Diego, pondering what I should do next and where would I go, an old Italian friend offered to let me stay in her villa in Toscana in a return for a bit of free consultancy. That was a wonderful opportunity, so I flew back to Europe on the first flight out. After all, the United States did not pan out for me as I had hoped it would, so why not to go back to the dear Old Continent, those lands soaked in blood but adorned with magnificent Gothic churches, where food is as tasty as the French croissants in *Patisserie Claude*—a wonderful small bakery in the Greenwich Village, New York.

Boschi di Montecalvi ("Montecalavi woods"), where the villa stood, was in fact a compound that served as a bed & breakfast sanctuary in Maremma, the very heart of Toscana and where Etruscans roamed over a millennium ago. The weather was hot and dry, so the next brisk, early morning I went to the nearby San Vincenzo beach, where I had first heard her guttural voice, and then saw an incomparable creature the old Victorian warps would call the jammiest bit of jam, Sophie.

Sophie from Nantes

A gamut of emotions overwhelmed me when I saw her. It was love at first sight; it felt like a tipsy Cupid took a day off and threw all his arrows for that God given day straight into my heart. It was an explosion. Men would go to war for her, like they'd done for Helen of Troy. They would paint "Girl with a Pearl Earring" like Johannes Vermeer had, or create enigmatic "La Gioconda" like Leondardo da Vinci's when he did his famous, mysterious painting. Pablo Neruda would have stopped writing poetry had he seen her. She was beyond words. She defied description. I asked her to translate something movie-related as I had a conversation with a waiter and she was beyond kind, helping us out.

"Sophie," she introduced herself.

"Sophie!" I exclaimed. "No honey is sweeter than your name," I babbled embarrassingly, but recovered and told her that Sophia was a code name for Holy Ghost, as much as the fish was a code for the cross and that she must have been holding the key to the universe's utmost secrets. I made no sense at all, but she laughed, flattered. Once I learned she was a viola player, I regained composure. I told her a story about Prokofiev and how he had composed "Sugestion Diabolique."

"How?"

I wanted to grab her syllable and kiss the air that transmitted it. Yeah, I really made no sense at all after I saw Sophie. I managed to tell her how Prokofiev got drunk after his friend's funeral and suddenly started to yell, "He's alive!" certain that his friend was buried alive. No one believed him at first, for he was grieving and drunk, but he kept insisting. After a while, he persuaded the drunken horde of mourners to go back to the cemetery to dig up their late friend's coffin. They were in for a surprise. The man buried was found in a position of someone desperately trying to dig himself out of the grave. He was indeed buried alive after all.

Prokofiev later composed *Suggestion Diabolique* while remembering that event. Nowadays, his *Suggestion Diabolique, Op. 4, No. 4* serves as an example of Prokofiev moving the boundaries of musical expression, but this was the root of the pain that piece contains. Liszt's "Mefisto Waltz" is a devilish dance written as a nod to the great Johann Wolfgang von Goethe. Liszt had been repeating his tune as he had composed several versions of the "Mefisto Waltz" throughout his life.

"Do I have to tell you that another Sophie, von Lavetzow, was Goethe's last love at the same age you are today?"

Sophie was laughing, pleased by my profuse somehow extravagant compliments. The very sight of her intoxicated me, and I was soaring like an eagle over the Andes as I promised her "The Mozart Ghost," as we would call our grand opera for Viola and Sophie in G-string.

She giggled. "Are you a composer?"

"No, a mere writer. But I could write a libretto, and my Hollywood friend," it never hurts to drop a loaded term or two I thought, "Joseph Vitarelli, a film music composer who has been dying to write a grand opera at least once in his life since forever, would write music. Or perhaps Natasha who once wrote the most beautiful tune, *"Crossroads to Universe,"* also when she was at your age my Holy Ghost, would be even a better choice."

Truth to be told, I met Vitarelli only once for a chance drink in L.A. and he would have no clue who I might have been, but I was not ashamed of that white lie. All was allowed in love and war. Natasha, on the other hand, was a real friend and a real musician from Montréal where I spent one winter, colder even than a summer in San Francisco, who had indeed composed that tune. I always carry it in my phone, so I had Sophie listen to it. It's really a magical, albeit simple, piece of music. When I looked at Sophie with my pair of headphones on her, I thought I would die from beauty. I also had a recording of *"If you forget me"* poem by Pablo Neruda, read by Tom O'Bedlam in that melancholic Welsh voice, so my Sophie—did I dare to think "my"?—listened to it as well. She was able to deeply concentrate on what she was hearing and looked otherworldly. She was my supernova, only I had been the one exploding.

Tyrrhenian Sea

"Come with me, let's take a dive."

"Why?"

Ouch. Was she suddenly trepidatious, distant?

"Oxum," I said.

"What are you saying?" This angel capable of imbibing the universe with one breath did not get me at first.

"Oxum, the tattoo you have," I explained. "Its Orixá that rules the seas and the rivers. Best friends with Iemanjá. Let's catch them and take a selfie with them."

"How did you see my tattoo," she asked. An all-seeing miracle indeed.

"I see everything, the past, the future, your unborn children, your solo concerts in the Carnegie Hall, your laughter captured for posterity and placed in Vatican to heal the sick…"

"OK, stop it. Let's go for a swim. It's hot anyway."

She laughed. I conquered.

Maremma

I swiftly drove through the narrow roads toward my little fairytale-like hill house in *Boschi di Montecalvi* in Maremma, the very warm heart of Tuscany. As she held my hand, Sophie looked aside and up, admiring the hundreds of centuries-old cypress trees towering above us as we passed them by. Her breath was shallow and fast.

"Sybaritic Etruscan women come to my mind when I'm here," I said. She smiled. She said nothing. I glanced at the tiny blond Vellus hairs on her legs, barely noticeable but now awash in sunlight that poured through the car's window and were glistering like gold on her long, toned and tanned legs. What a picture-perfect moment. I got dizzy out of mad desire. I caressed her skin with the back side of my hand and then took her hand in mine. Our fingers intertwined and she squeezed my hand with a surprisingly powerful grip. I returned the squeeze and she chuckled. That chuckle did it—it was a guttural chortle that hid promises of eternal communion—and I was overwhelmed by tender emotions for her and wild lust for her body at the same time.

I pressed her hand to my crotch where I had an erection as big as the biggest cypress tree around. I wanted her with so much passion that I was as hot as Mt. Vesuvius, ready to erupt in ecstasy. I did not keep her hand there but almost instantaneously I moved her toward my lips instead and kissed her slowly and very, very gently. She moaned. Interesting. As I was moving her hand back to feel my erection again, my eyes met with her side-glance.

She looked surprised. Astonished, almost puzzled. But I was sure she had not been amazed at me or my boner; I was a mere tool on her way toward maturity. I sensed that she marveled at herself instead. She started to love and to live fully. Was that a bud of all future loves that would blossom in her noticeable and apparently timid smile? Was that barely visible glint deep in her eyes a figment of the children I might have had but that were already sliding past me to find life in her future with other men? I asked myself.

"Sophie."

"Yes?"

It wasn't a question, her "yes;" it was a yes-yes, she was ready, truly ready to jump into a tumultuous sea of lovemaking, cock-sucking, heart-breaking storms. I knew she was as erotically intoxicated as myself—her nipples were almost as hard as myself. I pulled over and kissed her with all the tenderness I could muster. She came so close to me that I felt like we were one. How in the name of God she did that, was able to get so close, was beyond me.

"Not in the car," I said. "The house is less than a kilometer away," moving away from her.

"Fuck me now. Fuck me here!" she demanded, surprising me. Again in that guttural voice, hoarse from desire. I thought I'd come in my pants that moment at the very sound of her voice, at the very touch of her lips. I have no clue, no recollection of us taking parts of our clothes off, I remember not how we started to fuck, but we did fuck, and we fucked hard. For a minute or for an eternity I don't know either—the time did not exist, or, at least, it did not matter.

However, I do remember how it ended. I held her around the small of her back and followed her wild movements, thrusting in and out, until she arched her back in an earth-shattering orgasm, followed by wild laughter and inarticulate screams of pure, maddening erotic joy.

"Roman," she said.

"Yes?"

"You made a slut out of me," she giggled like a little girl and concluded with, "Thank you."

She laughed, again with that sexy, guttural mirth that drove me insane, so I fucked my little gorgeous slut on the spot, all over again.

Chapter 24
SOPHIE'S CLIMAX

"Thy flesh and bones: howe'er thou art a fiend,
A woman's shape doth shield thee.[48]*"*

William Shakespeare, *King Lear*

Boschi di Montecalvi, Tuscany, September 9, 2018

The tawdry quickie in the car wasn't one of my most tender, considerate moments but it wasn't my last act of love making to Sophie either. What followed was a masterpiece of love and sex, not unlike Wolfgang Amadeus Mozart's last piece of divine music, *Requiem in D minor, K. 626* that is arguably the magnum opus of his incomparable oeuvre. When Christopher Hogwood was conducting the Westminster Cathedral Boys Choir and Emma Kirby, the Mozart's *Requiem* had reached heights of perfection never heard before. I had been pulling all the erotic strings in Sophie's body, up to heights of beauty and erotic ecstasy also never reached before. In that brief moment in time, with Sophie in my bed, for the first time in my life I was a lover and an artist. I was Niccolò Paganini to my mesmerizing viola player as I had—should you forgive me a tired cliché—played her body like Paganini had played his Stradivari violin—until it broke, burned and cried.

I looked at Sophie, gazing at her peaceful, childlike smile and her lasciviousness posture as she waited for my move, confident and terrifying

---

48   Translation into modern English reads:
       "Your flesh and your bones, but however evil you are
       Your woman's body protects you."

in her effervescent beauty. And I wept inside me, I wept in awe. How any creature could be so perfect, so beyond stunning eludes me 'til this very day. Even hundred years after my demise, I would remember how she looked as she smiled at me on that summer afternoon in Tuscany. If someone would've put Sophie in Pablo Neruda's bed, he would have never written the *"I shall stop loving you"* strophe. But she was in mine.

One should love Sophie throughout eternity.

She had little crooked teeth whose imperfection only emphasized her overall flawlessness. I lost myself in the wonder of a sight her ideally proportioned, young body etched into both my retina and my brain. I was dizzy; my head was spinning faster than a spinning nebula. She was there, stark naked after just being quick-fucked in my car a mere ten minutes ago and yet still full of innocence of an angel and prurient desire of a slut.

"Do you like me," she asked, like some naïve debutante would. But she knew, in all her pretended naiveté, she was aware of the power only seventeen years old girl possesses. She could crush the world with one finger if she only knew how to use that power.

"Do you like me," she repeated, a little bit miffed by my silence as I stood still in front of her.

Hell, yes!! "I like you. I love you. I looove you. I luv you. I leev you. I lust you, *mon chéri*. And I will fuck you now."

Requiem for a Dream

I always wanted to have sex with Mozart's *Requiem* as background music. Requiem and love might seem a strange choice but, after all, each time you climax, a part of you dies, never to come back. Mozart knew that better than even Marquis de Sade. Eros and Thanatos, these two life forces, like ego of that elusive self and its shadow, are never far apart in an endless embrace of this catastrophic doom called life.

That double fugue in Kyrie, when the male choir sings and then the cherubic female choir joins, only to again be overpowered with males starting again and singing all over them, resembles love making. I put Mozart in my CD player. She was a musician and recognized *Requiem* at the first note. She shot a surprising glance at me as her body stiffened with a tiny whiff of worry.

"Trust me," I told her, and she smiled. She trusted me. What more could a man desire from a woman? Well, one thing came to my mind as I stepped toward her: Good gracious God and the Blessed Virgin Mary, what a thrilling sexy smile Sophie flashed my way.

INTROITUS *"ad te omnis care veniet"*
You are praised, God, in Zion,
and homage will be paid to You in Jerusalem.
Hear my prayer,
to You all flesh will come.

For all I knew, it might be that all flesh will come to the good Lord so he could devour it at his whim. But what do I know. I prefer The King James's Version of our demise, as spelled out in Genesis 3:19 *"for dust thou art, and unto dust shalt thou return."*

Until Gods and worms alike start fighting over Sophie's decaying body decades from now, her lively flesh is mine. Zeus and Thor can keep their honors for eternity, but I will hold my Sophie in reverence here and now. As you think about eternity and not time, live in the present, children of God. And fuck, fuck, like there's no tomorrow, fuck. "Fuck—in a word—fuck! That's why you were put upon this earth!"

I channeled my inner Marquis de Sade as I grabbed Sophia's fine ankles with both my hands and forcefully yanked her, pulled her toward me. Neither my cock nor my body were touching her—just my hands and her ankles were in contact. Her eyes widened in both surprise, expectation and a hint, a tiny tinge of sweet trepidation. She feared what I'd do next, but like in a movie theatre while watching a horror movie, she knew she was completely safe.

Or at least almost safe.

I pulled her even closer to me, kissed both of her ankles and then kneeled before the "holiest of holies[49]," as I started pleasuring her orally. She moaned and moaned as I took my sweet time licking her peach-like pussy. I stopped every time she arched her back like she was going to come and then came back for more of that implacable sweetness.

KYRIE ELEISON *"Christe, eleison"*
Lord, have mercy on us.
Christ, have mercy on us.
Lord, have mercy on us.

49　The quotation marks Roman placed around this expression tell me that he's quoting Jules, a character from Quentin Tarantino 1984 movie *Pulp Fiction*. (note by Trygve E. Wighdal)

I don't need your mercy, nor would I give any to you, motherfuckers. I was now eating her, merciless to her begging. It was "too much" she cried as she implored me to stop, "Stop, stop, please, I don't wanna come," she begged. It was a call to arms, so I sucked on her clit, released it, and sucked it all over again, while my hands went up, squeezing her breasts. She moaned and had such a spasmic orgasm that she almost broke my neck with her wet thighs.

"It's not fair," she cried. She did not know yet that she possessed an endless supply of orgasms in her, be it fair or not.

DIES IRAE "Dies irae, dies illa"
Day of wrath, day of anger
will dissolve the world in ashes

Unlike King David, who killed one of his soldiers so he could take his wife, I killed no one so I could take Sophie. She came of her free will, horny as only a seventeen-year-old girl could be. So, yes, she might have been like Erythraean Sybil, but Maremma in Tuscany, where my little hill stands, is such a blessed place that I always thought God should spare Maremma once the world dissolves in ashes, in the manner of General Dietrich von Choltitz who, in 1944, spared Paris from Adolf Hitler's maniacal wrath.

Sophie, the immortal fuck, was shaking and panting, quivering in little convulsions and moaning in aftereffects of orgasm. She was jumping up and down on the bed, "Insane, that was insane," she laughed and cried and jumped to her feet to hug me. As she embraced me with her legs, she sensed my erected cock. "You did not come?" she asked.

"I will soon, in your mouth," I promised her. She did not object.

TUBA MIRUM "Mors stupebit et natura, cum resurget creatura"
Death and Nature shall be astonished
When all creation rises again
To answer to the Judge.

Indeed.

The tenor was already soaring over the Tuscany hills around our little love villa, invoking the trumpet's wondrous sounds just before judgement for our sins, when Sophie took it in her mouth and swallowed it whole. I grabbed her head and pressed her toward my body even more strongly.

She gurgled a bit, like choking on my cock, but did not stop the circular movements of her tongue.

Then I started to fuck her in the mouth and fucked her hard. She never seemed to tire. Mozart was roaring:

Quid sum miser tunc dicturus?	What shall a wretch like me say?
quem patronum rogaturus,	Who shall intercede for me,
cum vix justus sit securus?	when the just ones need mercy?

All the mercy I have ever wanted I had in the deep, sweet, wet mouth of my little angelic slut. Thank you, God. Thank you, Wolfgang.

REX TREMENDAE *"Rex tremendae majestatis"*
King of awful majesty,
Who freely savest the redeemed,
Save me, O fount of goodness.

Have you ever had sex with a deeply religious Christian chick? If so, she would have been, I am certain, calling or thanking God while having sex with you. A mighty erected cock is indeed a thing of awful majesty, under which women tremble in sweet dread—don't let anyone tell you otherwise. I seriously doubt Sophie, the quintessential iGenerational sun worshipper whose clergy is digital, believes in God, but she did invoke God many times as she came again, God bless her.

RECORDARE *"Recordare, Jesu pie, Quod sum causa tuae viae"*
Remember, blessed Jesus,
That I am the cause of Thy pilgrimage.
Do not forsake me on that day.

Even though it began in a perfect Mozart-like manner, with an entwined duet exquisitely executed: first for instruments, then for voices, Recordare is my least favorite. It made me remember Grace Kelly. *"Do not forsake me, oh, my darling"* song always made me jealous of Gary Cooper. He had gotten the most beautiful princess of all time, Grace Kelly. And her competition includes both Nefertiti and Princess Fawzia of Egypt. But here and now, over the course of that one sultry, amorous afternoon with a girl, I daresay the blasphemous truth, more beautiful than the Princess of Monaco, I found bliss. No man or woman should live their lives without at least one mesmerizing love making episode with a specimen as beautiful as Sophie. A small wonder that artists throughout centuries obsessed over beauty. Even that Russian mystic, Dostoevsky, proclaimed that "beauty will save the world," so here she was, the Saint Savior of the worlds, this Sophie Bauffremont-Barbançon, the mistress of God from Nantes. My lover. My love. My salvation.

CONFUTATIS *"Confutatis maledictis"*
When the cursed are all banished
And given over to the bitter flames,
Summon me among the blessed.

Banish the cursed for I am blessed. Could you hear this divine orgy Mozart has given us? Basses and tenors sing over the cursed ones and then, sopranos and altos enter and "kneel with submissive heart" as they pray. "Oh, my God, fuck me again, please, fuck me again," Sophie prayed trembling. I was all sweaty and shaking, but there was no way this sex could ever stop.

I grabbed her wrists, encroached her body, fully possessing her, and started the very last fuck in my life, only I did not know that at the time. I started to feel possessed as I was thrusting her harder and harder. I also started to feel disconnected from that angel I made love to. I just wanted, needed, ought to fuck that perfect body beneath me. Thanatos wanted in, he wanted to kick Eros out and rule alone, undisturbed.

Then the Lacrimosa came.

LACRIMOSA *"Lacrimosa dies illa"*
That day of tears and mourning,
When from the ashes shall arise
Guilty man to be judged.

"It hurts, Roman, please slow down, it really hurts," Sophie cried as I was squeezing her breasts, biting her lips and ravishing her. "No... please... stop... please..." she begged with the voice of a little girl, so I came back to my senses, eased my maniacal grip on her body, and gently kissed her, still making love to her, but slowly and deliberately, trying to bring her back to pleasure.

Too late. The magic of lovemaking was gone, the ecstasy all but evaporated. *Judicandus homo reus*, guilty man to be judged, Mozart told the universe, so I slowed my movements further, down to a gentle rocking of my body over her and finally I stopped without coming once. I kissed her again. Very, very tenderly, almost like it was out of guilt. She was a little hurt, somehow afraid and confused. I hugged her; I embraced the life I was losing as I clung on her wondrous body. "I love you, more than life, Sophie," I whispered.

I looked at her. Her velvety eyes widened, her heart palpitating like a little bird's, her breathing shallow. I was heavy on her, so I rolled over, still hungrily embracing her. I could not let her go, but deep down in me, something moved. The Presence announced itself and started to crawl up my spine from the netherworld of my own being. It was terror creeping up, unstoppable dark and gooey from the Kundalini chakra, ready to release all the dark energy I accumulated over the years of living in the squalors of my mind.

No! I cried silently, it can't be…

God, please do not let me lose this one, I beg of you.

LAUDATE DOMINUM

The music of Mozart that had been a soundtrack to our lovemaking wasn't from an original recording. I collected various pieces of music I loved and burned it on a CD. After the *Lacrimosa*, one of the most moving pieces of music, his *Desperate Solemnness de Confessor, K. 339*, started to play, rather its most famous movement, *Laudate Dominium*. I hoped Sophie, my beloved viola player, would appreciate Lucia Popp's heavenly voice. The version I had recorded was made in London, in 1967, with Ambrosia Singers and the Philharmonic Orchestra under Georg Fischer (Lucia's first husband).

Somehow it fell flat, even that divine music. It sang in vain to the God that had forsaken me. I looked at the sprinkled stars of Sophie's eyes with love and tenderness, but I felt uneasy. Sophie sensed it as well and dressed silently, shooting an occasional furtive glance at me. I stood motionless so this might have been upsetting to her as well. Despite her three orgasms, it seemed to me the beauty of lovemaking was making place for doubts, for she did not understand what was going on. Neither did I. I wasn't even aware that I was still standing naked in front of her, fully erected, while she was already almost fully dressed up. It must have been scary for her, poor kid, my dear, darling Sophie.

A strange sensation overcame me as the Presence crawled up my spine—a feeling of unspeakable dread. While Mozart spoke to God, I belonged to Devil. I looked at Sophie to find peace in her eyes, but she was busy putting her dress on, averting her eyes from my nakedness. Not even the curvature of that unmatchable young body that I'd relished and lavished with kisses and adoration just moments ago could put me at ease. I looked at her fine toes as she was putting her sandals on and I trembled with the universe that was growling inside me. A rare thunderstorm over Tuscany, perfectly timed like in an Akira Kurosawa movie, announced itself with a lightning strike. It was dark outside already, I noticed.

Down Memory Lane

Suddenly, like the thunderbolt over the Boschi di Montecalvi, the truth hit me. Sophie finally looked at me but at that brief moment I did not recognize her. I was overwhelmed with the sensation of dread, for I knew this stunning young beauty standing in my room and looking confused, yet I had no clue who she was. I was panic-stricken and feverishly scanning my brain for the memory. It was obvious she was with me seconds ago. I could smell her. I saw the unruly bed. I realized I was naked, but her face was so strangely unrecognizable. That dreadful sensation lasted for maybe a second or two, and then her face started to morph into the face of someone else I used to know.

At that instant I remembered!!

Everything came back.

The memories of murdered girl's cries started to flow through me, tearing me apart. As I stood in front of the pulsating image of perfection—Sophie's innocent, confused beauty—dreadful images of lifeless bodies I had left behind started to pop up in front of my eyes. Leslie, the wonderful Leslie from Tulsa, Oklahoma and her strawberry blonde hair floated around. Her face was punctured all over, bitten by venomous snakes. It was blue and red and decaying. I heard her first scream and wanted to scream myself to silence the horrible cries of her pain. Brigitte, that tall, slender, intelligent Dane girl looked at me silently and accusatory. Her neck was broken. She could not speak. Viridiana cried, "Pupi, why did you do that," spewing dark, water all over me. The stench almost suffocated me.

They were hovering around me, torturing me with their cries. I could've heard their weeping, their last breaths as they begged for life for the last time. I felt their warm blood on my hands. And all those eyes dying in front of mine were there, in the air, haunting me, piercing me, condemning me to Hell.

I fell down on my knees.

I stooped to the graves I denied them.

"No..." I cried out. "No... it can't be... it can't be..."

"Roman, what is happening..." I heard a voice coming from a floating stone million miles away. That was Sophie, drifting away on a rock, leaving me and abandoning my life. God bless you child of love, I wish you love. From the CD player, The Skatalites and their famous rendition of the *Que Reste-T-il De Nos Amours* ("What Remains of Our Love?") by Léo Chauliac and Charles Trenet started to play. The next song was the original; I recorded for my French Goddess from Nantes, mon chérie Sophie I was losing. Alas, she was never going to hear it.

I Wish You Love

I wish you bluebirds in the spring, to give your heart a song to sing,
And then a kiss, but more than this, I wish you love.
And if you like lemonade to cool you in some leafy glade,
I wish you health, and more than wealth, I wish you love.
My breaking heart and I agree that you and I could never be,
So with my best, my very best, I set you free.

As The Skatalites were singing, Sophie gathered courage, came to me, crouched down and held my face with her perfect hands and elongated fingers. She had been jerking me off with those saintly hands only minutes ago, I thought guiltily, and started to kiss and lick them, cleaning them of me. She raised my head as I was wailing and said, "Roman, what's wrong? Stop that please. You are scaring me."

I recognized her. The Presence had growled in me.

Sophie's neck was so beautiful, so white, so elongated and fragile, it would have been so sensual, so pleasurable to squeeze it and to take her life with me while it was still fresh, innocent and young. And so beautiful. I needed to take her again, to show her real me.

"No! you won't," I yelled and jumped on my feet. Leslie's deformed face came in front of my eyes, "Are you going to kill this girl as well, monster?"

"No... no, no..." I cried, "No, I won't, I can't... no..." the dread was overwhelming.

"Roman..." Sophie was also crying, terrified.

Oh, my love, let your life redeem mine.

Live and love, my Sophie, live and love. I looked at her and I wanted to rescue her like no one had ever rescued me. I owed her a moment of bliss and a moment of realization. She saved my life by her love and now I ought to save her.

"Out!!" I growled at her like a madman. "Get out! Leave, leave, leave…" I was screaming at her in an animal voice. She jumped on her feet, terrified and ran through the door and further down the hill. I followed her outside and kept yelling, "Leave, leave…" I screamed with the thunderstorm that was passing above our love hill. Sophie ran away.

The Elysian Fields

I looked at the silhouette of that perfect body as she ran away crying and kneeled in the pond of water in front of my little villa. My heart suddenly leaped—the pond was now a lake of warm, viscous blood.

Then, it immediately turned into a river and an endless streak of dead bodies appeared floating by. Their torsos were ripped; their chests were empty holes but pulsating and squirting blood. A terrible scream came from the forest. *God, I beg you, let it not be Sophie.* A few corpses turned their heads toward me and opened their dead eyes, gazing at me. One bloated, decomposing hand—was that Viridiana?—reached for me. I hit it with a rock I found sitting next to the hand and it broke into a myriad slime eel dwarfs that started to suck on my skin.

Another thunderbolt. I was kneeling in the river of blood, naked, the slime eels suckling me. Then, with a horrible thunder, appeared Ammit, the Bone Eater, sailing on a funerary boat. He had the head of a crocodile, the torso of a lion and the hindquarters of a hippo.

"Osiris Maàt, where are you?" I wept. She was nowhere to be found.

Amit was eating human flesh from the decomposing bodies he caught in the bloody river. Their hearts ripped off, their necks broken, they laid in piles beneath Ammit's feet.

"I laugh when I slay," Ammit brawls at me. "Thou cannot pass me by unless you tell me my name."

I was sobbing as I recited the words I wrote in that cursed screenplay.

"Darkness is thy name, oh Great Ammit. Thou are the Great one of the Path of the Shadows."

Ammit gobbled more flash and blurted out in a horrible demonic voice, "Zazas, Zazas, Nasatanada Zasas! Open the Gates of Hell."

Suddenly, the wild wind started swirling around, raising dust and blood and vapor and bodies and river into a dark chaotic whirlwind with me in the center of it.

Another thunderbolt lightened the woods as I kneeled at the center of a dark, hurricane-like whirlwind. The wind stopped as suddenly as it has begun. The black fog started to dissipate very quickly. The terrifying voice of Ammit boomed over my dear, mellow little Tuscany hill, and then the Moon appeared. Ammit disappeared into the ground, and with him, his boat, the bloody river with its corpses and the eels from my skin. The images of Brigitte, Leslie and Viridiana also left, leaving only memories in its wake.

I lied down on the ground, crushed. I still had a boner that started to hurt, so I got on my knees, stark naked and started to jerk off. I was deranged, torn apart and had to jerk the life out of my insanity and get a respite from the Hell, whose doors were wide open, waiting. I was beating it like the madman that I was and finally it came pouring out of me that I almost passed out. I crawled back to the house and plopped into the bed. It still smelled of Sophie. I hoped she was fine.

I curled into the fetal position and fell asleep, oblivious of the two white eyes that had been silently observing me from the sky.

Chapter 25

ALCHEMY & AYAHUASCA

"Nothing in life is to be feared, it is only to be understood."

Marie Curie

Boschi di Montecalvi, Tuscany, September 9, 2018

Sophie ran away down the hill sobbing and disappeared. Both Ammit the Bone Eater and Mozart were also gone. The Path of the Shadows I'd walked on for such a long time had been clearly lit, displaying the corpses of women I killed. I laid in silence, no images hunting me anymore. They were etched in my mind. I had clear memories of my murders. What a pathetic, cowardly loser I was, condemned to an eternity of loneliness in hell. And yet, I felt like I needed outside guidance—for want of a more accurate word—to help me out of the quicksand, even if the Presence would make me break another table or a long, white neck. No, you triple-cursed nincompoop, don't try to hide behind lame, quasi-jokes at a somber moment like this, and get serious.

I had to come to terms with my own life. For the remainder of it.

Even if I should try to emulate St. Simeon Stylites[50], who, in the 5th century, lived for thirty-nine years on top of a pillar ("Stylites" arrived from the Greek word *stylo,* form of *stýlos,* hence *Stylites,* pillar) near Aleppo in Syria and went to some cave to meditate over my life and its sorrowful last months, in reality, I had no time to do that. Saint Anthony of the Desert's approach would've been more appropriate for my taste anyway. What I am trying to say is that I needed to find out why I let all that happen. But what should I do?

I realized that I was triggered just before those murders. But, damn! I let that one woman fuck me over by her insane, selfish behavior and by doing so I let her totally ravage my life (and my mind) but that would be a sorry excuse for anything. Who gives a fuck? Was I the only one who suffered from the hand—words—actions of a wrongly, poorly chosen lover? Was I the only one who lived his life in pain? The questions were rhetorical. I'd done nothing to stop the pain, to liberate myself. I wallowed in pain and, I suspect, I enjoyed the pain, for I did not know what else would keep carrying me through life.

The hostage of pain

I sacrificed my identity on the false altar of deranged love, trying to salvage it, only to find it in that one word: murderer. The word itself carries such a heavy burden. It felt like it had been engraved into my heart with a hot iron. From then on, that all that was going to sit next to my name, a serial killer who took lives and then went on drinking in Las Vegas or Tijuana in an orgy of morbid celebrations. My remorse came too late. No repentance would bring me absolution.

> *PATER NOSTER, qui es in caelis, sanctificetur nomen tuum. Adveniat regnum tuum. Fiat voluntas tua, sicut in caelo et in terra. Panem nostrum quotidianum da nobis hodie, et dimitte nobis debita nostra sicut et nos dimittimus*

---

50 "Saint Simeon the Stylite was born in the Cappadocian village and how, when he was eighteen, received monastic tonsure and devoted himself to feats of the strictest abstinence and unceasing prayer. Saint Simeon spent 80 years in arduous monastic feats, forty-seven years of which he stood upon the pillar." (note by Trygve E. Wighdal as adopted from The Orthodox Church of America notes, *Lives of the Saints.*)

*debitoribus nostris. Et ne nos inducas in tentationem, sed
libera nos a malo. Amen*[51]

I could say, at the time, I truly did not know what I had done, but
no trauma could excuse me. I had vague ideas about the dissociative state,
"as a way of coping, dissociation occurs when the brain compartmentalizes
traumatic experiences to keep people from feeling too much pain, be
it physical, emotional, or both," (Robert T. Muller, Ph.D.) and knew that
a fugue state could explain my amnesia. Well, now I recall, so how do I
explain my heinous acts now? I dabbled into reading books on dissociative
disorder, even those of Dr. Ellinor Tyri Geliassen. It's a curse that seemed
to have been hunting me my whole life—after all, my hallucinations were
clear re-enactments of my own hallucinatory writing, but nothing made
any sense. Those hallucinations were damn attempts in writing, nothing
else. Stephen King did not dress as a murderous clown and go on killing
children around, no matter the horrors he had produced, scaring the living
shit out of millions.

Sure, Charlotte was a bitch, but who gives a fuck? I had ample time
to start forgetting her and to start rebuilding my life without her damaging
influence.

Eye for an Eye

I understood that I was irrevocably lost but I asked myself, was this
it? Was the realization of my monstrosities the end of it? And what if, once
Sophie's tears and scent are gone from my memories, I forget again? After
all, loving her, or at least being madly infatuated with her and making love to
her had, for some strange reason, brought all the memories back. Love was
again the curse, but it was a helpful curse. I was not ignorant of my crimes
anymore and could do something about it.

But what if, if I started to hate Sophie like I hated Charlotte, I start
killing in the future, newly and blissfully unaware of my crimes? No, that
can't happen, Sophie never hurt me. However, it seemed I was on the verge

---

51 *The Lord's Prayer* was given by Jesus Christ when the apostles asked him to teach them
how to pray. Roman seems to have been quite disoriented in the moments of writing
this Chapter. I was thinking of not including this Chapter, or at least parts of it, in
his Chronicles, but then decided against any editorial interventions. Especially given
what came next, so the processes of his mind might be of some use. (note by Trygve E.
Wighdal)

of murdering even her, my beloved, innocent Sophie? Does this mean my condition—whatever you might call it—worsened and that she was left alive only temporarily? I shudder at that thought. Shouldn't I just kill myself outright and stop this bloody madness that left corpses rotting abandoned all over the world?

I was a dangerous abhorrence unleashed on the world, a puppet on the strings of Evil.

But again, I noticed that I needed, longed for "something" or "someone" in my loneliness, anyone to help me with my loneliness. I had known the crushing might of lone living almost all my life, but nothing made me more alone than the realization I came to only a few hours ago, that I was a monster serial killer. This was not a documentary about Ted Bundy one watches in disbelief, this was my own life. "I'm the most cold-hearted son of a bitch you'll ever meet," he said, but I did not want to compete with him. I am not a cold-hearted son of a bitch like him. I did not plan my murders. I did not stalk those girls. I did not eat them or visit their graves. I did not keep the trophies. I did not derive any pleasure from killing them. I did not even know I killed them, until today. I used to have a big, open heart like a little puppy. Puppy! My God, am I losing it again, this is how I strangled Viridiana in Playas da Tijuana, triggered by the "puppy" and there I was, invoking it again, without any provocation? I was lost. I was mad. That was crushing…

How was that possible? Any of that? Where was my putrefied portrait hiding all that time? In which attic of doom was I decaying? But think man, think, stop this madness, write its last chapter and leave with some honor— if a serial killer could have any—kneel in front of the victims' families and repent, poke your eyes out, anything.

"Learn… learn… learn… from me"

Applicable to my horrendous story, the most profound words that came out of Carl Gustav Jung's teachings were, "Until you make the unconscious conscious, it will direct your life and you will call it fate." I realize it's Jung's take on an ancient quote taken from The Gospel of Thomas "If you bring forth what is within you, what you bring forth will save you. If you do not bring forth what is within you, what you do not bring forth will destroy you," but, unlike the Bible, Jung has given us a path toward self-realization. Opposite to Charlotte, who called everything "fate" and then did everything to mold it to her own idea of said "fate," not budging an inch, I do not think being a murderer was my fate. I was, I am almost sure, a puppet of the unconscious. Something I could've prevented only if I knew how. The triggers that led to my murders were obvious clues, but how could I get to the unconscious? How to unlock the doors? Where's the key?

I don't pretend I could ever, not even under the hanging tree, be nearly as noble as Leonard Lowe and I do not think my own suffering matches his own for a second. He was a catatonic patient who survived the 1917–28 epidemic of encephalitis lethargica. The book *Awakenings* by Oliver Sacks, and the movie of the same title made by Penny Marshall in 1990, tell his story. But when I look back, I think that I would've lived a completely different life had I not been unfortunate and had not met Charlotte. I am not shifting the blame. She was a perfect match for my own dark side and it only served to reinforce all my peculiarities, all my weaknesses and all the evil in me. But had I not been unlucky and had met a loving woman instead, the outcome of my self-discovery might have been quite different. I was already on the path of understanding, but unfortunately, once the fork on the road presented itself, I took the wrong path. Was my subconsciousness already doomed, having chosen her so the worst of me would break the surface from the depths of my soul and take over? That could also be the case, I truly do not know. [52]

But that night in Boschi di Montecalvi, after Sophie had left and I calmed down a bit, I faced a gaping hole that was my murderous past and had to make a decision.

Franz Kafka

"We are as forlorn as children lost in the woods. When you stand in front of me and look at me, what do you know of the grief that are in me and what do I know of yours. And if I were to cast myself down before you and weep and tell you, what more would you know about me than you know about Hell when someone tells you it is hot and dreadful? For that reason alone we human beings ought to stand before one another as reverently, as reflectively, as lovingly, as we would before the entrance to Hell," that tubercular sufferer who knew Hell, Franz Kafka, wrote to Oskar Pollak on November 8, 1903. Maybe you, my most sensitive reader, would be able to see a reflection of my Hell in

---

52 Despite all his unspeakable actions and abominable murders, his cynicism and his narcissism and his peculiar outlook on the facts, I believe Roman L. truly meant what he writes here. (note by Trygve E. Wighdal)

you and learn how to avoid your own and its devastating consequences on Earth, among those you love? But I would not presuppose.

Kafka unlocked the unconsciousness, at least parts of it. My dream of Kafka might help me unlock mine. I was wiped out after all that happened that day. I went from ecstatic love with Sophie to the most dreadful visions and even worse realization about myself, so I fell into a slumber. I was back home, on the bus line "32" from Rijeka to Lovran, where I went to see some young girl, not of a dissimilar mien of that of Sophie. It wasn't a romantic trip. I ended up in a trap. I followed her through a very narrow hallway; I could barely squeeze myself through and then she vanished. The hallway had two doors on both sides. I could not open either door. I knocked on one, then on another. In vain. I yelled for help but then I realized they were padded, the doors, sound-proof. No one could hear me. But strangely, I was able to hear people on the other side. They were talking about me. "He is going in circles," one voice said. "He'll never be able to stop," the other mumbled. "He lost his way," the first voice shrieked. Then the small hallway started to shrink and squeeze me. It was claustrophobic; I felt like I was in a murderous trap. Then a blistering white light appeared as someone opened the third door I hadn't seen and was unaware it existed. In the door stood Franz Kafka. "There's always a door. And it would always open only had you asked," he said and closed the door. The hallway squeezed and suffocated me, and I woke up in cold sweat just when I died.

Midnight run with Clarice Starling

So, I had decided. I was going to give myself up. I would confess. I would do that in Norway so before they decide on extraditing me to the United States of America, Denmark, or México, they would for sure provide me with care and insight. Once there I might even seek Charlotte, but that would not make much sense. If I'd try to share the blame with her (I wouldn't) she'd aikido me, being oh so innocent, that I might end up breaking her neck. I was done with killing, so I would research within, write a diary of it and that's it. Then I would commit suicide, as soon as I was able to leave any sort of comprehensive, coherent explanation of what had happened to me—a textbook that might help someone to avoid my destiny.

But before I did that, I was going to get to the bottom of my soul and my madness. I might have been avoiding going inside for all of my life, but that unexplored inside had taken over me and killed. Before it killed me too, I owed my victims at least the courtesy of knowing why and how it had happened. Dorian Gray had finally been made aware of his rotten portrait in the attic and he had to face it no matter the price. I felt like I had sold my soul to the Devil but I did not get beauty nor eternal youth. Nor unlimited knowledge or worldly pleasures came my way either. Everything that had happened had been like one long, heavy nightmarish play set up in the entrails of a gigantic devilish heart.

"You see a lot, doctor. But can you point that high-powered perception at yourself?" said Clarice Starling to Hannibal Lecter in *The Silence Of The Lambs* movie. "What about it? Why don't you— why don't you look at yourself and write down what you see? Or maybe you're afraid to..."

It was my time to stop being afraid. But the time was running out.

The Time is Running Out

The sound of that banal, trite expression whose value sits right alongside "don't cry over spilt milk" phrase reminds me of a washing machine that's just about to expire and meet its mechanical maker. A concept of time is a property of matter—think of that damn milk that would go bad after some time if you don't spill or drink it—given to us by the Big Bang so we can measure it both in awe and in vain. Kill a sacred deer. Imperfection of our measurements and words alike always bothered us, the humans. A rock art calendar in Arizona, "The Clock of the Long Now" and Ernest Rutherford's half-decay principle all represent our need to accurately measure time. How else would Hallmark Greeting Cards, which you use for your granny's birthday or Cartier jewelry you buy for your wedding anniversary, make their money? I was procrastinating, I was aware of it, but how to find a shortcut to the awareness? My mind was rushing senselessly.

I remembered what, in the 1840s, after reading Alfred Tennyson's poem *"The Vision of Sin,"* Charles Babbage wrote to the poet and what did he suggest in the name of accuracy:

Sir:

In your otherwise beautiful poem "The Vision of Sin" there is a verse which reads – "Every moment dies a man, Every moment one is born." It must be manifest that if this were true, the population of the world would be at a standstill. In truth, the rate of birth is slightly in excess of that of death.

I would suggest that in the next edition of your poem you have it read – "Every moment dies a man, Every moment 1 1/16 is born."

The actual figure is so long I cannot get it onto a line, but I believe the figure 1 1/16 will be sufficiently accurate for poetry.

I am, Sir, yours, etc.,
Charles Babbage"

Enter Mark Twain: "The difference between the almost right word and the right word is really a large matter—it's the difference between the lightning bug and the lightning." Yes, people always seem to go on quibbling over the subtlest meanings of words. "It depends on what the meaning of the word 'is' is," Slick Willie, also known as the forty-second President of the United States once famously said.

So I ask myself, what was the meaning of the alchemy I studied like some ancient mystic, if I was still unable to grasp not only its labyrinthian secrets but the maze my own murderous mind?

Alchemy and Mysticism

Lao Tzu was the first mystic that captured my imagination. Plato, even though his writing seemed to have arrived from the future, was not a mystic. Marquis de Sade could not care less because he was too busy fucking, but his erotic vision was still wrapped in debauching mystique. C.G. Jung might have been the first, but it would take us decades before we were able to really decipher what was obvious from his monumental legacy. Aleister Crowley was a mystic but also more of a depraved provocateur—that impish dragonite rogue also well before his time.

Heinrich Cornelius Agrippa knew that magic was *"full of most high mysteries, containing the most profound contemplation of most secret things,"* but somehow I prefer Wu Han's *"I've followed you on many adventures... but into the great unknown mystery, I go first, Indy!"* he spelled out with his dying breath in *Indiana Jones and the Temple of Doom,* and I chuckle.

I lived my life in temples of doom seemingly forever, cursed from the start. I wish to have died as Gaius Petronius Arbiter, surrounded by friends and female dancers as my blood was slowly seeping away, taking my life with it. Jepp the Dwarf, Tycho Brahe's vigorous servant would fetch us some Greek Malmsey wine while oxy would bring Albert Einstein to play Mozart Violin Sonata K.301. And we'd all be merry, like laughing squirrels from Tex Avery cartoons on our orgy of death. Perhaps even Woland would bring Margarita, and the elusive Victorian Ghost, so we'd have someone's feet to worship.

At the end, I thought perhaps Obelix, the Michelangelo of menhir sculptors, was the wisest man that ever lived. So what? What kind of nonsense is that? I was not getting any closer. That deranged babble was taking me nowhere. Rather neverwhere.[53]

What to do?

---

53 *Neverwhere* is Neil Gaiman's book set in the "London Below." Roman, who had briefly lived in the bowels of New York, used to refer to it as "New York Below" and his homeless times in NYC as *netherworld's neverwhere*. This is an obvious nod to Gaiman. (note by Trygve E. Wighdal)

Chapter 26

LA CONTESSA

"We're all powerless, none of us matters. And that's the great comfort."

Sir Anthony Hopkins

Boschi di Montecalvi, Tuscany, September 10, 2018

I had finally recovered my strength, so I made the bed and took a long, hot shower. It shifts the energy, showering. When I was done, it was past midnight, and everything was calm in my little villa in Boschi di Montecalvi. Tuscana is such a nice, sweet-tempered land of Dante, Michelangelo and Sassicaia red wine that I had no worries about Sophie. I was quite sure she had arrived home safely. She did not call or e-mail, though. Nonsense, why would she? I smiled as I thought of the poor girl and what an experience that must have been for her, seeing me flat out of my mind, and inspected what laid around me. No rivers of blood were raging outside, nor was Ammit, the Bone Eater gobbling human flesh. The villa and its surroundings looked calm and normal. Even the sky was clear and starry. A small wonder van Gogh painted Toscana sky next to the cypresses. The New Moon appeared over the hills, and the placid beauty and serenity of Toscana completely calmed me down.

The question, "what to do," did not pose any burning, soul-shattering dilemmas in my mind anymore. Not that I did not care about the previous day's revelations, for I was fully aware of everything that had happened, I knew who I was, I was cognizant of what had happened to me and I knew what I had done to others (murdered them senselessly), but somehow I was, no pun intended, dissociated from my own horrid reality. It was a strange feeling, like I was split, but without any rage present, almost like a grown up in me had to finally taken care of the child in me. Or one should say "children," given how many different entities seemed to have been living in me over the years. However, all of them were asleep now, spent and exhausted, so I enjoyed a moment of peace and solitude.

The Passion

I decided to do a Thoth Tarot reading. I am not an ardent Tarot practitioner, mostly because Aleister Crowley's over the top mischief in the *The Book of Thoth: A Short Essay on the Tarot of the Egyptians, Being the Equinox Volume III No. V* and, perhaps, because he and his magic sex partner C. F. Russell[54] had created the Choronzon Club. And Choronzon himself attacked me in the Joshua Tree Park where I had savagely murdered Brigitte. I shuddered at the memory but shook it off. Crowley and Russell were not a nice bunch to spend too much time with. Nevertheless, I shuffled the cards and the first card my in reading was a Major Arcana, card XI, The Passion.

"The Passion is the step into the second decade of the Major Arcana, the point where the journey into the inner depth begins. In other decks, this trump is called 'The Power', a symbol for the mastery of our own animal side. Crowley named the card 'Lust' - and most people don't really think of mastering their inner animal, but enjoy it full tilt," wrote Raven's Tarot about it. Crowley himself called the card the most powerful of all twelve Zodiacal cards.

I had to laugh. The Passion, or "Lust" per The Great Beast, another of Crowley's nicknames, with which "the journey into the inner depths begins" was the card that came to me that day, on the New Moon night, in the very day that marked the beginning of the end of my life? What a cosmic joke. Not the first one. It was not going to be a long journey, I was afraid. No, I truly did not find anything funny in this bloody grotesque that has been my life, but you should have heard this guffaw—a belly-laugh—bursting out of

---

54 Cecil Frederic Russell was a target of Crowley's malicious rancor as much as his sexual perversions. In his 1918 Diary (O.T.O. Archives) he wrote *"Now I'll shave and make up my face like the lowest kind of whore and rub on perfume and go after Genesthai (Russell) like a drunken two-bit prick-pit in old New Orleans. He disgusts me sexually, as I him, as I suspect… The dirtier my deed, the dearer my darling will hold me; the grosser the act the greedier my arse to engulph him!"* so it is clear why I did not take Crowley's Tarot too seriously. I probably should have taken more precautions while I was writing his story and carelessly invoked Chronozon into my life.

me as I looked at myself, a madman who kept asking himself, would it not be correct, at the moment of reading the Tarot, to assume that a deranged serial killer's self-introspection is the last thing the world needs? Get him a guillotine and gather hateful crowds to hurl insults, rotten eggs and delightful pleasure in sweet expectations of seeing his head nipped off at him. I could hear rightfully righteous judges think and I wondered: Am I clinically insane or not? Am I, am I really insane? For my "madness" had always made me drown in pain, its claws had been always producing excruciating pangs of a crushed mind, as if it had been torn apart, but now I am as calm and as sane as anyone. The Passion? Perhaps I had been unjustifiably dismissing Tarot? Well, I had also dismissed my life a long time ago.

I went out onto the porch made of a chalky stone, and the cool night air, smelling of evergreen cypress trees and umbrella pines fragrances, of earth and nearby sea filled my lungs. So, I thought to myself, this is the world poets were raving about over the centuries? This is the beauty of living, under the clear night sky and its crescent moon, on the hill filled with trees?

Don't you ever forget, the trees and puppies are angels

There's a house that would have been full of life, with a woman in your embrace as you sleep together, while your children calmly rest in the next room, knowing they were safe and loved by you? Add a dog or two as your guardians and you have your paradise worthy of poets' rhapsodizing rhymes. Every man is the architect of his own fortune, they say. Alas, instead of the paradise this balmy Toscana night sketched in front of my senses, I had built myself a nice little Hell out of human skulls, pain, grief and guilt. It was time for me to end all of that shit. And what land was the best land for anyone to look at themselves if not *Sicilia*, the mythical Sicily, the land of magic, mystique, monsters and beauty.

I sat in my old but reliable S-320 and bade farewell to the villa that hosted me over the summer, to the Boschi and its incomparable beauty and to the love I made with Sophie, by far the most beautiful girl in my life. It had happened only yesterday, but felt like an eternity ago. I turned the engine on and started my night drive for Erice, Sicily. I'd once met a magician, in Erice, I now felt I needed to see again.

The Buckingham Palace

Erice, Sicily, October 19, 2003

Erice, Sicily is a spectacular medieval hill town. Its Temple of Venus, in fact a fortress built by the Normans, stands at almost eight hundred meters above sea level and offers a spectacular view of both the Mediterranean Sea on its left and the Tyrrhenian Sea on its right. The ancient Elyminians people built Erice over a thousand years ago. Their ghosts have since seen numerous rulers battling over their majestic town: Greeks, Carthaginians and Romans, as well as Arabs, and the Normans. All had ruled Sicily and conquered Erice at one time or another.

Erice is also a little bundle of mythical mysteries. The goddess of love Aphrodite's own son, Erix, had died in a boxing match against no other but Hercules and was buried on the spot where throngs of tourists are nowadays taking selfies, imbibing these magnificent views from above and buying souvenirs. They are most likely unaware that Erix's demise had given Erice its present name back when he was being laid down in the Shrine of Potnia, the protector of nature and fertility. Be warned, once you see Potnia with a helmet or a sword, you realize that she was a powerful goddess not to be messed with. She was, at her time, protecting Mycenaean palaces and their cities, perhaps even the ancient, mighty King Agamemnon, the conqueror of Troy.

Such was Erice where I strolled around those cold, windy days of October. It was 6:45 AM on Sunday morning when I walked briskly through its narrow, cobbled streets. If an Elyminians ghost or two witnessed me, they did not make their presence known.

Or so I thought.

Down the Via Sales

I walked down the Via Sales when a lone white dove flew over me and landed on a column next to the Chiesa Di S. Pietro and started looking at me. Was that dove Daedalus's spirit, I wondered. After all, Daedalus had built the Temple of Apollo at Piazza Pancali in Siracuse, Sicily as well as the walls of the Castle of Venus (Aphrodite) right here, in Erice. He was Zeus's son and because, according to Homer—whom you should trust—Zeus had also fathered Aphrodite, Apollo was her half-brother. Apollo also sent a white dove to Odysseus, and to make even more connections, the dove was sacred to Aphrodite. Who knew? As I entertained myself with thoughts about all those labyrinthine affairs of old Greeks and Romans, an old lady, a shriveled, dwindling lady walking with a sword-like cane, appeared out of nowhere. It was rather from a tiny Discesa S. Carlo alley, but she just popped up out of the thin air. She carried a small bag with "The Buckingham Palace" embroidered in gold on it. I could not resist and asked her, in Italian:

"La signorina è una regina?" (Is the young lady a Queen?), pointing toward the bag with a smile. She laughed, and to my surprise, replied with a distinctive twang of her British accent in a perfect, posh Queen's English, with those long vowel sounds Americans are unable to muster.

"Gosh! No, but so lovely ('laahh-v-ly') of you to ask," she smiled and extended her withered hand for a handshake. I gladly shook her hand. Wow! The little posh lady had the handgrip of a blacksmith. I immediately liked her.

"That's some handshake. I see you're rather a lumberjack."

My lame joke somehow gladdened her, "Lumberjack," she laughed. "Jolly good, I'll take it."

So at that moment, she has become a Lumberjack for me. Her real name was Contessa Chiara Corsini, Ph.D.,—yes she was a real countess, a member of the princely family Corsini from Florence. She had obtained her doctorate in mediaeval studies in King's College, London but had lived in Erice for the last two decades. Incidentally, Signora Titi, the biggest landlady in Erice, whose small apartment I rented those days, had sold a mansion to the Lumberjack after she had moved back to Italy and settled on that magical Sicilian hill, where Erice had stood for ages. She never married. She had spent a decade in diplomatic missions in the United Kingdom. Rumor had it that Queen Elisabeth II was her friend in the 70s. Or was that rather Cornelius Orr, whose hobby was immortality? I forgot to ask.

We smiled at each other, the Lumberjack and me. She looked at her golden pocket watch, and then she asked, unexpectedly, "Would you like to join me for a Sunday Mass?"

Would you refuse a lumberjack, an Italian contessa, who used a sword-like cane and carried a golden pocket watch in her left vest pocket, if she extended such a kind invitation to you? Neither would I.

"Brilliant!" she exclaimed, pleased, and we went into the Chiesa Di S. Pietro and immersed ourselves into the liturgy. It felt nice to listen to Biblical stories in a language so close to Latin and in the company of such an enticing, noble lady as my Lumberjack. After it was done, I offered her breakfast.

"How chivalrous of you…" she smiled, pausing.

"... Roman." I replied.

"Delighted to make your acquaintance, Roman. My name is Contessa Chiara Corsini—Lumberjack for you," she smiled conspiratorially. We shared a secret.

She had to go and meet friends as that afternoon she had scheduled her Sunday's bridge game in Trapani. "Do you play?" she asked. Sorry to admit, I was only a humble chess player, unacquainted with the complicated game of bridge, so I had to tell her, "No, I do not."

"Blimey, it would've been nice to have someone younger than a hundred years in the club." She sighed, slightly disappointed at my ignorance but smiled and invited me for a tea later that afternoon.

A Dinner with Contessa

I brought her a bouquet of purple and scarlet anemone flowers. She was delighted. "Where did you find them at this time of year," she asked? I had my own secret sources; I smiled and she invited me in.

I often whine about my homeless years, but I'd also been living in the famous "Villa Frappart" in Lovran, for full three months when I was hiding and my government trying to chase me down back home—thanks to my violin player friend at that time, Ino M., a man who not only saved my life but who taught me all I needed to know about Glenn Gould and his rendition of Bach's *The Goldberg Variations*. I spent some time in a magnificent six-story limestone townhouse on the Central Park West and 85th Street in New York that belonged to a friend, Tanja D., where I was enthralled by her library with floor-to-ceiling bookshelves (she did indeed read, despite her wealth). I'd been to the "Copacabana Palace" in Rio de Janiero and to many opulent hotels all over the world over the years, but nothing had prepared me for the Contessa's abode and its indescribable quirky and quaint charm.

She had two real torches illuminating her marbled entryway and a real majordomo, Achille, who, appropriately, looked like he must have seen the Erix's boxing match against Hercules thousands years ago, as it happened. And yet, he looked somehow ageless. He escorted us into an adjunct ballroom. An old, kingwood Gaveau Grand Piano with a miniature copy of Rachmaninoff: *The Last Concert* statue stood on the piano. That impressive piano was the center peace of that magnificent room adorned with family portraits. One painting looked like Hieronymus Bosch had painted it, and another a fantastic replica of the *Adoration of Magi* by Pieter Brueghel.

"Incredible," I cried, surprised. "I saw the original in the Rijksmuseum in Amsterdam several years ago," I said, admiring the painting.

"Yes they still think they have the original," the Lumberjack Contessa said enigmatically with a smile.

"You are not saying..." I asked bewildered.

"I can only tell you that Achille is not only a dapper geezer you see, but that he also dabbles in painting old masters since forever," she said with a delightful smile as she took a biscotti from a silver tray. Achille, unperturbed by this talk about him, brought and offered me one as well. I wasn't sure if she was pulling my leg, and I wasn't to find out, for a motionless skull on the wall opened its glowing eye sockets and startled me. I almost jumped. As the Lumberjack Contessa giggled at my reaction, the skull opened and chimed seven times, announcing it is 7:00 PM, a time for dinner.

It was a damn clock hidden in that skull. We were off to a dining room.

O Sole Mio

The dining room was a comparatively small space, comprised of one antique cherry pedestal Tuscan table and eight Versailles cherry oak vintage faux leather upholstered armchairs. I had no clue what those chairs were, so I used TinEye reverse image search to find out and to add this info into my database. You should try it once, a great little tool.

She removed a copy of *Finnegan's Wake* by James Joyce that was on the table and placed it on the dining room's wine cabinet. Achille took a dusty bottle of "Donnafugata Mille e una Notte", a red wine I loved and have enjoyed ever since that evening, and poured us some.

"Cheers," the Lumberjack toasted.

"Salute," I replied.

Achille then served us a simple *sfincione* (think pizza but better tasting) and left us. Chopin's Nocturne Es-Major, Op. 9, No 2 immediately came from the ballroom.

"Achille also plays piano?" I asked, more and more astonished by that mysterious majordomo and his Lumberjack Contessa.

"Do you believe he played Marche funèbre with Frédéric Chopin? I guess they also dated together. Those two sexy bitches," she winked at me and burst into merry laughter. "So, be careful, when talking under the Full Moon, on the graveyard where the Dog of Darkness dwells."

"The Dog of Darkness?"

"Yes, Gwyllgi. The Mauthe Doog. He has a lot of names and could kill only with his appearance."

She had left me speechless, so all I could muster was to raise my glass and take a bite of *sfincione*. It melted in my mouth. How do those Italians manage to make every morsel of food to taste so exquisite? Achille started to play *Tu Vuò Fa' L'Americano* and my extraordinary Lumberjack Contessa made me sing. When I, after another glass or two, insisted on singing *Non ho l'età* by Gigliola Cinquetti, the Lumberjack clapped, and we started to sing long into the night. *Nel Blu Dipinto Di Blu* (Volare), made famous by Domenico Modugno, *Il Cuore e' una' Zingara* (The Heart is a Gypsy) by Nicola di Bari, and then *Buonasera signorina* by Fred Buscaglione, *Nel blu dipinto di blu* by Peter Van Wood. I wanted *Parole, Parole, Parole* by Mina and Alberto Lupo and then *Ragazzo della via gluck* by Adriano Celentano. I never had so much fun in my life like that night I spent singing with the Lumberjack.

When we were tipsy enough to start with *O Sole Mio*, Achille, still playing in the adjacent ballroom started to sing in a very Enrico Caruso[55] voice. I had to check that he was not playing a CD. Who, in the name of *Svaligiata, la Madonnina dei Pescatori*, was that man? His voice was so beautiful and powerful that all the Gods sleeping on the hill hosting Erice awoke and joined us on our impromptu festivities.

Ayahuasca

"Only those who forget why they came to this world will lose their way. They will disappear in the wilderness and be forgotten," Lumberjack told me. It was a quote from the Gogyeng Sowuhti, Spider Grandmother from the Hopi Indian myth. I never forgot that quote and some years later went on researching it and even used in my screenplay located under Machu Picchu in Peru. Until this day, in which I realized that I forgot why I came to this world, I treasured that quote without really understanding it. Ahh, only

---

55 A sensational opera singer, Enrico Caruso (1873–1922) is still 'til this day one of the best tenors, if not the best of all time. When he died in 1922, over 100,000 people, including the King of Italy, attended his funeral paying a tribute to the singer that changed how opera is enjoyed. Bear in mind, opera singers at that time were stars as big as any Hollywood star that followed.

if I could live again and correct my numerous mistakes. Alas, *You Only Live Twice* is James Bond's privilege.

Why did I travel the world like a madman[56] while it was obvious I had ruined my life way back home in Rijeka. And now, when I intended to go to Norway, I took a crazy detour, traveling to Sicily. But I had no choice.

Achille announced that he was cream crackered and had retired for the night, and even the steely Lumberjack Contessa displayed signs of tipsiness. She decided to show me Heinrich Khunrath's *Amphitheatrum Sapientiae Aeternae* (The Amphitheatre of Eternal Wisdom) book, which I'd admired since the very first day I ever heard of alchemy. Khunrath's *"Tabula Smaragdina"* (The Emerald Tablet), was the first mysterious text I studied in some detail, but his *Amphitheatre of Eternal Wisdom* was a fascinating work. I often wondered if Jung had studied Khunrath. Contessa had a rare copy of the first edition of his work, published in Hamburg around 1595. I was amazed, holding that rare book in reverence, but I was also tipsy myself, so I tried a joke, asking the Contessa: "Did Achille write it with Khunrath?"

"It would not surprise me," she answered with a smile. It was at that moment she offered me to try Ayahuasca, under her guidance. She was an Ayahausca shaman who studied with Carlos Castaneda and his famous teacher Don Juan.

To my eternal shame, I was not just tipsy, but rather sloshed, and I was afraid, not ready. I had so many powerful visions myself, without any chemical substances to help me, so the stories of Ayahuasca-induced hell frightened me. I always believed that hell is a construction, a very real concoction of our minds and not that cartoonish religious depiction and I feared going there. Ayahuasca meant traveling inside and I wasn't ready to do it, until this very day. Such a shame. What alchemists took centuries to discover, an Ayahuasca trip might reveal in hours. And I felt I had only hours to get to the bottom of my inner hell that had spilled out and turned me into a murderer.

"Shame," my dear Lumberjack said impatiently and dismissed me. The evening was over. The next day she went to Rome and I never saw her again.

---

56 Roman had visited in between fifty-seven and eighty-three countries and lived, for long periods of time, in Argentina, Brazil, Canada, Croatia, France, Germany, Kenya, Italy, México, New Zealand and the United States of America. I was never able to establish the exact number of countries he did visit in real life and which ones only in fantasy. (note by Trygve E. Wighdal)

On the Road, September 10, 2018

So, that is the woman I was going to meet in Sicily. I truly needed help and no one in this world was able to give it to me but the Contessa Chiara Corsini, my Lumberjack from Erice, Sicily. My Merc was gobbling up kilometers, and the night was magical, ideal for driving but it felt like I was leaving my life behind.

"Objects in Mirror are Closer than they Appear"

Chapter 27

DARK NIGHT
OF THE SOUL

"You know what I hear, Danny? Nothing. No footsteps up the stairs, no jet out of the window, no clickeyty-click of the little spiders."

Lamar Burgess

Erice, Sicily, September 11, 2018

"Before I fell in love with Anna, I was hoping for an Italian girl. They tend to come with these incredible Tom Waits voices," Philipp G. told me once in Berlin as we discussed the differences between Liguria I did not know at all and Toscana he had never visited. Such discussions made much more sense if they took place in the *speiselokal* "Tulus Lotrek," nested in my most favorite street in Berlin, *Die Fichtestraße*, under the watchful eye of matchless owner-maître, Ilona, whose mastery in pairing wines with food is matched only with the exquisite skillfulness owner-chef Max displays with every unique and ingenius dish he prepared. But those were *tempi passati* of earthly joys that this murderer was not likely going to indulge again in this life, as he was on his way to the center of his cursed soul.

So I was there, already in Sicily, driving like a man possessed from Messina, where I crossed the Strait of Messina on a ferry, toward its easternmost peak, Erice, and my Lumberjack Contessa whose Ayahuasca I was finally ready to take. I was tired and had Tom Waits blasting from all nine speakers in *la mia machina* to keep me awake. Around Palermo my Merc was like a giant surrounded by hundreds of little aggressive cockroaches, these funny, puny, disrespectful Italian cars.

Abbey of Thelema and *La Chambre des Cauchemars*

"Had you been to Cefalù on your way here," asked Achille, after I'd knocked on the Lumberjack's mansion doors, which I'd last visited fifteen years ago. Those were the words with which he greeted me.

"No, why?" I asked the old majordomo, who looked exactly the same as he did that night of singing and drinking so many years back—all frisky and impeccably dressed. He let me in and escorted me to the ballroom where he served me a tea. The piano wasn't there. An icy cold needle pinned my heart. The piano-less house was looking somehow decrepit. Where's the Contesa, I asked myself, not saying anything.

"In 1995, Contessa went with Kenneth Anger to Cefalù and the Abbey of Thelema, as his guide and translator. He was filming a movie about it then," Achille told me.

"Speaking of which," I said, looking around meaningfully, "where is Contessa? Playing bridge again?"

"Her spirit might still inhabit Crowley's *chambre des cauchemars* in Cefalù, as she dances with the hermaphroditic goblins she loved so much back in the fifties." It made no sense what he was telling me, but yet the message was crystal clear even before his voice broke.

I realized that my Lumberjeck Contessa had passed. It was ten years ago. She had left him the mansion, a very generous gift not even the mighty Corsini family dared to challenge when they came to take her remains and have her interred in *The Cimitero degli Inglesi* in Florence. She was ninety years old when she died. That meant she was already eighty-five when I met her in 2003? What was I thinking coming here with so much hope that she'd help me get to the bottom of my murderous misery? It did not matter anymore, I guessed. This was just another botched attempt to understand something I seem to have been doomed to never be able to comprehend. I had to give up myself, and also give up any hope I would understand why my life turned out to be what it had.

Achille stood up, suddenly a million years older, and plodded slowly into the adjacent room. He turned and said, "La Contessa had left you a present." That sounded final, a parting gift I was expecting with curiosity and sadness. Then, for the reasons unknown, when a hundred-ton heavy weight whose name was loneliness fell upon my chest, I remembered Lamar Brugess.

Loneliness

No one was coming to rescue me. With the Contessa's passing, I was left to my own faculties and those were the first I had lost. There would be no voices of the angry gods Ayahuasca might have brought me to lead me through the maze of my soul; nor spirits of the sea, nor would my beloved Iemanjá ever speak to me again. The profound emotional energy had dissipated, never to come back. That was how I felt as I was waiting for Achille to return with my present.

How did she know I would be back? Well, for someone who had a doctorate in mediaeval studies, was a shaman, and danced in Aleister Crowley's room of nightmares, it might not be that surprising. I waited for Achille for quite some time, getting more anxious and sadder every passing moment. I'd already mourned Lumberjack Contessa's demise and I felt I needed to leave as soon as possible and let my mother's Little Music Box play in her memory, before I moved on and turned myself in. There was no more hope left.

My feelings of loss were quite strong given that I had met her only once— in fact twice, but over the course of that one day. But then, my whole life had been marked by loss(es) and death, so it was a small wonder the news of Contessa's death hit me like a tidal wave of tears I did not have in me anymore. Anyone who has suffered a great loss knows how I felt.

Finally Achille was back. To my astonishment, he carried the very *Amphitheatrum Sapientiae Aeternae,* Heinrich Khunrath's book, that I'd admired back then. That was my present? No way! Yes, it was. I was speechless, overwhelmed and lost in my emotions.

"La Contessa wanted you to have it," Achille said simply, handing me the book.

"But this book is priceless, how could I accept it?"

"Would you refuse *La Contessa* if she was handing you the book herself?"

Achille smiled at me. He had those deep, wise eyes that really might have seen Khunrath writing his words of wisdom, so there was nothing more for me to say but to take the book and to thank him, leave the mansion behind with Achille, whose eyes were gleaming as he escorted me out in Italian.

"Che Die ti benedica," (May God bless you).

I wanted to hug him, but that eternal man who had played piano with Chopin almost two hundred years ago exuded the strength of a lone oak tree that did not want to be bothered too much by anyone anymore.

"Thank *La Contessa* for me, will you," I said, leaving. I had no idea why I would say something like that. The doors closed behind me with a click. I swear I heard him sighing. Did he *know*?

Last Words

I came home to my small hotel, "Erice Pietre Antiche," a small, cozy, wonderfully taken care of gem whose manager, Massimo, was one of the kindest people I'd ever met. He knew I came to see *La Contessa* Chiara Corsini, but did not want to tell me that she had passed, letting that task to Achille. What a tactful man.

I put the *Amphitheatrum* on the desk and opened it with veneration. I still had problems processing that I had that monumental tome of alchemical wisdom in my possession. And, at that time in my life, at that. I opened it, afraid that it would break. It didn't. On the first page, I saw a dedication La Contessa had written down with her shriveled hand. Her handwriting was angular, her letters looked like they were falling backwards. Her inscription read:

> *"Never accept compromises, Roman.*
> Love,
> Lumberjack"

I almost swooned. Those were the very exact words my mother wrote to me on the last day of her life. In fact, the very last words she had *ever* written was her message to me:

> *"Never accept compromises, Roman."*

And then she breathed her last.

Chapter 28

IT HAPPENED
ONE NIGHT

"There is a love song of childhood
Brought up from the depths of the Uqhu Pacha
Where the dead and the unborn wait
There is a song known to all, but yet unheard off."

Willaq Inca Umu[57]

Erice, Sicily, September 11, 2018

I was in a state of profound shock. Having seen Contessa Chiara Corsini's words, almost half a century after I read those exact same words my mother had written to me, shook me to the core. Having no idea how to escape from that day and its recurring aftershocks, I tried to find a well-known respite by listening to the powerful and enchanting tune titled *"Dance of the Knights"* by Sergei Prokofiev. I listened to it over and over again. There's something deeply alluring and hypnotic in the music those Russian classic composers bestowed on humanity. Montagues and Capulets from Shakespeare's drama *"Romeo and Juliet"* were meeting for a showdown. One can hear the tension rising. Then, the subdued oboe solo, marking Juliet's

---

57 Willaq Umu is the priest in charge of reading the omens and making the predictions for the Inca, the highest position of the priesthood (willaq = anointed; umu = priest) who was appointed directly by the Inca. Ukhu Pacha represents the underworld and the end of death. (note by Trygve E. Wighdal)

entrance to the ball, reminded me of Mozart's oboe in the *Serenade For Winds, K.361: 3rd Movement* the one I loved so much. Wolfgang Amadeus Mozart, I said out loud, the most badass name in the world, and went back to the oboe. What an exquisite timbre that little instrument produces, unique in its fine subtlety. Just listen to Henrik Goldschmidt as he plays *"Gabriel's Oboe,"* Ennio Morricone wrote as the main theme for 1986 movie *The Mission* and I guarantee you, you would, unless you have a heart of a hard marble, fall in love with that delicate instrument. To me it's right next to the violin, with its heart-warming sound. It also made me think of Sophie, my beloved viola player and Charlotte, my triple-cursed demon. I also thought about my mother and my Lumberjack Contessa. I wanted to talk to all of them, but I had no words for any of them left in me.

So I took the Little Music Box out of my suitcase and let it play for *La Contessa* and—strangely, for he was still alive—for Achille. I never played my mom's music box for anyone alive but it felt like he needed music in his life, since he had to let his grand piano go.

"Do the Needful"

I used to spend time on Facebook, but afterward I always felt like I had been submerged under a huge pile of bird's poop and could not shake off the stench and nausea for hours, no matter how much I showered or puked. So I left that vile platform. How so many people all over the world are willingly submitting to its perverted version of the "Ludovico Technique" is beyond me. At least Alex DeLarge, a fellow murderer, had been compelled to aversion therapy, forcing him to watch violent images for a long period of time with the noble intention of healing him by torturing him. Felt quite like Charlotte's idea of "love." Alex's eyes were held open with specula, not letting him blink or look up astray. The idea behind the "Ludovico Technique" was to create negative reactions to the violence, and hence, to cure Alex of his own violent nature. Facebook and Twitter users are volunteering to the worst brain washing, social engineering tools ever invented by man and live in parallel universes of cute kittens, online hatred and virtual friendships alike, while at the same time their brains are being shaped by corporate ideas of social norms. This will not end up well for the societies around the world. My own brain, however, was coping with a sense of loss so overwhelming that I used a fake corporate account I had established for my online marketing work and went into stalking people from my past on that same mental poop producing Facebook. I needed to escape my own present, and I hoped to recover in the past. Well, if you dig up the past all you find is dirt. I should've thought of that before I logged in.

Once in, I went to the Facebook account of Charlotte's boyfriend before me, Devansh Balakrishnan, to do some old good research that everyone who had ever checked on a former lover or their lovers is quite familiar with. The people are funny—what used to pass as the most intimate secrets they now display online for posterity that is bound to bite them sooner than later. Digging around, I was in for a surprise. The very first post I read was quite an unexpected barrage of the most stunning revelations, even though I had to sift through its sometimes-incoherent drunken babble. Don't drink and post, good people of the world. This is what Devansh had written:

> "I have to do the needful my friends and tell you this. Forgive me. I am paining. You know my friends I belong to AA. I did not drink for 10 years. Yes, my friends, I am drunk now. I am sorry. I apologize. But I have to do that one thing and tell you all the truth about Charlotte Mørk."

WOW, that's some start, I thought. I might add a truth or two of my own. Let me see what else good Devansh had to say. I was gobsmacked by what I read next.

> "She left India. She left me."

"She left him?" I thought her leaving was my privilege.

> "She never reverts my e-mails. She gives me drink back. She was fucking Karl."

Cursed Karl again? Is this for real? It rang true. My jealousy seemed to have been founded in reality. And when I think how much guilt I had suffered because of my jealousy. I kept reading, lured into this strange world, so similar, or rather parallel to my own.

> "Every time she and Karl. But my friends that is not all. For the same time she telling me she loved me she was telling the same to Danny. Sorry. Donny. She tells him she loved him. The same to Patrick. Sorry. I typpe drunk. Sorry. Donny had a sex change. She never wanted him. Patrick killed himself. Sorrry

friends. He killed himself because he saw her with Karl. She was
with me, Patrick, Karl and Donny at the same time…"

Jesus Christ and Mary mother of Jesus and all the saints in high
havens. I did not know Devansh, only his online persona which hasn't been
an idiot at all. He posted quite a lot in one of Facebook's private groups,
mostly on the topics of Ayahuasca, Ibogaine but also on mescal, mecuna
pruriens and everyone's favorite, cannabis. He was a smart, coherent man
who did not drink or use any of those hallucinogenic plants but had a keen
interest in their ability to help addicts. His own brother was an alcoholic and
a junkie that had died of an overdose several years ago in some new opium
den in Laos. Thomas De Quincey called opium "the celestial drug" but Amit,
his brother, died of crystal meth in Vang Vieng during its most depraved
times, in some dungeon with a fancy name evoking romantic notions of old
opium poppy dens in Shanghai.

So Devansh's muddled rambling made me suspicious. Had his account
been hacked? Was he imagining-things-drunk? And why that ridiculous
Hinglish? Whom was he teasing by telling Charlotte's story from his
perspective in that moronic mockery? Drunk or not, he was an educated man.
That aside, a part of me wanted a confirmation that Charlotte was indeed the
monster I thought she was all the time she was "with me," but what Devansh
revealed in his ramble seemed too much, even for her. Even though, if I truly
ponder that notorious 84% of the time we were separated while "together,"
it was quite plausible that she had divided her time to four, five of us. She
traveled all the time, all over the world, from Europe to the United States, to
India and the Amazons, so it was possible. Of course she was mostly tired if
she had to juggle in between all those lives at almost the same time.

Yet, still incredulous, I started to dig around the group and personal
accounts of Donny, Patrick, Devansh and Karl. Devansh also described how
Charlotte, while very well aware of his history, encouraged him to have a
drink at some party. "I forgot," (about his alcoholism) she had stated after
he had relapsed as a result of that careless mistake. That reminded me of
an episode in Germany. We were driving to Italy through Bavaria when
Charlotte invited me to a lunch. In some ancient Bavarian Bierhaus she had
encouraged me to have a beer, given the waters or something special there.
After I had my third, she complained—vintage Charlotte—but her comment
was the same, "I forgot." (that I used to drink and how dangerous even one
drink could have been to me.)

So what Devansh had written started to make sense, no matter how staggering those discoveries were. I dug more into that vile, ignoble platform, myself. I found no pleasure in stalking Charlotte, but it was like watching a car accident scene. Only I was also involved. Karl's FB pages were almost empty, nothing of substance there, just him badly playing some idiotic music. I guess emptiness is sexy for those India-inflicted chicks. Donny posted only one comment saying, "I do not want to talk publicly about that person." Charlotte was absent from any of those pages and discussions.

Eager Young Minds

On Patrick's profile there were rivers of tears and condolences and those damn "thoughts and prayers," but only deep down, buried under hundreds of messages, a certain Amelia Daniels referred to Charlotte as "it was all that bitch's Charlotte's fault." Upon reading that, I sent her a private message and introduced myself. She was Patrick's young niece who readily accepted my friend request and turned out to be really chatty, eager to disclose as many of her departed cousin's intimate secrets as she was able in a short time. She wrote that Patrick had told her how Charlotte was always coming to him but leaving him soon after. The niece was so eager to talk that we eventually moved to video calls. What she told me revealed the same pattern as with me and with Devansh, et.al. Charlotte had been telling him how much she loved him, all of which I myself heard from her so many times. It was uncanny, the similarities of what she had been telling him and me, like she was a love spammer from Nigeria sending identically worded spam to anyone ready to open the message. However, she did not want to sleep with Patrick. I looked at his photos; the guy was as fit as a fiddle, much better looking than me. I would have thought, given how sexual she had been with me when she wanted to be, that she'd take on the chance to have another "fantastic lover" in Patrick like in me, another of her "fantastic lovers" she had in *Die Bergmannstraße*, Berlin.

To cut a long story short, she had been playing him like a fool. Amelia was certain she deliberately had driven Patrick to suicide, seizing upon and using his life tragedies. He had lost his first wife when she got killed in a car accident alongside her lover. He found out she was cheating on him on the same night she had died. Charlotte came into his life as a ray of light but had been rejecting him sexually since the start, while openly sleeping with other men so he could find out and suffer. Amelia prattled on, more and more excited with every word of that sordid affair.

That was beyond evil and worse than anything she had done to me—too painful to hear. I also could not listen to Amelia's squeaky voice anymore. It trembled with perverse enjoyment as she told me about her cousin's tragedy, so I thanked her for her time and info and, after I had to assure her we'd talk again soon, I went out for a walk to clear out my mind. I came to Erice to get to the bottom of my insanity, which had ended up with me murdering people, but a huge gap, an unexpected chasm opened in front of me. Its name was Charlotte's own insanity, something I always suspected to be true—that she was mad, but was never able to face it even when she was displaying all the signs of being mad in front of my eyes.

My fear of madness paved a road to perdition, to a self-fulfilling madness of my own by making me blind to the obvious. I could not stay inside, not for another moment, so I walked to the Castello di Venere and sat in the rain, pondering what I had just learned about Charlotte.

"The greatest sources of our suffering are the lies we tell ourselves."

It was a warm but rainy evening in Erice when I remembered Dr. Semrad's quote of self-deception and how it was a source of suffering. I realized at that moment that I must have known all along that Charlotte was sleeping with Karl, but I had refused to see the truth. At least I must have *felt* the truth. I should have known the real truth about her, the full truth, since the very first days of our relationship. I had no idea about Donny or Patrick but at least, given that I had never suspected she might have been back with Devansh even when she was in Tiruvvannamalai where he lived and where she used to go for months at the time, I should have listened to my gut feeling regarding Karl. Her behavior was so cruel, so callous whenever she met him that I should have known. I'd chosen not to trust my own feelings, my premonitions, my own realizations, so as a result, there I was, a cursed clown murderer, a *pagliaccio* whom she had taken on the ride of his life.

Ah! Ridi, Pagliaccio, sul tuo amore infranto!   *Ah! Laugh, Clown, about your shattered romance!*
Ridi del duol che t'avvelena il cor!   *Laugh at the pain which is poisoning your heart.*

"*Vesti la giubba*" (*Put on the costume*), a famous tenor aria from Ruggero Leoncavallo's opera *Pagliacci* I remembered as I thought of myself as a sad, rather murderous clown, made me cackle at the pain that did indeed poison my heart and my soul.

Why did I so blindly buy into her stories and endlessly deal with her real or imagined vulnerabilities, tolerate that ridiculous long-distance non-relationship? Was my loneliness so enormous, the hole in my heart so big that I was ready to fill it up even with the most obvious garbage she fed me with? Why did I put up with her behavior for so long? Did I feel she needed me to help her "heal," which was her mantra anyway? Did I sense that she needed rescuing and was fanatically trying to help her? Maybe my madness had hooked onto her own, hoping to negate each other and live free and in love? I see now how deranged my hopes had been. Perhaps, in order to assuage my sense of guilt I lived with since my mother had died, I had to believe in love's redeeming qualities? I felt guilty, for I was unable to help my mother. I vividly remember those futile attempts to help her as a kid. I had employed some magical rituals I'd read about in some quack's book, trying to keep her alive, and I'd failed miserably. When my father was dying, I was in America, unable to be with him, for at that time I was without a passport in the States, whose government was too slow in giving me a permit to travel. So he had been laid to rest without me present and I felt immense guilt. That sense of guilt was also prevalent over the years I had lived as an alcoholic. Were any of those reasons, or all of them, the reason for me clinging onto such a damaging person as her, only to end up fatally damaging others? I was going insane, for I could not even start to begin to understand what went so horribly wrong with me.

The next circle of hell was the emptiness into which I'd fallen that night I lost my Contessa and also Charlotte, the woman I knew, once loved and now hated was also gone; only that apparition in my mind represented a grotesque silhouette of someone I never knew but someone who did not want to leave me at peace. I had to find out who she really was and see her for the last time.

At least I felt like my trip to Sicily might have had a purpose.

The Void

"We are children of the void. The void is our destiny, our cradle, our nightmare, our fears, our hope and the space we are traveling in. The void is the beginning and the ending of all our power. Our souls seems to be one family, I experienced a lot what you were talking about Charlotte but there are not

many people in the world who have this psychic landscapes as their horizon," wrote C.V.E., a fantastic albeit quite dark artist from Berlin once in an e-mail he sent me to Paris.

God bless his and Alexander Shulgin's souls.

Pihkal: A Chemical Love Story

Oh, how much I missed Sasha Shulgin, the "godfather of ecstasy" who had unlocked so many paths toward the collective unconsciousness, and his wife, Laura Ann Shulgin, née Gotlieb, as I sat on that rain. I should've listened to Shulgin and tried those hallucinogenic drugs. Perhaps they would've healed me of my own hallucinations. Barbara, that untried lover I was destined never to make love to, once told me how she should write a book about what she called "our misunderstandings." Add our botched Zagreb encounter to that book, Barbara. At that moment, I had thought that my whole life was that of misunderstandings and missed opportunities to understand its very meaning.

Back in 2003, I had declined Contessa Chiara Corsini's offer to experience Ayahuasca just as I chose not to take up on Luna Palacios offer to teach me to dance tango back in 1998 in Buenos Aires. I was afraid of trying Ibogaine a friend had offered me in Tijuana before his untimely death near Carmel in California where a drunken driver killed him, his wife and brother. So this is a true story of my life: a fear of what's inside and a refusal to face it. And with refusing tango, now I know I also rebuffed a chance to encounter happiness. It was only natural that I had found utter misery with Charlotte instead. It took me all over the world, that life of mine, but not to the core of my being. Of course someone as insane as Charlotte would have taken advantage of such cowardice I displayed while thinking, pretending to be a brave man facing extraordinary challenges. Idiot. Again, I failed to see the obvious. I invoked them, those challenges, and each of those devastating events I experienced over my life were giving me a chance to learn, to finally get the message the universe had been so generously throwing at me year after year, trying to push me toward inner universes that I'd spurned. I also denied myself, I denied life.

It was too late now. What was left for me was a trip to Norway. Why Norway? I had to face Charlotte and what she had done to all of us and then I was going to put an end to all of this. I had no idea how, but I was sure the plan would present itself when the time was right. I went to my car and left Erice, Achille and memories of my Lumberjack, *La Contessa* Chiara Corsini behind.

Enna, Sicily, September 11, 2018

As I again drove like a man possessed, rushing to get to the north, I blasted the speakers so much that they almost blew up as I listened to Johannes Brahms and his romantic little tune, "Hungarian Dance No. 5," and sang the lyrics I invented as it boomed. I was driving along the wonderous Sicilian landscapes, so the movement, the music and loud singing—rather braying—had helped me live through the day. Just after I had to take a detour from the *Autostrada* A19 (one of the main Sicilian highways) on my way to Messina, I had a chance to brag about music, something I was waiting to do a long time. Two blonde angels, Anne-Mette and Margit from Copenhagen—those Danish people are tireless tourists as much as healthy, beautiful creatures—were hitchhiking so I stopped to pick them up. I was quite gloomy despite all the screaming, so I thought they might cheer me up. And a blowjob is always one drink away.

They were young, the Camila Cabello generation, about twenty to twenty-two years old, for whom *Havana na-na-na* was the artistic pinnacle in their iPhones so, quite naturally, they asked me what my music was. I told them and then expanded the story of that Hungarian dance by telling them that this Brahms composition was in fact inspired by a romantic *czardas* written by Kéler Béla that was titled "Bártfai emlék," I finished triumphantly. Nothing.

"Huh!" I exclaimed again, still proud of myself, fishing for a compliment. Still nothing. My brilliant morsel of knowledge about classical music fell flat. "I guess that's Vela's problem," Margit commented, and Anne-Mette burst into a colorful laughter, as though her friend had told us the best joke ever. *It's Béla, not Vela, you damn tool,* I heard a growl inside. Perhaps it was not such a good idea to pick them up. However, as they were prattling, excited over the immense beauty of Sicilian landscapes, that incessant babbling and unfettered love of life they exuded like happy kittens calmed me down. I could see how beautiful they were. Anne-Mette even caught my side-glance that slid down her cleavage, where her two perky breasts were jumping up and down as playfully as little puppies, and smiled unfazed. I would not say her smile was encouraging, not at all, but for certain she did not look disconcerted. Perhaps nothing bad happens to Danes, so they are not well prepared for this world's obscenities. I occasionally glanced in the back mirror at Margit, at her deep blue eyes, and every time I looked up, she gazed back, assessing me. I sometimes think they all have sensors, an ultrared vision, able to see through and constantly gauge the potential danger and the fuck-worthiness of every man they encounter—prey and predators in one at the same time. I felt regret that I was excluded from their world.

Calcutta in Sicily

Enna is in the heart of Sicily, overlooking from its mighty peak—at 931 meters above sea level—the magnificent Dittaino valley we were just passing through. Everyone should get to the Piazza Crispi in Enna and look at the Dittaino and Mt. Altesina on the other side at least once in their life and soak up all that mysterious beauty. Or at least try "Feudo Principi di Butera" wines. I prefer their intense ruby red Syrah. Imbibing the force and soul of Sicily in those great wines might help you better understand its story and the tale of Proserpina. This ancient Roman goddess of the underworld was taken by no other than the very ruler of the underworld, Pluto, from the shores of the Lake Pergusa near Enna. I told Proserpina's story to Margit and Anne-Mette, adding that we should go to the top and perhaps have a bite to eat, a glass of red Sicilian wine, or some such. Even my retarded vernacular I thought belonged to their generation fell flat. Damn, they were difficult customers to please. Or just too smart for me? Try too young, moron. I hope they were not "some such" cold bitches also in sex, or their Danish men have a steep mountain to climb. So, they refused my offer to wine and dine, stating that they had to get to Messina as soon as possible, to meet some friends.

Idiots.

The friends were some "spiritual" people that just came back from India. I mean, really, what's wrong with Western youth? They can't enjoy being prey of the corporate masters at home and pray in cathedrals? *Ego te absolvo* and all that stuff? Do they really need to replace "Amen" with "Om" and churches with shrines as they seek after fake gurus and typhoid fever that sub-continent provides in abundance to those naïve, mostly flat out of their mind spiritual throngs? I guess they were lured by the novelty and mysticism of Eastern religions but lacked enough critical thinking to see the parallels with their own religious heritage. Had they ever tried to deal with Indian IT consultants, they'd know what I meant.

I said something to that effect, a mild inquiry into the Indian obsession so many of them share, also trying to be humorous with the IT remark. Damn. Had I entered any kindergarten, telling the teachers that all kids need to be slaughtered for dog food the reaction would, for sure, have been less hysterical than that of those two blonde angels slash spiritual people slash raging maniacs. Being a white male, I was immediately accused of being a racist based on the color of my skin alone and by even a whiter female. I was also Indophobic. Is that even a phobia?

At first, I laughed merrily; it was funny that nonsensical rabid hysteria in a defense of a sub-continent they visited paid for by the generous Danish social structure, while mingling with other white "seekers." I asked if they cared for the sick and dying in Calcutta in order to repay the country for its generous spiritual guidance they had received and so magnanimously shared with me as they yelled like maniacs possessed? Did they cook for the homeless, perchance? Or at least, did they share some of their famous Danish pastry with them? I was saying that non-confrontationally, with a smile on my face and an occasional chuckle, but I only managed to enrage them further. "Did I know, what British did to India," Margit, a Dane, zealously asked me, a U.S. based Croat in Sicily. She was blissfully unaware what enormous luck and privilege it was for her to be born in such a rich country that enabled her to pontificate to a stranger while insulting him, without even being in danger.

Danger

That thought shifted something in me. "Danger." I remembered Brigitte, another Dane, who had died in the Joshua Tree Park in the United States. Damn, I'd learned to use the language of that murderous country and its "collateral damage" bullshit. No, she did not die just like that; I murdered her in a not entirely dissimilar display of idiotic rage as those two stupid Buddhist zealots are repeating so carelessly and arrogantly in my car. Brigitte was an innocent human being who, unlike these two, begged me to be nice to her. Guilt and rage were such a toxic combo and I felt them both.

"I advise you to be careful with your words," I snapped at Margit.

"Are you threatening me?" she yelled back. Boy, that escalated fast.

"No," I said as calmly as I could, while the well-known whiff of an old rage was back in me. I yet again felt how, from the deep downs of my guts, from the very root of my being, it started to slowly move up. I heard that familiar white rage again roaring in the distance. I tried mightily to contain it.

"I am not threatening, I am just telling you to be careful with your words, nothing else."

"Or else?" she challenged me.

Damn, is she insane? If she keeps insisting…

Mouth Full of Earth

Anne-Mette interjected herself, but she did not try to calm the situation. On the contrary, she poured some more water on the burning oil. "Are you even aware of how threatening you sounded?" she asked me with scorn.

"I-did-fucking-not," I said. The volcano in me was going to erupt. I need to stop this, this way or another.

"You men are all Nazis…" squalled Margit at me from the back seat. Stupid cow blew my stack in that instant. I could not let her keep squalling or I'd poke her eyes out, tear her chest open and eat her heart raw while it still beat, damn idiot. I broke maniacally. The two-tone car swerved like a toy. I almost lost control on that narrow side road, but it abruptly stopped in the middle of it.

"Not a single fucking word more. Not a fucking word!" I squeezed words through my teeth with such maddening hatred while my whole body quivered with rage that those idiotic girls finally got it and shut up. I got out. The damn Mercedes is a big car and, since it had stopped diagonally on the road, it blocked the way. I could not care less. I shook like a pit bull ready to tear apart anyone who dared to cross its path. I turned toward them, those moronic, yapping Chihuahuas and moved forward, filled with such a blind rage that I was certain I was going to break their little necks right there, right then, those fucking stupid idiotic bitches.

"Nazis?" Did they even know what they were babbling about? Margit rushed out from her back seat and was panicking, trying to get Anne-Mette out of her front seat, but she just sat there, aghast, staring at me, petrified. She was frozen and trembling in dread. She got it, but there was so much fear, so much pain in her eyes that it stopped me.

The White Eyes were burning in the skies but did not provide me with any guidance. Unsure what to do, as rage and guilt and grief were tearing me apart, I broke and fell down to my knees with an animal shriek. The birds flew away from nearby trees; their idyll was disrupted by my unnatural scream. I kept screaming to the heavens as I was falling apart, torn asunder by the mayhem in me. I almost killed them, but I did not want to—that is over, I was done and over with myself, but at that moment, I could not control myself. A part of me was losing its mind, eager for their blood, another part was enjoying the drama and the terrified expression on Anne-Mette's face, and yet another part just wanted to die and vanish once for all.

And then, unexpectedly to me as well, I stood up and started running through the green fields of Sicily, beneath the "navel of Sicily" as Enna was called since times immemorial. I channeled Alberto Juantorena, the famous Cuban athlete, and his unrivaled nine-foot stride as I ran. And not only the great Alberto, but also the unnamed protagonist of *Mouth full of Earth* book I read a lifetime ago. As I ran, I started to take off my clothes—they suffocated me. I ran and ran. I threw all my clothing away, then my shoes and my socks, and I kept running naked. My heart was pounding, my breath was shallow, but I feared not that I would die of a heart attack. I wanted to *be over with, this miserable wandering* or to, paradoxically, keep running. It seemed to me only as a cursed Flying Dutchman, always on the move like a shark, I could keep living without being hunted by ghosts.

In that insane run, somehow, it was also freedom. My feet bled, I was sweating so much that the sweat blinded me and, given that I was overweight, both my feet and my knees hurt like hell. I was losing my breath and limping, but I kept running. How to stop? For if I stopped now, where would I be? Where would I go? No one had ever invited me anywhere. Even worse, Charlotte threw me out of what I hoped would be my home. The homeless shelter people and my own country threw me out. Hunted, despised like an eternal homeless man on the Flying Dutchman's steering wheel, I kept running. I ran away from my own life; I ran away from the murder of Anne-Mette and Margit that I would have committed had I not ran. I ran, detaching from my own madness as I ran maddeningly. At the end I drooped as a flabby cock and fell on the ground. There, like in the *Mouth full of Earth,* I started to eat soil and grass and the bugs on them. I called, tried to invoke the spirit of GAIA as I ate her flesh—that fertile, wonderful Sicilian land—but she did not appear.

Who appeared instead were her sons, two nice young guys that ran after me, concerned over my little performance. The taller one, with a fledgling moustache on his gaunt face, was called Giulio. I forgot the other one. They laughed, *"Che bella giornata per correre"* (what a nice day for running), they joked like nothing odd had happened. Giulio handed me my clothing they'd picked up as they ran after me. They missed one of my shoes, but I had another pair in the trunk of my car. We slowly walked back and talked about weather and soccer. No, "Juventus" is not what it had been during Paolo Rossi times. No, "Ferrari" Formula 1 Scuderia is not what is had been. Such a nice young fella, that Giulio. No questions asked about my bonkers behavior or my car left in the middle of the road. They even parked it aside and set the traffic free. Thank you, guys.

When we were back, they made sure I was OK, greeted me and left. God bless Italians, the salt of this Earth, and those hard-core, rugged, no-nonsense Sicilians. I was grateful to them. I was also grateful that Anne-Mette and Margit were also gone. They had been one inch from death, saved by the skin of their teeth, so I hoped they would know how to appreciate life from now on. One day I would write them a letter.

Chapter 29

CHARLOTTE MØRK'S LAST DAY

"Happy girl! If a man ever wins your love, I hope you make him as happy by being everything to him, as you make me by being nothing to me."

Søren Kierkegaard

Svullrya, Norway, December 6, 2018

Alchemically speaking, demons are anti-life, since they have no life of their own. Demons hitch on the living, tear them apart and eat away all that leaks out of it, cackling like hyenas as they feast. The key to understanding these demoniacal vampires among us is to realize that nothing is ever enough for them. You can't satisfy their needs by being good to them or giving them your all. That's why problems with them always escalate. When we do not recognize them as spiritual demons, we might call them psychopaths or sociopaths among us. A bully tortures their partner, beats her up and feeds on her fears, pain and, ultimately obedience coming from the dread she feels all the time, but none of it is enough for the bully, not until he smothers the living life out of her and she becomes a spiritual zombie serving his own depraved soul or, ultimately, until he kills her. Hidden behind the farcical mask of a "spiritual seeker" propagandizing "healing," Charlotte had been like a very active demon, a shark procuring mostly those whose souls, hearts and lives had already bled and were weakened by it. Finely attuned to other's pain, she snuffed them out, like she had with Devansh in India, Donny in the United States, Patrick in Bolivia and me in Europe. She singled us out and chose us like a wolf would an easy prey and went feasting on them. By jumping from one to another Charlotte kept us as a jungle predator keeps its meat "fresh" by playing with it before the final kill.

The carnal nature of our cannibalistic species makes us vulnerable beasts. Our animal lust rules our interaction with the creatures of other gender(s) and we live, burn and die with our inner chaos whose pain we try to heal with so many failed remedies, out of which love is likely the strongest. If you don't believe me, ask Greta Garbo. Nothing can make ourselves stronger than gods but love. And nothing can make our life a living hell like lost, betrayed or false love, which is the same. Like there isn't enough of hell in our daily lives, we complicate and squander our time on Earth with ill-fated partners.

In the *Duchess of Padua* Oscar Wilde, in the Act V, wrote:
DUCHESS
We are each our own devil, and we make
This world our hell.

Jean-Paul Sartre exclaimed, "Hell is other people" to which Claude Lévi-Strauss retorted with, "Hell is ourselves." So there I was, on my way to a small village of Svullrya, Norway, ready for the showdown with the hellish mirror of my own infernos, the woman I loved and hated. It was not going to be a selfie worthy pinky-suck moment, for that I was certain. I was curious to see how she was going to react upon seeing me unannounced. She hated such spontaneities. Not a surprise, given how much meticulous planning must have gone into her insane interactions with four men over the same period, over years.

Antikk Shabby Chink

For no apparent reason whatsoever, I stopped at the quaint old *Ullern Gård* (Ullern Farm) an *Antikk Shabby Chick* (antique) store in Skarnes, north of the river Glåma (Glomma, Norway's longest river) and picked up an old Viking's morning star, a medieval weapon not really often seen in those Norse seafarers' pillaging pilgrimages. Given its cheap price, I doubt it was authentic anyway.

I did not plan to kill Charlotte with the morning star. No, my fantasy was to talk her up to sex, to make love to her for the last time and, as it became love making, grow more and more aggressive and then borderline vicious, to strangle her as I fucked her and fucked the living life out of her.

Fv 401 Road

Charlotte lived in a holiday cabin off of the Fv401 road, a little bit southeast of Svullrya. I pulled over and parked the car on a small lay-by on the road leading toward her house. I killed the lights and sat in the car looking at her cabin. She was at home. It was about 6:00 PM and pitch dark outside. I knew it was the time in which she would be making herself a cup of Darjeeling tea, her daily ritual. She drank that Darjeeling in gallons. I saw her shadow passing by the window and my heart started to race. Really?

Was I so deranged that I still loved or wanted her despite everything? It was not possible. But then, I had that mental image of a mighty redwood tree beneath which we made love one night several years ago in California. No, those were just memories and fantasy narratives still running through me, memories I was soon going to squash with all my hatred. But, damn, again… I was full of shit. At that moment I was not filled with hatred. I stopped and listened inside me. Nothing. Just silence. No one was talking to me, no burst of rage waited to explode. I was calm. I was as calms as the dead.

In fact, truth to be told, I felt like I was already dead inside, dead for a long time, or at least since that day on the Mountain Velebit in Croatia. One last step and *adieu*.

I've Heard That Song Before

I still sat in the car, motionless listening to the music. What did I want from Charlotte? Did I want to talk to her, like so many futile conversations before? Was I really going to do *it*? Or did I want her to tell me that she's sorry? Yes, that might be it, I might have needed her sorry, but why? She was incapable of apologizing; in her world every action she had ever made had a perfectly logical explanation and she stood fully protected by the rigid cage of her righteous beliefs. I did not know if she would even acknowledge that she might have been wrong in her actions. To me she was not only wrong, she was the most violent person I had ever encountered, plastering Ramana Maharshi photos all over her place and taking the spiders she found inside the house back to the outside world notwithstanding.

Non-Violent Communication

Marshall Rosenberg[58] once said, "What could be more violent than a language that implies we have no choice" and, by doing so, "deny responsibility for our actions." And she never had a choice, she claimed, but to run, avoid, babble, find excuses. Rosenberg further explained it by saying: "We deny responsibility for our actions when we attribute their causes to factors outside ourselves: Our condition, the actions of others, authority, group pressure, gender roles, uncontrolled impulses," and that was what Charlotte had been doing all the time, attributing her actions to outside factors.

I was curious if she knew that intimate partner violence was nowadays considered a human right violation. Please, my most cherished reader, place your eyes back into the forward position, for I knew you rolled your eyes upon hearing the murderer's brazen, almost deranged invocation of the "human rights." As you read this, I am dead already, but I did not forget the poor souls I deprived of their own right to live and love, even now as I burn in Hell. That's why I am gone. But I truly wanted to understand how things with one, two poor souls could have gone so terribly wrong.

What was the fatal attraction that brought two damaged people who, instead on going on repairing themselves with golden threads of love went, onto a destructive path?

Kintsugi

In Japan, instead of tossing broken pieces of an object in the trash, some craftsmen practice the five-hundred-year-old art of *kintsugi*, or "golden joinery," which is a method of restoring a broken piece with a lacquer that is mixed with gold, silver, or platinum. Kyoto-based artist Muneaki Shimode explains the *kintsugi*, *"Non-Japanese makers may not realize it, but we practice this philosophy when we see a broken object's potential, when we upcycle, when we repurpose, when we reincarnate an object that would otherwise likely be thrown away."* I asked myself, why don't people use the most precious thread known to men, that of love and repair themselves?

Too late.

---

58   Marshall B. Rosenberg, Ph.D. (1934-2015) founded and was for many years the Director of Educational Services for the Center for Nonviolent Communication, an international peacemaking organization. I do not think anyone got it, how the proper communication in between people might be conducted, as Dr. Rosenberg have. Regretfully, I have lost the language of life and compassion a long time ago.

Anyway, I still could not get out of the car. I had an old e-mail from her printed out with me and I re-read it again. I did not know why.

On Tue, April 16, 2014 at 6:15 AM <charlotte.mørk@yahoo.no> wrote:

> I think we see life and people and relationships and ourselves so differently, it is as if we lived in different worlds. And in each of our worlds our view is true, but it doesn't translate into the other person's world. I love you and you have touched and opened my heart so deeply; and I am in awe of your incredible beauty and I believe in you; I miss you terribly and I want you and want to be with you; I have never had such amazing sex before and I think this was just a taste of what is possible.
>
> xoxo,
> Charlotte

Vintage Charlotte. She knew compliments melted everyone's hearts, so she used them copiously. She also always started with a statement difficult to dispute but left it open. (she should've simply broken up with me if it was "impossible" to ever be "us" as she so believed) This was probably what I was looking for, sitting in the car, a reminder of how she had behaved throughout our miserable journey together. "What is possible" was nothing for she did not want anything. Only that she was too much of a coward to admit it. And she had repeated the same game with the other men she had destroyed by her selfish insanity.

I exited the car and knocked on her door.

Charlotte Mørk

"Puppy," she said, surprised, but added, "I thought you might get in touch after Devansh's post." There was no joy in her eyes, no fear, no hug, no invitation. I guess she would have described it as me "not being unwanted," like once after breaking my heart. I stood on her doorstep, in the freezing cold, not unlike Philip Latinowicz, and observed her. She was haggard and looked very tired. She'd aged. In those ragged clothes she did not look attractive at all—on the contrary. Only those eyes were still burning on her face.

"I guess it is getting cold inside," I said, quite meekly for a killer facing his *demon*. It's a letdown, this showdown.

I must have seen too many Tarantino movies.

"Sure, come on in," she finally invited me. She glanced at the morning star I had in my hand and looked up at me, quizzically.

"An old Viking's souvenir," I explained like an idiot.

"We both know why you are here," she stated matter-of-factly. "So let us just get on with it."

"Shoot!"

"I feel terrible having done this to you."

I said nothing.

"In the end I think what it was is that I was running again and going with fear instead of love. I was really afraid from the first moment I met you that we would have been too different to make this work, but I love you and this hurts like crazy. I can't believe this has happened, and I never wanted to hurt you."

"Are you demented? You were with four of us at the same time..."

"If you don't control yourself, we can't communicate."

I shook my head in disbelief. "Five, six years, over five, six years..." I started my rebuttal but then I myself heard how idiotic I sounded. I wanted to reason with her, to use data of how much we had been separated during the time we "were together." Moron. Nothing I ever said managed to penetrate the rigid cage of her thinking. So I stopped in mid-sentence and asked her a question instead.

"You were saying?"

She gave me a long, silent gaze, pondering. Then she slowly nodded, took a sip of the tea and said: "I have never experienced such a synergy and heightened perception of beauty than I had through you—it's like everything was suddenly bathed in light and a new dimension emerges and the world becomes so much more beautiful and meaningful through your love and the way you see beauty and the way you create beauty through language."

I felt like blood was draining out of my face. She really did not realize the magnitude of her actions? She continued.

"Do you remember how I told you about my LSD trip?"

I nodded.

"It's not that I had much interest in anything before the trip, I kind of liked literature and movies and music and was sort of curious about philosophy, psychology and brain research, but mostly everything seemed a bit pointless and dull and having to be there and go through the motions was a bit of a drag—or a huge drag, depending on my mood."

I felt like I was a traveler in an acid trip. What was she talking about? And why?

"Until then, I'd had a few bad paranoia trips just doing too much pot and wasn't ready for LSD because I was worried of getting stuck in a psychotic state. But at that point, I was so fed up with life that I didn't care anymore. And it turned out to be a marathon trip covering pretty much everything that's possible to experience on substances like this—starting with birth and traumas and tons of other subconscious fears and stuff, then through the religions and cultures and wars and symbols, et cetera, et cetera—up to a point of some kind of death experience which resulted in a total stopping of all movement and an incredible peace. And seeing that my whole world is just mind, there is no time, et cetera."

She took another sip of that stupid Darjeeling tea.

"And coming back after hours of tripping, I felt like what's the point of living anymore now—that's what you are supposed to see when you die, not when you just turned twenty-two. I was totally unprepared for this and for not knowing anymore how to function in this dream again, and it triggered some paranoia that lasted several months, on-and-off, until I met someone who gave me some spiritual books and then it all made sense. But still, it seemed to take the disinterest I had had in life a step further."

"And you are telling me all of this now?" I asked. "And why?"

"I thought you needed an explanation."

Collective Unconsciousness

Whatever was her explanation, it did not reach me. It missed the target. I looked at her somber, thin face, almost completely lost. Was this the woman I loved so deeply and the woman I came here to make her pay for her crimes of killing hearts and souls? And yet, I was standing there, disoriented, like a lost child in a forest. Those crazily beautiful eyes were still burning on her face, but she seemed absent minded. She looked at me like she was waiting for something. I was also waiting for "something," for a message, anything to provide me with some sense into this situation.

"That was an explanation? Your trip, decades ago?"

"What the time has to do with anything?"

"Well, nothing, I guess." She gets me every time.

"I am glad you agree." A hint of her fine sense of irony had not left her yet, I saw.

I stared at her. Should I just turn and leave? At that thought a thorn appeared in my heart and started to pierce it. I remembered the pain, the murders.

"Charlotte?"

"Roman?"

"Do you recall how you used to tell me that you do not have a need for publishing a science work for maybe you're contributing to the collective unconsciousness more this way, by just being? And I guess, thinking?"

"I still think the same."

"Don't you also think the damage you've done to me and the other guys is something we share with the collective unconsciousness as well? And that is our contribution, thanks to you. Moreover, our respective damages we might carry into other relationships, intimate or not, further in life. And then we hurt other people, damage them and the vicious cycle continues?"

"I disagree, but you have a right to your own narrative."

"Fuck the narrative. Devansh relapsed after ten years of being sober and is now a blubbering idiot. Donny is undergoing a sex change after you drove him insane by rejecting him. Patrick killed himself. I have killed several girls, triggered by your deranged nonsense. So kindly stop bullshitting me and take some fucking responsibility for your actions."

"Whom did you kill?" She perked up, genuinely interested.

A growl rose in me. "Charlotte, could you listen for a moment?"

"Sure. But try to be precise in what are you expressing."

I took a deep breath.

"Conscious exaggeration of our pain was pure evil. You have consciously, deliberately laid out a blueprint for harming people—don't you dare to tell me otherwise. Did you read what Devansh had posted? Do you have any idea what you have done to us, to me?"

"It's all just a narrative."

"A narrative? You are a damn psychiatrist. You know, or should have known better than anyone, that deliberately inflicting harm, repetitious inflicting of harm traumatizes and immobilizes people. That's why we were unable to break up with you, no matter how hurt any of us had been. Narrative?" I almost yelled my last words.

"Could you please lower your voice, if you really have to go on with your incessant ramble," she demanded.

Another growl, this time a bit stronger. But I did lower my voice and continued.

"That's the only damn narrative. You locked us in the cages of trauma, painted the walls with phony love to trick us and threw the key away. No one, in our respective lives, could have known that you were doing whatever it was that you were doing to us, deliberately, methodically, like some sort of Dr. Mengele of souls, with the sole purpose of harming us. So, what is that fucking narrative you speak of? What the fuck is wrong with you? Do you have any idea how deranged, damaging it was, what you were doing?"

"I think we see life and people and relationships and ourselves so differently, it is as if we lived in different worlds. And in each of our worlds our view is true, but it doesn't translate into the other person's world," she said. I was stunned, perplexed, stupefied. That was verbatim, what she had written in her e-mail from April four years ago that she sent me from Mallorca, the one I had just read in the car outside.

Word by fucking word.

I used to be greatly impressed by her mighty mind, able to penetrate deeper secrets of living and dying than many others. I admired her intellect even during the worst bouts of depression or hatred. Had I not had prior knowledge of her thinking, I would've thought that she's insane based on this interaction alone. But, while she might have been insane, she knew very well what she was doing. So I, the Idiot, just stood there and looked at her, frozen. "Our capacity to destroy each other is matched by our capacity to heal each other," wrote Charlotte's colleague, Bessel van der Kolk, M.D., so I was positive she was fully aware of that notion. After all, she had used a need for "healing" talk all the time she had been destroying the people she claimed she loved. All of that was beyond my comprehension. I could almost smell brimstone. But since when is an insect, attracted by a carnivore plant's shiny colors and its deliciously smelling nectars, who had fallen prey into its hungry clutches, able to understand why is he being eaten?

"I am tired," she said and sat on the kitchen table chair, observing me.

"I am also tired," I replied. I nodded toward the cocoon beanbag chair in the corner of her cabin, almost ten meters away. "Do you mind if I sit there for a moment?" Had I just asked her for permission? Yes, I had. And she had magnanimously granted it to me.

"No."

A Swim-Float Memory

I sat in the dark room. The only light was in the kitchen where Charlotte was sitting, still sipping on her tea. I looked at her slender silhouette, almost desiring her body. The minutes passed and we said nothing. I was in a haze, dizzy and confused. This was not what I was expecting at all.

But what was I expecting?

Then my mind started to drift away, like I was falling asleep.

With Charlotte present, I acquired a strange sense of seeing and feeling more deeply the world around me, like she was really that conductor, a portal to other dimensions of understanding. I used to have insights, like that one time I felt the animal's pain and fear in the slaughterhouse after I'd eaten a steak. The feeling was visceral, profound and frightening; I'd been that animal for a moment and the pain was beyond belief. I trembled before being butchered to pieces. I'd seen the pain in people's eyes and sensed the sources of their pain. Several encounters I'd had were confirmations of it— the people in such situations were flabbergasted; it was like I knew them better than they knew themselves. Alas, those insights, the talent I might have had did not develop, for Charlotte had always created a new drama and interrupted me until she ultimately ran away and let me cope with abandonment, pain and love e-mails that always ensued after she was gone. And despite everything, it was happening again. I left my body and glided away, far away from Norway, its darkness and its cold, endless winter. Soon after, I found myself floating in the Adriatic Sea, reliving what had happened to me on the tiny island of Mala Rava in June of 2015.

It was a day of The Hanged Man, Number 12 of Trumps in the Thoth Tarot deck, the perfect number, symbol of the Zodiac, 3 x 4, the heavenly three of our three dimensions multiplied by four. There are four rivers to Paradise, that formed a cross from which The Hanged Man hangs. He is a symbol for the turning points in life, showing a need to stop and assess a situation. I felt it profoundly, with all my being, as I meditated over that symbol of transformation. I was ready for it. There was no one on the beach. The sun had not set yet, but it was behind a little hill already and nothing existed but the sea, the clouds and me. There was no other way to put it. I'd entered that primordial placenta, a primeval soup that created all life before life itself. That was a sensation of what they might call surrender or nirvana (or it had been a surrender and nirvana of my own) and it was a moment of pure bliss. I was one with the universe. At moments I could hear my heart beating as I laid motionless on the surface and watched the crystal blue sky above. A swallow or two flew by overhead, a tiny little fishy swum beneath and there I was: no thoughts, no past, no present, no world, just pure being.

As I was one with the universe, with time, with love and life itself, Charlotte and her ethereal being were pulsating in, with, within me, outside in the universe, everywhere in multiverses, inside me and outside her and the sense of love, pure love, was overwhelming. She was my angel and I was her angel, watching over each other, healing each other, gently rocking our bodies on the surface of that ancient, magical sea, being one and all and everything at the same time—it was that kind of love, universal love. I loved Charlotte and she loved me like only God could have loved the first beings the primordial soup had produced, and it was a moment that gave meaning to life.

"Roman."

She startled me. I slowly came back from my swim-float memories into the present. That haggard, lifeless person clinging onto her cup of tea was for sure not someone who ever loved anyone. It took me a moment or two to fully get back to my senses.

"Roman," she repeated.

"Yes?"

"I am tired. I think it is best for you to leave now."

I shook my head in disbelief. She was throwing me out again. For the third time in that same room. I laughed, stood up, nevertheless ready to leave, but then I stopped, like someone who remembered that he had forgotten something important.

Morning Star

As I grabbed my "Viking souvenir," Charlotte glanced at it and looked back at me, gazing straight into my eyes. Her own were burning. As I gazed back at her, her eyes suddenly started to float away and were getting bigger and bigger in that space. And then, through them, I saw Leslie, I saw Brigitte, I saw Viridiana... them floating like ghosts of fate all over the room. Charlotte loved the song *99 Luftballons* by Nena, which popped up in my mind. What a flippant, vapid thought. These girls are dead because of Charlotte, I realized. Even those two guys, the anachronistic hippies from the Velebit Mountain, would not have been hurt if it were not for her. Their faces were blurred but are now getting more and more real as they looked at me.

"Roman," they spoke.

"Roman?" Charlotte spoke.

"What?" I cried out aloud, lost in images popping up all over the room.

"I think you should leave now," said an apparition that used to be the love of my life, my curse and my doom. I started to feel like I weighed hundreds of tons, the morning star in my right hand felt even heavier. I thought I was going to fall down, or have a stroke, a heart attack. I could barely move, trudging like through the mud. I even had problems breathing. But it wasn't mud that was impeding my steps: it was blood. All those girls I murdered in blind hatred for the apparition standing over there were bleeding again. And they spoke to me in my head.

"We are dead, and you are going to let her live?" They spoke in Ulrike's— our unborn daughter—voice.

"Ulrike?" I whispered.

Charlotte was finally moved out of her trance-like state she had been in since I arrived. She came closer to me.

"Did you just call Ulrike?"

She was so close I could smell her, Charlotte. I looked around, at Leslie, at Brigitte, at Viridiana, they were beautiful and terrifying as they bled. But I was searching around for Ulrike. Where were you? I saw the girls all over the place. But not Ulrike. "Where are you, angel? Where are you?"

"Roman," Charlotte came kissably close to me. "Look at me," she demanded, and I turned my eyes at her. I sensed she wanted to know more about Ulrike but then she took a small step back, like coming back from a trance. Her eyes were clear now and she *saw* me. Maybe for the first time since I had arrived. Or for the first time ever? And I saw in those eyes I used to love more than life that she *knew*. Finally, she realized. A spark of understanding and recognition burst into the flame of long lost love and, like in the moment of The Glance, when we first saw each other, the glance was now dying and with it both of us.

And there was no way around it.

Take This With You to Your Collective Unconsciousness

At that moment, I sensed Ulrike nearby and I turned around to see her. She was standing on the doorsteps.

"If you betray me, I will die," she said.

"Not this time," I replied.

I turned back to Charlotte, who stared at me with an unspeakable gaze. She was *ready*, even before I knew what I was going to do next. I did not even raise the morning star. I flung my arm from my hip, in a circular motion she did not even try to avoid, and hit her across her face. The blow crushed her skull instantaneously. She fell silently to the ground, dead before she hit the carpet.

I was enveloped in silence. And then, very slowly, I raised my morning star high above my head and smashed her dead body again. And again. "This is for Leslie." Again. "This is for Brigitte." Again, crushing her body, "for Viridiana," again, broking her bones. Then I hit her unrecognizable face again, and yet again. "This is for Devansh, this is for Donny, this is for Patrick." I was hitting her methodically, pulverizing her body with the precision of a meat-mincing machine. Then I hit her again, really, really hard. "This is for Ulrike."

Then I hit her yet again. "This one is for me."

At the last stroke, I felt that I was suffused with white light. Previously, that signaled that I was losing myself in rage, aggression, madness or Mozart, but this time it was different. It was like calm spirits of our long lost ancestors were embracing me. It was cozy, almost like the white light had approved my final showdown with Charlotte Mørk and its bloody outcome. I was accepted and received.

I wasn't alone anymore.

I was made whole.

See you in Hell

And that was it. Charlotte was finally gone, unable to hurt anyone anymore. I was all bloody as she lied bludgeoned to death next to me, but I could not care less for the mess I created. I sat on her kitchen table and drank from her cup of tea. It was disgusting. I turned my gaze toward the bloody mass on the floor. It reminded me of the dead mouse I almost ate in New York, her guts spilled around her. That mass of bloody, dead meat wasn't Charlotte anymore. She was gone. The woman I lived with in my mind for almost a decade was no more. So, what was next? Nothing, I guessed. I had better be going. I was calm but somehow also gone in the world of the living dead. I had no excuses, being a cold-blooded, premeditated murderer. All that I had left behind after those uncontrollable murders I'd remembered in Toscana after making love to Sophie, was pain, guilt and sorrow.

Sophie, my angel, where were you? I wondered for a second.

I started to quietly weep, tears pouring down my face. Yes, I was a selfish man, so while I wept for Leslie, for Brigitte, for Viridiana, maybe even for Charlotte I created in my fantasy world that I lost, I also cried over my life. I realized I was going to kill myself in the upcoming weeks, but I did not weep over what I was losing in the future that was no more. I cried over the completely fucked up life I had led. The corpse over there was no excuse; I had just let her be my demon. I invoked her and kept invoking her into my ravaged life to finish me off.

I knelt before dead body that used to be Charlotte Mørk, dipped my hands into her warm, velvety red blood and washed my face with it, purifying both of us from our sins. I wanted to cleanse myself, but I couldn't. She was poisonous and I was the same, but even worse than she had ever been.

Our sins will outlive us.

Chapter 30

THE BURIAL

"What if I should discover that I myself am the enemy who must be loved? What then?"

Carl Gustav Jung

Oslo, December 24, 2018

The ultra-secure wing of the Gaustad sykehus hospital was a joke. Not only that in the prison I had three rooms all for myself, but their security was appallingly inadequate, and on Christmas Eve it was even worse. They would not be able to keep a lazy opossum inside had he needed a walk like I did early morning that day. In fact, I had to do a couple of things before I killed myself, so I simply stole a doctor's coat and leisurely walked out of the hospital, and once outside, I flagged a cab. It's interesting how much respect people have for doctors. It was cold, I was scantily dressed, I spoke no Norwegian, but I wore a lab coat and that did it for them. I did not even have to tell the driver that I was a visiting doctor in residency whose luggage was lost by Norwegian Airlines, but I struck up a conversation with the driver, telling him precisely that. Me and my lost luggage story. It always works.

"You know how they are," I said with a smile.

"Ja, ja, de er fryktelige" (they are horrible, doctor), commented the driver, full of understanding. It was nice to be a doctor and not a patient for a change. I liked it. I had no worries anyone would recognize me; the media frenzy over my capture—surrender, rather—had waned since the start of the month and, unlike the serial killer guy from photos the newspapers were

plastering all over their front pages, I now had a beard, longer hair and was a respectable doctor.

"To Dressmann XL, vennligst, please," I requested politely. I needed to buy a few winter thingies.

The Mission

I also needed to snail-mail my *Chronicles* to Trygve E. Wighdal, a lustful Jesuit priest friend of mine back from times when we both lived in Paris. We were prowling the streets of the city of love and lured many an innocent looking girl into our horny nests. I recall how once we went to Germany, to visit The Basilica Church of St. Ursula in Cologne, Germany, where the bones of 11,000 virgins are arranged in beautiful patterns. Some girls we met in the train went with us on our unholy pilgrimage, and in that holy place, insisted on doing inexpressibly lecherous things together there—perverted sluts, madly aroused by his collar. Ah, those were the days... forgive me for being nostalgic on the penultimate day of my life. I did not trust the hospital administration, and for sure not the police, that they'd grant my wish and give it to him. So I had to do it myself.

More importantly, I needed to give a proper burial to my mother's Little Music Box.

Lake Movatn

It was a very cold day, around -10°C (14°F) but it was an easy stroll to the post office next to the Ullevaal soccer stadium for I have purchased a nice men's winter parka jacket and was quite warm in it. It feels nice to stroll outside, a man on the mission. Once outside the post office, it did not take long before one prudent woman left her BMW 5 Series running so it would stay heated as she rushed into the post office. I blush to admit, but I, ever a Mercedes man myself, stole that Bavarian car and drove to the nearby Lake Movatn. It's a small lake, but a short ride or walk from there is a wonderful Steinsdalsfossen waterfall with a romantic pedestrian path underneath. You can walk the path below it and stay dry. It is a very popular tourist destination that I once had visited with Charlotte, but I assumed it would not be that busy on that cold morning of Christmas Eve day, and I was right. I was almost alone there, so I passed beneath the murmuring purls of the waterfall unmolested by the throngs. The waterfall had not been frozen yet, so I stood beneath it and enjoyed the sights and sounds of nature for a while and then went into the woods.

The terrors of the forest, like all panic terrors, are inspired, Jung believed, by fear of what the unconscious may reveal. This is a notion that haunted me since the day in Lika, when I was maybe only a six-year-old, in which a bear chased me and my family from our picnic area. We ran for our dear lives as the big brown beast ran after our car. Since that day, I was always a bit trepidatious in the forests. I was always on the lookout for bears, even now during their winter hibernation. But I bravely walked into the forest, for I needed to find a place to bury my mother's Little Music Box. I could not let it fall in the hands of the "authorities."

I found a small plateau on the hill not far from the Steinsdalsfossen where a wonderful lone cherry tree slept her winter dreams. Back home we had a small, wounded, crooked but indestructible cherry tree that grew seemingly from the asphalt and, when the spring came, it had always blossomed at least two weeks before any other flowering trees. My mom loved that funny little tree (it never grew bigger) a lot. So it seemed a perfect place to lay her Music Box to rest—beneath another cherry tree.

"Nevermore"

I dug a hole in the soil with some effort. It was frozen, but I had a small shovel all Norwegians carry in their cars and that had helped me to dig faster. Once I was done, I wound the Little Music Box's revolving cylinder and let it play for the last time. When I put the Little Music Box in the hole I dug, and, covered it with soil while it still played, my heart broke. For forty-six and a half years, I had carried that little box with me all over the world, but now the Raven was telling me, with finality, "Nevermore."

When that tune that had been with me for all my life stopped playing, the world had also stopped moving for a moment. It was all over for me. However, for one blissful, undeserved moment of respite, I did not feel that I was a horrid monster, an insane murderer who had spent his life suffering, wasting it and, ultimately destroying it. For a moment, I was just a young boy whose mother had died. For the second time on that brisk, freezing Christmas Eve in Norway, a land so far away from all the others I'd hoped would be my home, the home I never found, she had died again and left the boy to wander alone and lost forever. I wanted to hug the twelve-year-old boy in me, the boy that stood on her grave on the day of her burial, and tell him that everything would be OK, but I could not lie again. I kneeled, my head drooped onto the miniature knoll, the Box's grave and a thought occurred. Perhaps I should just stay there, sit under the cherry tree and the Little Music Box resting place and die of cold? It would be fast; all I'd need to do is to take the jacket off? I entertained the idea for a moment, for that was it; nothing held me to the world I had soiled with my heinous crimes.

"Thud!" I heard.

I looked around, no, there was no one coming.

"Thud!"

Again? Only at the third "Thud!" did I realize it was the sound of the soil hitting my mother's coffin. I shivered. I heard the sounds like I was buried in the coffin with her. And as I looked up, yes, I was in the coffin, for I saw myself crying above, next to my father as we were both throwing clumps of soil on the coffin. Jesus, I had never seen so much pain on a human face before. My father kept his tears at bay, still gripping at my shoulder as if for dear life, but he was an image of a totally devastated man. I had never seen him like that, for I remembered how during the funeral, I never looked at him.

A Little Boy

Those thuds and the surreal feeling of me being in my mother's coffin—I did not feel her next to me, I was alone in that transparent coffin while I was burying myself—felt like a relief. So strange, usually I was a bit claustrophobic, but as I was saying farewell to my dad, after I bid a farewell to my mom as well and was leaving myself, I felt calm despite what seemed to be me being buried alive. I had been dying, but that was the end I had been hoping for since that moment in the Boschi in which I had *remembered*. I was still kneeling, with my head touching the Earth as I listened to the thuds. It felt like my heartbeats were ticking down their last, and deservedly so. The soil that I had kept throwing at the grave where I had lain started to obscure the sight. As I looked up, I did not see anything anymore. The thuds become stronger, but duller, those were the sounds of soil being shoveled over the coffin. I was still calm, ready to go.

Then, in that moment I saw, or rather, I felt a movement in me. I looked deeper and I saw the familiar White Eyes staring back at me but, for the first time, I did not fear them and their power. Instead I saw something else, someone else behind those burning eyes that usually provoked dread in me.

What was going on? What was that? Rather, *who* was that?

"Ulrike?" I was being buried alive and I did not want her to die with me. No, I saw it wasn't her. I strained to see better what was going on in the hidden depths of my soul when I saw—or more sensed—two other small eyes peeking behind the huge shadow with the White Eyes. Who was that?

"Who are you?" I asked the innermost part.

Nothing happened for a few moments that felt like several eternities and then, to my astonishment the White Eyes stepped away. Only two, I could saw clearly, little frightened eyes were left inside and looked at me, fixedly, not blinking.

"Who are you?" I asked again. But I already knew.

The little boy moved from the shadows. That was me, three and a half years old, lonely and frightened.

Elohim Gibor

My inner world had been illuminated in one sudden burst of understanding. My being was brightening by light and it felt like the Tree of Life burned in me. But what really burned was on the right side, where the Sephirot Five, the "Judgment" stood. The little me, the three-and-a-half year old, glanced toward that part of me, looking for solace. Or was that his protection? Do the White Eyes in me belong to Elohim Gibor, "the mighty God, punishing the sins of the wicked," which I had written in one of my screenplays?

No, all that goes back to Peter. "And God will open wide the gates of heaven for you to enter into the eternal kingdom," but I was not religious. I used a morsel of religion here, a crumb of alchemy there in my writing, nothing too deep, more tropes, or rhetorical devices that had helped me convey the message. And while I did not believe Elohim Gibor or Jehovah or any other God or Devil had appeared in me, I was sure of the presence of the little boy who did not want to come closer or talk. Did he even know how to talk at all?

As I pondered all of that, a flood of memories overwhelmed me. When I was that age, my parents sent me to my granny Kate for the summer holidays. Or was it winter? It must have been the summer—I was born in April. Then, I saw the day in which my mother came to pick me up.

I did not recognize her.

I hid behind my granny, not knowing that strange woman who called my name. I saw her just then. She crouched down, her face distorted in pain—her own son did not recognize her.

"Roman, angel, don't you know who I am?" She was on the verge of tears.

She opened her arms, inviting me in a hug. My granny told me to embrace my mother, but I did not know my mother.

She had left me.

She sent me away.

She abandoned me.

She did not love me.

I do not know her.

A few moments later, when she looked like her heart would break, I finally recognized her and ran into her arms. "Mommy," I exclaimed, and we both started to cry. But, and I know that now, as I kneel on my own Norwegian grave, the little abandoned boy stayed in me and never came back. When he ran to hug my mother, a part of him had detached and stayed inside. That part was not in that hug, not anywhere. That part was a seed from which the primordial "entity" in me was conceived in that moment of "abandonment." It became a part of the little child that had never had a chance to grow up, a child that wasn't even aware of himself, an "entity" that suffered, wandered in the dark, eternally terrified, perpetually lonely. It was so obvious to me now why my life had been that of a homeless wanderer who had suffered all over, the world reflecting the pain of that little child in me. When my mother died, I was twelve years old, but the real Abandoned Little Boy, that three-and-a-half-year-old child had gotten a final confirmation that he had, indeed, been abandoned for good. He was the Abandonment Entity, not the twelve-year-old as I had previously thought. Of course I could not, I did not remember my mother. I understood now why I had forgotten her almost completely. Three-and-a-half-year-olds have hardly any memories.

I was never there for him to help him remember. I had let him alone in that darkness. He had created Ulrike, so that "If you betray me, I will die" message weren't her words. Those were the words of my little self that I never knew existed.

The Praetorian Guard

The final truth dawned on me as clear as day. Abandoned by everyone, primarily by myself, the Little Boy had not only created the Abandonment Entity that ruled my life, but he had also created the White Eyes, the Protector, the Praetorian Guard always on duty. I knew with every fiber of my body that the little child had created the White Eyes to protect *me*, since I failed to protect *him*. The White Eyes were created and sent into my life by the three-and-a-half-year-old for it was evident to him I was not going to help us. And, because he was so frightened of women and all the pain they inflicted on me/us, he was determined never to let me become vulnerable to their manipulations and the suffering they had inflicted on me/us ever again.

The White Eyes grew stronger and stronger, the only real man in us, the only one with the guts and might to defend us all, and soon after, he had started to act independently in order to protect us. I was unable to do it, and the little child had no power, so the White Eyes acted and had killed everyone who resembled Charlotte and her behavior for he thought that they were going to harm and hurt me like she did.

That was a shattering revelation.

Had I not betrayed the lonely, abandoned little child in me and had I looked for him, nothing of what I told you in these *chronicles* would have happened. Leslie, Brigitte, Viridiana, even Charlotte would still be alive. The hippies, Henrik Olaf and Per Lund would also be alive, happily hitchhiking all over the world.

I would have never neglected a lost child on the street, not even a forlorn puppy. I always loved old grannies, puppies and little kids. In fact I would've died if my life was needed to save a child and yet, I had abandoned the forsaken, frightened little child in me. I never searched for him, I never looked inside and had never given him the help and love he had so desperately needed. I betrayed him. I asked myself, as I was kneeling on my soul's grave, if I was capable of betraying the child and therefore capable of betraying myself, why did I bother living?

To that, I have no answer.

THE AFTERWORDS

"If you betray me, I will die."

Ulrike B.

Paris, December 31, 2018

On that festive but cold, sunless Christmas of 2018 in Norway, Roman did not kill himself with the gun; he slit his own throat, slicing through the thyroid cartilage of the larynx and severing both of his carotid arteries, leaving behind only the letter "H" gruesomely written, rather drawn, in his own blood on the desk.

I wondered, why had he lied in his otherwise truthful *Chronicles* and almost chirpily wrote about the bullet that "mercifully" bore through his head, killing him instantly? I guess his flair for dramatic exits overpowered his devotion to purity of expression and accuracy, so it carried him away into yet another of his fantasy-induced episodes. It would not be the first neglect of authenticity by Roman; while I have taken vows of both poverty and chastity in service to Christ and am an ordained priest, he kept mocking me about copulating in various scenarios his restless mind kept inventing. Philipp G., his friend from Berlin, once said: "Roman was an excellent mixture of being polite, provocative and alienesque at the same time," and that explains a lot.

Assembling my acquaintance's murderous chronicles was a daunting but also a deeply personal task. My father had died after a long struggle with Alzheimer's disease. What most horrified me throughout his illness was to witness how his once prodigious mind (he was a physics professor) had been vanishing bit by bit and how it had been replaced by dementia. While there aren't many parallels with the loss of cognitive abilities that had stricken my father and Roman's cold, often calculated madness, mulling over the profound personality changes in those two men was enough to make this editing process even more painful.

I struggled with the very idea of publishing Roman's *Chronicles*. I could've just given it to the police to help them discover the remains of those unfortunate girls and bring a closure to the bristling dread their families suffered daily and stopped there. But then, his murders were in all the media so he had become a household name, almost as notorious as Peter Sutcliffe or Edmund Kemper in their times of horror. Roman confessed to his murders, but at first denied any knowledge of the remains' locations due to amnesia. That was a sick game he did not write about in his *Chronicles*. It's not that I would be giving him some special attention by publishing this tome. He had killed himself after all and, as he already lies dead interred in an unmarked grave somewhere in Norway, he would not have derived any benefits from this publication whatsoever.

Moreover, his *Chronicles* might be helpful for the students of human nature—my blood curls at the thought that I'd unconsciously just quoted Roman—it might indeed help someone somewhere to recognize what she or he is facing, either from the depths of their own soul or to detect a danger from without. Truth be told, I just wanted to get it over with it as soon as possible. Then, like in some contrived Hollywood plot, just minutes before the manuscript was to be sent to print, I received a note from Dr. Anja Sønstebø, Roman's first psychiatrist in Oslo and, almost at the same time, an e-mail from no one else but "his" Sophia. Both messages struck me like a thunderbolt. As I, on this New Year's Eve of 2018, sit in my small room, in a building adjacent to the Saint-Étienne-du-Mont church in Paris, a week after his suicide, I still struggle to finalize this book as soon as humanly possible and move on with my life. His letters had somehow helped me to get over my troubles, speed up the process of editing, and finally I am done with this burdensome task.

At least we have a direct juxtaposition of ways in which he dealt with women in his life. To witness firsthand the tender love toward Sophie, which he expressed in over the top maudlin tones, and then compare it to the strange letter written for "Anne-Mette and Margit" and addressed to the "Kingdom of Denmark" in which he expressed thinly veiled regret that he hadn't murdered them (he implies another murder but the person mentioned in his letter is not a real one—the police had checked it) and his maddening hatred toward Charlotte was a sight to behold. I decided to finish the book without further comments of my own by quoting both e-mails from Dr. Sønstebø and Sophie to me and by enclosing those three aforementioned Roman's letters.

I replicate them in their entirety henceforth:

On Tue, Dec 31, 2018 at 9:27 AM <anja.sønstebø@medisin.uio.no> wrote:

> Dr. Wighdal:
>
> We made a startling discovery – Roman's somehow bizarre, handwritten letters. One to Charlotte (dated a day after she has died, murdered by him), hidden in his coat's lining and another quite unhinged threat to the girls I do not recognize from his files (but he must have met them in Sicily) – so I thought it may be of help to your work. A transkripsjon of the letter is enclosed.
>
> In sympathy,
> Dr. Anja Sønstebø

Sophie Bauffremont-Barbançon's, Roman's "beloved" Sophie, e-mail arrived nine minutes after Dr. Sønstebø's.

On Tue, Dec 31, 2018 at 9:36 AM <sophie.b-b@gmail.com> wrote:

> Dear Trygve. I am Sophie. You maybe heard about me. I met Roman earlier this year, during my summer vacation in Tuscany. He wrote me a letter and asked me to give it to you. I am confused. But he sounded serious. So I am sending you his letter.
>
> Cordialment,
> S.

Roman's letter to Charlotte

Charlotte Mørk
Address: HELL

December 24, 2018

Nomen est omen. The name Mørk was the sign of darkness you carried in your already dead heart, but I was blinded by my love first and then by your deceptions second, since day one. I hadn't seen the obvious. Well then, you didn't either, you "did not see this coming," did you, you sick fuck? How many times you said, "I did not see this coming?" Let me help you: **EVERY TIME** you shattered us completely and threw me completely off the rails. You also had no idea you will burn in Hell, bludgeoned and hurled to there by a man you fake-loved? You yourself turned the same man who truly loved you into a monster with your demonic influence but still had the gumption to fake surprise that this happened. A small wonder you chose a profession the Urban Dictionary defines as "a practice of torturing, abusing, insulting and degrading other beings. A gigantic multi-billion dollar industry of death," i.e. psychiatry.

I hope there's a place, among Seventh (Violence), Eighth (Fraud) and Ninth (Treachery) circles of Hell (all of which perfectly depict your degenerate soul) for Hypocrisy that describes your sickening behavior to a tee.

The greater a hypocrisy, the more invisible it becomes. Your habit of running away supported the hypocrisy: you've been creating endless dramas (for "us"), recurring false resets (again for "us") and in all that messy hysteria you have been feeding your rotten soul with, you never allowed me to breathe, to rest, to calm down and to, in that calmness, see you for what you were: a selfish, hypocritical monster. You were playing your sick ruse with naïve men like myself all over the world, unmolested by our pain that you had created over and over again. Well, you won't be hurting anyone anymore anytime soon.

Upon further reflection, I realized that you were also a bully. Even some redneck that gets drunk and beats his wife bullshits "I love you," and explains himself with "I am like that." Alas, you have been even worse than a simple bully; he or she has moments of remorse; they are capable of saying: "I am sorry" when they feel guilty and ask for forgiveness, but not you. As a heartless vulture, rather as an emotionless vampire, you feast upon the living and destroy everything and anything that has love, light and life in it.

You spent your miserable life so self-absorbed that it seems you believe in the garbage you spew out like in that nonsense, when you claimed that it is you who suffer more, after casually breaking someone's heart, more than those you harmed ever so deeply? The bully suffers more than the woman whose bones he crushed and whose spirit he has broken? Can anyone be more dishonest, more deranged, more selfish that that?

That was a long-lasting puzzle to me. How come you've never ever said you're sorry for the outcomes (mostly pain in others) provoked by your behavior; how come you never took any responsibility for deep wounds you've been inflicting on others?

Then it dawned on me: über-selfishness like yours does not even recognize other people but through the distorted prism of your own lunacy. For you, anyone else, their lives, feelings, choices are only to be used and, at best, subjects of mild mockery and/or, more often, of disregard. In reality, unlike a simple bully that has moments of humanness and vulnerability in him, you never give a fuck about anyone else. Others are irrelevant unless they serve to feed you, but only in doses you prescribed.

Imagine how it would look if I were using your prescription. "I killed all those women only after they triggered hidden mines you planted all over my soul," and *voila*! I could now say I never saw that coming. It was their fault as much as it was mine. We are all equally guilty, let bygones be bygones and let us keep on going with our merry lives.

If burning in Hell is merry. You tell me.

Killing them was my language!

Killing those women was the only message that could penetrate your deranged mind; your regurgitated delusions; your callous lies. Killing them was my **PERPETUAL** message for you as much as bludgeoning you was my **LAST** message to you. The only one I could put across, the only one left to be bestowed upon you. Otherwise you wouldn't listen. You never listened to anyone or anything but to your own preconceived, quasi-spiritual garbage. I guess that dirt heap, your holy Arunachala hill did not contribute enough of its blessing into the collective unconsciousness. The sound of your crushed skull that sent you away was the only good thing coming from your rotten being, ever.

Killing them also meant killing **YOU** all over again because you deserved to die all over again, day after day and then once again and again and again and yet again with every breath you take in Hell and then again and again, in a perpetual Groundhog Day-like dying. You were the real black hole. No wonder God damned you back to Hell, you selfish, manipulative, phony piece of shit, forever.

Your Monster Child

This Hatred is what you conceived during mind games you played as you fucked around the world and lied to me and all of us endlessly. You were bullshitting and hurting me all over again, planting the seeds of rage in me. You did not want my children, but you had borne one anyway. This bastard son, the Hatred conceived in the bloody vortex of your deceptions now burns with you in Hell. For yes, only a hateful demon could have treated me, and the others, with such a callous disregard, hurting us in perpetuity, as you have, no one but a demon.

The Hatred reflects on how you trod on the others like a scumbag would, how you stomped on their feelings, their love, their lives as a murderer would. The Hatred lives as a monument to your disgustingly choreographed aikido movements you always used to shift the focus, never letting anyone see you, to see through you, to see the true nature of your grotesque, manipulative, degenerate selfishness. I hope the Hatred will, as you suffocate in Hell, feast on your dead heart daily.

No amount of dirt heap's phony spiritual pretentiousness or "sacred" fucks in the trailer trash parks where you went to feel "better" and more "superior" than anyone else would have ever given you a respite from the Hatred you carry in you, dead or alive. The monster child, your own Hatred, is there to stare at you with black, dead eyes reflecting your dead, black heart as it is eaten away.

The Hatred will also be there to stalk you and to hate you back, for you've given birth to pain and suffering to many, hidden behind that "I tried" delusional garbage, hidden behind the mantra of "poor me suffering *more*" than anyone else, especially those you directly hurt. Look at those dead eyes you have created, look at them carefully and in them you will see your rotting soul. I myself am living in the world I liberated from your damned presence and, unlike K. who thought the "shame would outlive him" as he was finished off like a dog, I am more like Caligula who, despite being stabbed to death by you, yells defiantly, "I am still alive."

Yes, you sick fuck, I am still alive while you will rot in Hell, forever.

Roman's letter to Anne-Mette and Margit:

L'CHAIM (for ladies only)

"I'm the most cold-hearted son of a bitch you'll ever meet."

Ted Bundy

Anne-Mette & Margit von Sicily
Address: Kingdom of Denmark

24 December, 2018

Roman L.
Tøyengata 15
Grønlands Torg
0190 Oslo, Norway

L'chaim!

To life ladies, to the gift you were undeservedly given by Pluto under the cliffs of Enna, a gift you ought to learn to appreciate in all of its bloody glory unless you want it slip away through your dilated pupils just before you're murdered on the way to Cairo. One place to die is as good as another, so instead of Cairo, you can fill in the blanks and put Paris or Taj Mahal, Aokigahara forest or Beirut or whatever pleases your gargantuan needs for romance in its stead.

A pulchritudinous librarian, Caitlin Brennan, once, as I was slowly unbuttoning her ridiculously old-fashioned silky skirt, goggled at my erection and uttered words that have outlived her: "just fucking fuck me already." You both, dear Anne-Mette and Margit, not unlikely dear Ms. Brennan once has, think mainly about the same, but are too much of hypocritical, self-righteous pussies to admit it.

> But please, please just fuck me already. Honestly, I appreciate your thoughtfulness. I like that you want to take things slow. I can totally get behind the idea of emotional connection, but dearjesusinheaven, FUCK ME. We've done dinner and drinks. We've gone dancing. We've cuddled and watched a movie. I'm

wearing a low cut shirt and you've been staring at my breasts
all night. Goodgodalmighty, get to it and fuck me. [59]

You live in a retarded age, my fair, well too often unfairly unfucked
ladies of the Kingdom, in sickly times that have seen swashbucklers replaced
by timid stroller pushers. Swords by iPhones. Intimacy by Facebook. Also,
the feminine ideal of physical beauty and attractiveness, in you ladies, has
been superseded by hoodies and pretentious "seeking" for higher truths.

Ego te absolvo a peccatis tuis...

The absolution I am offering you herein is, truth to be told, included
for comical effects. Forgive my joke but I know you fear dying in Cairo,
at least I am sure I saw in Anne-Mette's eyes that she fears. So I want to
lighten your load before the truth is unloaded onto your tiny shoulders. Call
me generous if you wish but I am only a humble purveyor of truth many
refuse to see, much less allow themselves to accept. For see, you're not in fact
absolved from any blame for the overwhelming societal castration of male
power that was going on in the beginning of the 21st century. You—average,
privileged Western ladies of your era—are unlike Victorian ghosts whose
sexual appetite was matched only with that of a succubi, chiefly flat out of
your mind. You try to ascribe a diagnosis to and describe a prescription for
any normal human condition, especially that of a desire for your flesh.

"They shall be two in one flesh" (Genesis 2.24) is an ancient blueprint
you refuse to build upon as you "focus" on your "spiritual search" careers,
despite all likelihood that it's just another soul eating "bullshit job" that
defines you.

Unsolicited Advice on Cock Fucking Honesty

You remind me of another Scandinavian—Lisbeth was her name.
She was from Stockholm and managed to turn a sumptuous, divine, rather
orgiastic dinner with a choice of wine that would make Caligula blush we

---

59   Originally posted on Craigslist on 2008-02-03 @ 03:29PM "Just fucking fuck me,
     already. (Seattle)" post mirrors your own thinking. So stop pretending, and as you read
     the post in its entirety, be honest with yourselves and admit: you want to be fucked. You
     always want to be fucked, no matter how political correctness or moral majority would
     frame your need "for love," "for family," for bombing Iran, for whatever, no matter what
     you just want to be fucked.

shared in Toscana once into a funny, albeit shocking parade of insults and insanity. (Her, aimed at me, quite loudly I might add: "Why don't you want to fuck me, you stupid, arrogant bastard. I love you. You disgust me," all in one, likely a 5.00 mg/L, breath.) What's wrong with you people?

As you told me before you ran amok in Sicily, you require of your men to be filled with tender understanding of your needs, a need "to be who you are," a need to be seen "as you are" (and accepted as such) but when they want to fuck you, you call it male aggression, presuming the libido is not the energy of life itself but rather some sort of mental illness that needs to be treated with utmost care and disgust until it's healed. At the same time you're not allowing men to be "who they are," it is the privilege you want only for yourselves, it seems. I imagine flaccid cocks as the ideal of the future you'd like to see.

But, fucking fuck girls, you're such a tangled mess as you live in a spiritual and an intellectual jam of your own making. And yet you dared to call an unknown man a "Nazi." You're an emotional and a hormonal mess and you have no clue who you are, who you had been 'til this point in time or who you might become in any of the futures in front of you. This is not damnation from an unmarked grave of a cursed man, there's the whole weight of scientific facts behind it. The whole humankind is just a cosmic joke in a vast sea of dark matter we do not even understand. A 90% of all that is in the whole vast universe is a deep secret even the brightest among us are not even close to comprehending. One hundred billion neurons in your brain match the number of stars in the Milky Way Galaxy. Multiplying your hundred billion neurons times 40,000 synapses is equivalent to the brain having more connections in it than there are stars in the whole universe.

So how anyone could "see you for who you are," damn it? However, you do not hesitate to keep insisting on bullshit and keep castrating your men with your superficial needs, as though you know what they are while the only real need is that of your genes, a basic biological need to procreate, that of a clear-cut fuck. Bullshit did not pan out too well for "my" *Bergmannstraße Demon*—you might agree with me on this if on nothing else—so it might not have panned out too well for you either.

Think about it as you thank Pluto, Thor, Shiva or *Det Radikale Venstre* (even though *Alternativet* might suit you better I think) for your life—it's a miracle you got away after spewing such garbage.

And if you, a sophisticated urbanite cringing over my insistence that all you really need is to fuck, let me share a secret with you: I'm dead! I have no genetic need to procreate any more. I do not need to seduce you with the sweet bullshit you crave in order to feel appreciated and for me in order to deploy my spermatozoids in an attack on your ovums. But, if I were alive and you were sitting next to me in a bland, phony, friendly but safe "Starbucks" as you sipped on one of your twenty-seven variants of coffee, I would, speaking of the same need to fuck, engage in playing your game and would have disguised the truth the best I could, neatly wrapping it up in some politically correct, spiritual balderdash your cock-losing generation loves so much. If you had been "seeking" some sort of "spiritual truth(s)" in India, I might have talked about the demon Kali, *Kali Yuga,* and about *Sahityadarpana* using a quote— "humans engage in activities only for their external fruits"—as a segue into, first, praising how unique your internal needs are, and second, into your pants so fucking you would suddenly be oh so different than the fucking of every other horny rabbit out there.

You are indeed special, and I will love you to death.

Ted Bundy School of Thought

A final word of caution. *"In spite of all the destruction he has caused around him, I still care what happens to Ted. I have come to accept that a part of me will always love a part of him. He is no longer a part of my day to day life, though,"* wrote Elizabeth Kendall in her memoirs, *The Phantom Prince: My Life With Ted Bundy,* displaying a perfect image of female derangement syndrome (FDS). If you'd allow yourself to be chased by the FDS, you're going to be prey for your delusions as much as for bad men for the rest of your days.

Do not enter a beige VW only if the guy is handsome and you "feel" that you might love a "part of him" afterwards. Suck on any cock as it is your last for it very well might be, whether you're destined to "happily ever after" live or die.

Roman's letter to Sophie:

Sophie Bauffremont-Barbançon
14 Rue Voltaire (deuxième étage, #9)
44000 Nantes
France

24 December, 2018

Roman L.
Via Alexander Nelson, 27
Erice, 91016 Erice TP
Sicily, Italy

Sophie, my beloved,
Now you already know, kiddo…
Every time I think of you, *mon chérie* Sophie (you are safe to assume that I think of you all the time), I have the most wonderful flashbacks. A scent of the Tyrrhenian Sea in which I first float-kissed you overwhelmed me with sweet memories. My heart skips a bit every time I re-live imbibing heavenly honey from your lascivious, cherry lips and feel your ambrosial tongue in my mouth. A miniature stingray just swam by and I giggle just like a little kid would. Do you recall how that tiny thingy startled you on the magical day of our eternal embrace? The sun had not set yet, but it was already behind a little hill towering *La Baracaccina* restaurant where we had a sumptuous *l'orata in crosta di sale* with your musician friends. Angus Dei, you light of the world.

You were so different from everyone else. The small Oxum tattoo on your left ankle attracted me as much as your pearly teeth. It sounds like a cliché, I know, those hackneyed "pearly teeth" but even your teeth aroused madly desire in me. Your husky voice of seduction, your natural kindness, your bemused glances, your vertiginous greyish-green eyes with velvet flecks; everything about you was special.

And **badaboom!** suddenly nothing else existed but you; then the two of us, the sea and our love. We were like Ares and Aphrodite in the net of sweet lust and tender love. You liked when I quoted from literature or movies, so here it goes: *"Just like a murderer jumps out of nowhere in an alley, love jumped out in front of us and struck us both at once! The way lightning strikes, or Finnish knife!"* said Master about his and Margarita Nikolaevna's love in Mikhail Bulgakov's sensational, incandescent novel, *Master and Margarita*. But I tend to believe Woland, the devil himself, would have known more about us, for I loved you even before I met you.

After I kissed you, not only had the outside world vanished for that moment but for the first time in my life I knew—in the core of my heart, in the deepest depths of what they call soul—that I loved you unconditionally. And that that you unconditionally loved me. No requirements, no demands, no expectations, just pure love woven into one single heartbeat we shared.

I was one with the world as time stood still; one with love and life itself; one with you while your angelic, ethereal being was pulsating within me. Everywhere in all the multiverses we inhabit, the sense of pure love was overwhelming. I loved an angel and an angel loved me. What else should anyone ask from life?

...

You were (are) not "just" the most gorgeous girl I have ever met; you are also an extraordinary virtuoso. If we are nothing but tunes in the vastness of space, you are the master of cosmic humming, those melodies permeating our universe. The viola comes alive in your angelic hands. You invoke his spirit and revive Mozart every time you play his *Violin Concerto No. 5 in A Major*. Or even Paganini *Caprices*. (no. 24 still awaits you, I know) Not even *Suggestion Diabolique* by Prokofiev scares you. The bravery of your heart comes on the wings of your music. You are indeed unique. Ah, how I wished to have been Niccolò Paganini and played with you. Alas, I am just a simple man, unworthy of your love.

"Art is a kind of innate drive that seizes a human being and makes him its instrument. The artist is not a person endowed with free will who seeks his own ends, but one who allows art to realize its purpose through him. As a human being he may have moods and a will and personal aims, but as an artist he is "man" in a higher sense— he is "collective man"— one who carries and shapes the unconscious, psychic forms of mankind," wrote C.G. Jung and that describes you perfectly. You are a human in a higher sense.

The universe you grace with your seraphic presence is a symphony of strings, as Kaku says. *Laudate Dominum* because you came out of the mind of God as her music resonates through time and space.

...

Even though, as I write you this letter, I listen to the magical *Clair de Lune* piano piece by Claude Debussy you introduced me to, I do not want to dwell on the past or on my love for you any longer. My eyes are misty when

I realize those are *I tempi passati* that are not coming back. *C'est la vie, ma chérie* Sophie. Regardless, I want you to fully understand that **YOU WERE NEVER IN ANY DANGER**, never!! You were always loved, you were always safe. I will always love you. I also want you to understand my motivation for acting so abrasively and why I chased you away from our little love hill barely a few moments after making love to you and in such an abrupt, rude manner. Before I met you, I was drowning in hate, self-hate and madness that made me kill.

But since the very moment I first laid my eyes on you and during every heartbeat I spent with you, I'd totally **FORGOTTEN** who I was: a monster whose name will forever be smeared in ignominy. I was completely, truly oblivious of my past deeds when I was with you. I am not a split personality, but with you I was like a different person. The other "me," the monster filled with hatred, the demon that murdered every time its deepest pains were triggered went away. Not for a single moment of being with you—I knew who I (also) was.

Once the ecstasy was over, I looked at the sprinkled stars of your velvety eyes with love and tenderness. Suddenly, the truth hit me like a ton of bricks. Out of the blue, I was overwhelmed with the sensation of dread: I remembered!! As I stood in front of that pulsating image of perfection— your naked body—I was immersed in dreadful images of lifeless bodies I left behind. They floated all around me, torturing me with their cries. I could've heard their weeping, their last breaths as they begged for life for the last time, I felt their warm blood on my hands. And all those eyes that were dying in front of mine were there, in the air, haunting me.

I cringed in terror.

No way in hell someone like myself deserved a single millisecond more with you. I had to let you go! You are still such a young woman, so very soon, despite my notoriety, I will be just a fleeting memory of a somewhat interesting fling you had one summer back in Tuscany. You will love and you will be loved and admired throughout your life as you deserve to be loved and admired so your brief encounter with me would have not left any lasting damage on your pure soul. This might not had been the case had I let you stay and continued our affaire.

It was that moment, a moment in which I held you and you held me in your arms, a moment that gave meaning to my life, even in death. You left in tears, dear Sophie, and I really am sorry that I hurt you on that rainy night in Tuscany. I've never been patronizing in my whole life, so trust me that I am telling you the truth: it was for your own good. Trust me also when I say that I want you to know that your tears felt like they washed away, not my sins for those deserve neither mercy nor forgiveness, but my delusions and my madness. Your tears **HEALED** me at last. Your love, as much as your pain, had **LIBERATED** me in those last instants of bliss.

"My God, a moment of bliss. Why, isn't that enough for a whole lifetime?" asked Fyodor Dostoevsky in *White Nights*. I feel like I lived all my life for that one singular second with you. That was also an instant in which I **FINALLY** figured myself out.

The moment in which I started to live was the moment in which I realized that I have to die.

Hence kiddo, I'm staying forever yours in love & death.

Roman

PS it is <u>important</u> that you share the content of this letter, in its entirety, with my friend Trygve. You can snail-mail him the letter to:

Abbot Trygve E. Wighdal, Ph.D.
30 rue Descartes
75005 Paris
France

I guess it would be more expedient should you just scan the letter and e-mail it to him as an attachment to trygve.wighdal@protonmail.com.

Made in the USA
Coppell, TX
25 June 2020

29381953R00184